¡VIVA LOLA ESPINOZA!

Ella Cerón

Kokila

KOKILA
An imprint of Penguin Random House LLC, New York

First published in the United States of America by Kokila,
an imprint of Penguin Random House LLC, 2023

Copyright © 2023 by Ella Cerón

Kokila & colophon are registered trademarks of Penguin Random House LLC.

Visit us online at penguinrandomhouse.com.

Library of Congress Cataloging-in-Publication Data is available.

Book manufactured in Canada

ISBN 9780593405628

1 3 5 7 9 10 8 6 4 2
FRI

Design by Asiya Ahmed
Text set in Narevik

For Irma, Eva, Araceli, Elba, Lulu,
Moises, Norma, Diana,

and Salustia.

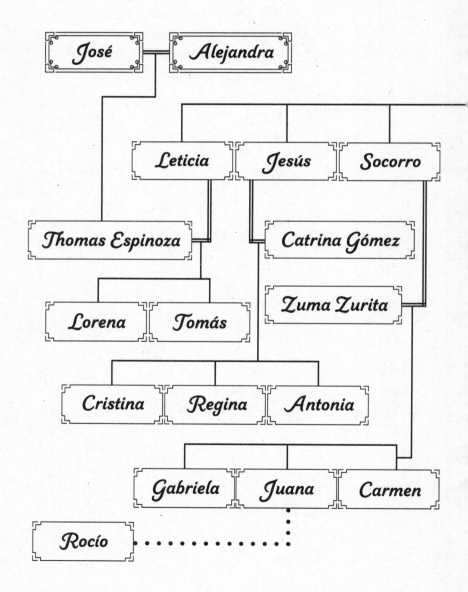

LA FAMILIA GÓMEZ CRUZ

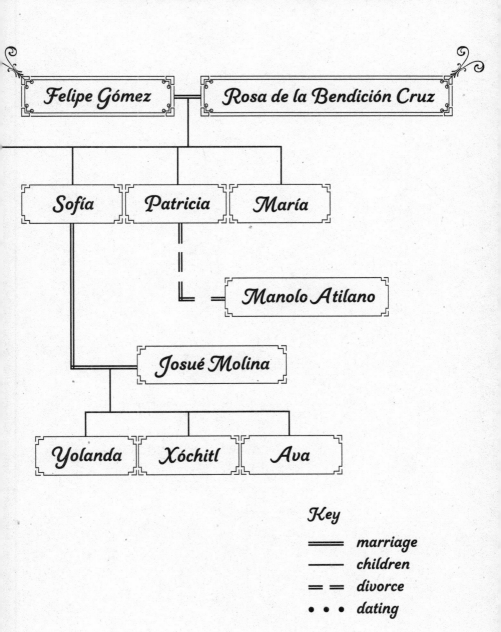

Felipe Gómez — Rosa de la Bendición Cruz

Sofía   Patricia   María

Manolo Atilano

Josué Molina

Yolanda   Xóchitl   Ava

Key

══════ marriage

────── children

═ ═ divorce

• • • dating

there's two ways to be a Mexican writer. you can translate
from Spanish. or you can translate to Spanish.
or you can refuse to translate altogether.

José Olivarez, "Ode to Tortillas"

CHAPTER 1

Twenty-seven minutes before the end of the last study hall period of the spring semester, a folded-up piece of paper landed in front of the book Lola Espinoza was halfheartedly reading.

Okay, she was using the book to hide her phone as she refreshed it. She wanted to be notified the second her grades hit her inbox. Not that she *wanted* to get her grades back. She just wanted to be aware.

She turned in the direction the projectile missive had come from and found Diego Padilla staring confidently at her. Diego—Padilla, as his friends called him—was one of the most popular boys in school and had been on the varsity soccer team since freshman year. Everyone knew Padilla. This was the first time he had ever indicated that he knew Lola existed, and they'd been in the same class since third grade.

Lola unfolded the note: *My party—u in?*

She read the words, barely legible in their smudged, stick-letter scrawl, again. Was she really being invited to the biggest end-of-semester party in the whole high school? She balked, buffered, and mentally reset. No, this note must have been for Ana, who always sat one seat over from Lola at the shared library table during study hall. Susana Morris was friends with everyone, a human disco ball refracting her light onto everyone around her. She was also, crucially, Lola's best friend.

Lola glanced at Padilla and motioned to confirm that he wanted her to pass on the note. He raised one eyebrow and shook his head.

Ana, who had been furiously shuffling a deck of oracle cards behind the book that served as her shield from Mr. Wesley, saw Padilla's facial expression out of the corner of her eye and snapped her attention toward the piece of paper in Lola's hand. "Is that a *letter*? From Padilla? What does it *say*?" She pushed the deck to the side and grabbed at the note. Her eyes lit up instantly. "You *have* to come with me."

Lola almost laughed at the thought. The last time she'd been to a party with Ana, she'd bopped her head awkwardly in the corner of someone's parents' living room before slipping out half an hour after she arrived. Could you classify it as "sneaking out" if only one person noticed you'd been there? Lola wasn't sure.

"There's no way I'm going," Lola replied. "No, let me clarify. There is no way I would even be allowed to go."

Ana sighed. "Come on! I can't remember the last time you *didn't* bail on a party, and we're going to be seniors next year. And Padilla invited you *personally*. The rules of high school dictate that you are obligated to attend."

Lola grabbed the note back. "Why would he do that? I didn't even think he knew who I was."

"C'mon, Espinoza. The two of you have been in the same school since before we were friends. He knows."

"But Padilla?"

"I don't get how boys' minds work—let alone the minds of boys on the soccer team—but sure, why not? You're cuter than you give yourself credit for. At some point, someone was bound to notice you. It's calculus or probability or whatever," Ana said matter-of-factly, picking the deck back up to shuffle it. A girl she'd been on three dates with had given it to her as a gift two years ago, and she'd gotten particularly obsessed with pulling a card before each final exam that semester, predicting how the test would go.

The verdict was still out on whether such a ritual worked or not. Grades were due by the end of the day, and Lola's phone had not yet buzzed, alerting their arrival.

Lola glanced over at Padilla again. Though she made the most thorough study guides of anyone in their grade, she did not have a road map for this. Boys didn't notice her, much less ask her to parties. The probability that they would was almost zero, and had been her entire high school career.

Not like she minded—anonymity gave her time to focus on homework. And while she spent her weekends watching makeup tutorials on YouTube, she always wiped off her handiwork before she left her bedroom. Not being known for her prowess with a cut crease ensured that her most defining trait at school was being Ana's best friend, as she had been since they'd sat next to each other in homeroom at the start of the seventh grade and Ana had forced Lola into having a conversation.

Their friendship was one of contrasts: Ana was on the cross-country team in the fall, the basketball team in winter, and doubled up on track and swim in spring. She was both the first one to make a joke in the middle of class and to rush to the center of the gym floor at every school dance. Ana lived for the spotlight—it only made her more formidable—while Lola fell to pieces if she had to speak during a group project presentation. During lunch, Lola studied in the corner of the quad while Ana made her rounds, only settling down so she could fill Lola in on whatever new drama had upended their classmates' lives. Lola liked it that way. She had a social life by proxy, with none of the stakes of actually getting involved.

In the four years since they had been friends, most of their classmates only ever acknowledged Lola when they wanted to get closer to Ana. There had been only one person who broke that mold: Christopher Yoon, whom Lola had sat behind in eighth-grade math. He was funny and owned the room the way Ana did; he gave everyone the same megawatt smile, and it made Lola's kneecaps disintegrate whenever she found herself somewhere in its light. He was the perfect boy to have a crush on because everyone had a crush on him—and because the only idea more terrifying to Lola than telling her parents she'd gotten a bad grade was asking if she could go out with someone.

She needed a crush like Chris. A safe one that was meant to be unrequited. That way, nothing could ever come of it, and she wouldn't have to be disappointed.

So when Chris asked Lola to partner with him on a geometry project, she heard herself saying yes even though the correct answer—the safe answer, and the one that her parents would expect her to give—would have been no.

It was that afternoon in the library when Lola learned how dark brown his eyes were, and that holding Chris's attention felt like the most special thing she could ever do. When he leaned over their textbooks and kissed her, her mind went blank . . .

And then she was hit by a wave of nausea so violent that she had to run to the bathroom before she deposited her entire lunch all over him.

Her parents assumed she had food poisoning and let her stay home from school the next day, a rarity in the Espinoza house. But she had to go back to school eventually, and she asked Sophie Acosta to switch seats in math when she did. Sitting within even a mile's radius of Chris made Lola's face grow as pink as her least-favorite blush. How could she have failed at her first kiss? Chris hadn't seemed to mind—he and Sophie started dating the following week—but Lola didn't forget so easily.

When she talked to Ana about it afterward, Ana

brushed off the incident as bad luck and pointed out that at least the kiss was memorable in its own way. Ana's first kiss, with Tara Guzman that same year, had been pedestrian by comparison; Lola had a *story*.

Yet Lola couldn't help but feel like she'd somehow been cursed to spend her high school years doing homework in an endless spiral, an academic purgatory with no salvation in sight. She studied so she could sign up for more AP classes so that she could then study for the next test, and the next one. There was no time for mall hangs, or homecoming dances, or parties, or, God forbid, a relationship. None of those things would get her into a good college on a scholarship, her parents often reminded her. And while Lola liked being smart, she also couldn't shake a specific sense of dread that she could be missing out on a world that existed beyond What Her Parents Wanted for Her.

Then again, Lola's identity was so wrapped up in school, she wouldn't even have known how to be anything other than a good student. Who was Lola Espinoza outside of that? She wasn't sure she even existed beyond the pages of her textbooks, or as the weird moon orbiting awkwardly in Ana's solar system. Really, the only logical thing to do was tuck any hopes of a social life—let alone romance—away and focus on her schoolwork.

She told herself she was fine with it.

And most days, she was.

Lola quietly folded up the note, but Ana snatched it out of her hand and scribbled something on it before Lola could put it away. *"Live a little!"* Ana had written below Padilla's invite, her effortless loops a direct counter to his handwriting.

Lola tried to suppress the small feeling growing inside her. The part of her that wanted to work up the nerve to ask her parents if she could stop by for an hour, the part of her that might actually want to go.

"It's just a party." She sighed.

"Exactly. It's *just* a party. So you should *just* come."

Lola sneaked a glance at her phone. Maybe if her parents thought her grades were good enough this semester, she would take Ana up on an invite or two this summer. Maybe, *maybe*, it would be fun to socialize—at least in a low-stakes, non-romantic, non-distracting-from-studying way.

An email notification from the Oxnard school district appeared on her phone screen.

Lola took a deep breath as she pressed the link.

She stared at the screen in front of her and kept refreshing the page, hoping it would change.

It didn't.

Lola Espinoza was not a C student. Lola Espinoza was not allowed to get C's, or even B's, not even an 89 percent. It was A's or nada.

Papi would not understand a C. And he would simply not accept a C in Spanish. That was basically like getting an F. And when Papi didn't understand, he grew quieter and more serious than usual. Mami called it being stoic. Lola called it something else.

Being the reason for his silence was mortifying.

Mami was the one who yelled. She had a knack for seeing each of her childen's shortcomings as yet another opportunity to remind them about the sacrifices she and their father had made, and continued to make, so that Lola and her younger brother could one day go to college—and this speech always lumped them into a single unit for some reason, even though they were two grades apart. It was together or nothing. Never mind the fact that they had different friends and liked different subjects (Lola: everything but PE and, okay, Spanish; Tommy: PE and lunch) and that Mami's disappointment in Tommy evaporated much more quickly than when Lola was its cause. She could hear her mother's voice growing increasingly melodramatic in her head: "Hacemos todo en esta vida juntos, o no lo hacemos."

The last time Lola had gotten a bad grade, it hadn't even been that bad, comparatively—a B- on a ninth-grade chemistry test in which the class average had been a crushingly low C. She came home prepared with that information, but her parents didn't care. Everyone else's grade should have been yet another reason for her to excel, her mother had told her. As for her father—well, he barely talked to her for a week, which was a worse punishment than being grounded given that Lola had nowhere to go anyway.

There was no way her parents hadn't already seen her grades—they would have gotten the same email she had, and Papi would have likely opened it instantly, too. She looked at the clock: 2:35 p.m. That meant she had approximately three hours and twenty-five minutes before she was tasked with defending herself, a one-girl stand-in for all of their hopes and dreams.

It wasn't as if Lola hadn't tried to get an A. She had put extra effort into her Spanish study guide—it had the most highlights, the most notations, and the most scratched-out attempts at sentence diagramming of any of her notebooks, and it was also the most dog-eared and flipped-through of all her guides.

And that was saying something, given how the only thing she ever did was study when she wasn't helping Tommy with his homework, or helping around the house so Mami didn't have to do more work, or sneaking a few minutes on YouTube before she dove back into another flashcard session. Other kids had sports or an after-school job. Lola had school.

Maybe that was for the best, because she spent so much time being the good daughter, the one Letty and Thomas Espinoza didn't have to worry about, that she had little time for anything else, even though an extracurricular or two would look good on her college applications. Hopefully, studying alone would be the key to a college acceptance letter and a scholarship rolled into one. Still, the pressure to succeed sometimes felt more like a burden than the opportunity her parents promised it was.

A ball of dread settled in Lola's stomach. A C in Spanish would mean *consequences*.

Lola's hand slipped from where it was propping her chin up, knocking her back to reality. She checked her phone's front-facing camera to make sure the lipstick she'd worn that day, a matte taupe-y liquid formula that would probably survive the apocalypse, hadn't smeared over her cheeks. It was still firmly in place—at least she had that going for her.

"You okay?" Ana whispered, which was ridiculous because Ana was loud in general and always louder than normal precisely when she was trying to be quiet.

"Yeah, sure," Lola said.

Sometimes things weren't worth explaining, especially to people who didn't get it. Even best friends.

Ana and her parents were decidedly more chill about her grades than Lola or her parents had ever been about hers. Ana was smart, too, but she didn't get straight A's, and she let B's and the occasional C roll off her like it was nothing. And not only were the teachers generally kinder to the athletes, but Ana was constantly finding loopholes that allowed her to coast. When they entered high school and signed up for the same Intro to Spanish class together, no one ever checked whether Ana was already fluent and could have skipped straight ahead to the college-extension course.

(She was and she could've, courtesy of a mother who

could trace her family lineage in Texas back twelve generations. But the teachers hadn't bothered to test Ana's knowledge of the subjunctive.)

Lola sighed again, a little too loudly.

"Miss Espinoza, Miss Morris, is there something you'd like to share with the rest of us?" Mr. Wesley asked.

Lola shook her head quickly. Mr. Wesley didn't expect anyone to actually answer him. He demanded silence.

Ana began focusing even more intensely on the oracle deck, which she'd been shuffling under the table. Her interest in such things had been sudden but sincere, and she liked to attribute the things their classmates did to the different planet placements in their birth charts. Lola was skeptical, which Ana said was typical for a double Sagittarius.

When the bell rang, Ana bolted upright and helped Lola pack up her things.

"So, party?" Ana asked again as they walked outside to the parking lot together. "You in, Lo?"

She was not letting Padilla's note go.

Lola sighed. "I got a C in *Spanish*, A. They're not going to let me go to a party after that. I'm telling you, when my dad finds out, it's going to be bad."

"What's going to be bad?" Tommy was leaning against Lola's car, trying to approximate as cool and disaffected a look as he could. Her brother was a lot of things; subtle was not one of them. "'Sup, Susana?"

The Espinoza children had the same warm brown

11

eyes and tan skin, and that was where their similarities ended. Fifteen-year-old Tommy was frenetic, excitable, quick with comebacks. His favorite thing in the world was roasting someone, but he had a particular knack for delivering his punch lines as a form of endearment. Lola, meanwhile, was more deliberate, perpetually stuck in her own head, weighing options before each next step. It was nice in her head, mostly. She could think through problems completely. She could plan.

"Your sister," Ana began dramatically, "has gotten a C in Spanish and is using that as an excuse to skip Padilla's party tonight. I can't believe my best friend is such a Sag."

"Okay, but . . . when was the last time Lola went to a party?" Tommy shot back, almost as if Lola wasn't both standing five feet away and his ride home.

She exhaled to remind him of her presence. Her brother laughed and reoriented himself to what was obviously the bigger issue.

"Yo, really? Lola, you got a C in Spanish? Spanish?! Mami's gonna kill you."

Lola felt her face getting red under her foundation. "I know. Just . . . get in the car, Tommy, please."

"Hey, if it helps, you can always tell Letty about the time señora Smith knocked ten points off my midterm freshman year because I refused to call a chamarra 'chaqueta,'" Ana offered helpfully. "It's not either of our faults they insist on teaching, you know, *Spanish* Spanish."

Lola said goodbye to Ana, promised to text her, also promised again to maybe at least think about the party (even if a promise was only a promise if you weren't halfway lying about it), and got into the hand-me-down Prius Papi and Mami had given her when she turned sixteen. It was quiet and unassuming, and though Lola had driven it for a year and a half, even she had trouble picking it out of the hundred other Priuses in any grocery store parking lot. In a lot of ways, it was Lola in car form.

She sat in the front seat for a minute as Tommy played with the aux cord, cycling through playlists until he found one he liked.

"For real, though?" he tried again. "In Spanish? Man, even I'm getting an A in Spanish. And señora Smith once called me a human dolor de cabeza. That's a headache, Lorenita. In case you need me to provide you with a traducción."

"Tomás, can we not?" Lola asked quietly, almost pleading. He scowled at his full name but got the hint.

Lola started the car, and together they rode toward home—Tommy to his dinner, Lola to her doom.

CHAPTER 2

Lola walked into the split-level that had been her home almost her entire life, dwelling on the C the way other people might fixate on a breakup or getting fired from a job. (As if she had experience with either.)

It wasn't that she couldn't understand Spanish. She mostly could. But she was not being graded on her comprehension of the chisme she overheard on her mother's phone calls to family in Mexico, an ability that did nothing to lessen the sting of her struggle. Spanish was the only class she ever really needed to work on to maintain her A, and while each test sank her further into the land of the dreaded B, she could usually do enough extra credit to bump her grade back up.

Not this time. This semester's final had gotten the better of her.

She found her mother working away in the kitchen. It was their standard after-school routine: Lola helped Mami make dinner while Mami gave her a minute-by-minute recap of her day. Letty Espinoza was a manager at the biggest Target in Oxnard, navigating screaming babies, seasonal decorations, and school supplies. Every few days, though, Mami would spend her dinner-making time catching up with one or more of her siblings instead of with Lola, and today she was FaceTiming with her sister Socorro.

"Mija, clean the elotes for me, please," Mami said by way of greeting. Some moms greeted their kids with hugs hello, but not Letty Espinoza. No "How was school today?" no "Happy first day of summer." She handed her daughter a metal bowl filled with ears of corn, and Lola knew better than to protest. Her mother was tiny, five foot one on a good day, but she was formidable.

Lola craned her neck to get into the phone frame to greet her aunt, then got to work cleaning the husks and silk threads off the kernels. Maybe this meant her mother *hadn't* seen Lola's grades yet. Or it could be the calm before the storm. It was impossible to tell with Mami.

"Lola! When are you staying with me? Your cousins will love having you around," her aunt called out from the phone.

It wasn't unusual for her relatives to mention the fun she would have in Mexico City, but rarely were the plans specific. Lola didn't read anything into it. As close as her mother was to her siblings, Lola didn't really know her extended family in Mexico City, and they didn't visit them all that much. She had a feeling that asking why was off-limits, like suggesting that she and her mother drive to a mall in Los Angeles for back-to-school shopping rather than using Letty's employee discount on the already-reduced sale rack.

Lola worked at the corn in silence while her mother talked with tía Coco about various nieces, in-laws, and cousins, and what she thought of their new boyfriends or girlfriends and haircuts and life choices.

Mami was the oldest of six, and she often wired money back to her mother and sisters, even if no one asked her to. But Letty also felt like those checks gave her the right to judge everyone and everything. She called it holding her family to a higher standard. Tía María, who was Letty's youngest sister and only five years older than Lola, called it exhausting—often to Letty's face when it was her turn to endure her sister's video call.

Lola could tell her mother was tired by the way her shoulders sagged a bit as she cooked. It wasn't enough that Mami managed the employees on her shift with the precision of a football coach. At home, she smiled her way through Tommy's newest comedy bits, which he insisted on calling his "material"; their dog, Churro, tracking mud and sticks and sometimes lizards into her otherwise spotless house; and a crackly video connection that made calling her mother almost as frustrating as an instantly sold-out special on Southern California's hottest summer commodity: sunscreen.

But Letty also loved talking, so Lola would listen to the employee gossip and the tales of demanding customers, as well as her mother's judgments on the rest of the Gómez family. Lola and the Guadalupe statue that lived in the center of the formal living room were Letty Espinoza's best audience. That statue had been the first and only thing her mother personally moved into their home while the movers had struggled with the rest. Sometimes she lit a candle in front of La Guadalupe. Sometimes she just said it reminded her of her mother's house. Of home.

That day, the special focus of Letty's's judgment—and Coco's melodramatic self-pity—was Lola's cousin Juana and the restaurants she owned in Mexico City. While Lola imagined that most families would be proud that someone owned even one restaurant, given how hard they were to keep in business, Letty was of the immovable opinion that two restaurants were twice the risk and therefore twice as impractical.

Lola indulged the gossip—not because she thought Juana deserved it, but selfishly because it bought her time. The more Mami talked about her family, the less Lola would have to talk about her Spanish grade.

"She could be an accountant, you know!" Mami yelled over a simmering pot of mole, several jars of her favorite brand of paste empty on the counter. The FaceTime with tía Coco had ended, but Letty had more to say. "Everyone needs someone to tell them what to do with money! But she's got this idea of serving your grandmother's recipes for the turistas. They could go to Taco Bell and they'd call it authentic."

If Lola had Tommy's bravado, perhaps she would have

offered that sometimes she'd pick those double-decker tacos over any other, more "authentic" option. But Lola wasn't Tommy, so she said nothing.

Anyway, Tommy picked that moment to saunter into the kitchen, a bag of Takis in hand. Mami dodged when her son stretched a radioactive dust-stained claw in her direction.

"What's this about Taco Bell?" he asked breezily.

Mami ignored the question. "Ya no comas eso, te vas a llenar."

Tommy continued to transport fistfuls of chips to his mouth. "Don't knock on Taco Bell," he said through chomps. "You're telling me the Baja Blast didn't come across the border with the rest of us?"

Mami glared at her son, and Lola didn't blame her. Tommy should know better than to joke about immigration with their mother, whose citizenship had only been formalized six years prior. She had been so happy when she got the letter, and so relieved—the Espinozas had heard too many stories of families waiting decades for an answer, or worse, getting the answer they didn't want. Lola could vividly remember the day Letty stood in that austere government building, one hand over her heart, reciting each word with a group of strangers like God or Walter Mercado or whatever higher power up there compelled her to do so.

"Tomás, ya te dije," Mami tried again. "Put those away. You're not going to be hungry for dinner." She took the bowl of shucked corn from Lola and began cutting

18

kernels off in long, starchy rows, oblivious as always to exactly how often she switched between languages. It made no difference how much Letty spoke to her children in Spanish—somehow, those words had barely imprinted on her daughter's mind.

Sometimes Lola imagined what it would be like for the Spanish words to make sense in her head without her having to translate them. She loved hearing Papi and Mami talk to each other late at night in rapid melody. And while Lola could understand most of their words, she could literally feel the little mechanisms in her brain working to process vocabulary and conjugation and tenses. It was exhausting. One day she'd get it. And even if she didn't, that didn't make her any less Mexican . . . right?

She hoped so.

Of course, she knew that proficiency in a language was not the sum total of her heritage, and besides, there were plenty of first-generation kids who didn't speak their parents' language. In that year's Spanish class alone, there had been seven other Latinx kids whose grasp on the language directly contrasted with what both señora Smith and the outdated textbook said. That didn't mean their Spanish was wrong—but it did mean they spent as much time being made to unlearn old habits as they did memorizing new vocabulary. Ana's chamarra showdown had been a prime example, and Monica Gutierrez had once petitioned the school to offer Spanglish as a language offering. Lola still remembered the impassioned speech

Monica made in front of the PTA about how knowing an in-between language didn't make her any less orgullosa de ser mexicana. It hadn't worked, but there had been a fun rally on the quad.

"Ey, Lola, did you hear me?" Her brother's voice punctured her mental spiral. "Lorenaaaaa."

"Lola, answer your brother." Mami sighed. She clearly hadn't had a great day. The last time she'd been in a mood like this, someone had spilled an industrial-sized bottle of Clorox across the freezer aisle.

Lola eyed her brother warily. "Anyway, as I was saying," he continued, clearing his throat dramatically. "Do you think it's 'Gordita Supremes' or 'Gorditas Supreme,' like 'attorneys general'? Or 'Gorditas Supremes'? The technical pluralization, I mean."

It wasn't clear if Tommy was walking her into a trap, though it was also entirely possible he had already forgotten about her C. The C she had absolutely not forgotten about. The one that would take her generations to live down, which Papi and Mami would use as a warning for her future children, and their children after them. That is, if they ever let her date to begin with.

Lola watched her mother out of the corner of her eye as she answered slowly. "'Gorditas Supremes,' absolutely. You pluralize both the noun and the adjective. But if you really want to translate it, it would have to be 'Gorditas Supremas,' because gordita is feminine."

"You're right." Tommy nodded sagely. "Though the

Fiesta Potatoes are really where it's at. Underrated secret menu item right there." He turned to leave the room, and Mami didn't stop him.

Lola's phone buzzed ominously in her pocket. And then it buzzed again. She glanced quickly at the screen. Somewhere on the other side of the Instagram algorithm, Ana was tagging Lola in horoscope memes, many of which suspiciously focused on parties and social lives.

Maybe if Lola promised her parents that she would spend her summer applying for college scholarships, it would soften the blow of the C. Would she officially have the least eventful summer ever as a result? Yes—even when compared against her usual summer plans, in which she pored over an AP workbook while waiting for Ana to get out of cross-country practice so they could hop from one air-conditioned café to the next, drinking so much iced coffee their teeth threatened to levitate out of their mouths. But for now, she had more pressing matters to attend to: Mami had told her it was time to set the table.

The Espinoza household plates were made of heavy terra-cotta, the kind found in Mexican restaurants that advertised themselves as being—there was that word again—"authentic." What did that even mean? And who decided it? Lola put the plates down and situated the bowl of jalapeños and carrots closest to Papi's chair at the head of the table. Almost as if on cue, her father walked through the front door immediately after she let go of the escabeche.

Thomas Espinoza, a solid sun-browned man who was perpetually exhausted by his work at an understaffed law firm that focused on farm workers' labor rights, shook Churro off him and deposited his keys under Guadalupe. Churro was undeterred by the brusque greeting. He had been a puppy with paws too big for his body when someone found him digging through the trash, and now his only worry was whether his new family would give him bits of their food at dinner. Papi had complained when the Espinoza children begged him to adopt a dog, but he baby-talked Churro more than anyone.

"Lorena, remind me to call the tree cutter tomorrow," he said. Again, Lola mentally clocked, no "Happy last day of school."

When Lola caught her father's eye, her stomach sank.

He already knew. Of course he already knew. If there was one thing señor Inbox Zero could be counted on to do, it was knowing.

Papi surveyed his daughter quietly as Mami bustled around the table and Churro staked out whose food he would be most likely to steal. Lola took her seat and focused intently on the napkin hiding her phone, which was currently threatening to vibrate itself off her lap thanks to Ana's incessant texting.

Other than that, the table was quiet. Too quiet.

"This Mrs. Smith . . . is she a fair teacher?" Papi began.

Lola exhaled. It was the beginning of her end.

She stared at a spot right above her father's ear, at

the graying hair he kept cropped close. It was easier to approximate looking at him than meeting his gaze. "Um, yeah, I . . . Usually I can get extra credit from her, but the final she gives juniors is thirty percent of the grade. So it's . . ." Her voice cracked. "It's kinda hard."

"And did you study for the final, Lorena?"

"Yeah, but . . . it's confusing. It's hard. It's supposed to be, right? To prove we learned instead of coasting through or something." Lola knew she was repeating herself, but her chest was getting tighter, and the only words she could force out were the ones she had already said.

The kindest thing would be for Papi to get it over with, take away her phone, ground her, tell her what she would have to do to make it up.

"And this English literature class, is that supposed to be hard, too? You got an A in that."

Lola looked at her mother, whose face was now as unreadable as Papi's had been when he first came through the door. Later, Lola knew, she would get the speech about sacrifices. She made a mental note to nod at the expected points. Maybe she'd get the condensed version that way. She just had to survive her father first.

"Do you like English more?" Papi continued. Or do you think it's more important than Mrs. Smith's Spanish class?"

"Lorena, why wouldn't you study harder for Spanish?" Mami asked. So she *had* seen Lola's grades, too. No wonder she wasn't coming to her daughter's rescue.

Lola looked at her father, who was winding himself up for another lecture on what it meant to be born in one country and to uphold the legacy of another. Maybe if she thought quickly enough, she could stop it before it began. Her mind cycled through potential options for a rebuttal: that it wasn't her fault her brain was at war with the imperfecto, or that she honestly considered *¿Dónde está la biblioteca?* to be the single most pointless phrase in her entire textbook. Spanish didn't come easily to her. If Thomas Espinoza considered her a traitor, so be it.

"I don't get it, okay?" she said. "Honestly, I don't. Señora . . . Mrs. Smith is fair, but it's a hard class and I don't get it and I was lucky to get that C. Which, by the way, is a passing grade." She sounded petulant, but she couldn't stop herself. "And look, one single C isn't going to sink my chances at getting into college. I got straight A's in every other class, just like I do every semester. I'm sure . . . I don't know . . . Berkeley or wherever will understand."

Papi was silent again. It was setting in, that quiet disappointment that Lola spent so much of her life trying to avoid, the one that felt so absolute.

Mami was stern yet reasonable, but Lola rarely understood her father. That wasn't to say she didn't love him—if she were forced to pick a favorite parent, she'd pick her father, while Tommy would claim Mami. Letty still indulged the baby of the family, but Lola's affinity toward her father probably had something to do with how they were wired to handle stress. They barreled through their problems, hoping the solution would come to them eventually. Why dwell on one problem when you could multitask on seven others?

Their similarities notwithstanding, there were so many things about her father that Lola didn't get. Why had he chosen to move to Mexico for college, for example, even though he had gotten into several stateside schools? (Ever the king of double standards, Papi had already made it known that Lola was expected to pick a college within the California state limits so she could still come home most weekends.) And why would he and his wife go to such great lengths to name their son Tomás when his own Thomas was right there?

Then there was the matter of heritage: An eighteen-year-old Thomas Espinoza's first-ever trip to Mexico had been when he moved there for college, and leaving his family must have been a serious culture shock. His parents—whom Lola had always called Papito and Mamita—had lived without papers for decades, almost their entire lives. The three Espinoza boys were the first in their family to be US citizens, and Thomas had moved to Mexico almost as soon as he reached adulthood.

But any time Lola asked him about why he went to school in Mexico, so far away from his family, and what that had been like, he only ever reminded her that it was how he and their mother had met. It was the conclusion rather than the exposition, and a story he often told factually and with little emotion. Papi wasn't often one for theatrics.

Even now, there was no drama on his face. Yet what stung this time wasn't his inscrutability. It was the unwillingness to hear Lola's side of things. She had tried to get a good grade and even offered to complete extra credit to make up for it. But the final had sunk a tenuous B+, and unlike the Ana Morrises of the world, Lola was not expected to treat that as "good enough."

Five painful minutes passed, during which the only sound was Tommy eating. When Papi spoke again, it was to Mami, his voice calmer and more measured than Lola had ever heard it in her seventeen years. "La suegra," he said, "would be good for her."

Her mother nodded. Like this was something they had already discussed and agreed on.

Lola must have misheard him or filled in the wrong blanks. Going to her grandmother's house? In Mexico City? There was no one else it could logically be but señora Rosa de la Bendición Cruz de Gómez, who lived in the same drafty house in which she'd raised her six children—which was exactly the opposite of where Lola wanted to spend the next-to-last summer of her high school career.

"You can't be serious!" she groaned.

Her C had been an obvious warning of danger ahead, but she never imagined this.

Tommy laughed incredulously. "Yooooooo, she's going to Buela's? Does that mean I can have her room? Or at least her TV? Lola, you won't mind, right? How could you? You won't be here." He happily began helping himself to extra mole, splattering the front of his tee as he did so.

The last time Lola had been to Mexico City was the summer before her sophomore year of high school, for her aunt's wedding. The trip lasted four days, and she had been introduced to more people than she could remember—so many cousins of cousins and aunts and uncles that she wished for a family tree to understand how they were or weren't technically related. She'd worn an itchy dress designed for someone four years younger and spent the big night in that special kind of fog that happens when you understand what's happening around you in concept but not in reality. It was like everyone remembered a younger version of Lola, one who still answered to nicknames like "Lolita" and who was not allowed to grow up.

By the end of the Espinozas' trip, Lola would have done anything for reliable cell service. That was the other thing: The Wi-Fi in Buela's house was spotty at best, which made tía María complain every time she needed to study at home rather than at her law school's library. But why should Buela worry about that? Her beloved TV antenna, which she used to watch her telenovelas as she cooked, was more than enough technology for her. She didn't want to learn to use anything beyond that, and she didn't want to move. So that house was where she remained, and where the Espinozas stayed on the rare occasions they did visit, often in tiny twin beds that should probably have been replaced thirty years ago.

Lola stared daggers at her brother before trying again

with her parents. "Come on, please. That's so unfair."

At that moment, Tommy's phone vibrated on his lap, because there was some universal rule that a phone would only ring when you absolutely didn't need it to. He brazenly checked his notifications. Papi had once again gone silent.

"There's got to be an alternative," Lola said, this time to no one in particular.

She looked up, and her own stubbornness looked back at her. "No alternative," Papi said. "You come back when you can speak Spanish."

In the safety of her room, Lola's exhale verged on a sob. Churro pawed at her door, but she didn't let him in. He'd get bored eventually and wander back to the dining room, where Papi would complain about the very concept of keeping dogs indoors before ultimately feeding Churro directly from his plate. Mami would admonish her husband, and she'd save Lola's unfinished plate in the fridge. Her family was predictable. Their world was small and known, and Lola liked it that way.

Mexico, though. She didn't understand why that was the first, last, and only choice available to her. *Duh, that's why you're going, because you don't understand,* a small voice in the back of her mind chastised her.

Lola told it to shut up.

Her phone buzzed again, and she looked at the screen. Ana was undeterred in her mission to convince Lola that going to Padilla's party and celebrating the end of the school year was the right choice for her.

LE: Can't

I'm more than grounded

My parents are sending me to my grandma's for the summer

AM: LOL seriously?

Wait, like as in Mexico?

Are you upset about this?

I'm sensing you're upset

You should take me with you

I'm sure my mom would say yes

Lo??

You there?????

Lola didn't reply, choosing instead to wallow in self-pity. She didn't want to look at this optimistically. She watched as the text bubble on Ana's side showed up and shorted out one last time, the three little dots signifying that her best friend was trying to figure out what to say.

Ana, mercifully, gave Lola space to stew.

CHAPTER 3

Lola had been given ninety-six hours after that fateful dinner to prepare for her departure, because when Papi decided something, it was as good as done.

Lola's summer plans? Canceled. Not that she had many to begin with. Even her last-ditch effort to appeal to her mother fell through: Mami had reassured Lola that she had cleaned her house just fine before she brought Lola into the world, and she would manage it again on her own for three months.

"So I start at six a.m. on Saturday, not at seven." She shrugged matter-of-factly. "Your grandmother won't let you clean a single thing, so consider yourself lucky, okay?"

And that party at Padilla's house? Apparently an epic, remember-forever blowout. Of course it was—and Lola found herself lingering a little too long on the photos Ana sent her, as well as on every other post on her Instagram feed. A party was only ever as good as its half-life, and the gossip inspired by this one would last until at least graduation.

The night before her flight, Lola opted to eat dinner

in her room again. It was the most basic form of protest she could think of, and it also meant she could text Ana as much as she wanted while she ate. Her best friend had already reinforced her status as the queen of her cross-country conditioning class and was busy sending so many microupdates about teammate drama that Lola's phone threatened to buzz right out of her hand. If Ana had a flaw, it was her habit of

texting

like

this.

Ana also offered her analysis of Lola's banishment as optimistically as she could: Going to Mexico for the summer would be an adventure. And for someone like Ana, it would have been. But Lola expected a very lonely few months surrounded by relatives who might as well be strangers and a language barrier that would bring any attempt at conversation to a painful crawl—not unlike the buffer plaguing an eyeshadow palette review video she wanted to watch.

Lola heard a knock at the door and a scuffle as Churro came barreling in ahead of Mami. He wasn't allowed on any of the beds, technically, but Lola's was the only room where he wouldn't get yelled at for inviting himself up anyway. He made a nest amid the jean shorts and tank tops that had yet to make their way into the half-packed suitcase lying forlornly on the floor, pleased with himself. When Churro was happy, there was no reasoning with him.

"Mija, are you packed? Are you ready?" Letty asked, looking at the piles of blue and gray and white and black that Lola had divvied up. "Is this really everything you're taking?"

She sat on the bed and picked up a mess of tanks so she could begin folding them. Lola watched as her mother's hands smoothed the cotton into neater folds than anything she'd ever mastered in her short life. There was something soothing about watching her mother take on tasks like folding laundry—how capable and pragmatic she was—even if Lola felt a pang of guilt for giving her yet another chore to complete.

After a few minutes, Mami tried again, in her own way. "You should take at least one dress, Lorena," she said.

There was a finality in her voice, one that cemented the fact that Lola was indeed going to Mexico City the next day. Letty took Lola's silence as an invitation to dig through her daughter's closet—the closet in her house that she let her daughter use, she would say. Before Lola could protest about something like privacy, Letty pulled out a dress Lola had forgotten she even owned.

It was an impulsive mall purchase, and the tags still waved wastefully from their little plastic strings. How did Mami even know it was in there? Her mother folded it efficiently and offered it to her. "Everyone needs at least one dress."

This was her peace offering?

Lola had been hoping for a reveal that, actually, she

and Papi had thought about it, decided the flight was too expensive, and their daughter could unpack her suitcases. Instead, she got a fashion tip.

"This feels kind of sexist, you know," Lola countered. "Would you tell Tommy that?"

"Sure. If he wants to wear a dress, why not?" Mami gave Lola a smile, another peace offering that helped a little but not enough. "Your father, he thinks this is important. You know, when I first met him, he had trouble with his Spanish. He kept telling people he wanted to hit the check, not pay it. But going to Mexico meant a lot to him when he was your age."

Lola contemplated the difference between *pegar* and *pagar*, and nudged her now-silent phone. Twenty-four unread messages, each one from the only person who ever texted her. "Yeah, well," she said. "I'm not him. It's not fair for him to think I should have the exact same experiences and priorities that he does."

"That's what a family is, Lorena," Mami said. "Just people who think they know what the people around them should be doing."

Coming from the woman who considered herself the expert on what *everyone* in her family should do.

"You could ask him why this is important to him," Mami tried.

"I know why it's important," Lola said. "I'm supposed to get straight A's and I didn't, so here we are."

"There's more to it than that, you know."

"Do I?"

"Try to talk to him," Mami said again.

"He'll just ask me to say it in Spanish and stonewall me until I try," Lola said bitterly.

"Spanish wasn't his first language, either, but he learned for me. Because it was mine."

Lola looked away, an apology not quite materializing on her tongue.

Mami took that as a cue to leave. "Think about at least one dress," she pressed before closing the door behind her. "Even if you don't wear it."

Lola packed the dress.

Her flight was at 3:00 p.m. on Tuesday, and she was supposed to meet Papi outside the house at 12:00 p.m. sharp. He had taken the afternoon off work to drive her and had texted his very terse directions that morning. Neither he nor Lola had spoken since his decision, and they only sent texts when they absolutely needed to. Tommy had somehow found the silent standoff to be hilarious, while Mami had grown more and more exasperated. It had been her idea that Thomas drive his daughter to the airport, and Lola had a feeling it was a last-ditch effort to get them to say something—anything—to each other.

She wasn't going to be the one to cave first.

At least she wouldn't in English. She had wondered

aloud to Ana whether her return at the end of August speaking flawless Spanish would be a moment for her to gloat or a reinforcement that her father had made the "right" decision. Lola had a sinking feeling about the latter, but Ana had pressed for the former: Mr. Espinoza would be shocked at Lola's mastery and apologize for his hard-line approach. Even señora Smith would be forced to acknowledge Lola's fluency. Until then, the real-time Lola couldn't think of anything in particular that her father needed to hear from her.

Yet by the time they reached the drop-off curb, she had definitely considered saying something to cut the tension in the car. That this was, in a way, her fault? That she was also disappointed in herself for getting anything less than an A-? Or should she offer a reassurance that she really was going to try to learn Spanish? Every possible opening was a concession in her head. She didn't want to give Papi the satisfaction of thinking he was right about this.

So she picked the stubborn option instead: say nothing. Lola leaped out of the car and yanked at her suitcases so she could head into the terminal and get the entire summer over with. She heard a gruff cough; Papi was asking her something. Was this the end of their standoff?

She turned to find him with his hands shoved deep into the pockets of a leather bomber jacket that was maybe as old as Tommy. "You have your passport?" he said again. "And what about your ticket?"

Lola lifted the backpack she'd repurposed from school accessory to travel essential. "All here, along with your written consent to let me leave the country and basically every other form of identification in case I get lost or decide to abscond to Europe and start a new life or whatever."

Papi's sense of humor was difficult to pin down, and Lola could count on both hands the number of times she'd heard her father really laugh. It was usually during a rare game of charades, when his brothers and their wives were over for Christmas and her younger cousins had all passed out from the excitement of so many presents. Lola loved those moments, when the stress levels in the house plummeted—toward the asymptote, according to her math study guide—and she could actually breathe for once.

This was not one of those times. Lola and Papi looked at each other for seventeen and a half awkward seconds before either of them spoke again.

"Well, text me when you land, and when you're with María," he offered, though he didn't move to hug her. There were men of few words, and then there was Thomas Espinoza. Lola wondered if he had ever spoken more than twenty words consecutively in his lifetime. Or if he had ever admitted to anyone that he overreacted or got things wrong.

She turned away before she could say anything. It hurt too much to admit she resented her father in that moment, and she was afraid whatever she could think to say would have tipped him off to that.

Lola spent the three-hour flight mentally reliving every moment of that agonizing car ride, applying a consecutive round of sheet masks in her tiny economy seat, and trying to ignore the white couple sitting next to her. They were busy planning their weekend vacation by plotting out the photos they wanted to take for Instagram, and the girl kept pronouncing Xochimilco with a hard ex-oh in the front. (Lola worried, for a moment, what words she herself mispronounced with her own rudimentary accent.)

Eventually, she drowned them out by speeding through a Spanish lesson on the language app she had downloaded two days prior in a moment of defeat. She murmured along, and the conjugations for the imperfecto lulled her into a trance until the flight attendants announced the plane's descent.

She passed customs, found her suitcases, and pushed her way through the exit, where a flood of people waited for other passengers, for the people they loved. For a second, Lola felt invisible, which was comforting in a familiar sort of way. She wasn't anonymous for long. Her tía María swung into view, waving her down excitedly.

"¡Lolita!" she exclaimed, using the nickname Lola had tried to outgrow the day she turned eleven. "¡Lolita, ya llegaste!"

Lola hugged her aunt as people milled around them. "Sola . . . solo Lola," she tried, cringing at how difficult such a simple word felt on her tongue. She had to try to use Spanish. If she didn't put in the effort, she'd be in Mexico forever.

"Okay, okay, *solo Lola*," her aunt replied, grabbing one of the bags and leading the way out to the car. "So tell me, how was the flight, how are you, look at you! ¡Ay, que guapa! Oh! Did you text your dad? He has sent me fifty texts in the last hour." The minute María switched to English, Lola felt her whole body exhale, even if the topic was her father. But her aunt didn't stop there. "¿Y el novio?"

María Gómez Cruz spoke as rapidly and as forcefully as her older sister did everything else in life. Lola kept grabbing sideways glances at the young woman who looked like Letty in every possible way. They had the same dark hair, identical sheets of black that Mami had also passed on to Lola. But where her mother was deliberate and self-contained, María crackled with an energy that her niece liked to imagine Mami had once had, too.

"There are no boyfriends, tía María."

Her aunt laughed.

"¡Tía! Ay Dios, I forgot I'm your aunt. From now, I'm Mari, okay? Better sister than mi sobrina."

Lola relaxed into that. There were so many years between the oldest and the baby of the Gómez family that for as long as Lola had known her, Mari had felt more like a cousin than an aunt. Mami sometimes talked about the ways the baby was allowed to follow the biggest dreams because the older children worked to clear the path. For Mari, that dream was to be a prosecutor, which she described as a desire to hunt down the bad guys who inspired her favorite *SVU* episodes, but which was really rooted in a serious hunger for justice. She was in her last year of law school, and there were textbooks and notepads piled up in the back of her car because school was school no matter where you were.

They loaded the bags into the trunk and got into the car. Up above, the sky was hazy and gray around the edges even though it wasn't cold. Mari messed with the dashboard until she found a station she liked, turned up the hip-hop, and expertly merged into the sea of traffic that defined the city's streets. As she drove, she shout-talked in two languages to fill Lola in on how Buela refused to set foot in Juana's restaurants and barely tolerated Regina's boyfriend and the at least eight ways in which tía Sofía's newest baby made Mari feel comfortable with being an aunt for the first time in her life, which was funny because she had technically been one since before she was born. The way Mari sped through everyone's big milestones made the world feel like it was going a million miles an hour.

They turned at an exit whose most defining characteristic was the auto repair shop at its corner, and made their way down the narrow streets to Buela's house and the faded pistachio walls that immediately brought a rush of memories back into Lola's still-bitter brain. Rosa's house was one of the few on the block with its own outdoor courtyard; it doubled as a car park and was marked by a metal gate that only opened by force. Lola hopped out of the car on Mari's request and struggled with the rusted door before shoving her shoulder into it. It was the most athletic thing she'd done all year. The gate's creaking gave way to music and laughter coming from inside the house.

"¡Ay!" Lola heard someone yell. "¡La gringa!"

She took a deep breath and tentatively went inside. Several aunts and her uncle, each of whom looked startlingly like Mami, were waiting for her. Tío Chuy was the tallest and held himself even taller, while tía Coco was squat and more cheerful than anyone else in the room. Tía Paty was Mari's senior by seven years but could pass for her twin; she wrapped Lola in a hug before heading toward the car to help her sister with the bags.

"Mira, Lola," she offered with a wink as she went. "La Señora está en la cocina."

Her grandmother's kitchen was old and showed wear if you looked close enough. On their last trip, Papi had offered to pay for a full renovation, but Buela hushed him and said it was well-loved. Rosa was busy stirring a large pot on the stove, but she immediately switched her attention to Lola, the oldest child of her oldest child. That was a special distinction in its own right, even though Gabriela, the first of tía Coco's twins, was her oldest grandchild—by a total of three and a half minutes, as Gabriela often reminded her twin, Juana.

"Lolita, ¡ven acá!" It was going to be an uphill battle

to get her family not to use that name, her grandmother most of all.

Buela was the kind of tiny that proved sturdier than people gave her credit for, and the warmth of her skin contrasted starkly with the solid white roots she hadn't yet been able to dye cinnamon-red. She had barely changed since the last time Lola had seen her, down to the apron guarding her neatly pressed slacks. Her mannerisms were the same, too. Without even asking Lola if she was hungry, Buela ladled something into a nearby bowl, topped it with a tortilla that she pulled from a pile wrapped in a cloth on the counter, and handed it to her granddaughter. Lola took it wordlessly. The rule was: Accept Buela's cooking or risk her wrath forever.

But before Lola could settle in, the house began moving again. There was a honk outside, and a rush of cousins and strangers that must have been their friends came pouring into the house. They laughed and yelled as they carted various boxes into the kitchen, and Lola recognized one yell in particular: Juana's laugh was unmistakable.

"¡Loli—!" she began.

Lola cut her off, preparing herself for the inevitable. "Solo Lola, ¿okay?" she pleaded, greeting Juana with a kiss on the cheek.

"No, I'm thinking I like Loli mejor," Juana replied with a wink. "Ey, Rocío, Loli is here!"

Juana's reserved girlfriend, a redhead wih fair skin and

knowing eyes, stood among a group of five other people, including tío Chuy's middle daughter, Regina, and her boyfriend, Adrián—the one Mari had said Buela wasn't fond of. She eyed him briefly, trying to figure out why her grandmother didn't like him.

The answer was most likely the simplest one: Adrián was a teenage boy.

Over the next twenty minutes, more and more family members arrived, eager to greet the person they kept calling *la gringa*, a nickname that chafed at Lola every time they said it. There was Juana's twin, Gabriela, and their little sister, Carmen, who together made up tía Coco and tío Zuma's three daughters. They were tall and looked like their father, a lanky Black man who taught economics at one of the city's universities. They also immediately put Lola at ease in the way Regina and her sisters, Cristina and Antonia, did not.

Those girls were each a year apart in age and often drove tío Chuy to ask the saints what he had done to deserve such worries. The Gómez y Gómez sisters showed up in coordinating Zara outfits and hardened, white-tipped nails—textbook telenovela villains. Cristina in particular kept eyeing Lola up and down. She was eighteen, the oldest of tío Chuy's girls, and clearly believed she was special. Lola rarely had to deal with girls like Cristina at school, and she didn't intend to start now just because they were related.

Instead, she focused on greeting her tía Sofía and Sofía's

husband, Josué, who were busy trying to corral two of their three children, nine-year-old Yolanda and seven-year-old Xóchitl. Tía Paty had taken over the handling of Sofía's youngest, three-year-old Ava, who laughed wildly as her aunt played la araña pequeñita on her belly. This was a small gathering by Gómez standards, though there was no telling who else might show up in the course of the evening.

Buela soon called everyone to the large table that took up almost every inch of her dining room. The family gathered around, passing the various bowls and plates of Buela's endless guisados and sopes as they chatted loudly. Lola took in the scene from the most inconspicouous corner seat, but the conversation was fixated on her.

"Lola's stuck with la Señora for the summer, so everyone be nice," Mari said, her comment directed toward Juana and her sisters.

Carmen scoffed. "We're the nicest. Aren't we, Lola?" she asked, sitting down next to her cousin.

"Ey, Lola, so what are you doing here this summer?" Rocío asked in English so crisp, it momentarily took Lola by surprise. In the same instant, however, she kicked herself mentally for anticipating anything else—the tourists on the plane weren't the only people who needed to check their privilege.

"I'm working on my Spanish," she said. It wasn't a lie, even if it was against her will.

Rocío smirked. "Entonces hablamos nada más en español."

"Yo prefiero un . . . un poco de inglés," Lola replied weakly. Her cousins erupted into laughter, though their conversation mercifully moved on from there.

As the meal went on, Lola took in her relatives one by one. Tío Chuy had zeroed in on his middle daughter because, from what Lola could gather, Juana had caught Regina and Adrián sneaking off into the back room at one of the restaurants. The speech needed no translation—his tone was proof enough that her uncle was not happy. Lola listened quietly as she loaded carnitas into a tortilla and spread one of Buela's many homemade salsas on top.

Mari, who was seated on Lola's other side, explained that Regina only landed her job as a waitress because Juana's worst business instinct was her firm belief that family and friends made good-enough staff. And while that meant service was sometimes slow, there was plenty of entertainment.

"I don't know," she added. "Maybe it works out. Her friends are fun to look at."

Lola almost choked at Mari's boldness and tuned back in to the primary conversation at the table. Coco and Sofía were interrogating Paty, who was currently living with her mother and sister, and whose divorce was so legendary, everyone felt entitled to mention it whenever they could. Rosa's children did not get divorced; they muscled through their misery in case the archbishop dropped by for coffee. Sure, that visit was about as likely as Lola's father saying sorry about anything, but the hyperbole had been enough to make Paty try to make her marriage work for a year longer than would have been healthy.

Rather than rehash her most disappointing daughter's love life, Buela chatted at Lola as she continued to serve everyone to the point of bursting, and while her words were in Spanish, her cadence so closely mirrored Mami's that Lola already felt at home. But Buela's rules came swiftly: Lola picked up that she was expected to sleep in the same room as Mari, whose bed split into twin mattresses, and that she wasn't allowed to so much as walk to the corner store without someone going with her. She was also supposed to adhere to a curfew, which felt redundant, given she needed a chaperone to go anywhere in the first place.

"Ey, Loli," Juana interjected conspiratorially. "If you ever need to get out of here, you can come work with us."

"Don't you mean, 'for me'?" Rocío asked.

Juana pushed her girlfriend's shoulder playfully.

"No importa. *We're* building the next Pujol! The new location is in La Roma, so you can handle the gringo tourists, Loli. Don't worry; it's not where these two work," she added, looking openly at Regina and Adrián.

The word *gringo* punctuated the air once more, a small reminder that Lola and her cousins were separated by more than distance alone. But rather than respond immediately—or even react to what she knew Juana did not mean with any ill will—Lola thought about what Mari had said: that Juana's penchant for mixing business and family often resulted in drama. If nothing else, working at La Rosa wouldn't be boring . . . though the idea of speaking Spanish to complete strangers, professionally, filled Lola with dread.

"I'll think about it," she said. Juana smiled.

By the end of the night, Lola was exhausted—from the long flight, from the whirlwind of her family, and from trying to keep up with the conversations as they overlapped. No one could talk like the Gómez family could, and she was more than ready for bed.

As she walked upstairs and settled into the creaky twin bed that would be hers for the summer, Lola was struck by how happy she was to be surrounded by her cousins, aunts, and uncles, and that their joy at having her could hardly be contained within that warm and lived-in house. Sure, she'd probably have to share the Wi-Fi with Mari while one studied and the other streamed social media posts, and she would certainly need the help of a cousin to get around, but she would figure those details out later.

She didn't want to jinx it, but as Lola closed her eyes, she threw a vague wish at anything in the universe that might be listening to intervene and keep this from becoming a long summer—or at least not a quiet one.

CHAPTER 4

If Thomas Espinoza had meant for the trip to Mexico to be a punishment, Lola was delighted to find that her first few days were anything but that. Buela simply refused to let anyone else in the house cook—she'd jump to so little as pour a soda for her granddaughter and routinely offered to make a four-course meal if Lola suggested that she was hungry. And where Mami often brandished the Swiffer at both Lola and Tommy to shame them into helping her clean, Buela scoffed at Lola's offer to help her with any of the chores she completed daily.

The only thing she expected Lola to do was join her in prayer in front of a painting of La Guadalupe that hung with reverence at the top of a wall of family photos in mismatched frames. She kept a bowl of salt and a white candle on a small side table next to where she knelt every day, and while Lola wasn't sure what those were about, she knew asking would result in an hour-long explanation full of phrases that had no emotional translation at all. So Lola didn't ask, and Buela was content to complete her rituals with a companion, but without interruption.

Because the Gómez matriarch didn't drive and said she was too old to start learning, everyone came to her, often with groceries or other necessities. Tía Coco, who lived six houses down, regularly brought plenty of gossip and pastries, including Lola's all-time favorite, orejas, whose small ice caps of sugar she would pick off as she listened to her aunt complain about anyone and everyone. It wasn't iced coffee with Ana, but it was an escape all its own.

The biggest downside to Buela's house was the shaky, unpredictable Wi-Fi system that waged a battle with every tutorial Lola wanted to stream. Practical Mari was too impatient to fight with it, so she would turn her phone into a hotspot when she was home—which, thanks to summer classes and a part-time job at a law firm, was almost never.

Lola didn't dare imagine what kind of roaming charges she'd rack up on her dad's cell phone plan if she did the same, so she spent the bulk of her days reading and trying to complete exercises on her language app in offline mode. Whenever she was able to turn her Wi-Fi back on, she was inundated with texts from Ana, who was busy running cross-country drills, stressing about a Stanford scout attending practice, and keeping Lola updated with gossip of her own. It was the same routine they would have had if Lola had stayed home for the summer—except this time, she was two thousand miles away.

But even she had to admit this was an extreme version of living life from her usual sidelines.

For once, being boring was, well . . . boring.

It was after three days of staying inside Buela's house and sporadic texting with Ana that Lola remembered Juana's offer. She texted her cousin shortly after Mari came bursting through the door on a particularly colorful tear about the traffic, and mercifully bringing the good Wi-Fi with her.

> **LE:** ¿Puedo trabajar contigo todavía?
>
> That's how you say it in Spanish, right? Anyway, let me know if I need to submit a formal application or whatever.

In return, Juana sent more GIFs than even the hot spot could keep up with, clearly not caring to honor the line between eagerness and spam.

It was settled: Lola would go to the new La Rosa on Monday for training, and Mari would drive her over. Lola made sure to ask her aunt for the ride only after she calmed down from whatever debacle she'd dealt with on the road that day. Mari was generous, but Lola already knew not to press her luck.

Though it had been less than a week and a half since classes had let out for the summer, Lola had already gotten used to sleeping in—so that first morning, she woke up only when a pillow made contact with her ear.

"Lola, ¡ya!"

Lola stirred awake to the sound of her aunt rushing around the room.

"Mari, what—"

"Late! We're late!" Mari grabbed a pair of jeans that were hanging haphazardly out of Lola's suitcase and threw them her way. Lola would have to talk to her about this habit of turning household objects into projectiles, no matter how soft they were. "Tengo un examen hoy. We need to go."

Lola rubbed the sleep from her eyes as she watched Mari finish getting ready, but then it dawned on her: She had somewhere to be, too, and if Mari was late, that meant *she* was late. She bolted out of bed, threw on the jeans, and hunted around for her phone, whose chirp announced three texts from Ana and an Instagram message from Mami, none of which Lola had time to respond to. Her link to home would have to wait.

She rushed through her teeth-brushing and hair-combing in order to meet Mari in the car, where her aunt spent the whole drive muttering to herself about some legal theory. Instead, Lola poked at the face that stared back at her in the mirror, trying to make the puffiness of sleep disappear with her fingers. There had been no time to put on any makeup, and Lola didn't dare apply mascara while Mari was driving so erratically.

Within twenty minutes, Mari deposited Lola outside a small building nestled on a quiet street in the colonia

Roma, with the words *La Rosa* painted above its front door. At that first family dinner, Rocío had explained that the name was in honor of la Zona Rosa, where the first La Rosa stood in la colonia Juárez, and for the matriarch who had ironically never visited.

Was it an act of defiance, then, for Juana to name her life's work after her grandmother, or an extreme show of deference?

Obvious and unspoken homages to Rosa filled the restaurant's main room, from the photo of her as a young girl that greeted Lola when she walked in, to the wall tiling that matched the ceramic work at her house, to the smell of dried chile and coffee that permeated the space. It was what Buela smelled like, and it was a comforting mix.

The space was only half-lit, and Lola's eyes adjusted to the semidark as she took in the plants and portraits that filled every corner. Of particular importance was a painting of Felipe Gómez, her grandfather, who stared somberly down from over by the bar. He had died almost two decades ago, when Mari was barely old enough to walk. It struck Lola that she had never heard her grandmother talk about him.

Lola stopped in front of the portrait and tried to imagine knowing this grandfather, whose memorial was far more serious than the crinkly-eyed memories she had of her Papito. Mami rarely spoke about her father, either—though Lola had a hunch that tía Coco would tell her stories if she asked. How strange it was to be related to someone you didn't even know, Lola thought, before realizing that the not-knowing was perhaps her fault for not asking more questions. She searched his face for any resemblance to her own; from certain angles, he looked like a sterner version of tía Paty.

But similarities didn't tell you how a person's mood changed when they were tired, or how they preferred their eggs, or what their favorite song was when they were sad. Anyone could be related or look like someone else. It took something more to be close, to be family.

The front of the building was quiet, amplifying the sounds that came from further within the restaurant.

"¿Buenos días?" Lola called out tentatively.

A boy stepped out of a back doorway. He beamed at her the way only strangers can smile at other strangers, his curls partially obscured under a beanie. Several organs in Lola's body threatened to flip themselves inside out.

"Tú eres la prima de Juana, ¿no?" he asked.

A crash sounded in the room behind him—the kitchen, Lola suspected—but the boy didn't turn his attention away. He was the most beautiful boy Lola had ever seen up close. He had high cheekbones and dark eyebrows that framed green eyes, which were distressingly locked on Lola.

She gulped away her sudden nerves and nodded. It could barely be considered encouragement, yet it was enough for him.

"¿Qué haces aquí?"

"Lo . . . lo siento," she offered, trying to avoid his gaze. She didn't want to risk what would happen if they made eye contact. "Mi español es . . ." The plaster walls bounced her unsteady pronunciation back at her tauntingly.

He only smiled wider. "Ah, she's an American."

A beat, and then: "Well, we all are. But you are the kind that calls yourself one. A gringa."

The comment momentarily snapped Lola out of the shock that a boy that looked like *that* would talk to *her*. She glowered before she realized what she was doing, and then immediately wondered if it was possible to disappear on the spot. Hadn't they invented an app for that yet?

He laughed. "Okay, she doesn't like 'gringa,'" he observed, and straightened himself. "Hi, American. I'm Gregorio, but you can call me Río. I'm training you today. Is this your first time at La Rosa?" It was like he could crank his friendliness up at will, and his voice balanced on the tightrope between recitation and sincerity.

"I, uh," she paused, trying to think about what would sound breeziest.

What would Ana say?

Probably not something that required an inner monologue to coach yourself through.

Answer him, Lola!

"Estoy aquí para el verano," she offered, wincing as she did so. Would he really care that she was only here for the summer? "Estás . . . Are you good friends with Juana?"

Río laughed and glanced at the clock. "Sí, algo así," he said. "But I didn't know Juana had a pretty American for a cousin. Better friends would share that, no?"

"So you're enemies, then; got it," Lola said automatically, trying not to let the fact that he might have just called her *pretty* short-circuit her nerve endings.

Río laughed again. He carried his beauty with confidence, the way Padilla and the soccer boys sauntered down the hallway, secure in their place at the top of the social order.

"Okay, so first lesson," he said, standing upright. He was tall and younger than Juana—he couldn't have been more than eighteen. "Come on, American, let's get started."

With that, Río began giving her a tour of the restaurant. Lola fumbled with her hair and was suddenly very aware of the mechanics required to walk. She immediately regretted not picking a cuter top that morning, even in the rush of being late and even though Juana had told her the uniform was black jeans and a black shirt. She was struck with a desire to know what Río thought about her *specific* black T-shirt. Were there differences in black T-shirts? Did he even care? Then it dawned on her that this boy was talking to her and, worse, expected her to reply.

"Y aquí tenemos mi oficina," he said, gesturing expansively at the bar. Lola made a mental note to never mention him to Buela. Her aversion to Juana's restaurant, boys in general, and probably the combination of boys and alcohol, too, meant Río was 100 percent off-limits.

Río motioned to turn a corner toward the kitchen. "So you are in Mexico for the summer," he said, echoing her weak explanation for existing here at this moment. "Why?"

One look at this boy, whose shirtsleeves were rolled up and who beamed at her expectantly for some witty comeback, compelled Lola to be honest. "My dad sent me here to learn Spanish. I got a bad grade in class, and . . ." He laughed. "I mean it! I got one C, and ta-da: Mexico."

"Well, it's good you learn," he offered.

"I guess. It felt a little . . . extreme, you know? I'm usually not the kind of girl to get a C."

Río raised an eyebrow. "What kind of girl *are* you?"

Lola felt her words stick in her throat. What kind of girl was she? An introvert? A shy girl? A girl who wouldn't know how to answer that question had anyone asked her, let alone a cute boy?

When she didn't reply, he began talking enough for the both of them, his body nudging close to hers as a way of guiding where they walked.

Río talked quickly and easily, and more about himself than the restaurant's routines. English had been his favorite subject in school, he explained, and now wasn't he lucky that he had the chance to practice with Lola? But before she was able to respond, he launched right back into the story of who *he* was, and it was easier for Lola to listen quietly than risk letting her nerves spill out in front of this stranger who suddenly didn't feel that strange to her.

As Río told it, he was an actor; he also worked at a Starbucks in the colonia San Rafael because he liked being near the theaters and because sometimes he'd book workshops in the area, so it was convenient that he hadn't been fired from the Starbucks yet—apparently they thought he was *too* friendly with the customers when he was trying to make conversation, but that was what happened when you were one of five kids, which also made it hard to live at home given that so many other people lived there, too, so he made coffee and bartended here and there for rent money, but Juana's restaurants were his favorite—his friend had gotten him the job, which he supposed was more proof of his good fortune.

It was a long and winding monologue, but one he delivered good-naturedly . . . and without ever taking his eyes off Lola. They now had only thirty minutes before La Rosa was supposed to open, and more and more staffers began filtering through the space and preparing it for lunch.

"Mira, American," Río said, grabbing a napkin from a nearby table and pulling his pen from a back pocket. "Ya tienes mi número. If you ever have a rough day and I'm not here, call me. ¿Tienes WhatsApp?"

Lola tried to make sense of the fact that this beautiful not-quite-stranger had really given her his number.

"Um, thank you?" she asked, and he laughed again.

Just then, Juana walked through the front door and made a beeline toward her cousin. "Loli, ¡aquí estás!" Lola cringed at the nickname. Either Juana was ignoring the face Lola made, or it had goaded her on. "Ready to work?"

"I . . . think so?" Lola said nervously. She didn't dare tell her cousin that she was now fighting a weird kind of fog surrounding her every thought, as if her brain were swimming through clouds.

"Let's see if Linares here did his job right for once," Juana said, pulling her away from Río and giving the boy a knowing wink. "Gracias, amigo."

"De nada," Río said, and Lola felt her stomach do that weird lurch again. "I'll see you around, American."

Lola followed Juana, sneaking one last glance at Río before any actual training made her too busy. She almost walked into a table as a result. Río was watching her, his smile bigger than ever. And it was a smile meant expressly for her.

Where Río had given Lola a crash course in Río Linares 101, Juana was much more focused on the intricacies of La Rosa, up to and including the story of how she and Rocío had decided to open their own restaurant to begin with. (It involved a terrible night at the restaurant where they first met and a contract written in eyeliner on the back of a grocery store receipt at three a.m.) Juana also wasted no time before grilling Lola on the menu and why it was special that their tortillas were made in-house and what to do if a patron didn't speak Spanish and couldn't decipher the menu, and why it was crucial that she highlight the chapulines to every table she could the second she seated them. Lola tried her best to commit every rule to memory. This was Juana's restaurant, and she was graciously giving Lola an excuse to get out of her grandmother's house. Whatever Juana said about the menu was law.

The next few hours were . . . well, to call them rocky would be an understatement. On top of trying to ignore her growing nausea, Lola was mostly shadowing Dani, an Asian man around Juana's age with dark hair and shirtsleeves rolled tightly to show off biceps the size of Lola's thigh. He usually split his time between the La Rosa in Juárez and the La Rosa in la Roma. "I have two rules for my hosting desk," he told Lola matter-of-factly. "Don't eat while you're up here, and remember that my bartenders are supposed to smile and flirt with everyone . . . including you."

As simple as the instructions were, the actuality of Lola's tasks was daunting. When a couple stopped her on the way to the kitchen to ask a question, she had to call Dani over to translate, and she had to guide not one but three parties back up to the front so she could study the map more thoroughly when she misheard the number of patrons in their groups. And she truly could not understand the body language that indicated whether people were looking for a table or simply trying to edge their way into the popular bar area.

Still, she hadn't dropped anything, or visibly offended anyone, or caused any irreparable damage in the variety of ways her imagination ever-so-helpfully supplied. She might not be a natural, but at least she proved she could learn.

Lola was only supposed to work the lunch shift that day, so after the restaurant closed to prepare for dinner, she stood around awkwardly, trying to find something to do and to stay out of the way of the more seasoned staff until Mari picked her up. So when Río beckoned her from behind the bar, she tentatively sat down across from him. (She couldn't get in trouble for sitting there, could she?) The nausea she had felt for hours was now a steady hum in the background of her body. Maybe Buela could make something to soothe it later.

"Don't worry, I'm not going to serve you alcohol—or tell anyone you drank it," Río offered as he wiped down a glass. Lola felt her cheeks burn with embarrassment. "So how was your first day?"

"Uh, I survived it, so I guess . . . ¿bien?"

"See? You are . . . How do you say it? Natural."

Río beamed and Lola felt herself relax, a tiny copy of his smile creeping onto her face.

Just then, someone behind Lola caught Río's eye, and he waved. "¡Jovenazo!" he called. "Aquí viene el príncipe de Nuestra Señora de la Rosa."

Lola turned around to see a boy around Río's age heading toward them. He was slightly shorter than Río, and his skin was a deeper, more golden brown—though, really, that wasn't difficult; Río was as fair as Regina and her sisters—and he looked as bored as Río looked engaged.

"This is Javier Ávila Idar. He's a server here, but we used to go to school together," Río said. "Javi, this is Juana's secret cousin. She's an American."

The boy and Lola made eye contact for half a second. There was something instantly judgmental in the way he looked at her, which she liked even less than Cristina's queen-bee shakedown from a few days prior.

Ever the master of timing, Juana picked that moment to swoop in with a platter of tostadas, demanding that Lola and Río taste-test them for Rocío. She greeted the other boy warmly and said something that sounded to Lola like a confirmation of work hours, before turning back to Lola expectantly.

"Well, are you not going to eat?" she asked. "I feed you, I pay you, and when I ask for your help making this menu perfect . . ."

Lola grabbed a tostada, and Juana beamed, placated. The boy, Javier, grabbed a seat next to Lola without a word. She hoped he wouldn't pick up on the discomfort that was now radiating off her.

Juana certainly didn't, because she switched topics with the authority of a news anchor. "So, Loli. What are you doing this weekend?"

Lola imagined herself sitting around in her grandmother's house, texting Ana and half watching Buela's telenovelas. "Nothing, I don't think," she said, feeling deeply uncool to admit it. At least she had left out saying *Same as always*.

Juana scoffed. "What do you mean 'nothing'? It's your first month in Mexico. We can't let you do 'nothing.'"

"You know what I haven't seen in years?" Río offered. "The pyramids."

Lola had been to Teotihuacán once before, with her parents. She remembered how massive they were to her little-girl brain, and she wondered what it would be like to experience them now. Back then, she had been too tired to walk any more down the Avenue of the Dead, and Papi had to carry her at least two-thirds of the way.

The idea of marching up and down a sacred historical site delighted Juana, whose very curls shook with their endorsement. "We'll make the cousins come with us— even Regina, who won't go anywhere without Adrián," she said. She looked at Río and Javier. "Y ustedes también, obvio."

"Sí, claro," Río said. "Fue mi idea, ¿no?"

Lola smiled at him automatically, which turned into a blush when he returned the grin. Javier, by contrast, looked somewhat put off by the prospect, though Lola also noticed his face held an intensity that matched Río's beauty. Whereas Río's floppy curls and openness were straight from a boy-band template, Javier's buzzcut turned his facial features—from his cheekbones to the lines of his mouth—into something singular and artistic.

Río nudged her, and the square inch of her shoulder he had made contact with suddenly felt more alive and alert than every other body part combined. "And we have the best tour guide in the city! Javier will give you the best tour you've ever had. You should have seen the way this man answered every question in our history classes. He loves those things."

Javier grimaced but said nothing. Lola looked from one boy to the other and back, trying to puzzle out how someone so open could be friends with someone so standoffish.

But that might be how some people at school thought about her and Ana, she realized, and began instead to study her cuticles in silent mortification.

"¿El sábado?" Juana asked.

Lola stole one more glance at Río as she weighed her options. If she felt this nervous around someone she had met mere hours ago, how would she survive an entire afternoon with him? *What would Ana do?* she asked herself.

Ana would take the risk.

"Sí, ¿cómo no?" she tried. "Let's do it."

Juana smirked at Lola's response for a moment—it was a flash of amusement that only Lola saw, but it didn't make her feel any less self-conscious that maybe she had gotten such a simple response wrong.

Rather than tease her cousin further, Juana changed the conversation, diving into updates about a romantic saga featuring people Río and Javier knew. Her cousin's Spanish was almost too quick for Lola, but she tried her best to keep up. Javier contributed the least to the volley, focused more on refilling the saltshakers that waited at the end of the bar than getting sucked into Juana's chisme, but Lola began to tune his energy out. It wasn't her fault if someone else was going to be sour about . . . about what? Her mere presence?

By the time Mari showed up to take her home, Lola was too full from the tostadas—which featured a fried squash flower that oozed cheese pleasantly when you bit into them—to move quickly. She said goodbye to Juana and Río, who smiled and said he was excited for Saturday, which, he added, couldn't come fast enough. (Javier had disappeared into the kitchen by that point.) Lola and Mari climbed into the Toyota, precariously placing plenty of leftovers on the already-cluttered back seats.

"Did you have fun today, Lola?" Mari asked.

Lola nodded. The day hadn't gone perfectly, but it had been fun anyway—a benchmark for satisfaction she wasn't sure she had experienced before. She was still nervous, about the job and about seeing Río again. But she decided that the uneasy feeling in her stomach was the good kind, for once.

Back in her and Mari's room, Lola flopped down on her bed with her phone. Ana had sent a few dozen texts, roughly half of which were concerned with whether or not she should take her mom up on a grand tour of colleges on the East Coast later that summer.

> **AM:** It would be nice to get away from 800 repeats for even a day
>
> Or maybe I should check out schools in Texas, get in touch with
> *my roots*
>
> Bet my mom would love that
>
> Go Horns, etc
>
> Wait, it's hook 'em horns, right?
>
> Better than Boston, I guess
>
> I don't think I could do Boston winters
>
> Anyway, how's CDMX?

Lola involuntarily shuddered at the idea of below-freezing temperatures. One of the primary perks of living in Southern California was the almost-comically pleasant weather, which was only marred by a heat wave or ten every year.

She began typing out her feelings about Ana's collegiate prospects—it was easier to have an opinion there, where her own future wasn't involved. And after logically pointing out that Ana would have at least one coat should she indeed go to school in a city where winter dipped below sixty degrees, she took a deep breath and started typing again. For the first time in a long time—maybe ever—she had her own news with which to report back.

> **LE:** You're gonna be so proud of me, A
>
> I met this guy who also works at my cousin's restaurant today . . .

In response, she received approximately one thousand !!!!!!!!s, as well as a few upside-down exclamation points for good measure. Even señora Smith would have to give Ana points for that.

CHAPTER 5

Cristina Gómez y Gómez, Lola quickly learned, was used to getting what she wanted.

Lola was almost impressed, the way she always felt a begrudging respect for movie villains who had very clear, rather understandable motives. But Cristina had a flirty giggle where most bad guys cackled, and the girl had somehow schemed her way into sharing the back seat of Javier's car with Lola on their trip out of the city. It didn't take a straight-A student to figure out why. Río was riding in the front seat.

That morning, an entire crew had showed up to Buela's, including Cristina and her sister Regina; Regina's boyfriend, Adrían, who grumbled that the only place he should be at seven a.m. on a Saturday was in bed; Río, who was wearing jeans and a T-shirt in the casual way that beautiful people do and grinning one of those toothpaste-ad smiles; and Javier, who looked like the non-famous cousin to Río's movie star and as bored as he had that first night at La Rosa. Juana had excused herself from her own plans at the last minute, claiming that if five of her employees were calling out, her restuarants simply couldn't spare her, too.

As was apparently now their custom, Javier had made eye contact with Lola, almost daring her to break the connection first again, which she did. She didn't understand why he took Juana up on the invite if he was intent on being in such a bad mood, and if she were braver, she might have asked him outright why he was there. Ana would have asked, she thought. Then again, Ana would have probably charmed him into friendship on day one.

Cristina, however, opted for strategy rather than charm. The oldest Gómez sister had assigned everyone to one of the two cars driven by Javier and Adrián—and by some feat of seniority, femininity, or witchcraft, her various relatives and friends listened to her. Conveniently, she'd seated herself with Lola . . . and the two single—and objectively attractive—boys in the group.

For a few miles, Cristina tried to engage Río and Javier in conversation. Javier either nodded his head or gave one-word answers, and every response Río gave was directed at Lola and paired with that same trillion-tooth smile.

A sulky Cristina eventually gave up, and rather than incur her cousin's wrath by breaking the silence, Lola satisfied herself with sneaking glances at Río whenever it felt like Cristina wasn't looking. He had exactly one dimple, Lola noticed from the back seat, and the asymmetry punctuated his face perfectly. The complete set would have been overkill.

It was even safer to steal glances at Javier, whose fingers tapped along to the Bad Bunny song on the radio as he drove. He and Río were the same age, that much was clear, but he seemed to square his body up against everyone else in the car, and perhaps against the world. It was only when the highway began to give way to roadside food vendors and the car tried to navigate unpaved gravel that the tension in his back snapped into something less hostile. Javier paid a man in a baseball cap and a long-sleeved polo shirt to let them into a parking lot, where he found a spot a few spaces down from Adrián's car and took his time putting the car in park.

Lola wondered if he was this deliberate with everything or if he was stalling.

Cristina, however, was operating on a different frequency than she had at the start of the day, and had gone from friendly to hurt to haughty simply because neither boy had flirted with her. She bolted out of the car and toward her sister the first second she could. "You understand, don't you, Lorenita?" she asked before turning to Río. "Take care of mi primita, Río lindo." The fact that she was ditching her cousin hung in the air like the dig it was.

Lola heard someone whistle in disbelief at her back. She turned around: It was Javier.

"Your cousin, la fresa—is she always like that?" he asked Lola. His eyebrow was arched—which was was the most emotion she'd seen from him all day.

Río scoffeed. "Who are you calling 'fresa,' fresa?"

Javier ignored him.

"I wouldn't know," Lola admitted. "This is the most time I've ever spent with her."

Javier's brow furrowed. "But you've been to Mexico before?"

"Well, yes," Lola tried. "Most of the time I'm with my parents and my brother. This is a different kind of trip."

"Different how?"

She could only stammer. Somehow, she felt like he wouldn't appreciate "I'm more bitter this time around" as an acceptable response.

Javier went quiet again, but Lola couldn't tell if he was satisfied by their conversation, if it could even be called that.

Río chose that moment to interject. "Why didn't you tell me your name was Lorenita? I like it."

"Because it's not," Lola felt a need to inspect the cuffs of her jacket rather than look at him. It helped the nerves a little. "It's Lola. Well, Lorena, but everyone calls me Lola."

Río's eyes sought hers. "Pero yo no quiero ser 'every-one,'" he said smoothly.

Lola almost choked on the air around them. From up ahead, she heard Cristina and Regina share a joke, their laughs mirroring each other's. The sound made Lola feel a pang of homesickness for Ana, who would have probably loved nothing more than to spar with Javi and to serve as guard against Río's lines. Lola could almost hear Ana in her head, grilling him on what his *intentions* were toward her best friend.

The Pyramid of the Sun loomed ahead of them, its tan bricks already baking in the sun. It was smaller than Lola remembered it from when she was little, though she was intimidated by exactly how many steps it would take to reach the top. Tourists crowded its staircases, and Lola could see some people striking yoga poses on the ledges.

"Anything for Instagram," she muttered.

Río nudged her lightly in the ribs with his elbow. His touch made her inhale sharply. "You want to go to the top?" he asked. "Come on, I'll take your photo."

Lola shook her head. "That's okay, I want to look at it from here first. Really soak it up mentally."

"You know, my family comes here every year during the . . . how do you say el solsticio?"

"Solstice?" Lola supplied.

Río grinned. "Sí. We don't eat anything, and by the time we get here, I'm always so hungry I could faint. But we climb to the top and hold out our hands and get our energy from the sun, the way the people who built these pyramids did. And then we climb back down and have a huge feast. It gives you energy for the entire year."

They had begun walking down the wide pathway past the Pyramid of the Sun and toward the smaller pyramid, the Pyramid of the Moon. Lola kept trying to sneak glances at Río without being obvious, but she had a suspicion that she was failing.

Río kept talking as they went, pointing out the vendors selling musical instruments and miniature replicas of the sun stone to the tourists walking by.

"My dad's got one of those hanging in the living room back home," Lola said. She could see Thomas in her mind's eye now, on the couch under the plaque, in that one spot he always claimed during football season. It was *his* seat, he said whenever Tommy or Churro tried to commandeer it. Miraculously, they would always listen and give it up.

A pang of homesickness hit somewhere behind Lola's heart. She and her father hadn't exchanged a single text since he dropped her off at the airport.

"Do you want one?" Río asked. "I'll buy it for you."

Lola shook her head. "I'm okay, thanks," she said, smiling quickly lest he think her no was a rejection. "Does that really work, though? Getting energy from the sun? Food would be a better way to achieve that goal." She tilted her face up and felt the sunbeams warm her skin.

"Why would the Mexica carve the entire sun stone if it didn't work?" Río boasted.

"I don't know. But, like, scientifically . . ."

From behind them, Javier scoffed. "Just because it doesn't fit with your science doesn't mean it's not worth believing in."

Río tossed a glare his friend's way, but Lola's eyes were locked on Javier.

"Science is science," she tried. "And hunger is hunger.

I'm just saying, if he wants energy, it makes sense to eat something."

Javier shook his head. "What's wrong with believing that you can find strength in the world around you?" he asked.

Lola balked, not only at his question but also because this was the most she had heard him speak . . . ever.

She could feel his eyes on her, waiting—almost daring her to reply. "Are you telling me you believe this, too?" she asked. "Is this what you're studying at college or something?"

"I study business," Javier said with finality.

"I thought Río said history was your thing."

An intensity flashed in Javier's eyes, making his cheekbones even sharper, almost dangerous. Río was pretty, but Lola could see how someone might consider Javier beautiful in a terrifying sort of way. That is, if they didn't feel a surge of loathing toward him, as she did now.

"Lorena, right?" The question of her full name caught Lola off guard. "Do you learn Mexican history at your school, too?"

She shook her head. "Most of the history classes I've taken focus on the United States, unless there was some global implication that affected us." She paused. "I know it's kind of narcissistic, if you think about it."

"Pues claro," he said. His eyes glinted pityingly, and Lola shuddered involuntarily. "You're from California . . . which was part of Mexico. Like Texas and Arizona. Does your American school teach you that?"

"Of course I know *that*," Lola replied, the forced light-ness evaporating from her voice. "And how before then, it was part of Spain, who stole it from the Native people already living there. Mrs. Parker in eighth grade called it, like . . . this great opportunity, the unknown frontier. It was definitely more of a revision than it was actual history."

"So a lie, then," Javier said.

"Yeah, I . . ." She tried to think of a way to end the conversation. "If they're lying to us so much, do you really think they're going to spend time focusing on other countries instead?"

"Is that what Mexico is to you? Just some 'other country'?" His voice was quiet, but she could hear the accusation in his tone.

Lola stared at Javier, her mind drafting a list of the things she wanted to say, of the things she felt this boy deserved to hear, and the ways she was going to recap this to Ana via text message later. Blue chat bubbles scrolled through her head in quick succession. But none of those words came out quickly enough, and anyway, the person she wanted to yell at most was herself.

Out of the corner of her eye, Río motioned that she should come with him, a silent offer to put physical dis-tance between her and his so-called friend.

Instead, Lola turned and made a beeline back toward the mouth of the Pyramid of the Sun, its crumbling stone staircases reinforced by guide ropes. She moved as quickly as she could around the laughing tourists, and even after

73

her legs began burning from the steps, she refused to stop or even look back down.

That her muscles were screaming halfway through her climb was fine by her because it matched the stinging in her eyes and dulled the queasiness she had felt around Río for two hours.

What Javier had forced her to admit to him—that her textbooks and teachers had a frustrating knack for lying to her and to everyone, and that the United States white-washed its violence—somehow made her feel ignorant and small. She wondered if the same was true of Mexican textbooks and of lesson plans in other countries, and she was reminded of the way Ana's mother often instructed the girls to say "California" whenever anyone asked what part of Mexico they "came" from. "We didn't cross the border, the border crossed us!" Mrs. Morris, who had been born in San Antonio, would yell with a whoop.

But how much did Lola really know about the steps she was climbing? What about the city behind them, whose colonias intimidated her and made her wonder if she'd ever know her way around on her own? How much had she ever cared to find out? Her parents had instilled a kind of hybrid pride in her and her brother from day one, reminding them every chance they could about the legacy they were building as Mexican Americans. Even so, the Mexico part of the equation had always been both a fact and an intangible, untouchable magic. It was the place her mother was from, and where she suspected

74

her father felt guilty for not having been born.

But now Lola was in Mexico, and her old life felt like the distant and foreign thing. Javi's words rang in her head, taunting her. It stung to think that maybe he was right, that she had been treating Mexico like something other and outside of herself, even a little. *Americans.* It echoed in her head like a curse.

She was also Mexican, wasn't she? Maybe not in the way Javier and Río were, but her heritage meant something. It had to. Her parents had said it did more times than she could count. But now that she was here, she wasn't so sure. Or perhaps she had misunderstood what that meant all along.

Lola pushed hot tears out of her eyes but didn't stop climbing until she reached the highest ledge she could. When she looked out at the horizon, her bitterness melted away. A few buildings poked out here and there from within an endless blanket of green, and she could see roads and the hint of a highway through miles of trees and mountains. Mexico stretched in front of her, in all the ways it had been built and destroyed and remade and claimed again and again for centuries. She gazed at the miles of land that were older than even the country itself, that had seen loss and heartache and betrayal but also rituals and holy days and hope.

She pulled out her phone and took a single photo. Everyone around her was focused on angles, dangling their feet over the pyramid ledge and taking selfies with outstretched arms and sticks, but something told Lola one photo was enough. A breeze picked up, and she felt the wind on her cheek where a tear had crawled a moment before.

Lola wasn't going to let one mean boy ruin her summer, she decided. Javier and Río weren't a package deal, and Río was not defined by his proximity to his friend any more than Lola was by hers to Ana. That was, she might not be if her classmates gave her a chance. Perhaps if she gave herself a chance.

After a few minutes, she headed back down the steep stairs, keeping her eyes on the horizon as she went and only looking down to try and spot Río once she neared the pyramid's base. He was waiting under a tree a few yards away from the glut of tourists. Javier was nowhere in sight.

Lola cautiously made her way toward Río, who smiled comfortingly. He was always smiling. Lola liked that about him.

"Ey, I . . ." He paused, lost for words. "Look, Javi, he . . ."

"Don't worry about it," she supplied quickly. She didn't want to make things weird. "It's okay."

"But this was fun." Río smiled. "The memory will make going to work this afternoon even nicer. I like spending time with you, American."

The fresh reminder that she was the American stung, but Lola smiled back anyway. Río had freckles across his nose that made the hazel in his green eyes pop; that's how close he was standing to her.

"Necesito irme con Javi, pero . . ." Río began.

Rather than finish his sentence, he leaned in and kissed her.

Lola stood there, trying to commit to memory how his stubble felt on her cheek and that he smelled like laundry detergent and some kind of mass-produced cologne. Usually, the stench of Wild Mountain or Pure Testosterone or whatever it was that followed boys down the school hallways gave Lola a headache. She didn't mind it so much this time—the feel of Río's lips pressed on hers more than made up for it. Though she was too surprised to kiss him back, the sensation was everything she'd imagined a kiss could be: warm and entirely thrilling.

Regretfully, she forced herself to pull away, annoyed and thankful for Juana's scheduling buzzkill all at once. Lola was scheduled to work that night, a baptism by fire as far as the Saturday rush was concerned. "I should go find my cousins," she said shyly. "But I . . . I had a great time today." And then, almost kicking herself for how silly and open she sounded, she added, "I hope I'll see you again soon."

Río smiled the easy, confident smile of a boy who was probably used to kissing girls he liked, who had every reason to believe the world would keep spinning comfortably on its axis if he did what he wanted. "Oh, American," he said. "I'll make sure of it."

CHAPTER 6

The car ride home was a giddy blur—Lola was so bewildered, she even ignored Cristina's pointed commentary about "las tipas americanas" and what separated them from las mexicanas orgullosas. Her cousin's voice was a taunting singsong, a monologue meant for herself. Lola tried her best to tune her out.

She focused instead on the queasiness that had settled in her body the minute she met Río and that had only grown in intensity now that he had kissed her. Her nerves sounded like heavy static in her ears, and the harder Lola ignored Cristina, the lounder the buzz grew.

She closed her eyes and took a deep breath.

The noise was still there. Dialed up to a hundred.

It almost sounded like whispering, but she couldn't make out what it was telling her.

The second she could escape the car after it pulled up to Buela's house, Lola ran straight to Mari's bedroom to text Ana and lie down for at least an hour. If there was ever a moment to send texts a few words at a time, this was it.

But Lola fell asleep the second she hit Send—and Ana's replies went unseen. Because when Lola's grandmother called her for dinner before she was expected to join Juana at La Rosa, she stood up, felt her stomach jump into her throat . . . and promptly fainted.

She came to five seconds or maybe five minutes later, and it took a moment to remember where she was.

"Lorena, ¿ya vienes?" Buela yelled again.

"¡Un momento!" she called down, trying to buy herself time. For once in her life, she had no idea what to do.

Mercifully, she had fainted onto her bed—the fall hadn't been onto the concrete floor. She tried to sit up and steady her breathing as she peered at her reflection in Mari's mirror across the room. Her face was a disturbing gray, even under a carefully applied layer of skin tint.

A sound came from the doorway. Buela was standing there, watching her curiously.

"Buela, yo . . ." Lola's voice dropped off. She wanted to tell her grandmother what was wrong, but she couldn't translate the words quickly enough in her head. What was the word for "fainted"? Hadn't señora Smith gone over that at least once?

Her grandmother moved closer to the bed. The look on her face was impossible to decipher—maybe it was fear, but what would Buela have to be scared of?

"¿Qué hiciste en las pirámides?" Buela asked.

Lola balked. She didn't think the pyramids had anything to do with fainting, or at least she couldn't imagine how. She really hadn't done anything unusual by normal teenage-girl standards: She hadn't even eaten anything beyond that small bag of chips she and Regina split in the car on the way back. And while she imagined the chile coating was filled with chemicals, she had eaten junk food millions of times before.

There was nothing she could think of—besides one major, world-altering kiss—that had been out of the ordinary for her, and certainly nothing that could cause her to lose consciousness, medically speaking. It wasn't like she suddenly developed an allergic reaction to Río—had she?

Her grandmother watched her, waiting expectantly for an answer. Then, after what felt like an eternity, the woman left the room, a whirl of skirts and orthopedic shoes.

Within minutes, Lola's grandmother was back with a small matchbook and a piece of palo santo, which she lit so that the stick glowed faintly with embers that did not want to go out. The room filled with the earthy scent of smoke, and Buela made the sign of the cross in her granddaughter's direction, muttering to herself about maldiciones and San Nicolás and Lola's mother.

Lola watched as curls of smoke twisted and faded away from the stick in her grandmother's hand. She had no idea what her mother had to do with saints, but she dared not interrupt Buela, who was waving the palo santo in one hand and tightly clutching the rosary hanging from her neck with the other.

Lola didn't like the idea of leaving her sudden illness up to . . . whatever her grandmother was praying to, especially not when she was strongly considering fainting again. But if she focused on her grandmother's voice, the static dulled just a little and she felt less disoriented than she had in days.

Buela sat down in a worn, overstuffed armchair Lola suspected was older than even Mami, and slowed her words as if she was considering both their meaning and gravity. Miraculously, Lola could understand almost everything. Perhaps her Spanish was better than she—or señora Smith—gave herself credit for.

Buela was saying that what had happened to Lola was no accident.

That the spirits—*What spirits?* Lola almost asked— were trying to talk to her.

The older woman's brow furrowed, and Lola began to understand.

Buela was saying that the Gómez women were cursed.

Without so much as a knock on the bedroom door, Juana came bursting into Lola's room, nodding toward their grandmother as a form of greeting. "Loli, Javier is watching the restaurant during dinner. ¡La pinche cena!" she huffed. "I can't let you already be sick. I just hired you!

81

Do you want for me to hire somebody else? I can do that."

"Juana, you're the one who suggested I take this job, not me." Lola tried to to sit up in bed but was immediately warned not to move by her grandmother, who muttered something to Juana and left the room again. She still had food in the kitchen and other family members that needed to be fed.

"¿Y qué, Loli?" Juana asked. "Is this how Americans treat work?"

Lola's brain caught up to the conversation. "Wait, who said anything about me being too sick to work tonight? Did Buela call you?"

"Be smart, Loli. I stopped here to pick something up, and Buela told me you had a sickness, but she did not say what. And I need my best host at work. ¡Trabajando!"

"I'm not your best host. That's Dani, and we both know it."

"Sí, pues . . . I need the hostess who makes my favorite bartender show up on time."

Lola felt her stomach do another somersault, this time in a not-unpleasant kind of way.

"I didn't know Buela said I was sick. I don't know what's going on, either. She just said I was cursed and . . . here I am."

Juana made a sound that sounded halfway between a squeak and nervous laughter. "A curse?"

"You know, like with spirits? What did she call it? ¿Una maldición? Well, whatever it is, I've been fighting

82

this weird . . . buzzing sound for days, and then I fainted."

If Lola were explaining this to herself, she'd call herself a liar. She waited for her cousin to do the same.

Instead, Juana exhaled and sat down on Mari's bed. It was a Saturday night, and Juana would eventually return to her duties, but Lola was her focus for now.

"Lorena, Buela is right," she said. "Did your mamá never tell you the Gómezes are cursed?"

Lola's eyebrows shot up before she could control them. Was everyone in her family in agreement here—and if they were, did they ever plan on telling her? Her mother had never mentioned any curse. Then again, Mami talked a lot about her family, but she hardly ever spoke about her life before she moved to Oxnard. For Mami, it was infinitely more useful to talk about what was happening in the here and now. The past was for people in the past.

"Don't look at me like that, Loli; it's true. The entire Gómez family . . . The women are . . . ." Juana's voice trailed off.

"But why?"

Juana shrugged. "No sé. You have to know I only heard this from mi mamá, y la chismosa . . . ." She sighed, the points of her shoulders hinting through her button-down. "My mother thinks it's tía Letty's fault. Buela was always a bit"—she whistled for emphasis, and Lola winced in defense of their grandmother—"but she got even stricter with her children when Letty left Mexico with your father."

Lola knew her grandmother was protective and cautious, but she had never considered it might have something to do with her mother. Did Buela feel abandoned by Letty? Was that why she doted on her family so completely? It didn't make sense that such coddling could serve as a talisman against spirits or a curse, but . . .

She looked up at Juana, trying to form her next question. And in that moment, she was hit with a memory—not of her mother, but of her cousin during one of the first trips to Mexico City that she could remember.

Lola had been around five or six, the age where plane rides lasted forever and she regularly asked her tíos and tías to take her to the store for candy. Buela's kitchen had been just as worn then. And while her sisters and their cousins had been tasked to look after Lola and Tommy, Juana spent her time in that tiled room, learning their grandmother's secrets. Buela had tried shielding her from the stove, warning she'd get burnt, that she was still too young to touch the blistering poblanos herself. But Juana reached in to turn a pepper over an open flame with her hand anyway, just like their grandmother always did. And Buela had beamed.

Maybe stories and memories were useful if they taught Lola something about the family she couldn't quite crack.

Ever the one to charge back into a room unannounced, Buela returned with a blue plastic tub, the smell hitting Lola's nostrils with a force. She laughed despite herself.

Of course Buela would suggest Vicks VapoRub as a cure.

"Gracias, Buela," she offered meekly. But she wasn't just thanking her grandmother for taking care of her. It was a comfort to think someone had the answers to questions she didn't even know to be asking.

"Dios te bendiga," Buela told her. She straightened to her full height of five foot nothing, reminding Lola faintly of the days she had been allowed to stay home sick from school, when Mami made her soup and circled over her protectively. "Todo va a estar bien. Vas a ver."

Easy for you to say, Lola thought. *You're not the one who just lost consciousness.*

"¿Buela?" Lola asked tentatively.

Her grandmother held her gaze steadily, with eyes that were so similar to her mother's and to her own. Words slipped out of Lola's mouth in a terrified whisper. In English.

"So you both really believe we're cursed?" she asked Juana.

Juana's answer was unmistakable: "¿Y por qué no?"

And why not indeed. Lola nodded as Buela moved toward a small altar in the corner of Mari's room, where a photo of Lola's grandfather took center stage. It was identical to the painting that hung by the bar at La Rosa, another tribute to a man who was now a memory, whose youngest daughter had barely known him. The image was faded with sunspots, an object of love.

Buela said something ominously, and Juana reflexively

laughed. Lola tilted her head, asking for a translation.

"She said, 'If the spirits can decide to curse you, God and Jesus can save you.'" Juana shrugged. "Sometimes I think she thinks we are characters in one of her telenovelas."

Then Lola's grandmother sighed and turned for the kitchen, back to the chores, back to the cleaning, back to the movement that her home—her entire life—demanded of her.

Lola had a million questions for her cousin, but she settled on just one: "And no one's tried to break the curse?"

It was the polite alternative to asking *And you're just okay with being cursed . . . forever?*

Juana gave Lola an apologetic half smile. "I think la Señora visited a curandera once to make it stop, and then she tried a bruja, but these things . . . Sometimes the magic is too big," she said simply.

Lola shot up completely. "What do you mean, too big? Isn't there, like, a deal with the devil we could make?"

"It doesn't work that way," Juana said. "Well, I don't think it does. The devil, he is real, but he's too busy for these things. These are the spirits, Lorena. The city where my father is from, Catemaco, it's home to a lot of brujos. They don't just wave their hands and go 'buuu' and take your money. The ones that are real? Los brujos and brujas, they're different from curanderos, but sometimes magic doesn't undo magic. Sometimes it is just . . .

like adding more salt to something that's already salty."

Lola stared at her cousin, who was every inch the grown-up and fully bought into this idea. And if Juana did, who was to say it wasn't true?

A dog barked outside, and a car stalled before revving back to life on the street. In the distance, Lola could hear the tinny recording of the scrap-metal man offering to pay for people's spare parts and construction cast-offs. The city would not stop, not even for supernatural family secrets.

Was it possible? Was everything bad that had ever happened to her a result of some long-standing family curse? But that was just the thing—Lola couldn't really think of a single interesting thing that happened to her, let alone *bad*. If anything, she was cursed to not have much of a life at all.

Unless . . .

"Juana, what kind of curse is it? Like, what happens?"

"It changes. La Señora thinks that everyone she loves will leave her—why else do you think tía Mari still lives here? And tía Paty's divorce? Tu mamá, maybe she was cursed in her own way. And *my* mother cries every day that none of her daughters are married. She thinks our love lives are her curse. I keep telling Rocío, but she won't propose *because* of Socorro's drama."

Lola laughed despite herself. Tía Coco *would* take that personally. "And tío Chuy? Is his curse only having daughters?"

"No, that's just tío Chuy being un baboso. Cristina and her sisters will support machismo more than any sons. Really, they are a gift to him if he would just see it. That is why I think the curse is just for the women."

Lola turned this information over in her mind. Maybe it was simpler to have something to blame, to believe that things were outside your control. Lola had never felt in control of her own life. Her parents had always had the final word.

Juana shook her head as if answering a question Lola had yet to pose. "If you want to talk the spirits into changing their minds, mucha suerte."

"What spirits?" Lola asked.

"The ones that are everywhere," Juana said simply. "Maybe some of them are even at La Rosa. Which is where I should be right now."

Juana stood up and stretched, her business-lite attire in stark contrast to the cracked plaster of Mari's room. "Que te sientas mejor, primita," she teased. "I need you back to work soon because I need Río to stay at work, ¿entendido?"

With a wink, she was gone, leaving Lola to her swirling, screaming thoughts.

CHAPTER 7

"Wait, for real?"

"Yeah, Susana, *for real*."

Lola had a hunch that telling her best friend she was possibly cursed required more than a text. This was a video call kind of conversation. And Ana had responded exactly how Lola expected.

"Oh my god, oh my god, oh my god. I crash for, like, sixteen hours, and the most interesting thing to happen to either of us happens . . . to you."

"Ana, interesting things have happened to you," Lola tried.

Ana shrugged over the slightly glitchy Internet connection. "Yeah, but this is, like . . . This is the interesting thing we'll talk about for the rest of senior year. So what are you going to do about it?"

"I don't know if there is anything *to* do about it. Juana said I shouldn't mess with the spirits. And, like, it's pretty unbelievable."

"But you believe her, don't you?"

Lola sighed.

"Well, don't you?"

"I don't know. My grandma wouldn't even tell me *why* we're cursed. Or why she *thinks* we're cursed. I have no idea why this is happening now."

"Maybe something triggered it. I can pull a card if you want me to," Ana offered.

"The last thing I want is to involve even more spirits. If any are involved to begin with."

Ana screwed up her face in thought. "Okay, I have to get ready for practice, but . . . we can figure this out on our own. What did you do right before you fainted?"

"I was texting you."

"Rewind the tape further, Lo. What happened before that?"

"We were at the pyramids."

"Yeah, but, like, did anything out of the ordinary happen?"

"Ana, you know that I . . . don't kiss people. I don't get kissed *by* people. That's not ordinary for me. How is that ordinary?"

"For most teenagers it's pretty ordinary."

Lola shot her best friend a glare that she hoped looked just as salty in pixelated form as she meant it to be.

Ana's face fell. "Wait a minute . . ." she said, and Lola braced herself for whatever she was going to say next. "What if you kissing that boy . . . is connected to this curse?"

"Just because I have, like, five seconds of practice doesn't mean you need to rub it in."

"I'm being serious!" Ana tried. "What I mean is, what if you got sick *because* of your make-out session?" She rooted around her room and through piles of clothes. It was the kind of scene that would make Letty throw a fit. "Do you remember what happened after you kissed . . . what was his name? Chris, right?"

As popular as Ana was, she was singularly horrible with names. "Yes, Chris. You had history and PE with him," Lola reminded her. "But that wasn't . . . I probably got food poisoning. The cafeteria in middle school was not good."

"What if it *wasn't* food poisoning? What if it was the curse?"

Not for the first time since she'd fainted, Lola didn't know how to turn her feelings into words. The logic she used every day of her life was slipping out of her grasp, and in its place was a small and unfamiliar *what if?*

She tried one last-ditch effort at rationality, trying to convince herself as much as she was Ana. "What if this is really bad anxiety or something?"

Ana nodded sagely as she sifted through her closet. "You do get anxious about like . . . actually, even if the check engine light goes off in that car of yours. You're the least chill person I've ever met."

Lola opened her mouth to protest, but Ana kept going.

"You know, the anxiety of kissing someone new usually goes away *after* I make out with her, but if . . . Oh! You know how there's that expression, *Takes your breath away* when something is, like, really intense? What if—what's his name? Río? Is he *that* good at kissing? Maybe I should take lessons on, like . . . the *theory* behind what he does. That's some potent technique."

Lola didn't dare look at her reflection in the screen's corner, but she felt herself blush. "It was like going to the moon and back," she mumbled.

"You were in front of the Pyramid of the Sun, I thought."

"Not literally," Lola said. If she didn't move, she could almost ignore how her brain itself felt blurred, like it was a pencil sketch and someone had taken an eraser to its lines. "I don't know what to believe."

"What if I helped?" Ana asked. "I could help you solve this curse; this is what best friends are *for*. Are you sure you don't want me to pull? I'm getting really good at reading."

It was just like Ana to think they could get to the bottom of . . . whatever was happening to Lola. Even on zero leads and with no idea where to begin.

⌒

Lola had never been good at sick days, partially because she had never been allowed to *truly* take them. Even on the rare occasion that she was allowed to stay home, no fever had stopped her parents from giving her homework anyway, whether it was a workbook from the school-supply section at Target or the actual homework she was missing from her teachers.

So when Lola was presented with a second day of actually doing nothing, well . . . she didn't know *what* to do.

She spent the rest of her Sunday afternoon refreshing Instagram, where her photo from the top of the Pyramid of the Sun was doing surprisingly well given her meager follower count. And while she tried to study Spanish through her app, Lola couldn't stop thinking about Río . . . or texting him, either. His WhatsApp messages kept interrupting her attempts to conjugate irregular verbs on her phone, and *those* were interrupted by a slow-motion mental replay of that kiss.

Lola clamped her eyes shut, trying to physically force herself to focus. She needed to study, because fluency was the key to going home.

But what if I want to stay?

Maybe Río could help her learn, she thought. Even if he liked speaking English to her as much as he said.

But Lola wasn't thinking about him strictly as a tutor, and that's what worried her. What if he tried to kiss her a second time? Should she dodge it, or did she dare risk fainting again? What if that happened in public? She certainly couldn't tell him that her grandmother believed she was cursed. Maybe he would think her family babied her, or that every last one of them was unstable or superstitious or both.

She wanted to talk to Río about everything else instead: about his favorite places in the city and if he'd take her to them, what kinds of foods he liked and disliked, how he could be friends with someone as argumentative as Javi. And she found herself wanting to know what he wanted to do with his life, and if maybe she could even be in it.

By the time Tía Paty dropped Lola off at the restaurant ahead of the opening shift the next morning, she had made her mind up: She wouldn't tell Río about the curse. She would play it cool. No, she would *be* cool. It's what Ana would do, and she took an exaggerated, bracing breath as she walked in.

She liked La Rosa in the mornings, before it came alive with conversation and the frenzied flight patterns of servers and busboys alike. The tile was cool and inviting, and some of the tables were still pushed against the wall from where the night shift workers had mopped.

But the space wasn't as quiet as it should have been. Juana had given her a key and warned her that she might be the first person at La Rosa that day, but someone had beat her to it. And that someone was singing along, rather clumsily, to a ranchera ballad. Their voice echoed from the kitchen.

Lola pushed the door open a crack. There was Javier, counting plates and glassware, pausing every minute or so to gesture during a lyric that particularly moved him.

Yes, he was bad at singing. But there was a certain

level of comedy at play in his performance—as well as an undercurrent of sadness that surprised her. This wasn't pain he was singing with, it was dolor, the kind that couldn't be translated.

And he was a completely different person than the scowling boy who had shamed her at the pyramids. Someone who might answer to the nickname that Río used for him: Javi. Someone she didn't want to automatically hate.

Lola laughed reflexively, more startled at her realization than amused at the scene in front of her. And though she tried to stifle the sound, Javi whipped around, his eyes narrowing quickly onto hers.

A barrier went up between them, so quickly that Lola might have thought she hallucinated what she had just seen . . . were it not for the music that continued to pulse through his phone on the counter. He grabbed the offending tech, slammed the screen, and scowled again. His posture was ramrod straight.

"What are you doing here?"

"I'm sorry, I . . . I was just . . . My aunt had to drop me off early," she offered feebly. "If you want to go back to what you were doing, I can leave."

His frown grew more pronounced, and Lola focused on the space around them rather than looking at him—at the cups he had been counting, the shelves of spices and chiles and dried goods, the empty sinks that gleamed and waited for the day's impending dishes. Eventually, she paused on the enameled clay plates in the corner, a big stack that reminded her of her parents' kitchen. Of home.

"Talavera, for the tourists," she heard Javi say. "They think it is more"—he paused, and Lola wasn't sure if he was searching for the right word or hiding his judgment—"authentic."

"They're pretty," Lola said, eyeing the intricate patterns.

"They have a story, too," he said, a softness in his voice Lola had never heard before. A kind of care. "Juana sourced them from Puebla; there's a studio of Nahua women who make my favorite talavera in the whole state. I think she should print that on the menu and teach people something while they're here."

"Well, maybe the tourists are too busy caring about getting the geotag right on their Instagram photos," Lola added dryly.

Javi actually smiled, but the look disappeared almost immediately.

"Río . . . He's not here, if you're looking for him," he said quickly.

Lola wondered how close Javi and Río were, and if that closeness meant Río had told Javi about the kiss. "I'm not looking for Río. I have the lunch shift today."

This time, she didn't imagine it: Javi visibly relaxed. "You're feeling better, then, yeah?" he asked. Lola looked at him quizzically. "Dani worked yesterday. He said you were sick."

"Oh, right. Yeah, I was sick," Lola moved to grab

silverware from behind Javi. If she was here early, she might as well get a head start on the place settings. "My cousin thinks it's a sickness without a cure, though. So TBD on if I'm feeling better."

Javi raised an eyebrow at her. "TBD?"

"You know, to be determined? We will see."

"We will see," he echoed. "Ya veremos. Because you're spending this summer learning Spanish."

Lola once again felt chastised.

"A sickness with no cure," Javi repeated, to himself as much as to Lola. "Sounds serious. Should we expect you to miss shifts every time Río kisses you, then?"

So he did know. Lola tried to think of a way to distract him, but her mind was fixated on one alternative topic.

"Do you think people . . . families can be cursed?" she blurted out.

There were a few options: One, and most likely, Javi would think that her question was the fevered rambling of someone who was not well enough to work. Two, he might humor her out of politeness until the kitchen staff showed up and he could go back to ignoring her.

Or three, and this felt like the most unlikely option of all, he might take her seriously.

Javi stared at her for a moment that lasted a decade. Could the spirits also stretch the concept of time into something torturous? "I don't see why not," he said. "Lots of things happen to lots of families. Why not curses?"

"But . . . even if there's a totally logical explanation for the things that my gra . . . I mean, people say are linked to the curse?"

"What I think, Lorena," he said, helping her with the cutlery even though she hadn't asked him to. "Is that just because you can explain something doesn't mean you need to."

She watched Javi out of the corner of her eye as he paired knives and forks. He was close enough to her that it made her posture a little straighter. On edge and nervous.

When he didn't elaborate on his grand theory regarding belief systems, she tried again. "Okay, so . . . Let's say my family is cursed. I mean, just hypothetically. And given this is my family's restaurant, have you ever . . . witnessed something strange here? Something kind of supernatural?"

"¿Como fantasmas?" Javi asked. A hint of suspicion crept into his voice, putting Lola at ease. Maybe non-believing was the answer she wanted. "Why, are you going to try to start scaring the customers?"

"Never mind," she said quickly. "It was something Juana told me yesterday about spirits, and I just . . ."

"If you want spirits, La Rosa isn't the right place."

"Then what is?"

Javi shrugged. "Las pirámides," he said. "Tepotztlán in Morelos, maybe. Pero aquí en México . . . yo creo que el Mercado Sonora."

"What's that?" she asked, perhaps a little too eagerly. "*Where* is that?"

Javi looked at her skeptically. "Why?"

Lola stumbled, searching her brain for a plausible reason, but she had none. More than that, she wasn't sure why she was still standing so close to Javi, let alone engaging in this conversation. She wasn't a fan of how he dangled just enough information in front of her while still managing to be stunningly opaque. And why was he grilling her like this family revelation affected him personally?

Javi laughed again, startling Lola back to reality. Maturely, she rolled her eyes and turned to leave. "Whatever, it doesn't matter. I'll figure it out myself."

"Espera." Javi took a step toward her. "Does that mean you're going to the mercado by yourself?"

"I don't need your permission, you know."

"I'll take you. Mañana. I have something after work today."

Lola started visibly, to the point that Javi imperceptibly mirrored her reaction with a flinch of his own.

"Why would you do that?"

He shrugged, yet even that didn't make a dent in his posture. He stood like he had been taught to do so, the mark of years of expectations and standards. "If I can save you money on an Uber, why not?"

Lola wanted to press him further, but she felt a buzzing in her pocket—Ana was probably asking for updates or complaining about negative splits or both.

"I should probably go." She motioned to her phone as

a form of apology. "Pero ¿mañana? ¿En serio?"

Javi laughed again. This time, the amusement made its way to his dark eyes and reflected there with a glint.

"En serio," he said.

It was a momentary peace offering. Even so, Lola studied his face, trying to find the fake-out or the clue. And while she found nothing that served as a warning or proof that he was lying, she still didn't believe Javi would follow through on it.

He'd wake up the next morning, forget about the market, and never think about Lola again.

And the sooner he did, the sooner she could focus on debunking or solving a family curse, whichever came first, and working up the courage to kiss Río again.

CHAPTER 8

Though Lola wasn't entirely convinced Javi would show, she found herself second-guessing her outfit on Tuesday afternoon, which also made her second-guess why she cared. Javi certainly didn't—at best, the things he said made her feel silly; at worst, he had nothing but disdain for her. Why try to impress someone like that? She eventually settled on her usual uniform of shorts and a hoodie. And while she might have been the world's most unremarkable dresser, at least she was good at makeup. Her eyeliner was even and crisp.

She could hear Buela and tía Paty downstairs, the former picking apart nearly everything about the latter's appearance. Did she really not want to wear makeup or at least some lipstick? What about ironing her shirt? Paty, for her part, stood her ground against the concept of ironing a cotton T-shirt. It was only when the doorbell rang that Buela slowly let up on badgering her daughter about a haircut.

"¡Lola!" Paty called. "¡Te hablan!"

Instead of going down immediately, Lola smoothed the

Dutch braids she'd plaited and unplaited and replaited. This was absolutely the worst idea she'd had so far this summer. But twenty-four hours ago, she'd been sure Javi would flake. Twenty-four hours ago, she had expected to only see him at La Rosa, where at least her cousin or, even better, Río could serve as a barrier.

Paty called for Lola again. This time, Lola heard Buela fussing in the kitchen loudly, in the way that let everyone in the house know she was winding up for a fight. Mami did the same thing, especially when Tommy was in trouble. She'd take her annoyance out on the vegetables, and Tommy would try to break the tension by telling her that rage made her cooking even better.

So to save everyone from the dramatics, Lola went downstairs. Javi stood in the living room, his hands shoved deep into his pockets, making as little small talk with Paty as was socially acceptable. Lola nodded a brief goodbye at her grandmother and tried to avoid Paty's questioning gaze as she moved past her and Javi both. Though it was a little rude, she had a single goal in mind: Leave the house as quickly as possible. She heard the door shut behind her. Javi had followed her.

"Hola to you, too," he said. "Or do Americans not say that?"

"I didn't think you were actually going to do this."

"I told you, I meant it."

"Yeah, but . . ."

"Do you always think so badly of other people?"

Words failed Lola. Instead, she moved toward the car that Javi had unlocked and watched as he got in. He had also worn a hoodie, as well as chinos and a leather jacket that was both supremely cool and visibly expensive. If he were a senior at her high school, he'd be the kind to ignore Lola entirely, which made her want to ignore him. She felt the barrier going up between them almost immediately as a result. If she kept to herself, the social hierarchies that guided the lives and decisions of people like her and people like Javi would remain undisturbed.

But Lola also reminded herself that Javi was doing her a favor and she should try to be as polite as possible. If nothing else, she could spend this afternoon learning about Río—where he went when he wasn't working, what kind of girls he liked, what Javi thought about his ex-girlfriends.

She paused by the car door long enough for him to catch her trepidation. "Are you getting in?" Javi asked. Lola looked at him through the window. "If you already changed your mind, I have other things I can do today."

"Like what?" Lola asked, her curiosity beating her hesitation. "Homework? You'd really rather deal with . . . economics? Is that what business students learn?"

"I should be offended," he said, revving the car's engine. "You think so little of me that I would find my coursework more interesting than a ghost hunt."

"Well, homework is interesting to me sometimes," Lola said under her breath. Javi smirked.

Save for the car's gentle hum, their trip began in

silence. Lola considered asking him if he wanted to listen to music, but something about the boy's demeanor—the ease with which he sat in the driver's seat, the way he only looked at the road—kept her from provoking him.

They said nothing for ten minutes exactly, because Lola watched as the car's clock ticked upward. Javi rolled down his window at a stoplight and motioned at a boy who was washing the windows of passing cars. But rather than let the child touch the window, he handed over a fifty-peso bill and quickly waved him off.

"Maybe it's enough for him to take a break for a few hours," Javi offered by way of explanation. "It's no good for them out here."

"That was really nice of you."

"You are surprised?"

Lola blushed. "Well . . . I just can't work out your whole deal," she admitted.

He turned his head to look at her.

"It's . . . like, what you're about, what you do, your whole *thing*," Lola tried. "I can't decide if it's weird or not weird for you to offer me a ride to this market even though you have better things to do."

"How do you know I'm not going to the market because I need to buy groceries?" Javi asked simply. He moved his hand slightly to pass her a piece of paper from the dashboard. There, in neat block letters, was a list:

CALABAZA.

TOMATE.

SALCHICHA.

ACEITE.

CHICHARRONES.

"My *thing*," he said slowly, "is that I work at La Rosa so I can pay for university."

"Right, business, you told me," Lola said.

"Exactly. The classes are free. But the books and the gas for my car . . . and the groceries."

"Why do I get the sense that you aren't too excited about school?"

"Would you be happy about studying something because your father tells you to?"

Lola nearly laughed. She was only in Mexico City because her father had demanded she study Spanish, and she would not describe herself as happy about it. But it felt like a rhetorical question, one Javi was challenging her to answer rather than expecting her to, and she didn't feel particularly inclined to meet his provocation.

Instead, she looked back to the road. Javi was what driving instructors would call an offensive driver, who maintained his composure behind the steering wheel but whose sharp turns and the way he defended against other cars trying to cut into the lane told another story. She missed her steady little Prius and the way Tommy never made fun of her for being so careful. Sometimes they would spring for McFlurrys after school. Whenever the ice cream machine actually worked, they considered it an act of divine intervention.

Javi's gruff voice snapped her back to the present. "When I was a child, my mother would tell me stories," he said. "She started with the Zapotec stories, because those are the stories her mamá told her when she was a little girl in Oaxaca, and then she would tell me the same stories from other towns and people. But they were always a little different, ¿me entiendes? When I was smaller, I liked the stories about Copijcha and the other gods going to war. But then as I got older, I really liked the way all these stories"— he paused, searching for the word—"overlapped."

Lola tried to sneak a glance at Javi from the corner of her eye. "Stories? You mean like La Llorona?" she asked.

"Sure, como La Llorona. What do you know about her?"

"Well," Lola said, trying to think back. "My mom would threaten me with her every once in a while, especially on Halloween, when I wanted to trick-or-treat. She said there was a ghost who lost her children and was doomed to spend the rest of eternity looking for them, and if I wasn't careful, she'd take me as a replacement. That's the short version, anyway."

"That's *one* version," Javi said.

"What do you mean?"

He paused. "It's like history, isn't it? It matters who is doing the telling. There's the version of La Llorona parents tell children to make them behave, and there are versions where she's a Nahua woman and the lesson is to not trust

106

the colonizers. Sometimes the story is both. Sometimes it is a story about La Llorona Zapoteca and how she and her true love were separated by the Revolution. My mom always liked that one, so I liked it, too. But my favorite version is the story about Cihuacóatl, the protector of Culhuacán."

"What's that?" Lola asked.

"*Where* is that," Javi corrected her again, and her cheeks flushed. "Cerca de Xochimilco. But hundreds of years and so many civilizations ago."

Lola sat with Javi's explanation, turning the different versions over in her head. "Does she still tell you stories?" she asked, the intimacy of her question hitting her in the heart the second she posed it.

He shrugged, almost imperceptibly, in his seat. "At first I thought she stopped believing in them," he said, his voice quiet and almost sad. "But I think she was just busy, and I was getting too old for stories. My dad got lots of promotions at his bank, and she had to host dinners for his bosses, and the stress was higher for her because the other wives at the parties . . . They look like your cousins. They act like them, too."

"And your dad wants you to do what he does," Lola added. "He wants you to work at the bank with him. Or at *a* bank, anyway."

"Sí," Javi said simply. "So I need to study business in college." Just as quickly, and as inexplicably, as he had opened up to her, he shut back down.

The next fifteen minutes felt like an eternity, and

the sight of the market's sign and vast walls came not a moment too soon. The Mercado Sonora looked simple enough from the outside, a rectangular building surrounded by tarped tents, with people streaming in and out of cavernous entryways. Lola fidgeted in her seat as Javi put the car in park and grabbed his list.

"Do you need anything while we are here? Food? ¿Cosas para tu cara?" he asked, barely looking at her as he climbed out of the car, though he did point in the direction of her face.

Lola shook her head awkwardly and kept a few steps between him as she followed him. Javi weaved through the crowd, just another person running another errand. The mercado was as loud as it was large, and the echoes of vendors reverberated off the walls, which had belied the sheer number of stalls inside. Rows seemed to stretch on for miles, offering as many ingredients and surprises a person could want.

It would be too easy to lose Javi—or for him to lose her—in the crush of traffic. So when he stopped to ask a gray-haired man about the nopales in one of his barrels, Lola let the crowd swallow her and moved on without him. Javi called after her, but she pushed past chiles and tomatillos, pottery and ornaments, toys and costumes, ignoring the pit in her stomach, trying to get a sense of whichever spirits might exist here. She was moving without a destination, willing herself to be swallowed whole by the noise of people paying for their purchases.

If she closed her eyes, the market itself almost faded away, and she was back in the busy hallways of her high school, invisible to almost everyone.

She only looked up as the movement around her slowed and the calls between vendors and customers grew muffled. There was a shift in the air. A woman with thin eyebrows and a weary face beckoned to Lola from a nearby stall. The smell of incense and candles wove a ring around Lola, and she considered turning around, though she had no idea if Javi was still following her, or even if he was still in the market at all.

If she could find the exit, she could find a taxi and head home. Her grandmother would be none the wiser that she had sought an answer to the curse without permission, and Lola could push the memory of the market to the back of her mind. She could forget she had even tried. But something about the woman's gaze convinced Lola to move closer.

English was the first and only language that came out of Lola's mouth: "C-can you tell me if a curse is real?" she stammered.

The woman looked at her curiously and motioned across the aisle to a younger woman with a kind, round face. Her skirts rustled as she walked; her hair was in a thick, glossy braid that extended down her back. The first woman said something in a language Lola couldn't understand. The second woman nodded and looked her potential customer up and down.

"She does not speak English," the younger woman explained to Lola. "But she says you bring with you a bad energy. She says she knows how to fix it."

Lola jumped at the opening. "Really? My grandmother thinks I've been cursed. Something happens whenever . . . whenever I kiss someone, and my buela says it's the spirits, and . . ."

The younger woman held her hand up and translated for her companion, who studied Lola and said something in a deep and comforting voice.

"She cannot undo una maldición," the younger woman supplied. "And she says you know this already. But she can confuse the spirits. Hay conjuros, una limpia. You have money, yes?"

Lola nodded, though her heart fell slightly. If these two women couldn't undo a curse, did that mean no one could? Did it mean Lola was stuck this way forever? She remembered Juana's comment about oversalting. And how could the woman confuse spirits that Lola wasn't entirely sure she believed in? Did limpias work for anxiety, too?

Before Lola could reach for her bag, she felt someone grab at her arm.

"Buenas tardes, señoras," Javi said from over her shoulder. "Discúlpenos."

His hand locked around Lola's as he pulled her away, the women following their movements intently with their eyes.

It took the length of half an aisle for Lola to snap back

to herself. "What are you . . . I didn't ask you to follow me!"

"What are you trying to do?"

"She said she could help me," Lola huffed. "She was *going* to help me."

"How?" Javi wheeled on her just as Lola wrenched her hand out of his. "By taking your money? Did you ask what she practices? What spirits she works with? Is she a bruja? A curandera?"

Lola's sight line only came up to Javi's shoulder. Still, she stood her ground. "It's my money. I can do whatever I want with it."

"So you're throwing it away on the first vela you're offered?"

"I wasn't going to buy a *candle*. I think I need something more heavy-duty than that."

"You know that's not the point. Asking her to do whatever you're looking for without showing respect for what she does? It doesn't work that way, Lorena."

They stared at each other, and Lola was transported back to that day at the pyramids, when the look in Javi's eyes had been something close to cruel. Lola screwed her features tightly to match his.

More than anything, she didn't want him to see her cry.

"Can you . . . please just take me home and forget about it?" Lola took a step to where she thought the entrance they had used was. She stopped. There were so many entrances, from so many directions. Suddenly she was unsure about where she was, and why she was even there.

He motioned with a shoulder. "It's this way," he said, his voice as rough and critical as it had been a moment before. "And don't worry. What is there to forget when nothing happened?"

It wasn't an invitation to explain. Lola filled the silence anyway. "This is going to sound so . . . I don't even know," she began, following Javi as he weaved through the crowd.

"Plenty of things sound that way." He didn't even look at her as he walked.

"No, like, really . . . Just go with me here." She took a deep breath. "My grandmother says I'm cursed. Actually, Juana says our grandmother thinks all the women in my family are cursed, which is its own thing to unpack. And I don't know if I am or not, honestly. Like, this is starting to feel real. Because Río kissed me and then I fainted"—Javi's shoulders jumped like he was suppressing a laugh, and she shot the back of his head a look—"and there's probably some totally logical reason why weird things happen whenever I'm in a situation that is anything close to romantic, like fear of intimacy or whatever, but I want there to be *a* reason. And this is as good a reason as any."

Javi was silent for a moment. Lola regretted everything she had ever said to him, getting in the car with him, even agreeing to go on this trip.

"We think different about spirits here, ¿me entiendes? It's not Halloween and ghost stories."

Lola balked. "So you . . . believe in this? If I say the Gómezes are cursed, you believe me?"

"Stop looking so surprised." They had reached his car, which he unlocked for her. She got in, less resistant now. "But if you want to do something about it, going to the first woman who works with spirits and smiles at you probably will not help."

"How do you know what will help?"

Javi shrugged. Lola decided she hated when he did that.

"But then what do we . . . I mean, what do I do?" she asked.

He laughed and put the car in drive. "Well, you don't tell Río about your . . . Did you really faint?"

Lola nodded, and Javi said nothing for a while. Instead, he sneaked glances at her as he drove, and Lola didn't jump to defend herself or to fill the silence anymore. Javi reached for the radio and fidgeted with buttons. But even as the music he ultimately landed on drowned out Lola's thoughts, she could tell he was still agitated. There was something he was not saying.

"Look," she said. "You don't have to help me if you're busy or something. I'm sure you have better things to do. I can try to figure it out myself."

"And let you waste your money? I know what Juana pays, and it's not a lot."

She gestured toward the direction of the market weakly. "I didn't know where to start. This was the only idea I had. And I *always* know. That's my thing at school. *Lola Espinoza's got the answer. Let the teacher call on her.* It's weird that I don't know now."

"It's human," he countered.

"It doesn't make it suck any less."

Javi sighed and pulled at the collar of his sweatshirt as he thought. "I will help, but you have to be more respectful. There's history here, and to a lot of people, it isn't a science. If you want only one answer, you won't get it. It's what you feel."

"But why do you even want to help me?" she asked. "You can't care that much about how I spend my money."

He flashed a smile that almost registered as a grimace, and Lola was unsure if she could trust it. It was the smile of someone who was doing it to be polite, who understood that a smile was the appropriate response for that moment, even if he didn't necessarily want to give one.

"Let's say it's for the stories, yeah?"

CHAPTER 9

Lola didn't know what else to say on the ride home, and she wasn't in the mood to try to fill the space between them with awkward, rambling fragments. It wasn't like Javi tried to hold a conversation, either, and once he pulled the car up to Buela's curb, he barely offered a quick adiós before driving off. Lola breathed a sigh of relief. If Javi had spent another second inside her grandmother's house, Lola was sure her aunts would never let her hear the end of it—and they would tell her parents.

But it wasn't tía Paty who gave Lola pause this time. She had barely stepped onto the sunny driveway when tía Coco rushed out of the house toward her.

"¡Ay, mija!" she trilled with a wink. "Está guapíííísimo el muchacho."

After a moment of trying to decipher her aunt's chatter, Lola realized that Coco wasn't talking about Javi—she was talking about Río, though her constant references to "ese chico" meant she could have been speaking about anyone. Coco loved to know everything about everyone, but she often left the most important details out of her dispatches and monologues. Lola tried to smile and nod her way out of the conversation and excused herself to head inside.

Tía Paty was sitting at the dining room table, working at a massive torta that reminded Lola how hungry she was. "La más chismosa," Paty said, nodding in the general direction of her sister's voice. If she intended to tell Letty about who Lola was spending time with, she didn't show it. In fact, the more pressing issue was her sandwich, a piece of which she offered to her niece.

Tía Coco's curiosity was nothing in comparison to the way the staff at La Rosa began shooting looks at Lola and Río whenever they worked the same shift. Two of the waiters went out of their way to ask Lola to put in drink orders at the bar for them, and even Rocío would give Lola a knowing look as they passed each other.

"They're bored, Lo," Ana offered over a video call during one of Lola's breaks. "You're the shiny new thing in town. Seriously. There's gonna be some other drama, and they'll forget about it in a week. Like . . . okay, so Courtney Torres puked after hill repeats two days ago, but now all anyone on the team wants to talk about is the Iowa State scout who might be stopping by. It's kind of like that."

"Wait, am I Courtney throwing up in this scenario?"

"She PRed that day, so it wasn't the *worst* thing that could have happened."

"Throwing up your breakfast burrito because of dehydration sounds pretty bad," Lola pointed out. The back office where Juana usually handled paperwork was mercifully empty. If Lola angled her phone in a particular way, the Guadalupe statue and the candles that Juana kept in the corner stayed out of the camera's view. Ana would ask about it, and Lola wanted to avoid anything that might remind her of the curse, at least for a little while. "It's different, is all. This place isn't like school, where something happens at lunch and everyone's attention moves. Right now, I *am* the lunchtime thing. I don't like it."

Ana laughed and called to someone out of frame. "Is that really such a bad thing, though? One of these days, you're gonna have to get used to being the center of attention, Espinoza."

"I'll leave that to you."

"Fine by me. Hey, I've got to go. Coach wants us to get in a few more miles before it gets too hot out," Ana said, panning her phone around the dusty track for effect. "I'd say you're definitely not missing anything with this heat wave, but I know you're missing *me*, and that counts enough for everything," she added.

"*Bye*, Ana," Lola said, not really meaning the annoyance in her voice. Because she did miss her best friend, and she missed waiting for her in the parking lot, safely tucked in a book and under no academic obligation to physically exert herself.

"Who is Ana?" a voice behind her asked, so suddenly that Lola almost jumped.

Río stood in the doorway, that signature gleam in his eye. The slight buzz of nausea that Lola had been fighting for hours cranked itself right back up.

"She's, um, mi mejor amiga," she offered. If she clenched her fists tightly enough, she could focus on that discomfort rather than whatever else was taking over her body. "Ella vive . . . She's back home. In California, I mean."

Mercifully, Río ignored her stumble back into English. "Tell me about your life in California."

"Well, it's . . ." She paused. How was she supposed to explain that her life was filled with obligation and expectations without coming off like she didn't have much of a life at all? Deflecting felt safer than letting Río know she was a nobody. "What are you doing back here?"

"I'm looking for you. Isn't it obvious?"

Lola's cheeks flushed, betraying her attempt at anything close to coolness. "The dining room isn't as fun when you're not out there," Río said, a boyish kind of bashfulness on his face. "Plus, it's pretty empty, so I don't think they'll mind that I take a break, too."

"You can't tell Juana I had anything to do with that decision," Lola said. "She would fire us both for insubordination."

"Juana won't fire me. I'm her favorite bartender."

"You seem really sure of that."

Río's smile was as devastating as it was teasing. But Lola's break was over, and as sure as Río was about his job security, she wasn't as confident that Juana wouldn't discipline her for slacking.

As they walked out of the office, Javi glanced their way and Lola chose to ignore how she thought she saw him roll his eyes. She resumed her station at the hostess stand, pushing down the feeling that her stomach was flipping itself inside out. The last thing she needed was to pull a Courtney Torres in the middle of the restaurant.

Instead, she repeated the welcome Juana had instructed her to offer as guests walked in the door, and tried to absorb the Spanish and English that flowed around her at varying speeds. While she needed to practice her pronunciation and given how often she mixed up conjugations, even she had to admit she was getting better at the actual work involved in a restaurant's front of house.

⌒

"Not bad, American," Río offered a few days later after Lola rattled off seven different drinks for a particularly busy table, only tripping over an inflection once. "Maybe you should stay here with us even after the summer ends."

The feeling Lola had begun to associate with Río threatened ominously somewhere between her organs.

"Maybe," she said as she grabbed water glasses for another table. "I'd miss my dog, though."

Río lightly wrapped his hand around her arm. "And what about how I will miss you?"

She laughed incredulously. "You don't know me well enough to miss me."

"Not yet, but I will."

Lola busied herself with filling the glasses, the water sloshing up the sides and almost spilling over. He was smooth, she had to admit. Almost impossibly smooth, but then again, maybe boys like Río were wired this way, and Lola was too inexperienced to know any better. Dani had said on day one that the bartenders were supposed to flirt with everyone.

But Río had also told her he didn't want to be everyone.

Lola thought back to the handful of other times she had felt something even close to what she was feeling now. There were two such moments: that kiss with Chris, and a disastrous game of seven minutes in heaven that she'd played at Ana's suggestion during a house party in ninth grade. When the bathroom door closed behind her and Danny Arroyo, she begun stammering that they didn't have to make out if he didn't want to, so Danny suggested they forget about it and spent the remaining six and a half minutes on his phone. She appreciated that he had taken anything less than a yes as a no, but his instant change of mind still stung.

Lola was determined not to let anything embarrassing

happen again with Río if she could help it—and that was exactly the problem. She couldn't control whether or not her body would forcefully reject the attention. Was that weird feeling butterflies or her stomach threatening to upend her breakfast . . . or, the thought kept playing in the back of her head, an actual curse leveled against her family?

She thought back to the grave look on her grandmother's face and to the way Buela was resigned to shoulder something impossible and greater than herself. What did it feel like to believe in something that much, no matter how little you understood or could explain it? This was bigger than Santa Claus, or the threats of El Cucuy that her dad had sometimes invoked to keep his children quiet on long car rides when they were little. A person could base every decision they made for the rest of their life on a belief like this.

It was yet another reason for Lola to play things safe. She was good at safe.

But if she was honest with herself, she also wanted to take a risk at least once.

"Hey, Mari?"

"¿Qué onda?"

"Tengo una pregunta . . . Well . . . Can you promise not to tell anyone what I'm about to tell you?"

Lola's aunt shoved her phone away and sat up on her bed. "Lorena, no voy a ser metiche. It's my sister who's the gossip, not me," she said, eyeing her niece suspiciously. "Is this about that boy you were kissing at the pyramids? The pretty one who makes the drinks at Juana's place too strong?"

"I wouldn't know, I haven't . . . Did Regina tell you I was kissing him?"

"Come on, it's not like things stay secret in this family for long. Paty knew your mami met your papi the day after it happened. She takes one psychology class and ¡pum! everyone knows about this boy at school making eyes at Leticia. I was two, so I didn't remember this," she added, cutting Lola off from asking more about her parents' courtship. "Pero ¿las mujeres Gómez? We decide and we do something. And Letty decided on your father, and on California. And here you are now."

Lola's curiosity stretched itself in two directions: wanting to learn more about how her parents had met and asking her aunt why this was relevant. It wasn't like she wanted to *marry* Río and move to Mexico like a great reversal of her mother's path.

As for Mari's analysis of their family, when was the last time Lola had made a choice for herself, let alone seen it through?

When Lola didn't answer, Mari tried again. "Cristina and Regina told Antonia, who was loud enough about it for her papá to hear, and Chuy told Paty to watch over you, so now every Gómez knows." Her tone was playful but held a small warning. Lola was being monitored. Why was her family nosier than people in high school? "Don't worry about it, nena. Besides, he's cute, no?"

"That's not really what I'm worried about, Mari. Well, it is, but . . . Tía Paty acting like my keeper isn't the top of my priority list right now. Has . . . has your mom ever told you she thinks the family's cursed?"

Her aunt exhaled. "Is that what this about?"

"Yes . . . Wait, you know about the curse?" Lola's head stopped spinning slightly. "You know I came home from the pyramids, and I fainted, and that could have been me being dehydrated or whatever. But Buela immediately said it was because we're . . . cursed in some way. And I don't get it." She paused, trying to complete an impossible equation, to solve for X and Y concurrently. "Mari, is this the Buela version of El Cucuy?"

"No, Lola, the Buela version of El Cucuy es El Cucuy. Trust me, the number of times she threatened me with that monstruo . . ."

"So then what? I know she doesn't like anyone's boyfriends. Is this why you don't date? Because of her?"

Mari raised a single formidable eyebrow, almost daring Lola to keep going. "If I wanted to date, I would. But between school and my job and making sure this family doesn't kill each other? I have enough in my life. I don't need a man to make it worse."

"Have Cristina or Regina ever brought a boyfriend

home that Buela liked? Or what about tía Sofía and Josué?"

"She likes Josué. Why wouldn't anyone like Josué?" Mari looked thoughtful for a moment. "Your grandmother, when she doesn't like something, she lets you know."

Lola smiled. "Another thing the Gómez women have in common?"

"Now you're getting it!" her aunt replied with a grin.

Lola sat down on the squeaking twin mattress that was now hers and looked around the room. There were some touches that clearly came from her grandmother's decision-making—the flowery bedspreads, for one, as well as the sturdy wooden furniture and, of course, the altar—but most of the space was puro Mari. A desk was piled high with equal parts books and makeup, and a jumble of heels burst from the closet doors. On one wall, Mari had taped a collage of mementos, including school-era photos filled with kids in identical uniforms and a snapshot taken at Disneyland. Lola remembered that trip; they'd begged for identical sparkly Minnie Mouse ears and spun in the teacups until they couldn't walk in a straight line. Four-year-old Lola hadn't quite understood that her nine-year-old cousin was really her aunt; the divide barely mattered now.

"I'm sorry if it's weird that I'm basically asking you to explain your mom to me," she tried.

"It's not weird. My mamá does weird things. And you have questions," Mari said matter-of-factly. "My grandmother, your bisabuela, she was very religious. Everything bad that happened in her life was brujería. To her, everything was about los demonios. And the masses she made us sit through, they would go on for hours. The last time your grandmother sat through one was her mother's funeral. Now she prays in front of that wall of hers. But some of those old ideas stick, you know? Especially the ones that make it easy for you to not blame yourself for things you can't explain."

"So you're saying . . . it's not real?" The promise of a superstition dangled itself in front of Lola. Maybe this was like one of Javi's childhood stories, one that had survived through generations.

But Mari shook her head, and the hope Lola had felt disappeared as quickly as it arrived. "I didn't say that. Sometimes if you believe something, it's enough to make it real. And my mamá, she sees these patterns in her life, these things she thinks are bad happening to her hijas and her nietas, and she thinks it's the demons, or cualquier maldición." She sighed. "Don't let my mamá get to you. She shouldn't stop you from having fun this summer. That's not what the Gómez women do."

Lola shrugged. "I guess."

"This is where you say 'Gracias, Mari,'" her aunt chided playfully. "And where I say 'De nada, mi amorcito.' Hey, la Señora is a bit loquita, but she knows how to cook. I'm going downstairs for food. Do you want to come?"

Lola shook her head, and her aunt left her to her

thoughts. It was reasonable enough to hold a superstition, but the fervent deference her grandmother showed her beliefs didn't sit right with Lola, either.

If it was a justification Buela wanted, there had to be reasons for everything, ones that would satisfy her. Sure, sometimes people left one another for the sake of leaving, but everyone in Buela's life had been pulled away from her for something else. Love, for example. Or death.

Maybe the curse was more concrete than Buela knew. Maybe the spirits knew each Gómez woman's worst fear and the specific rules they followed when making decisions and taking risks and living their lives, and turned them into full-blown nightmares. Juana didn't want to lose her restaurants. Paty hadn't wanted to disappoint her mother. Coco . . . maybe she was afraid she wouldn't ever know what it was like to be a grandmother. Lola didn't quite care to learn what Cristina and her sisters were scared of.

And Mari didn't seem to be afraid of anything.

Lola wasn't confident in her ability to track down a doctor who could explain why her body forcibly rejected any romantic attention like the back side of a magnet, but she was sure she could at least find a way to prove to her grandmother that being 5 percent less protective wouldn't result in her granddaughter abandoning her, too.

CHAPTER 10

The second La Rosa location had opened its doors in April, which meant it was still enjoying its status as one of the newer restaurants in the colonia—and that made Juana giddy, Rocío permanently harried, and kept Lola busy whenever it was her turn to work. There was always another party to add to the wait list, another table to swap out, another carryout bag to hand off to a delivery person or office worker trying to get back to their desk in one of the buildings nearby.

At first the flow was overwhelming, but there was something comforting in shutting her feelings off to focus on work. If how her body reacted whenever Río was around was a matter of biology, then hosting at La Rosa was an obstacle course in PE—and while gym was tied dead-last for her least-favorite subject, Lola was still determined to get an A here.

There were still small pockets of downtime, during which she could observe the world that Juana and Rocío had built together. She especially loved watching the groups of friends that came in as a break from shopping or their first stop before heading out for the night. Their laughter was loud and infectious, no matter the topic. Crushes, partners, horrible bosses, overbearing parents, siblings that owed someone money, other friends who weren't at the table, the significant others of those other friends, dream jobs, haircuts, relationships that were going better than anyone thought possible, relationships that ended several months ago but still needed to be dissected postmortem— everything was fair game at a La Rosa table.

And while plenty of American tourists flocked to the restaurant, many people spoke Spanish—and not the sterile version that señora Smith taught, where the vocabulary of the week informed the students' stilted and unimaginative sentences. Here, customers, who often weren't older than Mari, goaded one another with sarcasm and slang that took Lola days of repeated listening to decipher.

And for everything she couldn't understand, there was her cousin. The Juárez location had been Juana's first success story, and she was determined to make lightning strike again a few miles away—though the minute the kitchen doors closed, she could often be heard groaning about that week's shrimp prices bankrupting her personally.

"Hey, Juana," Lola said as she waved goodbye to a party of eight—one of whom had spent the better half of two hours showing everyone photos of some social media disaster she'd been forced to deal with at work, at a decibel that meant Lola overheard the play-by-play as well. "What's . . . oso?"

Juana laughed. "Vergonzoso, Loli," she supplied. "Es como. . . . embarrassing, shameful."

"Sí, como . . . qué oso que we're not out dancing right now," Río called from behind them.

Juana rolled her eyes. "Río, cielito lindo, that's not vergonzoso. That's qué *mala onda*. And if you go out dancing, then I won't have my favorite bartender, and my customers will be mad at me. How about you can do whatever little cumbia you want from behind the bar until Sebas comes for the late shift? As for my Loli, if I let her out dancing with you, I won't have *any* customers because her grandmother will kill me."

Lola's ego evaporated like a water drop on Rocío's hot stove. "She's your grandmother, too," she mumbled.

The real shame was how the Gómezes insisted on treating her like a child, she thought. For the first time she could remember, she actually *wanted* to have a life, but there were more than a dozen obstacles standing in her way. And most of them were related to her.

If Río felt embarrassed for Lola or judged her for her cousin's protective ways, he didn't show it. Instead, he returned to the bar, his hips rotating dramatically in a little two-step to prove a point. Lola laughed and immediately turned back to her seating chart, a living algorithm she used to distract herself from what she had begun to call "the Río problem." Did it dissolve the dizziness she felt when he was near? No. But it made it easier to stay upright.

She couldn't get over the fact that he wanted to pay

attention to her, much less kept finding reasons to talk to her. It wasn't like flirting with her would endear him to his boss—Juana clearly already loved him. Nor did Lola ever feel witty or sparkling, even though he was all too eager to set her up for easy responses. They had known each other for less than a month, but already they had established a rhythm: Río initiated and Lola reacted. He had kissed her, and because she had the bare minimum of experience in that department, she had just stood there and let him.

She should have returned his kiss and been a more active participant in the single most romantic moment of her life. She should have . . . Well, whatever she should have done, Lola didn't like to think about that day in front of the pyramids because it also made her remember how Javi had made her feel not only foolish, but ignorant.

That was another set of questions to unpack: If Javi didn't like Lola, and if Javi and Río were friends, wouldn't that matter to Río? Or maybe Javi's surliness was a test, and Lola was failing that, too. She tried to imagine a world in which she liked someone Ana, or even Tommy, disapproved of.

That thought exercise always ended before it began. Because that would require a world in which Lola let herself like anyone.

Later that night, it was Dani who cut the tension between Lola and her own thoughts. "Oye, morra," he called out toward the end of Lola's shift. "Did you not remember my second rule? ¿Qué onda contigo y Gregorio?"

Lola faltered. "Uh . . . ¿nada? I mean, I don't think anything is happening with Río. Or between us."

"Or you don't *know* what is happening?"

His question took Lola so off guard that her only reaction was to be honest.

"*Yes,*" she replied. "Or no, I don't know what's happening. Or why. If it's obvious that something is happening, I have no idea how it started. It definitely wasn't me. I'm not supposed to be liking anyone right now. I'm here to learn Spanish."

"¿Por qué no los dos?"

"Have you met my family? It's not like they're holding the door open for me to be the next Bachelorette. It's . . . Actually, it's the exact opposite."

Dani laughed. "What family isn't like that? You're their little princesa. I tell my parents once a week to stop worrying about me, and I don't live with them anymore."

"You mean this is how it's going to be for the rest of my life?"

"And when you're dead, why not?"

Lola groaned. Dealing with a curse felt like a hurdle on its own. Overbearing parents until the end of time? At some point, the universe was bound to cut her a break . . . Wasn't it?

"Mira, güey," Dani said as he began stacking menus for Lola's next table. "That boy is a flirt. *He* is why I have rule number two. Just take care that you know what *you* want from this, too."

But Lola wasn't sure if there was anything to get out of liking, or even being liked by, Río—not because she was going back home at the end of the summer or because she had never been in a relationship before, but because of the risk that came with every interaction. She had learned to mask the two-second buffer she felt when a wave of nausea overtook her, the way someone might balance on a boat in a storm. Less pleasant was the minor current Lola felt if Río got too close, like he was an exposed wire and she was holding on a second too long.

And while she wasn't sure if she believed in the curse the way her grandmother did, what else could it be? It was easier to imagine that somewhere, some spirit was angry at her—and at her entire family, for good measure—than it was to unpack why she was so scared of being the reason someone else lit up.

But Lola also had to admit it was nice that Río's eyes brightened whenever he saw her, even if his eyes were always lit up and dancing. Even if the summer had to end and they would have to say goodbye. That was, if his interest in her lasted that long. Surely there was a limit to how enthralling she could be.

Another idea began to form in Lola's brain. Juana had said Buela believed she was doomed to lose those she loved. And after talking to Mari, Lola suspected that the spirits somehow knew what each of the women in her family most feared. Maybe if she learned why Río liked her, she wouldn't be so afraid to like him back, and then the spirits would have nothing to take. Maybe understanding was the key to undoing the entire curse.

Her shift ended at ten that night—one of Buela's stipulations to Juana about Lola's employment was that she be home as early as possible, even on weekends. But before she could find her cousin to ask for a ride back to their grandmother's house, Río intercepted her.

"¿Tienes hambre, American?" he asked, his dimple on full display. "Let's get tacos. You can't come to Mexico City without trying this place a few blocks from here."

There were two reasons why Lola wanted to say yes: She hadn't eaten anything in hours, and, well, he was Río. Asking her.

So it hurt when she heard herself say, "I have to get back to my grandmother's house." That only made Río smile wider.

"What, and you're not allowed to grab food on the way home? I'll drop you off right after, te lo prometo. Mira: I stopped working. You stopped working. It's fate." He gave a little wave to the other bartender, Sebas, who had taken his place behind the bar for the late-night crowd. "I'll take care of it with your cousin."

Juana, who was trying and failing to control the chaos like a conductor without sheet music, jumped at the idea of not driving Lola home. "I'm not giving you a raise for this, Linares, but ask me in a month or two, eh?" Dani smirked over Juana's shoulder.

"¡Vámonos, pues!" Río led Lola out of the restaurant,

casually draping his arm over her shoulders. "We can't get separated. I'm responsible for you now."

Lola's skin prickled where the weight of his body pressed into hers.

The crowds outside La Rosa were as lively as the ones inside. No matter where Lola looked, there were people making their way to the next bar or club, with music and dancing spilling out onto the sidewalks. Every so often, Río gave a nod and a shout in one direction or the other—he was clearly popular, and Lola wondered what it was like to know in the core of your being that you had friends everywhere. She didn't even have that in a small high school, and here he was holding court in a city of millions.

Eventually, they made their way to a side street whose crowd was attracted to something other than the neon nightclub signs illuminating the path. Spotlighted against the ancient houses was a taco stand, its awning spanning a stately brick wall. The specialty, their boards proclaimed, was al pastor, but the full list of guisados and salsas was enough to make Lola's head spin.

"Déme seis de pastor y tres de bistec, con salsita de la picosa, porfa," Río told the taquero. He turned to Lola. "The true test is if you can handle this salsa."

Lola thought about her brother's habit of putting salsa on everything—back home, Tommy would put salsa on salsa if he could. "What do I get if I pass the test?"

"All of my love and affection."

The hissing nerves that felt like the background track to

134

Lola's life made the pressure points behind her ears ache. Río clearly took her silence as agreement to his terms.

A taquero handed their order over quickly, with a salsa so loaded with jalapeños it almost stopped Lola from inhaling one of the drippy tacos off their shared plate. Almost.

"So?" Río asked, waiting for his praise.

"Way better than anything I've ever had back home," Lola said. "The pineapple definitely helps."

He beamed. "Tell me about home."

It was the second time he had asked.

"It's okay, I guess," Lola said, trying to guess what Río would find interesting. "We have a dog—his name is Churro, and my dad says he doesn't like him, but he's the baby of the family. And school is . . . I don't know, it's probably the same everywhere," she offered.

"But you're going to school in *Los Angeles*," he said.

"Not really—we live in Oxnard. That's not Los Angeles," she corrected him. "We're really far from Hollywood and . . . the celebrity stuff. There's a lot of farmland in Oxnard. That's what my papito, my dad's dad, did for work for years."

"You're closer to Hollywood than I am, though," Río pointed out, ignoring Lola's family history. "Well, not right now, pero . . ." He polished off another taco. "An agent told me once I should go to Los Angeles. I could make it work, I think. I'd book a few jobs, send some money back to my mother. She doesn't want me to be an actor, but if I made American dollars, I think she'd change her mind."

His voice dripped with confidence. Lola didn't know what else to do but agree. "If that's something you want to do, why not?"

It was the encouragement Río clearly wanted. "Pues it would be painful to not know anyone," he said. "So that's why I haven't done it yet. But now I do know someone, and how lucky that she's very pretty."

Lola blushed and reached for another taco, the second tortilla pulling its weight under a mountain of steak. Rocío was constantly turning out inventive riffs on tacos at La Rosa, each one tiny and delicious, but there was something beautiful in how this taco stall's ingredients came together so easily and so simply. The taqueros were confident. They knew they didn't have to improve upon something that already worked.

Río, meanwhile, was content to offer another mono-logue to Lola. "When we studied Shakespeare, la maestra, she showed us the *Romeo y Julieta* that was filmed here in Mexico City, the one with Leonardo. Everyone else liked John Leguizamo and the Capulets, but me? I liked Leo. He got the girl in the end, didn't he?"

"Not really," Lola said, suppressing half a smile. Shakespeare she knew. She'd gotten a 105 on a unit about iambic pentameter—extra, extra credit. "The point is that he and Claire Danes both die. So they don't actually get each other. It's kind of a famous ending."

"Okay, but in real life, the girls swoon over Leo. So in a way, he gets the girls. And now, six years after that class, here I am. I learn the lines and I go to the auditions whenever I can. I think next year I'll get a telenovela. Y después, Los Angeles."

He beamed at her, the kind of smile that could easily inspire a million fancam videos. Lola blinked herself back to her senses.

"But . . . do you like acting?" she asked. "I mean beyond the part where you get to be the heartthrob."

"What's not to like about making the audience feel what you want them to feel?"

Lola, who had trouble naming her own feelings most days, once again didn't know what to say.

The tacos slowly disappeared, and Lola and Río made space for the ever-widening crowd, many of whom danced along to the music blaring from a hidden speaker. Río tried twirling Lola around once before she tripped over her own feet, unsure how to take the right step when she needed to. He laughed and opted to show her the steps instead— "Como that scene in *Selena*, ¿ves?" he offered, exaggerating the hip swivels to make her laugh. Lola tried to follow along and felt her body loosening up as the songs went on. It was only after she could keep up with a very basic step-touch that Río flagged down a cab ambling down the road.

"You heard Juana," he said. "I have to get you back to la Señora or else . . ."

Lola tried to hide her disappointment that the night was already over. "Oh, well . . . I had a great time?" she tried.

"What are you talking about? It's not goodbye yet," he

said, climbing into the back seat with her. "I have to make sure you get home. Otherwise I'm really fired."

Lola gave the driver the address that Mari had forced her to memorize on day one. She watched from the window as the city passed by in a blur of light and noise, nodding every so often to Río's narration of what they were looking at and how it compared to the rest of the city.

Most of all, Lola was struck by the vast differences in the buildings, the way the skyscrapers along Reforma challenged the smaller buildings in her immediate sight line. It felt like some kind of shorthand for two very different worlds that somehow existed in one. She thought of the people who stayed in their own little world, either unwilling or unable to visit another, and of the people who passed between them. In some ways, she was part of the latter group. It was a privilege, but not one she had asked for—and not one she knew what to do with.

Eventually, the familiar street corner came into view, and they pulled up to the pistachio-colored house, where a light waited in the living room window. She glanced at her phone: It was past midnight, and she hadn't texted anyone that she would be late before she left the restaurant's Wi-Fi radius. Río paid the fare as she scrambled out of the car, trying to think of a way to say goodbye as quickly and as discreetly as she could, and her heart flipped again when she heard him close the taxi door behind him, too. There was no way she was getting away with a wave and a promise to WhatsApp him later.

"Gracias para todo," Lola said, wrapping her arms around her body as if to create a barrier. "Is it 'por'? Or 'para'? But either way, you were right; I couldn't be in Mexico without trying those tacos."

Río leaned in closer to her, and Lola instinctively backed up, the metal of the driveway gate behind her back. The faint, sweet smell of the neighbor's jacaranda lingered in the air, mixing with Río's cologne. Lola held her breath.

Before anything could happen, Lola heard a door slam open behind her. "¡Lorena!" tía Paty almost shouted, the tenor of her voice forcing at least a foot's distance between Lola and Río. "Tu abuela está enojada; you need to get inside now."

Lola stole a glance at Río as she moved toward her aunt. His face betrayed a temporary disappointment before resuming his signature grin. "I'll see you soon, American?"

Lola winced. "I'm sorry, my grandma is . . ." Protective? Overbearing? Convinced the family would one day have to answer to forces greater than their own? All of the above?

Río nodded knowingly. "Don't be sorry. I know better than to fight with a grandmother." He winked at her and turned to the corner—whether to go home or to find another party was unclear. Lola swallowed her nerves and followed her tía Paty inside.

And in that moment, she made a decision: If she could help it, Río would never find out why she was so scared to kiss him even though she really wanted to. Because she would change her fate first.

CHAPTER 11

"I remember my high school boyfriend," Vanessa Corinne said perkily, like Lola was her best friend in the world and not another anonymous viewer watching her Glowy Prom Glam video through a phone screen. Lola wasn't even sure if she wanted to go to her senior prom, but the gleam of highlighter in Vanessa's thumbnail had caught her eye. What she hadn't been banking on was a monologue about first loves. And Vanessa Corinne had a lot to say about that.

"His name was Andrew, but I called him Andy," Vanessa explained in front of her perfectly lit backdrop. "He played on the basketball team, and I was ob-*sessed* with him. We went to prom together junior year and senior year, and honestly, I wish I had YouTube to teach me back then because my makeup? Oh, it was not cute." Vanessa laughed melodically as she buffed tiny triangles of concealer into her skin with a brush. "But I figured that part out, and! I also figured out that Andy just wasn't The One, you know?"

Lola brushed away fallout from her eyeshadow, a glittery orange that was concentrated in the inner corners of her eyes. ("It's fun, and you can totally mix the colors up to match your dress," Vanessa said.) She wasn't supposed to go to La Rosa that day, and tía Coco had ushered Buela off to the supermarket an hour ago. Except for the sparkly cheeriness of a beauty influencer, the house was the quietest Lola had ever heard it, and the only things that stood between Lola and as many of Vanessa's tutorials as she could manage were the number of brushes she could use and reuse until she had to wash them and the buffering of her grandmother's Wi-Fi.

Lola still remembered the first time she had tried to use makeup—real makeup, not the plastic accessories that came with the dolls her parents bought her for her birthdays. Mami had brought home a bag of slightly damaged but perfectly useable creams and powders at the end of one of her shifts, and ten-year-old Lola had sneaked a bright red lip liner from the stash. She had used it to fill in every inch of her lips, a little imprecisely but not terribly. The girl in the mirror smiled at her. And even if Mami yelled at Lola for thirty straight minutes when she found her later, greasy red still smeared on her cheek, the risk had been worth it.

"Here's the thing about those high school romances, though," Vanessa Corinne said, cutting through Lola's memories like the friendliest cheerleader on the squad. "Even if they don't last—and they usually don't—they're totally worth it. You're going to want to burn the photos, and egg their car, and sing angsty breakup songs into a pint of ice cream . . . and trust me, I've been there. I was there last week, you know what I'm saying?" She gave the camera a little wink before dusting another layer of highlighter onto her already-sculpted cheek. "But you shouldn't get rid of those memories just because they hurt now. You're going to want them when you're my age."

"I think I want them *now*," Lola said to Vanessa Corinne, even though Vanessa Corinne could not and would not hear her. Because she was mostly admitting it to herself.

Three hours later, Lola climbed out of Mari's car, a box of groceries in her arms, conscripted by tía Coco to take groceries to Juana's apartment in Roma Norte. The command was the only spark Mari's self-righteous fuse needed.

"She is old enough to be my mother, but that doesn't mean she should *act* like my mother," Mari huffed as she carried a bag of bolillos up toward the front door, ranting about her sister like a human windup toy that had been kept from taking off for far too long. She probably didn't get the space to vent about Coco, or any of her siblings, at Buela's house. There, the only person allowed to complain about Rosa's children was Rosa herself.

"How long are we staying here?" Lola asked as Mari rang the doorbell three times in quick succession. "Just so, like, if you want to go and you need me to stage a diversion or something . . ."

"Oh, we can catch up with Juanita for a moment. I haven't heard what Socorro tells her about me in a while. Por cierto, I like that . . . lo que hiciste con tus ojos," she added, pointing to the burgundy smoky eye that Lola had just finished before being dragged along on their errand.

"I meant to wash it off, but you were in such a rush."

"No, I like it. Pareces vampiresa. In a good way."

Mari rang the buzzer another three times before the crackling sound of "¿Qué chingados, María?" let them into the building. The lobby was bright and airy, covered entirely by a paneled skylight toward which overgrown bird-of-paradise stretched. Mari motioned for Lola to follow her up the stairs and down a hallway to a door that was already ajar, ostensibly so Juana wouldn't also have to deal with Mari's incessant knocks. The smell of roasted garlic drifted their way, mellow and sweet and inviting.

"Qué chingados yourself, Juana Octavia," Mari said as she greeted her niece. "Lorena and I bring these groceries here from your poor grandmother's house, and this is how you thank me? Soy tu tía, ¿recuerdas?"

"Sí, but I'm older," Juana teased in return. "And a business owner. *Entonces,* I am more important."

"Ay, keep that energy for your customers; you don't have to prove anything to me," Mari said with a wave of her hand.

Juana ignored her and offered Lola a hello. "Loli, put that box on the table. The bathroom is in the back to the left and the Wi-Fi password is Buela's first name in capital letters."

Lola did as she was told, while Mari, who was clearly used to making herself at home in the space, disappeared down the hallway. The apartment was just big enough for two people to live comfortably in without tripping over each other and featured an entire wall of windows, their industrial iron casing identical to the skylight downstairs. The clean lines of a wooden table and plenty of chairs provided a contrast to the steel appliances and countertop that lined one wall. Juana was busy using every inch of the kitchen space, happily surrounded by the chaos she had created.

"Who are you seeing with that makeup?" she asked Lola as she transferred blistered and burst red peppers from a sheet pan to a blender.

"No one, this is just for me. I wanted to practice," Lola supplied, knowing Juana was mostly teasing her. "What are you making?"

"Vodka sauce with red peppers. Did my mamá give you the crema?"

Lola rummaged through the box and found a carton of cream that she passed to her cousin, then watched as Juana worked, her shirtsleeves rolled up to her elbows. Small scars that served as reminders of splattered oil, hot pans, and a burgeoning career in kitchens dotted the smooth brown of her forearms, and her hands worked methodically and confidently from one pan to the next. Like their grandmother, Juana was moved by a feeling rather than a recipe. If she was figuring it out as she went, she was having a lot of fun doing so.

"Don't tell the critics who come to La Rosa," she said conspiratorially, dropping a hefty pinch of salt into a pot with tomatoes that seemed to melt as they simmered. "Every article they write about the restaurant says the same thing, about how Rocío and I are adding to la cultura with tacos and enchiladas and sopes and inventive ingredients, but some days I want Italian food."

"Well, if you think about it, vodka sauce is kind of like a salsa borracha," Lola suggested.

"Now you're thinking like a cook, Loli. But tía Letty would get mad at me for putting you to work on the line. There is a big risk of injury back there, and we're supposed to return you with the fingers you came with still attached."

"What are you saying about putting Lorena to work?" Mari said as she sat down on the overstuffed couch that was positioned close to the glass wall. "You're already giving her enough work; I hardly see her at my mami's house as it is."

"If you spent less time at school, and working, and studying for school and work, you'd see more of her," Juana replied. "Or you can always study at La Rosa. I might make you work during your breaks, though. Clean a few tables, mix a few micheladas, ¿qué dices?"

"I say what I said every other time you asked: No. I'm going to be a lawyer, like my sister was supposed to be before . . ."

Mari's voice dropped off. There was no mistaking which of her sisters she meant. Lola avoided her aunt's gaze, feeling guilty even if she wasn't sure she needed to.

The buzzer snapped the sudden, awkward tension in the room. Juana wiped her hands on a towel and let whoever was downstairs in. "Oh, you move quickly when you know it isn't me," Mari wheedled.

Juana smiled beatifically. "No, tía," she said sweetly. "I know how much you like being annoyed at me, or at your sisters, or the entire political system. If I make you wait, that's my way of helping you with your purpose in this world."

Before Mari could respond, a knock on the door announced Juana's other guest: Javi, a backpack slung casually over his shoulder and a laptop tucked under one arm. Lola busied herself with studying the artwork on Juana's walls as Javi greeted his host.

"¿Tienes hambre, compadre?" Juana asked. "I'll make you a plate while you work." She grabbed a bowl before he could answer, a trait she had inherited from Buela.

"Buenas tardes, María," Javi said, exchanging a cheek kiss hello with Mari before he offered Lola the same perfunctory ritual. His eyes flitted over her makeup, and Lola thought she felt a spark of electricity as Javi's cheek touched hers, where the sensation of stubble should have been.

"And why are we so lucky for you to join us today?" Mari asked, watching Lola more than Javi.

Before he could answer, Juana countered her aunt's question with another question. "Do you know the smartest thing I ever did when I opened La Rosa?"

"Doing it with Rocío?" Lola offered.

"Okay, sí. The love of my life is the most important thing. But second was hiring a business student. Don't tell Dani, but half the time it's Javi who runs my second location; half the time he makes sure I'm not losing my money too quickly." She clapped Javi on the shoulder and motioned to the heaping serving of pasta on the table.

"And I spend *all* of my time telling you that your father would be better at this than me," Javi said, pulling out a chair and unzipping his backpack so he could shuffle a few things around inside. Clearly he'd been to Juana's apartment before, because he moved to grab a filing box from the corner of the room nearest to Lola before he sat down. "Besides, business and accounting are two entirely different things."

"Sí, but they're both about numbers and money, right?" Juana asked.

"I can see why you need someone to do this for you," Mari volleyed.

They bantered back and forth for a few minutes, hitting a cadence that was clearly familiar to them. Mari and

Juana fought like siblings—but while Lola's brother was quick-witted and happy to spar, Lola rarely met Tommy with the same kind of energy. Watching two people who were equally matched was like watching a verbal ballet.

"Are they always like this?" Javi asked quietly so that he wouldn't interrupt the conversation. Lola might have been the only one who heard him.

"I think they are." Lola took a seat a few spaces down from him at the table. He had already spread receipts and papers in front of him and only paused the process of plugging numbers into a spreadsheet to work away at his food.

"That is exhausting, no?" It was a statement more than it was a question, and Lola wondered if whatever wall he kept up was exhausting, too.

"Do you not have siblings you fight with like that?" she asked.

Mari's voice cut through the almost-conversation before Javi could answer, hitting a certain singsong to mark what she clearly thought was impractical. ". . . y además, what are you doing telling Lorena about this 'Gómez family curse'?" Lola turned to look at her aunt, who was still sitting on the couch but gesturing to Juana as if she were out of her mind. "I told you years ago, it's not anything to worry about. Every family is cursed some way or other, so why would you let this fantasy stop you from living your life?"

"Wait, you believe in the curse, too?" Lola asked. "I

thought you considered it just a Buela thing?"

"Mari doesn't believe the curse is strong enough to stop *her*," Juana said, placing a steaming bowl in front of Lola. "She's probably right. I've never seen anything stop her from something when she decides to do it. But the rest of us, mucha suerte."

"If I can do it, you can do it," Mari said. "We're Gómezes, aren't we, Juana Octavia Zurita *Gómez*?"

Lola held her hands up before they could start in again. "But what *is* this curse about?" she asked. "All anyone does is talk about being cursed, and no one will tell me why or give me any answers." She thought she felt Javi's eye on her for a moment, but when she glanced his way, he was looking at the computer screen.

Juana sighed and sat down next to Lola. "There aren't really answers to give, Loli," she said. "It's not a science, you know. Let's just say the curse has made things . . . difficult for the family when we want to do the things we love. And especially when those things are not what's expected of us."

"Wait, what happened to each of you, then?" Lola asked.

"Nothing to me," Mari said simply. "I do what I'm supposed to."

"That's easy enough if you're a perfect child," Javi intoned. He didn't look up, but Juana punctuated the sentiment for him.

"María the angel," she said. "I, on the other hand . . ."

149

"Ay, here she goes with the drama," Mari muttered, the look of amusement on her face undercutting the annoyance in her voice. "And if I am the perfect daughter, at least someone is. Go on, Juanita, what has the curse done to you?"

"It's made opening my restaurants very difficult!" Juana said, crossing her arms tightly in front of her. "It almost bankrupted me, my hair is going gray above my ear, I have to deal with seventeen problems a day." Almost as if on cue, her phone chirped with a text message. "¿Ya ves? It's always something."

"Juana, how is that different from any other restaurant?" Javi asked. If the Gómez family was a Greek tragedy, he was the chorus. "And did you really buy this many cases of mezcal for Roma's first two months?" He let out a low whistle. "They're gonna drink you out of your lease, jefa."

Lola stifled a laugh as Juana leapt from her seat, threw her hands into the air, and walked briskly back to the stove, where at least the flame and the food understood what she meant and what she wanted to do.

"I'm telling you, it's the curse," Juana said. "It feels different from normal restaurant things. Sometimes when the spirits are really angry, I can hear them whispering at me to do something else."

"But how is opening La Rosa off your path?" Lola asked. "I thought you loved the restaurants."

"Yes, I love them, but that doesn't mean they will

150

make me money. Maybe my path was supposed to be to be like Mari's, or like Javier's." Juana nodded toward the paperwork on the table. "Running a restaurant is good work, and I give people jobs. But the spirits wanted something else from me, I think. Because our family wanted something else from me."

She leaned against the counter, looking almost defeated. Mari took that as her cue to ladle Juana's sauce into a bowl so she could dunk a piece of bread into it like it was a dip. "And you're doing what you want to anyway," Mari said. "You see what I mean? You're not letting the curse stop you."

"Sí, pero . . . it could certainly be easier without this hanging over my head."

The questions came to Lola in escalating importance, a puzzle with only rough edges and no corners. "What about the rest of the family? What about Buela? Does she get sick, too? Is she doing something the family doesn't approve of?" Her voice only wavered when she sensed that Javi's eyes were on her and not on his computer screen.

Like he was trying to figure her out, too.

Mari gave Lola one of her hell-if-I-know looks. "If anyone was born to suffer in silence, it's my mother," she said. "But I suppose it affects her somehow. That day you fainted was the first time she talked about it in years. She might forget it exists, like I do."

"How did the curse start?"

Mari shrugged. "Everyone has their theories, but

nobody really knows. But it doesn't matter. Let me tell you, Lorena: You will be just fine, with or without this curse."

It was the resignation that made Lola snap. "So you're just . . . happy living like this?"

"I'm not happy about it, Loli, but it's what we have to do," Juana offered.

"No." Lola's voice rose and her cheeks grew hot with determination. She wasn't used to challenging things—in fact, the fight she'd gotten into with her parents at the beginning of summer had been the first time she could remember ever talking back to them. "There has to be some way to fix it, some . . . some spirit we could talk to, or a bruja who can uncurse us, or . . ."

"Lorena, please don't go running around Mexico City trying to talk to every spirit you can find," Mari said, pushing a basket of the bolillos her way. "The spirits do what they want, and we have to do the same."

From the corner of her eye, Lola saw Javi stifle a smile. He was the only other person who knew about their trip to the market, and she had a sudden vision that she would be ratted out in one devastating second. Fortunately, Javi lowered his head back to his spreadsheet, and she could no longer see the smolder in his eyes.

Juana nodded. "I tried to break it for a time," she said. "I lit candles in the basílica, I prayed in front of the ofrenda, I did lots of things. Some families are just cursed. It's not so bad once you make peace with it, Loli. That's the truth."

Lola tried to picture a future in which she followed her family's advice—or rather, one in which she kept following it like she always had. A future where she was okay with fainting whenever Río kissed her and with the whirring feeling that came over her whenever he was around. She got the hint, sure enough, that liking Río was not what the spirits, or even her family, expected of her. But she was so close to having a life of her own and memories she might want to hold on to forever. All she had to do was let herself fall into it.

"Most families have, like, recipes they pass down, not curses. Couldn't we just have something normal to deal with?"

"We have that, too," Juana said. "Where do you think I got the recipe for the mole amarillo at La Rosa?"

CHAPTER 12

The next morning, Lola arrived at La Rosa with mere minutes to spare before her shift, a snag that Juana seemed to take personally after the warmth she'd shown her cousin the day before.

"Ay, Loli, ¿dónde estabas?" Juana asked as Lola rushed to the front, relieving her of hosting duties.

"Nowhere, *Juanita*, why?" Lola asked, a little too brightly. "Is Buela blowing up your WhatsApp with questions?"

Her cousin scoffed. "Ya sabes, la viejita doesn't believe in cell phones. Mi mamá, on the other hand . . ." As Juana spoke, she noticed her cousin's attention had drifted toward the restaurant's main room, where Javi was already attending to a table. "Listen, Loli, you think I don't see, but remember: Nothing is secret here. You'll have to pick between los dos amigos. If my mom finds out about this little triangle you have?" She whistled between her teeth.

Lola stopped herself from laughing just in time; Juana

was her cousin, but she was also her boss. "There's no triangle. Javi and I . . . I think he hates me more than he likes me," she said.

"Qué sexy," Juana said, and Lola glanced nervously over her shoulder, almost on reflex. "No te preocupes," Juana added. "That boy is my best server. He's not paying attention to our chisme. But tell me, if not him, then qué haces con mi Río favorito? He's cute, no? How is *he* romancing you?"

Before Lola could find the words to answer, she and Juana were interrupted by a cloud of clashing perfumes and multiple pairs of high heels. In through the front door came Cristina, with several friends replacing the sisters who usually flanked her. They were laughing the way the popular kids did at Lola's high school, a sound that was as intriguing as it was alienating.

"Cristina, ¡ya te dije!" Juana chided. "If you come here, you pay for your food. All of it. No family discount!"

Cristina pouted dramatically for a moment. "Juana, who said we weren't going to pay?" she asked. "My friends and I were out shopping and I was hungry, but also I wanted to introduce them to mi primita, la *gringa*."

Rather than squirm under her cousin's imperiousness, Lola tried to steel her nerves as she was introduced to Cristina's friends, who offered cheek kisses hello as they gave Lola multiple once-overs close up. She doubted she was passing any kind of test they had assigned to her.

Juana relented and motioned that they follow her to a table. Cristina passed Lola and smirked, batting her eyelashes dramatically.

"Not a big fan of your cousin?" Dani asked from behind her. His bag was slung over his shoulder; the shift change meant he was done for the day.

"It's not that I'm not a big fan of her, I . . ." She hunted for the words in Spanish. "No sé lo que yo hice . . . I don't know what I did to get her to not like me."

Dani nodded sagely. "We don't get to choose our families. And sometimes that means God gives us people we don't care for . . . or who don't care for us. But I think maybe you know." He raised his chin in the direction of the restaurant's bar, where Cristina was talking to Río. "You keep saying nothing is happening between you and that boy, but that doesn't mean it couldn't happen. Anyway, ya me voy. Cuídate, Lorena." He gave her a pointed nod and left.

That doesn't mean it couldn't happen.

What if she took Mari's advice and stopped letting things—like her nerves, or her family, or curses—get in her way?

So without thinking it through further, she walked straight to the bar and gave Río a warm smile that surprised even herself.

"I was wondering when you would say hello to me," he said, returning her smile with his own bright one. "How's my favorite Gómez girl?"

"She's not a Gómez," Cristina said quickly, her hands gripping the countertop slightly.

"Aren't you primas?"

"Sí, pero . . ." The older girl's voice trailed off. "Your papá's last name is Espinoza, right, Lorenita?"

Lola nodded. "But my mother is still your dad's older sister. Which means, technically, I'm a Gómez, too."

"But not *fully*." Cristina's smile held nothing friendly. "Not like the real thing." She flipped her hair with a perfectly manicured hand, and Lola had to bob her head away from the whip of golden strands.

"Remind me not to make a Gómez mad at me." Río laughed. "One of you will curse me in my sleep."

Lola blanched, but Cristina didn't notice. She shrugged as if already bored by Lola's presence and turned back to Río, making him promise to mix margaritas the way she liked them before sauntering back to her table, where she could more fully be the center of attention.

Lola watched her warily, trying to figure out exactly what her angle was. "Tío Chuy picked the wrong daughter to call Regina," she muttered under her breath.

"Don't worry about her," Río said, pulling out bottles and getting to work on Cristina's order. "If you let her get to you, she wins."

Lola nodded politely. When had anyone actually, successfully implemented such advice into their life?

"Oye," Río added as he handed a pitcher to Lola, ice and limes bobbing at the top of their chartreuse bath. "I meant what I said. You're my favorite Gómez."

The skin on Lola's arms crawled, either threateningly or pleasantly. Maybe both.

If only Cristina's friends were half as amiable as Río when they held court in the middle of the restaurant, constantly beckoning to Lola so they could add one more thing to their order even after she explicitly told them it wasn't her job and that someone else would help them instead. Juan Carlos changed his mind multiple times about what he wanted, while Sonia and Maricela spoke quickly, using slang Lola had never encountered before. Rodrigo was simply loud enough to distract anyone trying to focus on anything else, including the party Lola miscounted and needed to move after they were halfway seated. Jaime, the surly busboy, shot her an annoyed look when she explained they needed to reset that table, but he did it all the same.

Juana had told her repeatedly not to use her phone at the hostess stand, but Lola pulled it out anyway when she finally got a moment to herself.

> **LE:** Pretty sure my cousin and her friends thought Mean Girls was an antihero story

> **AM:** Lo, it is here I once again give you my best and most trustworthy advice

What

Would

Ana

Morris do!

Actually, no, don't listen to me,
I'd probably plot a way to overthrow
her in a way that was both needlessly
intricate and devastatingly effective

Can you systematically make her
friends your friends and have them
turn on her?

"¡Lorenita!"

Lola turned when she heard her cousin trill her name, bracing herself for whatever Cristina and her friends wanted next.

It happened in an instant: She crashed directly into Javi, who was carrying a full tray for one of his tables. Rice flew everywhere, including on Lola's clothes and, she was pretty sure, her hair.

"I'm so sorry," Lola said quickly, trying to gather the pieces of a plate that had shattered on the floor. It was one of her favorites, with a kaleidoscopic flower blooming from its center in turquoises and reds. Now it was several splintery fragments and dust, impossible to put back together without ruining the design. "I was distracted; I didn't mean to . . ."

She reached for a glass, but Javi blocked her from helping further. "Go ask Rocío to make the order over again," he said. His voice was stilted and formal, the kind reserved for a stranger.

Lola heard even more laughter from the middle of the restaurant, and the buzz she'd felt earlier was drowned out by embarrassment.

It took Lola hours to fall asleep that night. She stared at the ceiling, following a crack with her eyes back and forth until she had mentally transformed it into a canyon. Maybe that crack was how the spirits got in. She imagined them twisting and turning their way throughout the house, keeping an eye on each member of the Gómez family. Did their hold on someone grow weaker if they left her grandmother's house?

And if so, was that why Lola's mother had never mentioned anything about it to her? Was she simply too far away for the curse to affect her anymore? Was the easiest way to break the curse simply to go home?

But Lola knew she would be no closer to talking her father into booking her return flight than she would to growing wings and flying home herself.

Her phone dinged, brought to life by a WhatsApp notification from a number she didn't recognize.

+ 52 55 5555 5284: There are books if you want to read them, and places you can go.

      LE: ¿Qué? Who is this?

+ 52 55 5555 5284: This is Javier.

Historians study these beliefs.
There are a lot of spirits in the history of México.

Maybe there is an answer in the past for you.

Lola's fingers paused over her keyboard, trying to find the right combination of letters to pick. What was she supposed to say?

At least he wasn't mocking her. If anything, Javi was treating her grandmother's superstition—and by extension, now hers—with a scholar's rationality. It was an impulse that she understood, one she tapped into when essays for English class just didn't flow. Mari's pragmatic resignation existed at one end of the spectrum of possible reactions. At the other end was Juana, who maintained a fervent and slightly fatalistic belief. Lola decided in the moment that she wanted to exist somewhere in the middle. Academia was her in-between.

      LE: Do you really think that will help?

+ 52 55 5555 5284: It's as good an idea
as any.

LE: Ok, fair

So . . . what do we do?

+ 52 55 5555 5284: I will help you.

Lola waited for an elaboration, but the app didn't
indicate that Javi was typing. She squinted in the yellow
light of her phone, saved his number in her contacts, and
rolled over, trying to will sleep to come to her through
the crack in the ceiling and the whispers in her ear.

CHAPTER 13

It was a small consolation prize—really, one by matter of technicality, a participation trophy—that Lola wasn't the only person Javi treated with indifference. She had taken to watching him when they worked the same shifts at La Rosa, and he was always unfailingly polite, with a veneer of professionalism that gave his friendliness a limit. This was his job, and he was going to complete it because he needed to, while hitting every mark in the process.

And yet his silence was more loaded than Río's flirtatiousness. His customers tried to win over their somber waiter, and La Rosa's other staff laughed off their coworker's formality with good-natured jokes.

Lola wasn't exactly comforted by Javi's apathy, but she was more comfortable *with* it, she realized one day as she deposited a family at one of his tables. Going unnoticed was what she knew. She was used to indifference from boys, Padilla's personalized party invite notwithstanding.

It was when a boy liked her that she didn't know the answers. An SAT coach had once told her to pick option

B when in doubt. Her option B was simple: Shut down so that the boy in question gives up and moves on. Problem solved.

"Juana's girlfriend calls them Diego y Gael," she told Ana the next morning on a video call, holding her phone up in the tiny corner of Buela's kitchen that held a decent Wi-Fi connection. "Though I'm not sure which one Río is supposed to be and which one is Javi. Or even if that analogy works. And I really don't get why they're friends."

"That's a vintage movie reference, right? Maybe I should watch that this weekend." Ana was curled up in her bed, the familiar quilt that Lola had flopped down on after school so many times barely inside the camera's line of sight. "But I get what Juana's going for. It's like . . . Zack and Cody, or Archie and Jughead. Blair and Serena. Sometimes combos just work."

"Zack and Cody were brothers, A."

"You know what I'm saying. There's always one friend at the center of the party, and the other one is brooding protectively from a distance."

"You mean like us?" Lola said quietly. She and Ana rarely talked about the mechanics of their friendship because it felt awkward, like touching the wet paint on a masterpiece before it dried, messing it all up.

Ana smiled thoughtfully for a moment. "Yeah, well, I call Serena. Chaos is more fun. But this whole Javier-guiding-you-through-a-mythic-quest thing. That other boy . . ."

"Río, you mean?"

"Yeah, him. He said Javier was into history in school. Maybe it's a history-student thing to nerd out on this stuff." Ana scrambled out of bed and began her late-morning routine. "Like . . . this is some great anthropological quest or research for a college thesis or something." Spoken exactly like someone who had gotten a B- in history last semester, and could not be bothered less by it.

If this was an extended field lesson for Javi, and if he was at least upfront about it, Lola might understand. But the ire he'd shown her at the pyramids was difficult to shake. If he could be that angry at a relative stranger, why couldn't he be honest with her about everything else?

Ana paused in the middle of combing her hair back into a high ponytail. "Well, if you're not going to ask him what's up, I'd do it for you. If only . . ." A scheme flitted across her face.

"Ana, what if you came down to Mexico?" Lola said quickly, finishing the thought for her. "Like, for real. You can visit colleges and charm track coaches anytime, can't you?"

"And stay with your grandma, too? I don't think your dad would let her open her arms to me."

Lola felt her hope wilt as soon as it had bloomed. "You're right," she said. "This is supposed to be a punishment for me."

"I keep telling you, you should look at it as less like

punishment and more like an opportunity," Ana said. "The rest of us are stuck at home, and you're off . . . solving ghost stories and eating real tacos and stuff."

"The tacos in Oxnard are real, A, you know that. And they're not ghost stories," Lola said before she could stop herself. "They're . . . Well, it's . . ."

How was she supposed to explain something she didn't fully understand herself? Her grandmother and her cousin took it seriously, though, and that felt like reason enough for her to take it seriously as well.

Thankfully, Ana got the hint. "Hey, look, so I'll figure out some way to talk my mom into some kind of summer vacation in Mexico City for the culture. Until then, Espinoza," she added, looking pointedly into her phone's camera, "have some fun with it, okay? You're still thinking to yourself, WWAMD, right?"

"Ana Morris wouldn't be overthinking every single move."

"True, but that's why I keep you around, Jughead. To do that overthinking for me."

The call ended, and Lola switched her phone back over to the makeup tutorial she had been watching. There was something soothing about the transformation process, especially when the end look was subtle. "The amped-up version of yourself," Vanessa Corinne called it.

Lola wondered who the amped-up version of Lola was. Maybe that girl could see a C for what it was—a temporary setback—or kiss someone without feeling like

166

the ground would rush up to meet her. Maybe she didn't have a grandmother who thought every female member of her family was cursed. Maybe the amped-up Lola wasn't afraid of *living*.

Lola sighed. She wanted to believe that Ana could talk her mother into a trip to Mexico City, but if there was one person she wanted to see most, it was her own mother. Mari was a solid stand-in for explaining the particularities of Buela's habits, and Ana loved nothing more than to scheme fantastical revenge plots over text, but Lola missed Mami's gentle straightforwardness.

There was no way that Lola could talk to her mom about Río, of course—at least not without inviting a million questions that she didn't feel like answering—but maybe Mami would issue her judgment against Cristina's reign of terror. They could even talk about the restaurant, and maybe Lola could convince her mother to see that what Juana and Rocío were building together was a legacy all its own.

Lola texted Letty a short Te extraño, her typing slow and uncertain, as if to confirm the proper conjugation and the wiggling accent.

¿Ya puedes hablar español? came Letty's reply, along with a few emojis whose faces found their sender's wit hilarious.

Lola groaned and put her phone back down. In the living room, she could hear her grandmother clicking through television channels and talking loudly on the phone. Lola could only pick up every fifth word, but she wasn't particularly in the mood to try to decipher everything, and besides, being able to understand someone didn't necessarily mean she should listen in.

"¿Qué pasa, Lorena?" tía Paty asked jovially as she entered the room and made her way to the fridge. "Is your trip to Mexico everything you wanted it to be?"

"Oh yeah, totalmente," Lola intoned moodily before adding to herself, *How can it be everything I wanted if I didn't want it to happen?*

Paty laughed. " 'Por supuesto' is probably better," she said. "Gives the ¡pum! of sarcasm que buscabas."

Lola looked up at her quickly, chastised. "Lo siento, tía, solamente . . ."

"It's okay, Lorena. I understand. Sometimes things happen to us that we didn't want, and we have to figure them out anyway."

Lola's mind jumped to the thing that they weren't supposed to mention in Buela's house, the legal formality that had turned something into nothing, a connection into a once was. Did tía Paty regret the divorce as much as Buela did? Few family members took the time to ask her aunt how she was piecing her life back together after her marriage ended—and now Lola had no idea where to begin.

"¿Sabes qué?" Paty asked, clearing her throat. "You young people, you are the same. You want the answers, and you want them now. And you know how I know? I was young, too, and I wanted the answers to everything . . . science and philosophy and where I would be in fifteen years. And now look at me."

"You're not that much older than Mari, tía," Lola pointed out.

"Claro que no, pero to you I might as well be a viejita. What I mean is, don't be so busy trying to know everything that you forget to live, too."

Lola tried to work through what Paty said, but her phone buzzed midthought. A WhatsApp banner blinked across the screen. Paty smiled at her knowingly.

"¿Cuál chico es ahora? Don't worry, I won't tell mi mamá."

Ignoring her teasing, Lola looked at her screen.

> JAI: Probably better for you to come
> outside, no?

Lola peered out the window. The same car she'd climbed into for that disastrous trip to the market was idling at the corner. Before her suspicion could take hold, Lola said goodbye to her aunt and shouted a quick "¡Ahorita salgo!" to her grandmother, darting through the driveway to avoid more questions. There, in front of the gate, was Javi, his hands crossed impatiently against his chest.

"I'm surprised you're here," she said before she could stop herself.

"¿En español?" Javi asked dryly.

"Qué sorpresa que . . ." She paused. No, that didn't

169

sound right. Annoyance crept in, both at herself and at the boy standing five feet away from her. "Why are you here?"

"If you do not want me here, why did you come outside?" he asked, a look of amusement on his face. Lola couldn't make sense of the fact that he somehow found this funny.

"Well, where are the books you promised?" she asked. "Aren't you just dropping them off?"

"Buenos días a ti también," Javi said. "They don't teach you manners back in California?" He turned back to his car and opened the door. "Are you getting in or no?"

"Where are we going? I should probably . . ."

"You can tell your grandmother you're picking up books to study," he said, glancing at the phone Lola clutched in her hand. "*Those* are at my house, and we have another stop to make after. I cannot imagine what la señora Rosa is like when she doesn't know where you are."

"Are you speaking from experience?" she asked.

"I have had grandmothers mad at me before. Sometimes at La Rosa, sometimes other places. You'll see." He fell silent for a moment. "¿Ya nos vamos o no, Espinoza?"

A sound caught Lola's attention and made up her mind for her. Tía Coco was bustling down the street, her nylon shopping bag announcing her arrival as much as her voice and slippers did. Lola helped herself into the passenger seat, and Javi mercifully peeled away from the curb before her aunt could interrogate them both—even though tía Coco had already seen them, which meant Lola would need to brace herself for double the number of questions later.

How was she going to explain Javi's visit to her aunt, and to the family at large? Then again, Coco would be too happy to explain it to everyone else. All Lola had to do was land on a convincing-enough story for her.

"Oye, what do you want me to call you, anyway?"

She snapped to attention, bracing for another one of Javi's interrogations. "What do you mean?"

"Lorena, Lola . . . Your cousin calls you Loli. The other one, she called you Lorenita."

"And American," she supplied, thinking of Río.

The glower was back. "Mexico is still part of North America. Are we not Americans?"

That first, fateful conversation with Río replayed in Lola's mind. "He said something to that effect once, too," she mumbled. "First he tried *gringa*, but he landed on *American*."

Javi surveyed her, her own judge, jury, and gallery. "Entonces, ¿cuál quieres?"

"Lola's fine," she said quickly.

Javi nodded, repeating the syllables under his breath before focusing on the road again, his eyebrows as furrowed as ever. Lola tried to take the silence as an opportunity to decipher what he was thinking, but he was a language all to himself. She wasn't even sure if she wanted to be the person to translate him.

Before she could think of a way to continue their stilted conversation, Javi broke the silence with another

171

question of his own. "Can I ask why you came here? Unless it was your idea to spend your summer working at your cousin's restaurant."

"My dad sent me here," she said. "Kind of like grounding me by a magnitude of two thousand miles."

Kilometers, Espinoza, she thought. But she didn't know how many kilometers she was from home. It might as well have been a galaxy away.

Javi glanced at her. His was a face made of angles, the kind of points that made him look older than he was. More hardened, too. But there was something familiar in his particular flow of Spanish and English, the way he used the words he was comfortable with in each moment. It reminded Lola of her mother, who still used whatever words she felt fit her feelings best. "And your dad, he decided to send you for no reason?"

Lola sighed. It was worth at least trying to be honest with him. What else did she have to lose? "I got a bad grade," she said after a moment. "In Spanish."

Javi let out a low whistle. "So he thinks Mexico will teach you Spanish better. Even if Spanish is not the only language we speak here."

How could she explain to Javi that trying to understand her father's logic was like trying to understand the way a brick wall felt and acted? "I guess. I don't know what he thinks. It's . . . it's so unfair—I tried really hard and I studied and I didn't want to get a C"—Javi glanced at her, trying to decipher if that was good or bad—"like, not the *worst* grade ever, but not the best. The rest of my grades were great. It was just this one."

The whine of her explanation clung to Lola's tongue like something slick and rotten. Javi nodded, but if he was annoyed, he didn't show it. Lola would have to get used to his silences, as uncomfortable as they made her feel.

"Tu papá," he began after a moment. "Is he from Mexico, too?"

Lola shook her head and stared out the window at the stream of people walking on the sidewalk. "As much as I'm from Mexico," she said. "His dad . . . my grandfather came to the States from Jalisco with his parents when he was a kid, and my other grandmother came when she was around my age, I think. But my dad came to college here; that's where he met my mom."

"And neither one of your parents taught you Spanish at home?"

Lola certainly hadn't been prepared to get into her family history with Javi when she woke up that morning, but she was going to meet him where he was at. And no matter how she felt about getting shipped down to Mexico without a say in the matter, she wasn't about to let Javi think her parents were neglectful people.

"They speak it at home. I never picked it up," she said defensively. "My mom constantly switches to Spanish, especially when she's annoyed. But she was also learning English at the same time I was, basically. She'd sit down and do my vocabulary homework with me. It took me a while to realize she was using it as a way to practice."

She thought back to the nights a much smaller Lola had spent with her mom at the kitchen table, laboring over three-syllable words.

"My brother can totally speak Spanish," she added after a beat. "*I* should be able to speak Spanish. It doesn't . . . it doesn't click," she said, not bothering to hide the frustration in her voice.

"Pero ¿lo entiendes?"

"Más o menos." Lola shrugged even though there was so much more to say.

"So what was the plan?" he asked. "You show up, spend this summer not even trying to speak Spanish, and go back exactly the same?"

Lola stared straight ahead, but she could feel a glare sharpen on her face. She thought about telling Javi how tired she was of trying to master something impossible. *Well, with that attitude, of course it will be,* a voice in her head pointed out.

There was her whole backstory she could tell Javi if he really wanted it: the one about her parents' expectations and that getting obnoxiously good grades at least gave her something to *do*. But even if being a star student came easily to her, she still didn't know if it added up to saying much about who she really was.

And anyway, Lola had a feeling Javi would love nothing

more than to poke holes in her logic, no matter what she told him

Mercifully, he stopped the inquisition, and Lola turned the volume up on a song with a reggaeton beat. Mari would have loved it, though it filled Lola with a kind of bravado that she didn't know what to do with. She also sneaked a glance at the back seat of the car, where the backpack Javi had hauled to Juana's, as well as clothes stuffed unceremoniously into a separate bag, lay in a heap.

At last Javi's driving grew more precise: They had already exited the freeway and were now taking deliberate turns through tree-lined streets. The buildings were old and clearly loved, and Lola marveled at the architecture, the brightly painted walls, and even more greenery threatening to burst out of both interior courtyards and planters along public sidewalks.

"Estoy viviendo con mi abuela," Javi offered as he parked the car in front of a house whose brick front was only just visible behind bouganvillas and vines. "Su casa está más cerca de la universidad que la de mis padres, así que aquí estoy."

Before Lola could decide if his Spanish-only explanation was some kind of petty test, he motioned her to follow him.

CHAPTER 14

The house was filled with intricately carved furniture, all of which had been polished to a shine. Clearly, someone whose relentless dedication to cleaning rivaled Buela's lived here. Sometimes grandmothers really were alike, Lola thought with a smile.

Almost as if on cue, a frail but foreboding woman with paper-white skin and hair the color of burnt honey came slowly out of a nearby room, an apron affixed over her blouse. "Javier, ¿ya hablaste con tu padre?" she asked, not even registering that Lola was there. "Te sigue llamando."

Javi's face tightened, the shadows of his cheekbones growing even more pronounced. Lola wondered what kind of conversation he was avoiding, but she felt an acute sense that it would be rude to ask. Instead, she studied the stately woman, who was in every way Buela's opposite, yet her role in Javi's life was unmistakable.

"Lola, te presento a mi abuela, doña Pilar. Señora, Lola es una . . ."

Before he could finish explaining who exactly Lola was,

however, a second woman entered the room. Javi started. "Mamá, ¿qué haces aquí?"

Javi's mother was smaller and far more tan than Doña Pilar, and her formal warmth filled the room almost immediately. Javi's grandmother shared his bone structure as well as his skepticism, but there was a way his mother held herself that she had clearly imparted onto her son. Her posture was perfect, and though she smiled kindly at Lola, the curve of her mouth did not extend completely to her dark eyes. A soft wariness wrapped itself around her like a second skin. Lola wondered if it was a matter of protection, of self-preservation.

Javi's mother said something softly to Javi as he embraced her with a kiss on her cheek—he had squared his shoulders subtly, and stood straighter, too—and he nodded over to Lola. "Es una compañera del trabajo. Lola, te presento a mi mamá, Esperanza Idar de Ávila." He turned to Lola slightly and dropped his voice. "She brings us groceries sometimes, but my abuela acts like she doesn't need us to help her."

Lola managed a nervous nod, and Esperanza returned it knowingly. Doña Pilar, who hadn't stopped looking Lola over as if she were judging her in a beauty pageant, said nothing.

"¿Tienen hambre?" Esperanza offered after a moment in an attempt to bridge the silence. The two women turned back to what had to be the kitchen, and Javi motioned to Lola that she should follow him, a slightly pained look on his face. Maybe he wanted to get this visit over with as quickly as she did.

Perhaps that made four of them: Javi's mother and grandmother wasted no time in laying out a platter of milanesas on the table by the couch, as well as a cazuela of fragrant rice and a bowl of salad. Yet the steely, territorial way with which doña Pilar moved around them undercut the entire meal on offer. Hers was hospitality with a limit, that of a woman raised to be a good host. She motioned for Lola to take a seat in the middle of the table while she moved to sit at its head and nodded at Javi and the water pitcher so that he would lift it for her.

He obliged, but he did not sit down, even after his mother asked if he was sure he wasn't hungry. Lola didn't know whether she should eat, but she sensed it would be rude to not take at least a small piece of chicken from the platter.

"My parents live in la colonia San Rafael," Javi offered as he moved toward a nearby bookcase and began pulling out a textbook here, replacing another one there. "It is closer to La Rosa, but I would have to drive to get to school, and here I can walk or bike. Plus, I like the museums. I go there sometimes when I have the days to myself."

It was the first detail about himself Javi had offered up to Lola that wasn't an absolute necessity. "Which museums?" she asked.

"El Museo Diego Rosales, el Museo Anahuacalli—that's Diego Rivera's museum—el Axayácatl . . . the university museums. I don't like every exhibit, but it's important to be honest about history. And that includes the uncomfortable things." A look that wasn't entirely confrontational flashed across Javi's face, and Lola wondered if he was talking about their fight at the pyramids.

Before she could bring it up, doña Pilar interrupted with a "tch" and arrogantly waved a hand at her grandson's books. "Ya lo pasado, pasado," she muttered before quickly turning her gaze to Lola. "¿Y usted?" she asked. "¿Qué estudia?"

Lola busied herself with her milanesa, trying to avoid looking at either Javi or his grandmother—that was, until Javi spoke.

"Doña, Lola es gringa," Javi said. "Ella no entiende español."

"Sí entiendo," Lola shot back, but neither Javi nor his grandmother paid attention. Instead, they mirrored each other with barely polite stares. Lola wondered if that was what she and her father looked like over the dinner table sometimes.

It was at that moment that Esperanza decided she was finished rushing back and forth to the kitchen. "¿Qué libros agarraste?" she asked, nodding to the growing pile on the floor. "Mira, este es mi favorito." She pointed to a paperback by Isabel Allende and extended a hand to clasp her son's shoulder, a show of affection that lasted half a second. Other books in the stack were older, their spines cracked with wear. Did Javi really expect Lola to read each one cover to cover? And how was she going to admit to him that reading Spanish was as difficult for her as speaking it? She didn't want to give him the satisfaction.

Doña Pilar peered over the titles herself and sighed dismissively. At least she was consistent. Knowing what little she did of Javi's mother, Lola wondered if his grandmother was just as contemptuous with her, or when other members of their family were around.

But then again, maybe company didn't matter.

Doña Pilar began carving her milanesa with determined force as she spoke. The history books at Javi's feet, the woman contended, were no better than La Llorona or the Chupacabras—stories that benefitted parents who didn't know how to discipline their children effectively. Why did he insist on buying them and bringing them into her house, she asked, especially given that his future would have nothing to do with ghost stories?

Javi pointed out that his mother used to tell him about La Llorona, his voice now measured and flat. It was the tone of someone who had spent a lifetime trying to change someone's mind and had perhaps only recently decided it wasn't worth it.

"She's got a point about the discipline, though," he said, turning to Lola. "My parents used to threaten to take me to la Isla de las Muñecas and leave me there, too. That one usually came out when I was being loud at Sunday mass." He said something to his mother, who smiled slightly.

"Solamente cuando andabas de diablito," Esperanza said.

Lola tried to imagine a miniature Javi acting out anywhere, much less at church. For some reason, she could only picture a child-size Río causing a stir, not Javi—who she could only imagine had been as stoic as a child as he was now. "What's . . . ¿Qué es la Isla de las Muñecas?" she asked.

Doña Pilar interjected again, this time talking at a rapid clip about the need to clear that island—whatever it was—out. Esperanza tried to intervene—Lola thought she said something about keeping a spirit at peace—but that only set doña Pilar up further. How ridiculous it was, the older woman opined, that people indulged the tourists who wanted so badly to believe that ghost stories were everywhere. Couldn't they spend their time seeing better parts of Mexico City, she asked, ones that showcased the city's power and not its decay?

Javi stood up abruptly, a pulse working at his jaw, and motioned at Lola to grab some of the books, which she did quietly. At the top of the stack was a language workbook clearly meant for small children, its cartoon animals on the cover out of place in the severe room.

"Ya nos vamos, abuela," Javi said politely, offering his grandmother a curt kiss on the cheek. "Voy a regresar después de la cena." He motioned with his shoulder for Lola to head for the front door.

Lola thanked both Esperanza and doña Pilar for the

meal and bobbed her head awkwardly again, feeling the older woman's hawkish expression on her the entire time.

After spending a few seconds lingering closer to his mother, Javi followed. Lola had been too far away to hear what they said to each other, but it didn't matter. Some conversations were better left between family, and this one wasn't Lola's.

Birds chirped in the trees as Lola made her way to Javi's car, and she was struck by how pretty the street was—and how well-kept. *Expensive* was probably the word she was looking for. The families who lived here had done so forever. They were settled, in both their station and their ways.

Before long, Javi joined her and leaned against the car frame for a second. It was the first time she had ever seen him slouch, like something in him was depleted by the visit. "I like to forget she thinks like that sometimes," he said eventually.

Lola looked at him expectantly, waiting for him to elaborate further on the source of his grandmother's unprovoked ire.

"She is my father's mother," he offered, which Lola registered as neither an explanation of doña Pilar's attitude nor an apology for her manners. "My whole family, for centuries, they've . . . ¿Cuál es la palabra? Se asimilaron a la nobleza. Everyone except my mother, but I think she believes some of it now, too. That folk stories and traditions are somehow beneath them." He paused, discomfort flitting over his face. "That they're not worth remembering or keeping alive."

"That's why your grandmother wants to demolish . . . what was it? Las muñecas?"

"La . . ." he said slowly.

Lola gave Javi a sideways glance, then echoed him. "La."

"Isla . . ." he continued, "de . . . las . . . Muñecas. It's in Xochimilco. This man, he built a tribute to the spirit of a girl he never met until after she died."

"How do you meet someone after their death?" Lola asked. "Do you mean like a ghost?"

The thin line of Javi's mouth twitched slightly, but he said nothing. Determined not to sit through another silent car ride, Lola tried again.

"So is that why you like history? To challenge whatever your family stands for?" she asked. She could certainly think of less worthwhile causes he could dedicate his life to. But nursing a hobby to spite his family seemed . . . Well, it seemed awfully lonely.

Javi shrugged. "Supongo," he said. "My father, he wants me to study business like him. So here I am, studying business to make him happy. He also wants me to call him with updates. I think to make sure I am showing up to my classes. But it's summer now. So I am not sure what he wants."

Lola didn't know what to say to that, nor did she know if she was the right person to offer advice about what parents wanted for their children. Javi busied himself with making room in the back seat for Lola's books while she thought things through.

She decided the best, or at least the kindest, course of action was to change the topic as much as she could. "Well . . ." she said slowly. "If your family doesn't believe in curses but mine does, what does that mean? Is this something you opt in to? If I say I don't believe in this curse, does that cure me?"

"You can try it, but . . . that's the beautiful thing about it, no?" Javi asked, a small smile pushing its way out of the corner of his mouth. "People find what they need from whatever they believe. Sometimes people find the same thing as others because they need the same things. And sometimes they decide they don't need it, so they find other things. Money, for example. That's what my family believes in."

"I don't know what I believe in," Lola said defeatedly, like she had exposed something raw about herself that she wasn't sure she liked.

"So you say your family has a curse, and now you say you don't know. Which is it?" he asked.

"I'm trying to figure out what I think. It would be easier to believe the way Juana believes. Or how Mari doesn't. I'm somewhere in the middle."

Javi shook his head as he lowered himself into the driver's seat and leaned over to open the passenger side door from the inside so Lola could climb in. "For someone who doesn't know if they're cursed, you're spending a lot of time focusing on it."

He turned the car on and pulled away from the curb determinedly. Lola got the sense that not only was Javi driving her somewhere else—he was specifically headed away from whatever family drama she had just unintentionally witnessed. Buela might be a little stubborn, but she meant well. Doña Pilar, on the other hand . . .

The tension that remained on Javi's face was reason enough for Lola not to ask him about it.

His family was a challenge he didn't know the answer to. She had a small idea of what that felt like.

So instead, she reached over the center console for the grammar workbook. It was the smallest of olive branches, and the only one she could think of that didn't require any words at all. Javi smirked before reaching to turn the music up.

Lola hadn't planned to spend a whole day with Javi—though at least she didn't feel as unmoored when he was around as she did with Río. She couldn't remember the last time she had been spontaneous about anything, though there was usually nothing to be spontaneous about. Her life was predictable and planned, and she was normally pretty good at hitting the marks.

Until this summer, anyway.

This was the summer she shoved herself into a car with a boy who demanded she speak Spanish whenever she tried to start a conversation and who possibly considered their excursions the worst babysitting gig ever.

"¿A dónde vamos?" she asked, trying to placate him.

His eyes were as fixed on the road as they ever were. But he shifted both the car's gear and something within himself. "Tengo una idea," he said ominously.

Was that her only hint? Did he expect her to be up for anything, on something as meager as an idea? Her mouth set itself into a displeased line.

"Te pareces a mi profesora, la señora Smith," she said moodily.

"You're not going to get better at Spanish unless you practice. And you have to practice if you want to go back to California, no?" He shrugged faintly. "De todos modos, ya llegamos."

Javi parked the car and motioned for Lola to follow him. They weaved through people selling and buying food from carts, adults admonishing children for running too far away from them and toward the groups of people posing for photos in front of the colorful boats dotting the twisting canals in front of them. Lola thought back to the couple she had sat next to on the plane—if she checked the Instagram geotag, would she be able to find them?

"Javi, what are we doing here?" she asked.

"Visiting la Isla de las Muñecas."

"I thought you were scared of this place."

"Scared the way little kids are scared, and that was a long time ago. And being scared isn't a reason to not do things, no?"

"Can you stop answering my questions with questions?"

"Is that what you'd like?"

Lola shot him her most withering glance, not that he seemed to notice.

"If you're going to run to every corner of la ciudad to talk spirits into taking pity on you, why not make it easier and bring you to them?" he added. "If they curse you more, they curse us both, so at least you won't be lonely."

Lola did not feel comforted by his answer's grimness.

She had been to Xochimilco before, on a family trip when she was little. All of Rosa's children and their children had joined the Sunday outing, and Lola and Tommy had spent the bulk of their time trying to find their own names on the colorful trajineras. Almost out of habit, she now scanned the embarcadero for a "Lola" or a "Lorena." Again, she came up empty.

But her attention snapped back to reality because Javi was having a difficult time booking two seats on any of the boats, and he had resorted to haggling with one of the men guiding people on and off shore.

"Queremos *bajarnos* en la Isla de las Muñecas," he said again, trying to sound conspiratorial. "¿Cuánto por dos personas?" Lola sensed his frustration was only perceptible to her—did she already know him well enough to notice that?

The man motioned to the other people sitting at the table in the center of his trajinera before pushing the boat off the dock.

Javi turned back to Lola. "He won't do it until everyone else is off the boat," he said simply, like he understood the reasoning but didn't like it. "Come on, let's find another."

The man who eventually said he would let them off at the island eyed Lola warily as she climbed aboard the flat-bottomed boat and sat gingerly on a chair at the end of a long table. The boat bobbed precariously in the water as its driver prepared it for voyage, like he had done thousands of times before and would maybe do forever. An image of the River Styx, which Lola had read about during a mythology phase in fifth grade, popped into her head. Javi had told her about overlapping histories—maybe he knew other stories about boats that ferried the living to a world just beyond their senses, too. Maybe she was on that boat in this very moment.

Her old memories of Xochimilco lacked details and focus, but she could tell that the banks of the canals were worse for the wear than the last time she had seen them. Clumsily, she tried to ask Javi what had happened, and the look he gave her made it seem like the answer should have been obvious.

"It's climate change, pollution, the population growing . . . the government not caring, either. They want the tourists to come here"—he nodded in Lola's direction, and she immediately felt her defenses rise—"but they don't want to put money in and help the people who work here.

"It's a shame," he added after a moment. "There's so much culture in this area, if you know where to look. This one museum nearby, it's just one dead woman's personal collection of Diego Rivera's work. Frida Kahlo, too. And Zapata and Pancho Villa met here, over a hundred years ago. Eh, not *here*," he said, motioning to the boat under their feet and the water that swirled murkily under it, just out of sight. "But somewhere close."

He looked out across the canal, and Lola studied him for a moment. He spoke with reverence, like he was proud to have learned what he knew, and with an endearment that Lola had never felt toward her own schoolwork. Sure, she had risen to her parents' constant expectation to get good grades, but had she ever once stopped and asked herself if she liked what she was learning? Maybe she liked English, she reasoned. But the fact remained that she was a good student because studying came easily to her—Spanish grade notwithstanding—and Javi studied because he cared.

"Oigan, ¿qué quieren con las muñecas?" the trajinera operator, a stocky man whose skin had turned tough and wrinkled in the sun, jutted his chin at Lola. She hesitated for a moment. How could she explain to this stranger about the spirits that gripped her family's imaginations and about her own uncertainty and her fears?

Tentatively, she asked him what had happened on the island, her mouth tripping over *maldición*. The *c* hissed tensely out of her mouth, betraying her nerves.

The man shook his head. "No es una maldición," he said definitively. "Es un encanto." Lola made a mental note to ask later why *charm* was a masculine word and *curse* was feminine. Javi might know the answer, or he might tell her she was reading too much into it. And she was totally comfortable not caring about his judgment at all.

But she listened to the story of the man who lived on the island and who spent half a century decorating the entire place with dolls he found in order to appease the spirit of a drowned girl. He thought he heard her, the boatman stressed, sometimes in the water or through the trees. The man was dead now, but the dolls remained. And so did the voices, if you listened closely enough.

"And your family thought it was funny to threaten to leave you here if you were bad?" Lola asked Javi. "You must have been a terrible little kid."

"I never said I wasn't," he said, the beginnings of a smile on his face. She counted that as a small win.

Lola thought for a moment. "Can you ask him what the difference is between a curse and a charm? I mean, how do you tell which is which?"

Javi obliged, and the man looked at Lola suspiciously before speaking.

A *charm* is made with respect, he said, but what he didn't say made the silence heavy and thick. Lola looked away quickly, shame running down her spine.

It was painful to think that her family could be bad people, though it was less of a stretch to imagine that someone somewhere in the Gómez family's history might have earned retribution. But the implication—that an ancestor's actions were awful enough to mark their descendants for generations—wasn't easy to sit with.

From behind her ear, Lola thought she heard a whisper, a voice reaching out from the horizon. She tried to listen, but the sound disappeared as soon as she heard it.

The boat rocked and pushed up against a makeshift dock. "Aquí estamos," the man said. But now that Lola could see the limbs and heads of dolls through the bamboo gates that marked the island, each one marked with weather and wear, she had no desire to go farther.

If she was cursed and the island was charmed, she didn't want to risk it. Ana would say it was mixing vibrations, or like pulling two cards that could only be interpreted as an omen. And while Lola felt that she was acting as her own dead end, a voice passing through the trees and into her heart told her that turning back was the right thing to do.

She shook her head. "Yo . . . quiero regresar," she said quietly, terrified Javi would try to convince her otherwise. But if he was taken off guard, he didn't fight her request, and shrugged to the boatman that it was already time to head back. Lola tried her best to ignore Javi as they went, her body vibrating at an embarrassing frequency.

She pulled her phone out and opened the camera. Maybe tourists had a point, she thought as she watched the screen and waited for the right moment and angle to appear.

She hit the button. The camera pixelated the image but not the feeling that came with it. By preserving the moment, she didn't have to live in that reality.

⌒

Lola forced herself to wait for the trajinera to dock completely at the embarcadero before she bolted off it, trying to put as much distance between herself and the boatman as she could.

Every touristy thing she'd done so far this trip had been a bad idea. She was better off spending her time going between the restaurant and Buela's house, with no in-between. Her life would be boring, a mirror of her schooltime commute back home.

From behind her, she heard Javi shout "Lola, wait!" She slowed, realizing she had no idea where he had parked the car. "You cannot walk off like that, ¿sabes?"

"Javi, I'm really not in the mood to be spoken to like I'm a child," she tried.

"But aren't you acting like one?" he asked. And while the simplicity of his logic demanded a protest, or at least a dazzlingly witty comeback, she was too tired to fight him.

"Look, I'm really sorry about that back there," she said. "I just . . . I heard a voice . . . or, voices or . . . I couldn't do it. And I know it's a waste of your time to drag me around the city like this, so while I appreciate it, you really don't have to anymore."

"I heard the voice, too."

Lola had to stop herself from reeling. "You did? And you wanted to see the island anyway?"

"If you do not bother the spirits, they will not bother you. The people who keep these traditions alive say the spirits have been here longer than we have. They are everywhere; we're the ones in their world."

"I think you've been watching too many movies about the supernatural or something. If spirits are everywhere, why don't we know it?"

"If you believe it, you know it," he said simply.

There it was again, the promise of belief. It felt more like an unsolvable riddle at this point, or a single line drawing without a start and without an end, one that did not want to let her into its world. It taunted her, more than the boy standing in front of her was capable of. He, at least, could answer her questions—even if he did have that frustrating habit of also asking questions she did not have the answers to.

"Why are you helping me, really?" she asked. "I know I already asked and you said because you couldn't let me waste my money and because you wanted the stories and then you did one of those annoying shrugs of yours. But that's not an answer. So why?"

"I didn't think I shrugged that much," he said.

At least it wasn't a question.

"First, it's safer if I help you. You don't exactly know this language, and I doubt your family needs you getting into trouble," he said with a bluntness that Lola almost expected at this point. "Second, classes start in a few weeks, and I'd prefer to spend my summer doing something I have interest in rather than studying marginal gains. So in a way, it's selfish for me."

"Why can't you change your . . . are they majors here?" Lola faltered. "I mean, the thing you're studying."

Javi smiled, and the expression reached his eyes in a way she hadn't seen before. "For the same reasons you don't explain to your parents that you can't learn Spanish."

Lola laughed in spite of herself. She had to admit he had a point.

"So what?" she asked. It was dawning on her that she had no leads and no ideas where to turn next. If anything, the haughty boy in front of her was her one and only lifeline, not to mention her ride.

Javi shoved his hands in his pockets, searching for his car keys. "We'll work on your curse in time," he said. "Primero, comemos."

CHAPTER 15

As Javi drove, he tapped his fingers along to a song Lola vaguely recognized as señora music, the kind her mother often listened to as she cleaned. After days of listening to the artists Tommy favored when he played passenger-seat DJ—both Mari and Paty shared her brother's taste in music—the throwback took her momentarily by surprise. But it was the next song that floored her.

"Y ahora . . ." the over-enunciating voice of the radio host said through a slight crackle of connectivity, "Aerosmith."

Lola laughed out loud as the sweeping chords of "I Don't Want to Miss a Thing" began filling the car. Javi drummed the beat on the steering wheel.

"¿Qué?" he asked, raising an eyebrow at her laughter.

Lola looked at him sideways. "Aerosmith? Really?"

He shrugged. "The American songs stay around for a while sometimes. We love a classic."

Dramatically, he turned the volume up right as Steven Tyler hit the anguished chorus, and sang along with the same effort he had given the ranchera performance in the

La Rosa kitchen. Except this time, he had an audience. And while Lola was too aware of herself to join in, she hummed along.

"Where are we?" Lola asked for what felt like the millionth time that day when the car pulled into the parking garage. She hadn't paid attention to the traffic signs as Javi drove, assuming he'd drop her off at La Rosa and consider his work done. Instead, they were in a part of the city Lola hadn't yet seen.

"Bienvenida al Centro," Javi replied, getting out of the car and handing the keys to the waiting attendant. "It's my favorite place."

"Let me guess: There's good museums here, too."

He laughed, and for once there was no malice in the sound. "There's good museums everywhere, Lola. But here, everything is history."

Javi led the way down the street and toward a wide city square, where a huge Mexican flag waved high in the center. A gigantic cathedral towered over the hundreds of people milling about, and buildings competed with one another in their ornateness.

"It's el Zócalo," Javi said, slowing slightly so that he could fall into step with her. "All of these buildings are centuries old, but the ground is even older." He pointed to something, and as they neared it, Lola noticed the exposed ruins of an ancient temple, its walkway crammed with tourists. "El Templo Mayor," he added. "People used this ground before the Spanish marched in and took everything. The city changes a lot, and some people who lived here twenty years ago cannot afford to anymore. He paused and took a breath. "Pero la tierra es la misma de siempre." His voice was reverent and quiet, as if he was thanking the land for persevering.

Lola nodded, quietly committing his tour to memory. There was something special about knowing that the spirit of a place could endure no matter what humans did to the buildings on top of it, or to one another.

She followed him out of the crush of people and down yet another side street, to a corner shop with a few seats in the back. Javi greeted the women behind the counter warmly and pulled out two chairs at the end of a single, long counter.

"Everything's good here, but the tamales verdes are my favorite in the city," he said. "I told Rocío that once, and she spent days trying to make better ones. She couldn't do it."

"Is that how she and Juana come up with the menu? Riffing on their friends' favorites?" Lola asked, taking the seat closer to the door. "I think she does that with my grandmother's, too. Did you know Juana started cooking with her when she was, like, ten years old?"

"That doesn't surprise me," he said. "Who knows food better than a grandmother who is always feeding people?

But I think your cousin is trying to . . . preserve the food she grew up with, too. She and a lot of other people, they don't want these colonias to lose their history. Mexican food is a blend of so many cultures. That includes the ways people make their food at home."

For the briefest of seconds, it felt like they were in on the same secret. But then Javi looked back at the menu, and the connection shattered.

Lola's stomach knotted, the chicken Esperanza had offered hours ago a memory. She heard herself ask the question before she could stop it from escaping her mouth: "Can I ask what was up between you and your grand . . . I mean, with doña Pilar?"

He barely looked at her. "You picked up on that, yeah?"

"It was hard not to," Lola said tentatively, biting back what she really wanted to say: that his grandmother had been cold and almost willfully disagreeable. But she was also his grandmother, and Lola knew it would be rude for her to say that, too.

Javi didn't answer. Instead, he waved one of the women behind the counter down and asked for three different kinds of tamales. But Lola had been too busy trying to figure Javi out to decide what she wanted to eat, so when the woman turned to her expectantly, she froze.

Mercifully, Javi stepped in and asked for even more variety. "We'll split them," he said after the woman walked away. "You can tell me which you like most."

Around them, the restaurant was loud and warm, the

bite of salsa permeating the air. It was the kind of place that might appear on a "best-kept secrets" list on some trendy restaurant blog, or else would only ever be a place that the locals kept close to their hearts.

Javi exhaled and stared at the wooden countertop for a moment. "La doña has ideas about what everyone should do with their life. And not just their path, like your curse, but every decision and every day. People listen to her, too, which I think is about respect, but it's also about money. Like most things are. And la doña, she has the money. I think the first time someone did something she didn't like was when my father met my mother."

Lola arched an eyebrow, afraid that if she spoke, Javi would realize that he was doing the unthinkable—opening up to her.

And it was here that he told Lola the story of how his parents met. How his mother was from a tiny Zapotec village near a town in Oaxaca called Mitla, and most people who lived there only spoke Spanish to the outsiders who came through town. How she moved to Mexico City, found work in a restaurant—"Como tú," he added with a small wink—and met his father while out dancing one night.

Javi spoke about Esperanza protectively and with reverence. She was vividly alive in Javi's storytelling, and Lola wondered if this was the part of herself that Esperanza kept guarded in front of his grandmother, and in front of her, too.

"Actually, she spilled a drink on him, I think the story goes. He says it was on purpose. But she talked him out of being mad, and they danced that night. Se enamoraron luego luego. And my father was making enough money at the bank that he didn't need la doña to give her blessing, which is good because he probably wouldn't have gotten it. She expected him to marry some güerita like my aunts."

Javi paused just long enough to swirl the ice in his water glass around so it clinked against itself. "My father says he married my mother not to make la doña angry, but because she helps him remember there's more to life than doing that," he said at length. "Anyway, it doesn't matter. Now he's the one with the money, and people listen to him to earn his respect. My mother did it when she stopped telling me her stories, and now I'm doing it at university. It's one big circle."

There was resignation in Javi's voice and throughout the line of his body. Lola would have understood if that weight had been bitterness. But he had accepted whatever fate came with a business degree and a future spent high above the city in one of those glass towers. His future had been decided for him. It had never been a matter of choice.

"But aren't they happy that you're at least *going* to college?" she asked.

Javi's eyebrows shot up in a question, as if he had never before considered whether they were happy. Maybe that was an answer of its own.

"The only thing my parents talk about is me getting

into college," Lola added. "Well, actually, my brother and me getting into college, even though he has a few years left to go."

"And then what?" he asked.

Lola thought about her mother, how Leticia Gómez had worked her entire adolescence to become the first in her family to go to college and had devoted years to her studies. That she decided to follow the boy she'd fallen in love with in one of her classes to a country whose language she hadn't yet learned. It couldn't have been a popular decision, but Lola wasn't sure if her mother had ever worried that she was going off-script or wondered how her life might have been different had she stayed in Mexico.

It might not have been a bad life, necessarily. But it would have been different.

"I don't know," she said. "That's where the conversation ends. It's about getting into college, and going to college, and getting a scholarship for college. But never about what I'm going to do when I get there, or anything beyond that. It's like a road map missing the destination."

"You have freedom to choose, then."

Lola laughed involuntarily. "That's pushing it. I'd like some direction, I guess. But maybe they're as lost as I am."

Javi stared at the wall ahead of him. "My father, he works with investments and thinks that's what everyone should do. So he sends me to one school, then another, then the university with that future in mind. I think I was sixteen when I stopped wanting to follow along. It's easy to know when something isn't for you. It's harder to stop."

"What would you want to be studying instead?" Lola asked.

"History," he said simply, like the word could wrap itself around the world. "Especially the history of Mexico. I want to know what I wasn't told, what my mother and her family kept alive for so long. She doesn't visit them anymore. But everyone talks about these people, these tribes and cultures, like they are gone, and I want the world to know we're . . . they're still here. Who knows? Maybe if I can make enough money and can move out of la doña's house, I can also find the courage to tell my father no. But like I said, it's easier to know than it is to stop."

Lola studied him. Maybe there were several paths that could be right for a person, and it was up to each one to decide which was the best path for them.

"I think it's brave, what you're doing," she said. "Even if you haven't told him yet. At least you know there could be a way. I mean, I can't move out, and it's not like I even know what it is I want to do, but . . . I think my parents get so focused on what they think is best for me, they forget that it's what *they* think. And my dad *really* forgets that my brother and I aren't him."

Lola paused. She would have never guessed that she and Javi had something in common that was this tender, this raw. Finally, she added, "It's so easy for them to forget that we're going to want different things than they do."

"They?"

"I mean we *both* know what it feels like to disagree with our fathers in particular," she said.

Javi nodded but fell back into his moodiness. The woman behind the counter, who had an innate sense of when to interrupt conversations and make her presence known, had deposited a basket of tamales and a few plates between them. Lola helped herself to one, its corn-husk wrapper steaming. She used her fork to cut it in half and offered one end to Javi, who accepted the plate wordlessly.

Lola took a bite: There was chicken studded through the masa, which was as light as it was flavorful. She made a mental note not to tell Juana or Rocío about the meal—this could be a place just for Javi, and now for her.

The next time Javi spoke, Lola wasn't sure where his logic was going. "That day at the pyramids, you had been here maybe a week?"

"Probably closer to two," she said slowly. "It already feels like so long ago."

He ate some more of his tamal. "I'm sorry for how I was that day," he said eventually. "That place is filled with so many tourists, and I thought you were like the rest of them. The gringos I get, but I wasn't prepared to see it from someone whose family is here. But if I had been in a new country for only a few days, I probably wouldn't want a history lesson from me, either."

"If I was being dragged along to play tour guide against my will, I'd probably be in a bad mood, too," she said. "Though I don't know what I could convincingly give a tour of. Maybe the Sephora at the mall back home."

Javi's face pulled into a frown.

"Okay, not that," she added quickly. "I guess that proves my point."

"Someone should really tell Río there's no use impressing someone with his friend the historian," Javi said between bites. "That's not why girls like him anyway."

Lola blushed. It was obvious that Río was paying plenty of attention to her, but hearing Javi call her on it felt oddly personal.

"You and Río . . ." she began.

"Fuimos a la misma prepa," he said simply. "Everyone liked Gregorio there. What's not to like about him?"

Something prickly had crept into Javi's voice, nursing a question in Lola's mind. She shoved it down as she took another bite of her tamal. If he was being nice to her, she wasn't about to push her luck. The way her summer was unfolding, she'd need it for something else.

CHAPTER 16

"I don't usually come here twice in one week, but the new quesadilla is too good," Cristina proclaimed, loudly enough for the entire restaurant—as well as the kitchen and the back rooms—to take notice of her arrival.

Lola was ready to bet three Saturday night shifts, as well as all of the orejas in her grandmother's house, that her cousin wasn't there for the food.

Antonia, the youngest of tío Chuy's daughters, gave Lola a withering look as she followed her sister into La Rosa's dining room, a trail of complementing perfumes following them like a warning. Antonia was younger than Lola by a year, and her devotion to her older sisters was obvious, from the way she dressed to her habit of punctuating each comment with a hopeful "¿Verdad?" It was approval by mimicry, conditional and changing.

"Well?" Dani asked, nudging the laminated menus into Lola's hands. "Are you showing them to their table or not?"

Lola groaned and followed her cousins to the table that Cristina had picked herself, at the center of the restaurant.

"What would you be doing in Los Angeles if you weren't here, Lorenita?" her cousin asked, her eyes trailing judgmentally over Lola's black jeans and T-shirt, as if it were a personal choice and not the restaurant uniform. "What a shame you can't be doing it right now."

"It was the quesadilla for you, then, yeah?" Lola asked, trying to ignore Cristina's bait. She wasn't supposed to take orders, but getting chastised by one of the waiters seemed like the lesser of two very annoying evils. "And for you, Antonia?"

Cristina shook her head, a smile on her face. "I almost forgot," she taunted. "We need to be speaking to Lorenita en español. That's why tu papá sent you here, no? And he won't let you back into the country until you can talk like the rest of us."

Antonia smirked, clearly pleased to provide backup. "Para mi también una quesadilla, porfa."

"*Dos* quesadillas, Lorenita," Cristina emphasized. "That means two."

Lola heard the sisters laughing as she walked away, two girls who understood their power. After passing her cousins' orders off to Rocío and the kitchen staff, Lola stole away to the small alleyway in the back, desperate for air.

It wasn't fair, she kept telling herself as the anger settled in her lungs, threatening any breath that might calm her down. It wasn't fair that Cristina could act like she owned La Rosa, or that she could be so cruel to Lola for no discernable reason, or that Juana didn't see a need

206

to curb her antics. It wasn't fair that going home was still out of reach, and that she was at the mercy of everyone's whims but her own. She was seventeen—didn't that give her a say in how she wanted to spend her summers?

Cristina's question singsonged in her ear. What would she have been doing in Oxnard at that moment? Most likely, she would be stacking flash cards full of the single-spaced notes she'd taken while reading the literature her new English teacher had assigned, partially as a way to kill time until she and Ana could eat burgers in a takeout parking lot somewhere. Maybe Tommy would be texting her, begging to be driven to meet up with his friends. Lola wouldn't have minded playing Uber, really, she thought.

> **LE:** I can't take it anymore. Can I come back yet?

> **AM:** Not before I come down!
>
> I've almost convinced my mom
>
> IT'S A RESCUE MISSION!!!
>
> I've got a Whole Plan
>
> It's gonna be great
>
> Like a montage scene in a spy movie

Lola smiled right as she heard the back door open on its squeaky hinges—probably Dani, who no doubt was going to scold Lola for leaving him to deal with the restaurant alone. She shoved her phone in her pocket and steeled herself to apologize.

But the familiar feeling that began somewhere between her stomach and her heart warned her of someone else's presence. She looked up: Río leaned against the doorway the way he had when she first met him. If it was his signature move, it was a good one.

"¿Qué onda, American?" he asked, a smile playing on his face. "¿Por qué te fuiste?"

Lola swallowed her feelings with a shrug, the way she had her entire life. "I'm sorry. I'm coming back in a second; I just needed air."

Río's smile widened and showed his dimple, his grin making her stomach do a backflip that had nothing to do with how she usually felt when he was around. "Cristina is jealous. Don't pay attention to her."

"I wouldn't call it jealousy. She's in there making my life a nightmare, and her sister is helping her."

"I did not say it is easy," Río said, raking a hand through his hair. "Pero es la verdad. She's jealous. Here you are, on summer vacation, seeing everything Mexico City has to offer with a very, very handsome young man"—he paused for dramatic effect, saving the line from sounding too conceited—"and she's doing what? Laying claim to her cousin's restaurant like it's the only thing she has going on in her life."

Lola sighed. "But why does she have to be a . . ."

"¿Pendeja? ¿Cabrona? ¿Mamona?"

"I was going to go with *monster*," she said. "I think if I called my cousin anything worse than that, my grandma would find out, and then I'd be in even bigger trouble."

Río cocked his head. "You are in trouble? Why?"

Lola closed her eyes, annoyed at herself for coming perilously close to bringing up the curse.

"I . . . My aunt told her about you dropping me off at home late. She's not a fan of me hanging out with boys," she covered.

"Did she know it was me, though?" Río countered. "Las abuelas me aman."

"You're cute, but I doubt Buela is going to make an exception for you."

"So you think I'm cute?"

Lola blushed and looked up. Río was now standing extremely close to her—so close, she might not have known what to do with the dwindling space between them just a few weeks ago. But now she didn't just want Río to kiss her—she wanted to kiss him back.

Should she warn him about the curse? Stop him before it was too late?

Río leaned down before she could make a decision either way, and Lola felt herself leaning in, too.

It was every cliché at once: Her knees went a little weak, and she felt his hands at the small of her back. The secret part of her brain, the one where the things she really wanted were locked away, took over. It was the kind of kiss they showed in the movies, where the camera panned around the couple, and they lived happily ever after. And while Lola highly doubted that this was a happily-ever-after moment, she couldn't deny she was happy for one complete minute.

Maybe this summer didn't have to be so awful, she thought. Maybe this would be the summer she actually learned what life was like outside of her schoolbooks. And maybe the best time to start was right now.

Lola spent the rest of her shift nervously scanning her body, bracing herself for a betrayal or for the earth to split in two right where she stood. When Cristina and Antonia eventually left—and did not tip Jaime, who swore about it the second the kitchen doors closed behind him—she busied herself with the silverware toward the back of the house. And when Dani asked why Lola was hovering by the restroom, she tried to play it off as being worried about something she ate.

"¡Aguas!" Dani said, his hands on his hips creating a near-perfect impression of Lola's mother. "Be careful you don't get whatever is going around." Lola looked at him quizzically. "Tu amiguito Río, he went home earlier because he was throwing up. Dijo que algo le cayó mal."

Lola paled. Río was sick? How long had that been true? Was he sick before he kissed Lola, and was she now going to come down with whatever he had? Or was it that . . .

No, she told herself firmly. Río was not a Gómez. There

was no way he could have gotten caught up in the curse, too. Spirits had to have better aim than that. Whatever was meant for her was still on its way, a special-order package of familial shame and disappointment made real.

"It's coming," she muttered to herself, slumping against the wall.

"¿Qué es 'it'?" Dani asked, concern in his voice.

Lola shut her eyes tight and counted to five. But something Juana had said earlier—that nothing stayed secret at La Rosa—echoed in her head.

"Do you believe a person can be cursed?" Lola asked quietly. People at La Rosa gossiped, but she wanted someone to talk to anyway.

Dani nodded, and Lola let out a single breath in surprise. "Everyone believes in something. Sometimes it's the limpia con un huevo; sometimes it's los santos and el Papa. Even believing in nothing is believing in something, you understand?"

"¿Un huevo? You believe in the egg thing?"

"Hey, if you believe in it, it works. Además, what's going to happen when you need a limpia and the spirits know you laughed about them?"

"Then I will recant and beg for forgiveness," Lola said.

Dani laughed, but Lola could tell he wasn't amused by her sarcasm or whatever skepticism lingered in her voice. He shooed her away from the door, telling her that if she wasn't going to be useful at the host stand, she might as well go home early.

She had never been so grateful for her shift to end and for Mari to take her back to the house. Lola was silent during the car ride, and her aunt mercifully picked up on the fact that she wasn't in the mood to talk.

After hurriedly kissing her grandmother hello, Lola sped up to her side of Mari's bedroom and began sorting through the books Javi had given her, trying her best to decipher the titles or put them in context based on the covers. She scanned the pages, too, but the letters on the page felt thick and distant, the words meant for someone else. There was no way she could possibly open any of the books to a certain chapter and find the answer, least of all in the massive anthology of folk stories that glared at her from the bottom of the stack. She wasn't in the mood for parables and morals. She wanted answers.

Mari had said it sometimes, that if a person believed in something enough, it could become real. Maybe Lola had done this to herself, and to Río by extension. Which meant that now she would have to stay away from him for good. That was, if he wanted anything to do with her after this.

She sat down next to the bed, willing the feeling of the cool floor to ground her. She didn't want to have to avoid Río. She wanted to do the opposite, and there was less than a summer's worth of time to do so. Javi's words rang in her head—what was not to like about Río indeed?

But a force greater than herself had ruined everything.

And Lola doubted she could get revenge on a spirit without something backfiring horribly.

Her phone buzzed, and she fished it out of her jeans pocket, mentally composing an explanation of the day's events to fill Ana in on them.

But it was a WhatsApp message that waited for her, not a text—and the notification told her it was from Río.

Nervously, Lola opened her phone, almost too afraid to peek at the message. It was a selfie in which Río was propped up on a couch somewhere. Even gripped by illness, he managed to find his angles.

> **RL:** I guess this is what Americans
> mean by "lovesick"

She began typing, then hit send before she could talk herself out of it.

> **LE:** I'm so sorry, I should have told you

> **RL:** You knew Rocío's menudo
> would make me sick?

> That's the last time I follow
> menudo with calabaza frita

> Ya estoy muy viejo para tanta grasa

Lola braced herself.

LE: I think it was me that got you sick, not the food

Lola watched the screen nervously. This was it. This would be the final straw: On top of her drama with Cristina, and the fact that Lola and Río were coworkers, and that she would be headed back to California at the end of the summer, he would decide that a girl who caused him to throw up wasn't worth paying attention to. That his time was better spent with girls who didn't need him to repeat some of his sentences more slowly and whose laughter didn't come after a three-second translation delay. Girls who didn't feel the static of spirits in their heads whenever he was close to them.

In other words: girls who weren't Lola.

Four minutes and no reply. Had Lola lost connection somehow, or had Mari stepped out and taken the good Wi-Fi with her? But no, eventually there was the familiar buzz of her phone, and there was his reply—which neither asked her what she meant nor even engaged in the possibility.

RL: You were the best part of my day ;)

Lola felt her own smile mirror the digital one.

If Río wasn't going to be deterred simply because he'd gotten a bad stomach bug, she wouldn't be, either. Even if she knew the truth and that his sudden illness was so much more.

CHAPTER 17

If there was anyone who liked gossip more than tía Coco and her daughter, it was the staff at La Rosa, who passed it on with alarming speed. Someone must have seen Río and Lola in the alleyway, because not only did Lola have to contend with questions about her boyfriend during her shift the next day, she also had to navigate jokes about making that boyfriend sick.

To the first point, Lola didn't know how to answer— she wasn't even sure Río *was* her boyfriend. And to the second? Well, Lola figured if she told the truth about why he'd gotten ill, the laughter would only multiply.

So she smiled and nodded when Jenni and Fernando, the line cooks, asked her if she had seen Río that day, and busied herself by studying Rocío's ever-changing menu and looking up the ingredients she wasn't familiar with. The different cuts of meat were the most difficult to keep straight, and Lola had a fifty-fifty success rate when it came to identifying which tacos were made with cabrito and which were meant to be served birria style. She was maybe a thousand words into a cooking blog in which the author was reminiscing about their grandparents' rancho when she noticed this was the first day at La Rosa that she hadn't needed to fight any Río-induced nausea.

She should have been relieved. But it felt damning in its own way. As if in his absence, the spirits were making their point.

Isn't it better this way? they might as well have whispered.

You don't have to feel like your skeleton is about to jump out of your skin at any moment.

All you have to do is stop liking him.

As if it was as simple as that. And so soon after, she had admitted to herself that she liked him, too.

She only looked up when she heard someone call her name in a deep voice: Juana's father, tío Zuma, stood in the restaurant foyer, an impeccable suit jacket folded over one arm. He had a closely shaved head and the undeniable cool of a 1970s rock star. Of everyone who had made the risky decision to marry into the Gómez family, he was the clear favorite, and the comforting hug he offered his niece as a greeting was just one of the reasons why.

"Lorena, look at you! Look at this place!" he said, gesturing to the walls around them. "My daughter is doing well, no? You watch, with a little time, they'll print Juana Zurita Gómez's name in every website and magazine."

As if on cue, his daughter rushed out from either the back room or the shadows, trying to intercept her father's needs, the only one immune to his contagious pride.

"¿Qué haces aquí, pa?" Juana asked, trying and failing to disguise her nerves as concern. "¿Dónde anda mi mamá?"

Zuma grasped his daughter's shoulder, clearly used to the task of calming her down. "Relax, mi vida. It's just me today. Is this not the perfect opportunity for you to show me what you've been building? The two of you can join me for a very late lunch," he said, guiding both Juana and Lola to a nearby half-set table. Juana raised an eyebrow at Lola's slow handiwork.

"I have to get back to . . ." Juana tried weakly.

"The paperwork? I'll do it for you later. And Daniel can help the other customers while we borrow Lorena. Right now, we eat as a family."

Juana's body relaxed 80 percent of the way, as if she were still waiting for the criticism she would so readily give herself. She tried to reason with her father and talk her way out of the meal, but Zuma waved her off as he greeted or introduced himself to every member of the La Rosa staff who passed his way. He spent a full five minutes talking to Javi, whom he called one of his favorite students in recent memory, and gave him advice for the professors he would have next semester. Javi tried to defer the compliment but was clearly pleased, because Zuma's spotlight made everyone feel that much better about themselves.

Zuma also ordered their meal directly from Rocío, who

had come out to greet him and simultaneously reassure Juana that La Rosa would still be standing if she took a thirty-minute lunch.

"This is a place where people eat, mi amor," Rocío said kindly, in a tone that was reserved for partners and parents. "You should try it sometime."

"Exactly what I keep saying to her, but no one listens to their fathers anymore," Zuma said, showing a kind of investment in the restaurant in a way the other members of the Gómez family rarely did. No wonder Juana was incapable of trusting his pride in her—and Lola wondered if that included whatever support she did or didn't give herself.

Zuma asked Rocío to bring out whatever dishes she was still experimenting with and turned his attention to Lola. "Y tus papás, ¿cómo están?" he asked.

"Papá, Loli no habla español como nosotros," Juana tried.

It was the second time in less than a week Lola had heard that sentiment in front of her. "Pero yo entiendo, Juana," she said, and while she struggled through her response, she managed to tell her uncle that her parents were doing well. She did, however, neglect to tell him that she hadn't talked to her mother at length in a few days, much less communicated with her father at all, worried that such a confession would cloud the way tío Zuma was beaming at her for trying. It was a warmth she wanted to live in a little while longer.

But when the conversation turned to how Lola felt about working at La Rosa, she stumbled. She was not a naturally gifted host, and when tío Zuma insisted that was reason enough to practice, she shook her head.

"I'm only here for the summer. It would just be a waste of time," she tried.

"So? The summer is still part of your life. You still need to live in these months," her uncle countered.

Juana, who until that moment had been inspecting the huitlacoche in her taco with the precision of an archaeologist on a dig, decided to rejoin the conversation. "Don't worry about Loli, she has enough to take care of," she said. "I told you, she has the Gómez curse, too. The spirits don't want her to have a boyfriend."

Lola would have been angry that her cousin had gossiped about her to every member of the family, but she was struck by her uncle's measured nodding. That she could, or even would, be cursed did not surprise him.

"Tío, how can you believe in the curse?" she blurted out. "Doesn't that, like . . . I don't know, contradict everything you teach?"

Zuma laughed kindly. "Lorena, these curses and the rituals around them, they are older than anything I can tell my students. In my economics courses, we study why people do things and the point at which they are influenced to do something else. It's human nature, and sometimes the easiest way to describe why people do things is because they believe it is what they should do. Do any of the theories in my books allow for the possibility that a spirit is influencing the person? Of course not, but that doesn't mean it's not possible."

"When did you first hear about the Gómez curse?" Lola asked.

"The minute I met your tía Socorro." From Lola's left, Juana groaned. Apparently the only gossip she preferred not to hear was the story of how her parents met. "Your grandmother gave me a warning immediately that I could not love her daughter, and that if we got married, I'd have the Gómez curse, too. For weeks, it was the only thing I heard. But Socorro let me fall in love with her anyway, and here we are. Three daughters, two restaurants, and at least one fantastic niece. If that's a curse, I am okay with it."

"No eres Gómez, Papá," Juana countered.

"If you marry a Gómez, you are a Gómez. I am smart enough not to fight your grandmother about who runs this family." Zuma turned his attention back to Lola. "Este joven, Javier, what do you like about him? Is he worth the pain of the curse?" he asked.

Lola stared at her uncle, trying to calculate how he would have decided it was Javi that turned her world pink at the edges.

"It's that Gregorio who has a crush on Lola. He's one of my bartenders, so please don't tell Buela about that tiny detail," Juana interjected.

Zuma let a silence hang for a moment, analyzing it

with the same precision that Rocío applied to plating her dishes.

"Lorena, in economics we have a problem called the prisoner's dilemma," he said. "It's a very famous exercise; I make my students do it every year."

"Ay, Papá, this is lunch, not a study hour," Juana tried. "My workplace is not your workplace."

"You can listen to this, too, Juana. The prisoner's dilemma is very good for explaining price points for your restaurant. There are ideal prices that keep your customers happy and keep you in business, but if your customers think you have the wrong prices, or if you think you are charging your customers the wrong prices, one of you will be hurt.

"Mira," he added, waving Javi over and asking for a pen and a piece of paper. "The government has locked up two men. They tell each of the men they will be freed if they betray the other but will serve the same amount of time if neither says anything. There are four options: two where one man betrays the other, who does not say anything and spends more time in jail while the betrayer goes free; one where each betrays the other, and both spend more time in jail; and one option where neither man says anything because they trust each other, and they both spend the least amount of time in jail. Which one do you think is the most likely?"

Lola studied the boxes he had drawn on the scrap of paper, each with corresponding causes and effects.

"Betrayal," she said slowly. "No matter who says something, it's more likely that at least one person is going to betray the other."

"It's human nature to be so afraid of getting hurt that you hurt the other person first," Javi's voice intoned from behind her.

Zuma nodded emphatically before circling the square in which neither prisoner betrayed the other and each served equal time—the most improbable yet most hopeful option. "Love and business are the same in a lot of ways," he said. "You need to be fair to the other person and believe that the other person is being fair to you. Si tienes eso, who cares what a curse tells you? That's how your tía and I stay together."

"Sí, and because la Señora would kill you personally if you divorced," Juana added. "You see what she's doing to tía Paty, and she's her daughter."

"Pues yo la di nietas," Zuma said with a wink.

The conversation moved its way back toward the personal dramas of various family members—Juana's favorite topic, and one tío Zuma approached with a measured logic and a generous benefit of the doubt for the absent parties. Though she didn't turn her head, the way Javi's voice carried told her he had left the space behind her and was back to checking in on his tables, as if catching up with his old professor had been just another task for his job.

Lola, meanwhile, kept studying the scrap of paper. She didn't know if her connection with Río was meant to last as long as her aunt and uncle's relationship had, or even if it was love, as her uncle had called it. How could she be certain that she and Río were both working from a place of trust without it blowing up in her face? How could she avoid being one of the people who betrayed the other or the one who was betrayed?

From the back of her head—or maybe even from within the walls of the restaurant itself—a voice whispered to Lola that she wouldn't know until she tried. She tucked the paper into her back pocket and finished her meal. Tío Zuma insisted on paying, without a family discount.

In the brief interim between the afternoon and evening seatings, La Rosa closed its doors and most of the staff escaped for a quick break. Lola had taken to hiding in Juana's office so she could text Ana and scroll through her Instagram on the rare occasions her hours bridged both services. In some ways, it felt like she was back at the edge of the quad during lunch, watching as her classmates flirted and fought and took control of their lives.

As she stepped into Juana's office to grab her bag, carefully avoiding the white candle that was flickering in the corner in front of the miniature Virgen statue, Dani crowded in behind her, determination in his eyes.

"Uh, ¿hola?" Lola asked, surprise and suspicion mixing in her voice. Dani was strict about taking his break between shifts, explaining it helped him find balance, especially on busy days. "I'll be right out. I'm just getting my—"

"And have you on my floor with whatever mal de ojo you have?" Dani shook his head as he tightened a red bracelet around his wrist and took Lola's hand in his. "Mira, stand here," he said, gently guiding her to the middle of the small room. It had been cleaned recently, so thoroughly that it still smelled of something industrial-grade and antibacterial. Dani surveyed the room. Exactly what he was looking for, Lola wasn't sure.

"Are you going to tell me what's going on, or . . ." she tried again.

Dani moved past her and stood in front of Juana's altar, taking a breath that seemed to reach his toes. "Your cousin is worried about you. She cares about you, but she won't put a barrida on you. I think she's too scared to do anything about this. So you and I will have to protect you without her."

"A . . . Sorry, a what?"

Dani picked up an egg that had been sitting in a small bowl in front of the candle. "Lorena, has anyone ever done a limpia con huevo for you before?"

Lola stared at the small white oval cupped gently in Dani's hand. It was just an egg, she reminded herself, identical to the eggs she had seen possibly thousands of times before in her life. "No, no one has ever banished a curse with an egg for me before," she said slowly.

"Con esa actitud, claro que no," Dani said. Though his

words were brusque, his smile softened the sting. "You don't need to be nervous, Lola, but you do have to believe that this will work, or it won't. Can you do that?"

Lola hesitated. Dani had never given her bad advice in the few weeks she'd known him—and he was the only person who didn't get angry when she made seating mistakes—but this was so far out of her realm of experience than she wasn't sure how to proceed. "Dani, if Juana doesn't want you to do this . . ."

"Juana does not want to be involved, but she wants to help you. There is a difference." Dani's voice was calm and even, and his presence was enough to ground Lola's pinballing emotions. "It is your choice. You say no, I take the egg and go."

Lola looked from Dani to the egg. She thought about the curse, and about kissing Río, and about how she'd like to do the latter without worrying about the former. "If I do believe, it will work?"

"Maybe, maybe it will take more time. But it's better that we believe, otherwise why do anything?"

Dani waited until Lola nodded her head, then he took a deep breath and closed his eyes for a moment. "Entonces, voy a pasar este huevo por tu cabeza y tu cuerpo también. Y tú necesitas creer que se te está limpiando el mal de ojo mientras lo hago. ¿Está bien?"

Lola was too busy trying to understand what Dani had said to answer the question. Even so, she got the sense that it wasn't one she could say no to.

Dani touched the egg lightly to Lola's neck and rolled it down to her shoulder blades methodically and slowly. As the egg moved, Dani murmured words so quickly that Lola doubted they were meant for her. She worried for a moment that the egg might slip and crash on the floor, but it never did. She let the sensation lull her into a sense of rhythm as she thought about how Dani could be right, and she might as well believe this would work.

That it was better to do something about what was happening to her than accept it, than do nothing at all.

So Lola took a deep breath and then another. Her gaze settled on the candle in the corner, and though she had no idea what she was doing, she tried to focus on her heart and how it thrummed in her chest. If she really listened, that pulse felt like her heart was saying something, the way the buzz of her body had felt like someone trying to get through to her whenever Río had come too close. Lola had no idea what her heart was trying to tell her now. But had she ever really known? And what could she do when whatever her heart told her changed midsentence?

Dani pulled himself up from where he had been rolling the egg in circles on Lola's shoes. He closed his eyes and exhaled.

"So is that it?" Lola asked, but one raised hand from Dani made her go quiet again.

Dani moved toward the tiny altar and cracked the egg into a waiting bowl. Lola couldn't see over the lip and inside it, so she watched him as he furrowed his eyebrows in concern.

"Whatever is happening to your family, this is not just one curse," he said slowly. "Whoever is doing this to you, they are doing it over and over. This is a curse with layers; it goes very deep. Perhaps whoever is doing this knows you're trying to undo it," Dani paused and locked eyes with Lola. "That may be why they keep redoing it."

"Dani, how do you know this?" Lola's voice was startlingly loud in the tiny room.

"Mira," Dani said, holding the bowl out to her. In the egg was a constellation of reddish-brown spots forming an imperfect but steady line across the yolk. "Whatever the egg picked up from you has a purpose. This isn't just one spirit. This is something with effort."

Lola's heart fell to the bottom of her chest. "And you're saying there's no way to fix it?" she asked slowly. "If . . . whoever is doing this is just going to do it over and over again, is there any point in trying to undo it?"

Dani shook his head. "There might be a way. Why not? But you'll be okay today, or until they put the curse on your family again. So I would tell you to enjoy it for now."

"Wow. Thanks," Lola offered weakly.

"I know this wasn't the answer you wanted, Lorena," he said kindly. "But isn't it better to have an answer than is to have only questions?"

"But we don't know who is doing this, or even why," Lola tried.

"No, pero . . . you know you are safe now. That's good news."

On that lukewarm sentiment, Dani left the room, his arm outstretched as if to keep the bowl and its contents as far away from his body as possible. She could hear him calling out to the servers, already moving back into business mode.

But Lola was not wired the same way. She was built to overthink.

Why stop at half the answer when she could have the whole thing? It was better for her to believe that she could find the other pieces of the puzzle and a complete cure than to accept a temporary reprieve.

It was thanks to Mari that Lola was even allowed to leave the house that night, especially after Río had brought her back so late the night of their first real date. In a stroke of genius, Mari had told her mother that she was taking Lola to dinner but that she had to run errands at school first and could not fetch Lola herself, so wouldn't it be easier for her niece to meet her later? Miraculously, Buela had relented, which meant tía Paty would drive Lola to "dinner."

Lola took extra time on her makeup, looking more for a boost of confidence from the ritual of blending and shading than for hope that Río would appreciate her hard work. Not that there was anything wrong with the barefaced Lola, but the version of herself that wore false lashes and a hint of blush on the bridge of her nose had a kind of armor the other didn't. She burned an incense stick she'd found in Mari's drawer as she got ready, the copal imparting a bright, grounding scent to the space.

Lola's aunt was quiet during the car ride, and instead of talking, they listened to the brassy notes of a banda album whose singer belted on and on about infidelity and heartbreak. It was only when the car neared their destination that Paty lowered the volume and turned to Lola.

"You're not meeting Mari for dinner, are you?" she asked simply.

Lola tried to stammer a cover, which made her aunt laugh.

"Está bien," Paty said kindly. "Just stay safe. My sister will be in a lot of trouble if la Señora finds out she lied, and you will be in trouble for whatever it is I don't want to know that you're doing."

Lola nodded gratefully and climbed out of the car. She could already see Río waiting for her at the entrance to the mall.

"There she is!" he said as she approached, his arms outstretched. "¡Mi americana!"

Lola smiled. "I'm glad you're feeling better," she offered, wondering if she was too sincere to be unaffected and cool. "I'm so sorry, again."

It was what she didn't say, that her family's curse had reached out its arms and latched on to him, that hung in the air.

Río waved her off. "What is there to be sorry for? Normally I have an iron stomach, but every man has his off days." He wrapped his arm around Lola's shoulders and guided them into the shopping complex, which was filled with people bustling from store to store. The curse made Lola's nerves feel like a fireworks show inside her heart. Dani had said the limpia might take time, she reminded herself. When she squirmed to knock some of the tension loose from her body, Río laughed and squeezed her tighter.

A movie and an ice cream at the food court was the kind of night that teen magazines had decided was the gold standard forty years ago—but that didn't mean it wasn't still a fun way to spend an evening. Lola felt slightly sheepish when Río insisted on seeing the one movie being shown in English with Spanish subtitles, but he waved off any apology before she could offer one. They held hands through almost the entire movie, and while Lola's skin prickled with excitement, it was a feeling she liked.

Río led their conversation as they walked through the mall, and Lola didn't mind serving as an audience to his animated storytelling. For every question he asked about her, he supplied three details about himself that Lola committed to memory like historical facts she might be tested on later. The way he talked about his school days and his family, it felt like she was the first to hear any of this, that his memories were expressly for her. She almost dared anything to go wrong now.

So Lola wasn't worried when Río pulled her toward him as they left the complex at the end of the night, and she didn't dodge or steel herself for catastrophe when he leaned in to kiss her. In fact, she found herself leaning in once more and kissing him back.

It was a moment that made Lola's stomach once again perform a somersault. But while it could not last forever— they were standing fewer than twenty feet away from where Mari had told Lola she would park her car to pick her up— its end did not bring the sky crashing down around them. In fact, Lola felt better than fine.

What she felt was happy.

CHAPTER 18

The happiness, Lola soon learned, was not meant to last.

The next morning, she woke feeling sick—stay-home-from-school sick, a violent flu that racked her whole body and made her head feel like it would split in two. She barely managed to drag herself out of bed and to the bathroom, and it wasn't the cold tile making her shiver.

Could the curse reset this quickly? Or maybe Dani was wrong and the limpia hadn't worked at all, she thought as she stared at her gray complexion in the mirror. If anything, openly defying the spirits had made things worse.

"¡Querida, mírate!" Buela cried with concern when Lola finally made her way downstairs, though she only had enough energy to curl up on the couch. But while her grandmother continued to mutter to herself about the curse, she relished tending to Lola. Helping a sick family member was clearly where the woman felt most useful.

According to Buela, the only possible remedy for Lola's spiking fever was to go straight back to bed and stay there until she felt better. She already had the phone in one hand, waiting to call Juana to explain why her host wouldn't be coming in today. Gratefully, Lola pulled herself back upstairs. She didn't have to hear the conversation to know that it would be far more effective coming from their grandmother than it would have been had she tried telling Juana she was sick.

For the next few hours, Buela busied herself by checking in on Lola constantly, each time with another task to help her feel better. First came the now-familiar tub of Vicks, then came a delivery of apple soda Lola hadn't asked for but appreciated anyway. At one point, Buela asked if Lola had enough pillows, and she not only brought Lola a steaming bowl of caldo de fideo, but made sure her granddaughter ate it.

Lola was too exhausted to fight the constant hovering, but it would have been futile. Besides, she was grateful.

It was only when she had begun to doze that Lola got a message from Río, asking why she wasn't at La Rosa. *You're my favorite part about going to work now*, he added.

The rush Lola felt from that comment mixed uncomfortably with her body's aches.

LE: You mean you didn't get sick again, too?

RL: I'm better than new, I ran 10 kilometers before work and feel like Superman.

This time, the curse hadn't missed its target. Even texting with Río felt like she was testing the spirits' wrath, like they were simply waiting to issue the next bolt of bad luck.

"I get the hint, God . . . or whoever is up there," she muttered at no one in particular.

> **LE:** I woke up feeling like a nightmare, so watch out, I guess.

> **RL:** Nothing to watch out for ;)
>
> Let me know when you're better, yeah?
>
> There's a new restaurant my friend works at, I can get us a discount
>
> You're going to love it

Lola put the phone down, trying to shake the frustration creeping into her chest. Boys were dense sometimes, but she hadn't anticipated that Río would be so cavalier about her sudden illness. Hadn't he lived through a similar fate only a few days ago? Shouldn't he have understood?

She was forced to push the thought from her mind when Mari came clambering up the stairs and into their room. "Mi hermana quiere hablar contigo," she whispered dramatically, pointing to the phone in her hand, where Letty's pixelated face filled the screen.

"Lola, what happened?" Mami asked, the concern its

own decibel in her voice. Like Buela, like mother, Lola thought.

She shrugged. "I woke up sick. Don't worry, Buela is taking . . . really good care of me."

Mari smirked good-naturedly on the other side of the room.

"Lola, can I have your car yet?!" Tommy called from out of frame.

Lola watched as her mom shook her head but didn't chastise her son for yelling.

Letty Espinoza ran through the checklist with Lola— Had Buela given her Vicks? Was she eating anything? Did she have enough water? How bad was her fever?—before deciding she was satisfied with the care her mother was offering in her stead. "If I could be there, I would in a heartbeat. You know that, Lola, right?" she asked.

Lola fought back the pang of homesickness that had cut its way into her heart. It hadn't gotten to her before, but now it was a feeling—no, a reality—she couldn't shake.

Letty, who could predict her daughter's moods with startling accuracy, launched into filling Lola in on everything that had happened at work since she was gone. On and on Letty went about the new hires she needed to train and the repeat customers she had to put up with, whose nicknames were familiar to Lola given their regular appearances in her mom's stories. But Letty was also tired: There was so much inventory turnover that she wasn't sure when the store would get a break, she said.

Lola leaned back and listened to her mom's stories, almost as if she were back in their kitchen, helping to prepare dinner. When Letty complained, it was pragmatic—she rarely began a story without knowing its resolution, could be counted on to end on a happy note or with a joke, and was almost always justified in her frustrations. Hers was righteous anger, Lola's father said sometimes. If she was mad, it was for a good cause.

It was only when a lull formed in their conversation that Lola chimed in. "Hey, Mami?" she asked tentatively. Her mother, who was clearly cleaning something in the living room, murmured an affirmative. "Do you ever think how different your life would have been if you stayed in Mexico? And if you had been able to actually use your degree?"

"Who says I'm not using it now? I learned a lot of things at university, you know. Sometimes the fights I break up between shift leaders feel like litigation."

"I know, I just . . ." Lola tried. "You know what I mean."

Her mother sighed. "I do think about that, Lorena. But then I probably wouldn't have had you or your brother, which is really where my life would have been different. Easier sometimes," she added with a wink. "But very different. Why?"

Lola shrugged. "I didn't know if you ever resented your job. It's not *exactly* what you went to school for, I mean."

"We do the jobs we have to do sometimes, and sometimes

longer than we intend to. Besides, it's a good job. That I didn't plan for it makes it a surprise."

"Why did you decide to go to the States, then? If it was going to be so hard to start from zero."

"Gómez women do a lot of things that scare us for love," Letty said. "The men, too, come to think of your tíos. Chuy is the biggest scaredy-cat I know."

If there had ever been a time to ask her mother about the curse, it was now. But Letty interrupted her daughter before Lola found the words. "Is my sister still there? I want to talk to her and la Señora about looking after you."

Mari's outstretched hand accepted the phone, and she left the room as she picked the conversation with her sister back up. Her voice took on a different tone when she argued with her siblings, one that exposed her more as the baby of the family than the capable law student, and it reached that pitch now with Letty.

Alone, Lola waded through the ways the curse had impacted her family. Buela had found love but lost it, leaving fear as her constant companion. Lola's mother had followed love to a new country, leaving behind family and the degree she'd worked so hard to achieve. Tía Paty had tried to keep her love alive, but her marriage collapsed anyway. Mari insisted she was too busy with her career to entertain a relationship, as if acknowledging she had to pick one or the other, and while Juana was happy with Rocío, the stress of running their restaurants clearly took its toll. And Lola was sitting in bed, willing her grandmother's soup to stay in her stomach.

The origins of the curse might be unknown, but Lola feared its rules were becoming increasingly clear: If a Gómez woman wanted to forge her own path in life and in love, there would be a cost.

Lola would have done anything to go back to the high of the night prior, when she thought she had risen above whatever was dragging her down, that she had outsmarted the forces at play by simply believing she could. But now here she was back at square one, with no idea where to turn.

From the corner of the room, the powdery smell of Mari's incense wafted enticingly. Lola wondered if lighting another piece would help, but the thought of getting out of bed made her head spin.

Instead, she turned to her text thread with Ana, who was busy planning everything she wanted to do in Mexico City, from visiting the Barragán House and Frida Kahlo's Casa Azul, to watching the mariachi play at Plaza Garibaldi—and while Mrs. Morris hadn't yet given the official okay, Ana was optimistic in that and every respect. She was a one-girl Google search, and her list of places to go and restaurants to try was so long, Lola hadn't heard of most of what made the cut. There was so much to the city she didn't know about, and so much more to learn.

CHAPTER 19

It was going to take a miracle for Rosa de la Bendición Cruz de Gómez to let her granddaughter out of the house once she was well again. What Lola didn't know was how to make that miracle happen.

"Buela, no te preocupes por mí," she pleaded for the fifth time in three hours. The bug, whatever it was, had passed in a day, almost to the minute, yet Buela wasn't convinced that Lola was entirely better. "Mari, can't you tell your mom that *I'm fine*?"

Mari looked up from her laptop and shrugged. "If my mother thinks there's reason to be worried for you, then she's worried for you. You try talking sense into a stone."

Lola sank back into the couch. She was supposed to go to a party with Río, who had promised her the most fun she would have that whole summer. She hadn't been sure how to break it to him that she was bad at parties—what if admitting it revealed to him that she was a loner back at home?—so she hedged a worry that she wouldn't know anyone there. But he had insisted, over and over again.

They're going to love the American as much as I do ;), his last WhatsApp message read. Lola had looked at the text on her screen dozens of times, almost as if to make sure it was real, before sending a screen shot of the message to Ana.

> LE: He . . . didn't mean love like THAT, right?
>
> Or like . . . did he?

> AM: What do you want him to mean?

Lola didn't quite know.

It took her longer than it should have to craft a text letting Río down. The word *love* magnified itself in her mind as she typed and deleted variations of the same thing. At first, she'd written "Lo siento" but back-tracked. It was Javi who insisted, annoyingly, that she use Spanish.

> LE: I can't go tonight. My grandmother won't let me even leave the house . . . ever, I think.

> RL: :(:(:(:(:(

At least he was as upset about it as she was, Lola told herself. That was a comfort of its own.

It was tía Coco's intervention that delivered Lola from her grandmother's house. The next morning, her aunt came bustling into Buela's kitchen, tía Sofía's middle daughter, Xóchitl, at her side. Tío Zuma strolled in behind them, a bag of groceries meant for his mother-in-law in his hand. He gave Lola a wink hello as Xóchitl made a beeline for their grandmother, clutching at the woman's knees before offering the perfunctory kiss hello.

"Ay, ¡mi nietecita!" Buela cried, pausing her cooking long enough to smother the girl in kisses. Xóchitl beamed under the attention, the chocolate on her round cheeks betraying the Gansito that her tía Coco had already plied her with.

Tommy and tío Chuy were each the only boy in at least two generations of Gómezes. And while Socorro, Chuy, and Sofía had been convinced they would each have at least one boy, their trios of Gómez girls said otherwise. If Buela was holding out hope that Paty or Mari would break the streak, she would have to keep hoping—Paty was nowhere close to dating again; and Mari, who was neither maternal nor romantic, was far more interested in telling anyone who would listen how a child would derail her career. So Buela spoiled tía Sofía's children doubly while she waited for the next set, and her other daughters helped.

Tía Coco sighed dramatically and deposited her bag and coat on the table as she herself sank into a chair, complaining about her feet. "Lorenita, tráeme mis otras bolsas," she said, waving to the other room. Lola followed her directions and brought back two gigantic nylon bags, each filled to the brim with produce. "El . . . ¿cómo dices . . . el market? It was so busy, Dios mío," she groaned. "¿Y con Xochitzintli? I was thinking I would never leave."

"Tía, podemos hablar en español," Lola said as she pulled tomatillos and poblanos from the bag. "Estoy practicando."

"And you are la única que necesita practicar?" her aunt snapped. "I know my English. Juana, she spends so much time talking English around my house, thinking that she can get past me. So I learn, too!" She cackled happily. "Tu tía Coco, she knows everything."

"But she will not tell you where she learned it," tío Zuma added as he helped Buela sort through her groceries. "That was my fault, Lorena."

"¡Y mira! Now I know what you two talk about when you do not think I am listening."

But the pull of Spanish was stronger as Coco began relaying the gossip she had amassed since her last visit. Lola's grandmother multitasked between her daughter's stories, her caldo on the stove, and Xóchitl's explanation of a complex game she had learned at school. Zuma calmly added asides meant for Lola more than anyone else. The cacophony reminded Lola of her mother's video calls back home, of words creating a chorus over the sizzle of a busy stove.

She was snapped back to reality by tía Coco's insistence. "Lorena, ¿tú qué piensas? Is Rocío going to marry my Juana or no?"

"Ay, Socorro, ahorita no . . ." Zuma tried.

"Yo . . . no sé," Lola said, trying to hide a grin.

"¿Y por qué no?" her aunt continued. "She owns *two* restaurants, she has her own business, even if a mi mamá no le gusta. My Juana, she's special. And me? Quiero nietos también." She nodded toward Xóchitl.

"Tía, Juana's only twenty-six."

"¿Y? That means I'm getting old, too. I was her mother at that age. Oye, those naranjas, they go to La Rosa. Rocío las necesita para una receta nueva. Lorena, take those with you on your next shift, no?"

"I can't." Lola sighed. "Buela doesn't want me out of the house."

That was enough for Coco to turn her attention squarely on her mother and launch into an interrogation that rivaled Letty when she suspected Tommy was up to no good. No wonder the woman had dirt on everyone—her questioning was relentless, even if Lola understood only three out of every five words.

"Sabes que no me gusta ese lugar," Buela huffed, turning back to her stove.

"True, but we do. It's a good thing, too. I gave Juana her first loan to start it," tío Zuma said conspiratorially. Tía Coco winked at Lola.

"Pues mira, Lorenita," she said breezily, as if she

243

hadn't just disagreed with her mother. "Take these naranjas to La Rosa; tell Rocío I sent you. I'm ordering you un Uber now. It says . . . Marco Aurelio is five minutes away." With a smile she added, "It's your job now to also find out when la novia becomes la esposa, ¿entendido?"

Lola nodded and rushed out of the room to change her clothes and grab her bag before Buela could stop her. Your mom is letting me come, I can do my shift, she messaged her cousin, bracing herself for the inevitable moment in the near future where she would have to deal with Juana's questions.

The Uber ride itself was a blur, and Lola was grateful when the puttering Toyota deposited her outside the familiar building. She barely remembered to grab the oranges from the back seat before the car sped off.

"Lorena, ¿dónde estabas?" Dani asked suspiciously as Lola shoved her things behind the hosting desk.

"I'll explain later, but it begins and ends with my grandmother," she said, which earned a knowing nod.

"It's always grandmothers, no? I love mine, but that woman . . . Every time I stop by her house, she acts like I abandoned her and she'll die because of me," Dani said. He nodded towards Lola's bag. "What's in there?"

"Oranges for Rocío. Have you seen her?"

"¿Coco?" Dani asked.

"Coco."

"If Rocío's not in the kitchen, she's out back. Tell her

I want the first taste of those churros recién salidos o lo que sea que she's dreaming up now. ¿Me escuchaste, Lorena? ¡El primer bocado!" Dani called after her.

Lola waved hello to the kitchen staff as she poked her head in, but Rocío was nowhere to be found. "¿Saben si la jefa está en la oficina?" she tried, to which Fernando shook his head. So Lola turned to the door that led to the alleyway . . .

. . . where she saw Río, his mouth suctioned firmly on the mouth of a girl she'd seen in the restaurant before.

Lola remained rooted to the ground for longer than she should have. Whether it was for ten seconds or twenty minutes was anyone's guess. "I . . . I was looking for Rocío," she stammered weakly to no one, not even sure that Río or the girl had noticed her, before turning back inside and slamming the door behind her. She pushed her way through the restaurant, and it was only when she was out on the sidewalk in front that she heard someone call her.

"American, wait!" Río said.

She turned, as much as she didn't want to. "It's Lorena" was the only thing she could think to say. "I mean, Lola."

Río offered her an easy grin. "Well, which one do you like more?" he said.

Lola felt herself reach a limit she hadn't known existed. "Really?" she asked. "I see you . . . and her . . . and . . . and now you want to ask which name to call me?"

"Relax," Río said, the ease in his voice a sting. "Janet's

a friend from one of my acting classes. We're having fun, como tú y yo."

His smile was stretched across his face, his dimple winking cruelly.

"You're kidding, right?" Lola tried to find a comeback or a withering one-liner stored somewhere in her brain. What would Ana say? How would she react?

Well, Susana Morris would have been the one doing the heartbreaking, not the other way around. She wouldn't have invested her feelings that deeply in the first place, much less worked so hard to solve whatever curse had tried to stop her from ever coming close to heartbreak.

The pain in the middle of Lola's chest, the one that made it hard to breathe, had a name.

"Leave me alone, Río," she said, feeling exposed on the sidewalk.

"American, I . . ."

"I said it's Lorena, and I said I want you to leave me alone. Or do you need me to say it in Spanish?" she said, surprised by the bite in her words. "Déjame en paz."

Río's smile faltered for a moment. Then, with a shrug, he turned and walked back inside.

Lola hugged her arms around her body and stared at the ground, trying to calm herself down before she was forced to work an entire shift with Río at the bar. She had looked forward to escaping her grandmother's house for La Rosa that morning. She had actually been excited to go to work.

The morning version of her had been a fool.

The whispers she'd endured behind her back, the teasing about her so-called boyfriend . . . it had been for nothing. Río had made that very clear the moment he told Lola they had been having fun. How fun was it when one person didn't know the specifics of their arrangement? The sun was shining brightly down on Lola, but she couldn't help but feel like she'd been in the dark the whole time.

CHAPTER 20

Juana begrudgingly acquiesced when Lola asked if she could be removed from the schedule at La Rosa for a few days, but she was the first person to tell her that under no circumstances was she going to fire Río.

"He's my best bartender, Loli," she stressed from the doorway of Mari's bedroom two days after the incident in the alleyway. She had stopped by to see how Lola was feeling, but the latter noticed that Juana seemed wary of moving any closer to her cousin lest she throw a shoe. "I am sorry for what that pig did to you, but you try finding someone who makes micheladas as good as he does."

"Weren't you complaining last week that he pours double the shots he needs to?" Mari asked as she folded clothes in her half of the room. Lola watched as her hands hit the exact hypnotic rhythm that Lola's mother found when she did the same chore back home. "¿Que qué?" Mari emphasized. "'Ay, pinche Río, pouring my money away in mezcal.'"

"People buy even more food when they drink more. It's a smart business decision," Juana protested.

Mari rolled her eyes and continued to fight with Juana on Lola's behalf, pulling her generational rank as the two squabbled. Lola groaned and hid her head under the bed's single pillow.

"Well, if you're not going to help, you might as well get back to your restaurant, Juana," Mari said, looking over her shoulder at Lola. "I'll take care of your cousin because you won't."

Juana looked like she was about to enter the room but thought better of it. "Bueno," she said eventually. "Un día más, Loli," she said. "Solo uno."

"Un día más," Mari singsonged after her, closing the door in her absence. "You see how she acts? Like it's her burden to be la jefa? She loves this, though, this chisme. Es la hija de Socorro." She huffed and put a small stack of folded clothes on the corner of Lola's bed before nudging her niece's legs to the side so she could sit. Lola appreciated her aunt's quiet comfort, which was less direct than her mother's but no less aware.

A few minutes passed during which Lola heard her grandmother's voice rise from the floor below, the sound likely directed at Juana. But as easy as it might have been to be mad at her cousin, Lola's disappointment was not Juana's fault. She could only blame herself for reading so eagerly into Río's flirtation, when everyone—including Dani, the spirits, and she herself—had warned her against it.

How did her classmates live with feeling so terrible about every breakup and crush? At school, the aggrieved parties would not only be forced to tend to their feelings and pass each other in the hallways, but they'd be expected to finish their homework, pass their tests, and show up to practice. Lola could barely go downstairs for breakfast—Buela had been bringing her cereal up to her for the past two mornings.

Lola felt Mari's hand on her shoulder and took it as a cue to sit up. Her aunt had her own life, and the last thing Lola wanted was for Mari to feel obligated to dote on her.

"Mari, I'm fine," she tried to say, the exhaustion in her voice betraying her. At least she hadn't thrown up, or developed hives, or broken her leg, she thought. Physically, she was in one piece—and she supposed that was something to be happy about.

"You're not, and you don't have to pretend to be," Mari countered. "Las mujeres Gómez, why do you have to be strong all the time?"

"You're a Gómez woman, too, Mari," Lola pointed out.

"Sí, and I have the good sense to not be strong when I don't feel like being strong. If I want to cry, I cry. I don't go blaming any bad thing on espíritus or santos." Mari moved back to the half-folded laundry, muttering to herself.

Lola sighed again, replaying the moment in which Río had smirked at her on the sidewalk. It was the only thing she had been able to think about, his detached, almost haunting nonchalance. Ana had suggested Lola find a way to transfer the curse onto him. Lola wasn't sure that his cruelty wasn't a curse of its own.

Mari handed Lola another stack of clothes. "Do you have anything other than jeans?" she asked. "We're going out tonight, and you can't wear these."

"We're going out?"

"That's what I said, didn't I?" her aunt replied, inviting herself to poke around Lola's suitcase. "There's a party at a friend's apartment in la Condesa. I won't let you stay here with la Señora another night, and you can't wear what you have on now."

Lola opened her mouth to protest, but Mari had already found the dress that Lola's mother had insisted she pack the night before her exile. She held it up against her body, examining it like it was her own.

"Oye, ¿y este vestido?" came a familiar trill from the hallway. Lola tried to collapse back onto the bed as Cristina came bursting through the door. "Está padre ese vestido," she cooed, offering Mari a cheek kiss that was mostly air. "It's new?"

"No, it's Lorena's," Mari offered with a head nod.

Her cousin stifled a noise that sounded suspiciously like surprise. "This is yours, Lorenita?" she asked. Mari rolled her eyes again, clearly annoyed that no one took her statements at face value. "It's cute. Why don't you wear dresses more?"

"Cristina, ya," came Mari's warning.

Cristina shrugged and picked her way around the room, examining items like they were hers before she got bored and moved on to the next thing.

Lola heard herself ask the question before she realized it was rude. "You're coming with us?"

Her cousin scoffed. "Why would I miss a party? Lorenita, I *am* a party. You'd know that if you visited more often."

Mari clicked her tongue disapprovingly, which made Cristina spin on her heel toward her aunt.

"¿Qué?" she asked, challenging Mari. "Es la neta. Su familia no nos visita. ¿Debería sentirme feliz cada vez que ellos están aquí?"

"Be nice to Lorena; she's sad about that Río boy," Mari said pointedly, tossing the dress in Lola's direction and moving to one of the bags Cristina had brought with her, which was full to bursting with clothing. Perhaps it wasn't worth pointing out to Cristina that borders and airline tickets were more difficult to navigate than piling into a car every weekend.

"Do you get like this over every silly guapo?" Cristina asked. "That's a lot of wasted time, no?"

"There aren't any other boys," Lola replied, hoping that her honesty would shut her cousin up. "I study for school and do my homework. That's my life back in the States. My parents wouldn't let me go on a date. Not that it matters, since no one asks me out."

Cristina arched one precisely penciled brow. "So why not ask them out?" she countered.

It was a simple question, but it reminded Lola of the many ways in which Cristina talked her family into giving her whatever she wanted, whenever she asked. Apparently, dates were no different—nor was Lola's makeup bag, which her cousin had helped herself to without an invitation.

"Lorenita, ¿me lo prestas?" she asked, holding up an eyeshadow palette. She didn't wait for the answer before moving to the mirror.

It was clear to Lola that she wasn't going to spend another night scrolling through Instagram at home if her cousin and aunt had anything to say about it. Maybe she could go with them for fifteen minutes before shaking them off and hailing a taxi back home. Begrudgingly, she got off the bed and moved to get ready.

Mari clapped her hands at the development. "Vas a ver," she told Lola sagely. "That Gregorio, Río, o como se llame, he doesn't deserve you, Lola. What's your saying? ¿Hay otros peces?"

"You mean there's more fish in the sea?"

"That's the one!"

"What do fish have to do with men?" Cristina asked suspiciously. "Río es un baboso, pero no huele a pescado."

"No mames, no es una frase literal," Mari chided her before pushing Lola toward the bathroom so she could change. "And hurry up, okay? Rafa's place is very cool. We're going to have fun tonight, you'll both see."

CHAPTER 21

After Mari convinced her sister to drive them to Condesa and interrupted Buela's nightly prayer in front of her wall of portraits to tell her they would be out together past Lola's curfew—but only an hour at most, she had pledged—the girls claimed their seats in Paty's car. Cristina sat in front, cycling between checking her phone for notifications and touching up her lip gloss in the rearview mirror. That, too, had been Lola's, but the tube was now tucked away in Cristina's purse—"It looks better on me, ¿no crees?" she had asked, holding her fair arm up to Lola's tan one in petty comparison.

And Lola's cousin didn't let the antagonism stop there. "Oye, did Rafa say it was okay to bring more people to his party?" Cristina asked over her shoulder as tía Paty navigated through traffic.

"Rafa would be disappointed if *everyone* wasn't at one of his parties, Cristina Luisa," Mari said matter-of-factly before turning to face Lola. She was wearing one of Cristina's blouses and a skirt that was far shorter than anything Lola had seen her wear so far that summer. "Rafa's sister and I went to school together," she explained. "Her little brother is Cristina's age, but he goes to the same school Juana and her sisters did. It's a big city but a small world. I think that school is how Juana met el feo and his other friend, too."

"You mean Río and Javi?" Lola asked, trying to avoid Cristina's glances toward the back seat.

"Ah, sí," Mari said. "Look, I know we hate him right now, but I meant what I told you before. They're both cute."

"Juana calls them Diego y Gael."

"*Juana* has two skills in this life: turning any ingredient into the best meal you've ever eaten, and making friends with attractive people. And what are you doing driving around with Javier anyway? Don't tell me you aren't."

Nothing Lola thought to tell Mari felt believable enough. "I–I'm . . . He's teaching me more about Mexican history," she tried. "As, like, a supplement to the Spanish lessons." She wasn't particularly in the mood for Mari to tell her that chasing down spirits was a waste of time.

Cristina's attention moved back to her phone, and Lola made a mental note to bring up homework the next time her cousin got on her nerves.

"My sister warned me about this," Mari sighed. "Letty told me you would always want to study something. But tonight, there's no studying. Tonight we're having fun."

"Lorenita, you'll have to tell us if our parties are like American parties," Cristina said.

Before Lola could admit that she wasn't the right person to ask, the car stopped with a jerk. "Ya llegamos," Paty said, nodding in the direction of brick walls painted a bright white. An open gate led to a house illuminated by lights.

Lola thanked her aunt for the ride and climbed out after Mari, who had been right about the size of Rafa's parties. There were people everywhere inside the house, laughing and yelling and dancing to a playlist being piped through hidden speakers. Cristina excused herself to say hi to someone almost immediately, leaving Mari shaking her head in her niece's wake.

"I told her tonight would be about family, and there she goes," she scoffed. "Cristina means well, pero . . . My brother, he spoils her. And her sisters."

"It's all right, really," Lola said. "I'm kind of used to la princesa by now."

"Is that what they call her at La Rosa?" Mari asked, her eyebrows shooting up in amusement. "And you're not used to it, I can tell. But come on, let's get you a drink." She paused. "Does my sister let you drink? Ni modo, I will get you a Sprite."

Though Lola knew a grand total of two people at the party, it soon didn't feel that way. Mari quickly introduced her to a number of friends, including the infamous Rafa and his sister Karla, who had long black hair and was extremely willing to help her guests drain her parents' alcohol collection. And while it would have been easy for Mari to forget Lola existed, she made sure to include her in the conversation. None of Mari's circle let Lola fade into a dark corner, either, and they asked her plenty of questions about life in California and the difference between home and Mexico City.

"Mira," Esteban, a curly-haired boy of around Mari's age, said. "Cuando quieras, you can show me los Estados Unidos."

"Esteban wants to leave like Lola's mother—my sister— did," Mari interjected. "She met su marido, y se fueron. And now we have our Lola. A true Mexican American."

The conversation migrated into such emphatic Spanish that Lola couldn't quite keep up with the pace, but she tried to nod along as much as she could. Her plastic cup was now filled with more melting ice than soda, and she motioned to her aunt that she was going to try to find the kitchen and get a refill.

"We'll be here waiting for you," Mari said.

Lola smiled. For perhaps the first time in her life, she was having fun at a party.

I went to Mexico and became fun, she thought as she made her way through a crush of people. Would Ana believe her when she told her about going out with Mari? Or would she be annoyed that Lola had never loosened up the same way at the parties she'd dragged her to back home? The uncertainty lodged itself in Lola's brain, but her attention was pulled by a bout of laughter from a corner of the courtyard outside.

Lola looked through the window and did a double take when she saw Javi surrounded by people, including Jaime, the busboy from La Rosa. Some of the boys were talking animatedly, and though Javi wasn't as engaged in the conversation, he at least didn't look like he was there against his will, the way he did so often around Lola.

Resolving not to let neither him nor Río ruin her good night, she turned her head and mustered up the courage to ask someone for directions in as practiced an accent as she could attempt. The kitchen was filled with even more people. "Cómper," she tried, moving toward a table covered with buckets of ice and not-yet-cold beers. The scene was like something out of a '90s movie, the kind where the main character got a makeover and found themselves at the center of the dance floor. Where the party served as shorthand for a point of no return.

As the thought occurred to her, Lola looked down at her dress, the stretch of its cotton hugging her body and reminding her why she had shoved it to the back of her closet for months after buying it. Because she had never had the courage to actually wear it until this moment.

But to everyone here, she was the exact kind of person who would wear that dress. To everyone here, her dress was part of who she was and how they'd remember her, if they did at all.

"¿Qué onda, Javier?" said a voice over her shoulder.

Lola spun around as Javi entered the kitchen, flanked by a few of his friends. He greeted the girl who had called his name, and Lola tried to use the distraction as an opportunity to escape the room unseen. Javi was clearly having a good time on his own, and she didn't want him to say hi out of a sense of obligation to her.

She moved toward the door right as someone changed

the song blasting on the sound system outside. Half a dozen people turned their heads to look either through the doorway or out the window, and Lola froze midstep when Javi's eyes met hers.

"Lola, ¿qué haces aquí?" he asked, excusing himself from his friends to greet her, polite as always. Lola returned his cheek kiss warily.

"Mi prima . . . Well, my aunt is friends with Rafa," she tried. "And my cousin is around here somewhere."

"¿La fresa?" he asked, the skepticism in his voice mirroring Lola's feelings about Cristina. "I went to school with Rafa's brother, Alejandro," he added, nodding toward one of the boys in his pack, who smiled and waved happily.

Lola tipped her empty cup to Alejandro briefly. "I'll let you get back to your friends," she said quickly, her exit catching in her throat. "I was looking for a drink."

Javi looked down at the plastic vessel in her hand. "And you didn't find it? I'll help you; ven conmigo."

Lola sighed and followed Javi back to the table, where he found the bottles of soda that Mari had helped herself to earlier. "Are you allowed to drink alcohol back in California? Los Angeles, ¿no?" he asked as he poured.

"No, but I'm not really from Los Angeles. Even though . . . I'm not allowed to drink here, either."

He nodded. "Sí, I remember. Oxnard isn't Los Angeles. Well, wherever you're from, you're in Mexico now. But I will make sure no one mixes anything into your Sprite if you don't want it."

Lola took the cup from him, unsure what to say next. She was not good at small talk, but even she knew *So how's your judgey grandmother doing?* wasn't appropriate party conversation.

Before she could try to excuse herself again, Javi cut in. "Hey, I'm sorry about Río," he said, his dark eyes meeting hers awkwardly.

Lola paused. "What do you . . . How do you know about that?" Her cheeks burned. Was her rejection common knowledge by now?

"Tu prima," Javi supplied simply.

Lola felt her eyes roll into the back of her head. Of course it was Juana.

"That, and Río does that kind of thing a lot. A new girl-friend every day," Javi said after a beat. "He's a . . . how do you say it in English? ¿Un mujeriego? A player?"

"Well, here I thought it was me and the whole being cursed thing," Lola chirped, the sunniness in her voice a brittle distraction from the hurt she was trying to choke back down.

"Does he know about that?" Javi asked.

Lola wrapped her arms around herself, careful to not let her cup slosh against her dress. "No, I never told him about any of that. Which I guess is a good thing. It's almost easier to know he was already running away instead of it being something I did."

Javi scoffed and leaned against the countertop behind him. "You didn't do anything," he said. "But he is more of a pendejo than I thought he was."

Lola knitted her eyebrows together. "If you think he's so awful, why are you friends with him?" she asked.

"Now you're defending him?"

"No, I . . ." The conversation was making her head spin. "If you aren't friends, then you two hang out a lot for a pair of enemies," she tried.

Javi helped himself to another beer and popped the cap off with a key from his pocket. "We were closer when we were younger," he said slowly, clearly thinking through how much he wanted to tell her. "But I told you, everyone loves Río. He's good at keeping the friends he wants. And then when he needed a job, I was already working at La Rosa, so." He shrugged. "I need to pay for my schoolbooks, and he needs to help his family with their bills. If I could help someone, why wouldn't I?"

Even though his tone was casual, Lola got the impression that there was some rift in Javi and Río's past. Maybe Río had dated a girl Javi liked. Or maybe Javi simply didn't approve of Río's plans. Wanting to be an actor was far riskier than being a banker. Lola wouldn't have been shocked if Javi also judged his friend for that—or if perhaps he was jealous.

As if he were reading her mind, Javi spoke again. "Río did something similar to my cousin Ruby. But I think he broke up with her after a week instead of kissing some other girl in a back alley."

He said the last part with a small smile. But if that was his attempt at making Lola feel better, it wasn't a good one.

"So, what? Everyone knew Río does this and they . . . let it happen to me?" she asked, acid creeping into her voice. "No one thought it would be a good idea to warn me? God, Juana really does love her drama, doesn't she?"

"I think your cousin liked seeing you happy," Javi said. "Besides, would you have listened if I warned you?"

Almost as if the word *cousin* were a summoning force, Cristina burst into the room. "Lorena!" she cooed over the clacking of her high heels, her charisma oozing into the corners of the room. "¡Aquí estás! Mari and I have been looking for you everywhere!"

She linked arms with Lola and helped herself to the drink in her cousin's hand. "Javier, did you make this?" Cristina asked, looking more toward Javi's friends than to him. "Está buenísimo."

Javi raised an eyebrow first at Cristina and then at Lola. She tried to hide her obvious confusion at Cristina's dramatic entrance, but it was too late: Javi had seen it . . . and it amused him?

"Gracias, I call it 'refresco,'" he said, shaking his head and moving back toward the courtyard he'd come from. "Adiós, primas."

Cristina waved obliviously at Javi's friend Alejandro as the group left. "¡Nos vemos!" she trilled before steering Lola toward another room. "Lorena, ¿conociste al hermano de Karla?" she asked happily. "Está guapo, ¿no?"

Lola had barely noticed.

CHAPTER 22

The rest of the party had passed by in a blur. Mari and her friends welcomed Lola back into their conversation, and Karla pulled Lola out to the dance floor for more than a few songs. At first, she hadn't known what to do with her body, but she focused on the music as it pulsated through the room. Sometime after midnight, Mari guided her out from the sweaty mass of people and toward the door. Lola's aunt slurred her words slightly as she complained about Uber prices and how her mother was going to take them both out of this world and into the afterlife for breaking Lola's extended curfew.

Lola wouldn't have changed a single second.

Mari had passed out with her makeup on almost immediately after they'd crept back inside the house. Lola, on the other hand, hadn't slept at all. Several hours after they had returned home, she was still studying a photo that Cristina had insisted someone take of them and four of Cristina's friends.

Lola remembered the moment vividly: Cristina throwing her arm around Lola's shoulders, hitting a practiced pose, and insisting her cousin do the same. "Move your chin down like me," she had told Lola, adjusting her entire body like a doll between photos. "¡Ándale! That's much better."

Lola had practically frozen herself in place until Cristina was satisfied with her photo, which was only evidenced by the latter swiftly selecting her favorite out of dozens of nearly identical images from her phone. "La Karla, her eyes are always closed," Cristina had told Lola conspiratorially, dismissing her audience only after she had asked for her cousin's Instagram handle. Predictably, she returned her focus to a semicircle of boys at the periphery of the party, who were either too cool or too awkward to dance.

And there it was on Lola's screen. Proof that she had indeed gone to a party, although she barely recognized the girl standing in the middle of Cristina's friends. There was something hard and plastic about the way she held her body, and the waves that Cristina had pressed into her hair had already deflated slightly. The girl was a slightly nervous clone of the other six girls in the photo, who had identical hairstyles and half-vacant facial expressions.

But that almost-robotic look on Lola's face, the one that had shown itself after Cristina had bossed her into an adequate pose, felt familiar to her anyway.

It was the approximation of someone who was afraid to have fun.

That hadn't stopped Cristina from posting the photo to her thousands of followers, or from replying to almost every comment and compliment with heart emojis and declarations of mutual obsession. And while she had tagged Lola in the picture and devoted her caption to her "primita americana," she hadn't followed Lola herself.

But it wasn't the only photo Lola had been tagged in that night. Someone else had posted a carousel of partially candid images, a collection of people either smiling wide or acting too cool for the camera. And there Lola was, in the middle of the dance floor, flanked by Karla and Mari, each of them wildly and electrically alive.

She couldn't remember the exact moment the photo had been taken, but her arms were outstretched and she was clearly singing along to the music, the joy on her face matched by that of the people around her.

Lola clicked through to the profile that had posted the photo and sat up in surprise: What was Javi doing taking photos of her?

Even so, her confusion couldn't obscure the feeling that he had captured something about her she hadn't known existed. Like maybe she had let her guard down for once, and that it was worth the minor drama of her cousin's performance, and of coming face-to-face with Javi, to have done so. She took a screenshot of the image, adjusted its borders, and made sure to tag Mari where she appeared.

At the last second, she added Javi's handle in the corner and the CDMX geotag before hitting post.

⌒

She woke to a lit-up phone screen and comment after comment from classmates who had clearly never considered that bookish, quiet Lola Espinoza could get dressed up. Ana had left an encouraging **WHO IS SHE?!?!?!** and even Padilla anointed the post with a **Holaaaa Espinozaaaa**. Lola felt herself blush before hitting the heart next to his comment.

Other people offered likes, but their acknowledgment of Lola's existence, and the fact that they were now following her on Instagram, felt significant. It was the most many of Lola's classmates had ever spoken to her, if she didn't count the times they had a question for Ana or had been teamed up with her in a long-since-forgotten group project. And while she regularly followed the posts and memes and milestones of the other kids in her grade, this was the first time she could remember that they had been interested in something *she* had posted.

Six feet to Lola's right, Mari shifted in her bed. It was a miracle that she could sleep through the cars honking outside and the shouting of street vendors as the city woke up, but this was the only home she had ever known. She was used to the chaos, and its absence would be uneasy and eerie.

No, Lola revised. Mari wasn't just used to the chaos, she was contributing to it. Asserting her presence and adding her unique noise, even if only in a small way, even if only one other person heard.

CHAPTER 23

"Karla says you're welcome at any of her parties," Mari said as she drove Lola to La Rosa two days later. "And I think Esteban was serious about wanting a very personal tour of the United States." She nudged Lola with her elbow.

"Mari, no," Lola said. "He's your age; that's weird and not legal. *You* date him. Besides, I'm done with flirting or . . . or whatever, for a while now."

Her aunt made a face. "Why? Because Río is a cochino? You can't let one bad story ruin your fun."

Except that's what I've always done, Lola thought.

Mercifully, Mari did not ask about either the Instagram photo that Lola had tagged her in or its photographer, and dropped Lola off in front of the restaurant with only a few minutes to spare before her shift started. True to her word, Juana hadn't fired Río—and Lola didn't blame her, given the fact that Río technically hadn't done anything wrong as an employee—but she did give the lunchtime hours to Sebas, who was from the Dominican Republic and practiced choeography as he worked behind the bar.

The shift change meant that Lola would see Río less, but she heard about him just as much as before. The La Rosa staff couldn't stop talking about their breakup—not that Lola was sure it could even really be called that. The only person who didn't ask about her about the fight with Río was Javi. Instead, he self-appointed himself as a tutor and pretended he didn't hear Lola unless she spoke to him in Spanish, and then he corrected her verb tenses until she echoed him accordingly.

Lola didn't protest—anything was better than talking about Río—except when the restaurant was busy, because the grammar lessons ate away at the precious seconds she could have been using to keep the flow of diners happy.

"Please, just take the molotes to the couple at the bar," she asked Javi, rushing to seat one table and bracing herself for the backlog at the door. "Rocío said they need to be served hot; it has something to do with the chorizo, and I don't want her mad at me today."

"¿Y en español?" he asked.

"Puedes llevar . . . Dude, can you please do me a solid this once?" she pleaded, glancing at the restaurant's entryway. It was already spilling over with people waiting for tables.

"¿Qué es 'dude' en este contexto?" Javi's eyebrow rose tauntingly.

"Like, hey, my guy, my man, my buddy, my compadre, my pal, do me a favor and I will owe you forever."

Maybe it was the use of *compadre* that convinced him, but Javi ran the plate where it needed to go.

Even as the reluctant student, Lola had to admit that her unlikely teacher's tactic wasn't unfounded. It wasn't only that Javi was constantly drilling her to *speak* Spanish—he wanted her to think in it first, and to focus less on translating. To trust rather than to doubt.

But verbal sparring with Javi wasn't the worst way to spend an afternoon. Not only that, she found herself almost ready for his prompts as the days went on—and she was almost pleased whenever she noticed he was watching her, even if sometimes the look on his face made her feel like she was perhaps a walking chapter in one of his history textbooks.

And because Lola didn't want to go into the alleyway anymore if she could help it, she started spending her breaks at the far end of the bar, closest to the kitchen, the somber portrait of Felipe Gómez watching over her. She'd been unsuccessful at finding a trace of her own face in his, but more than a few of the details reminded her of Letty if she looked hard enough.

"¿Te acuerdas de él?" Javi asked one afternoon, making the most of his annoying habit of standing right behind Lola before she registered his presence. She jumped in her seat and swiveled ungracefully toward him. He jutted his chin up at the painting. "Tu abuelo, do you remember him?"

Lola shook her head. "He died before I was born. And

my tía Mari, the one you met at the party, she was really little when it happened. So every memory she has of him, he was sick, and I don't think she likes to remember him that way. My grandma never talks about him, either. Basically no one in my family does."

She said it matter-of-factly, but there was something profoundly sad about the admission that surprised her. There was so much her family didn't talk about. And maybe it wasn't for lack of wanting to. Sometimes there weren't words to convey how a person felt, or maybe time hadn't yet transformed the feeling into something solid and understandable.

Javi nodded, his eyes still on the painting that stared back at them from its place of honor. "My mother doesn't talk about her family, either," he said. "I don't know if it hurts her too much, but I always thought it would hurt me more to not talk about the people I love. It's a different pain to forget."

"Did you know them?" Lola watched Javi as he moved toward the seat next to her.

"Sí, los conocí," he said. "I have memories of the village where she is from; we would go every year when I was very small. Pero . . ." His voice trailed off, and his shoulders loaded themselves with a weight he didn't like. "Maybe it became too difficult for her to come back to her life in this city. She has to be someone else here. All my memories of mi mamá in Oaxaca are of . . . She was a different woman."

Shadows appeared on his face, hinting at the memories he wasn't turning into words. Lola tried to imagine how it must have felt for Esperanza to bid her family goodbye every time her visits ended.

"She was happier, I think," Javi added, "whenever we visited her brothers and sisters. They had kids, too, and they would play with me because I was the baby. But most of what I know about Oaxaca are the things I have studied at school."

"Would your family have ever moved back there?" Lola asked. "I guess your dad's job probably wouldn't let him, but . . . Or maybe *you* could move there. Take a year off school. Find yourself, or whatever."

Javi raised an eyebrow at her. "Are you trying to make me go away?" he asked, a hint of bemusement in his voice.

"No, I just . . . I mean, if the city didn't work for your mom, why did she move here?"

"She once told me it wasn't about *leaving* her village. It was about going somewhere else. She wanted something different, so she came here. Sometimes it's simple. And then she married my father, and he became her home. They're very different people, but they do love each other. Sometimes I don't see how, but . . ."

"But love isn't about understanding," Lola finished. "It's just believing in the feeling."

"Algo así."

Lola looked back up at her grandfather and tried to picture him standing next to Buela, replacing her mental image of a small woman holding space for a memory and a ghost. But her imagination stopped short. The only version of her grandmother she had ever known was the one who was scarred by her husband's death. That loss had taken something from Rosa. And whatever hole was left gave rise to an overwhelming need to protect her family and a fear that something like that could happen again.

It was a crater, the mark of a love that had nowhere to go but inward.

And Lola thought about tía Paty, whose wedding was still a fresh memory. She and her husband had rented a community room with a low ceiling and mismatched folding chairs, and people had dropped by to congratulate the couple throughout the night. At the center of everything had been Paty and her husband, who had been so in love and so sure of what they were doing together. It was like nothing could have touched them—except now Paty was back at her mother's house, navigating life in the aftermath.

There was a difference, Lola thought, between feeling like luck simply wasn't on your side and feeling like you had failed. Maybe belief in the curse was Paty's way of living with the gulf of disappointment that lay in between. And maybe it was Buela's way of filling the pain of losing her husband before she was ready.

When Lola turned her head, though she wasn't quite sure what she wanted to tell Javi, she was met with an empty chair. He had gone back to work like it was nothing, without even letting her know.

CHAPTER 24

"No mames," Dani said matter-of-factly during a slower moment the next night. "There had to be some point when you spoke Spanish as a baby."

Lola shook her head and continued studying the seating chart for irregularities. Another waiter, Samson, had accused her of loading "the good tables" in her "best friend's" section, though Lola wouldn't have classified the friction she felt around Javi as friendship. It was too complicated to explain. Their . . . Well, it was more circumstantial than friendship, and she was okay with that.

"Not even when you were chiquitita?" Dani tried again.

Lola shrugged. "No, not really. My parents must have tried to teach me when I was little, and a lot of people in our neighborhood only speak Spanish, but my mom says I always replied in English. That I was stubborn like my father, in the opposite direction or something. It's weird, but Spanish gets stuck between my ears and my mouth. I can hear it, but it . . . It's like I start running up a hill, lose momentum, and fall back down the way I came."

Dani laughed. "Someone should write a book about you American-born kids. You spend your whole lives thinking you're one thing and then, ¡pum! You come down here to *find yourselves* or lo que sea. I see it every day—you are as easy to spot as the turistas. But you are the same person in both places. And nothing you find changes who you are. It only makes you more you."

He offered Lola a knowing look before picking up a stack of menus, putting on his best this-isn't-just-my-job-I-really-am-happy-to-see-you smile, and greeting the young parents who were trying to coax their fussy toddler into a rare afternoon lunch out.

Lola leaned against the host podium, its solid weight a soothing counter to her own instability. This trip wasn't meant to be about finding herself, even though she seemed to be questioning who she was more and more with each passing day.

Of course she knew the broad strokes, the things that college applications would ask her: her name, her age, that she was an incoming senior with a 3.9 . . . well, now a 3.8, GPA, thanks to señora Smith. She knew that her YouTube history and her shopping habits directly over-lapped and that she could usually apply mascara in a moving car without stabbing herself in the eye or getting those little smudges on her eyelids. And she knew that the sum total of her identity couldn't be whittled down to those little demographic boxes—that she had been raised not to choose between her two overlapping cultures.

"You are Mexican, and you are American, Lorena," her father would say, often while stressing to Lola why she had to strive for A's or get into a good college. "And you are also an Espinoza."

Sunday afternoons at Buela's were sacred. There was a routine: Her grandmother would finish cleaning her living room and dive straight into cooking. Five of her six children were tacitly expected to make an appearance, as were their spouses and children, no matter what else was happening in their worlds and lives. The open invite was how Rocío was so familiar with Buela's cooking, and each weekend the house would be full to bursting with laughter and good-natured verbal sparring.

Because while some people reveled in celebrating birthdays and anniversaries, her family made every occasion special if they could. Cooking and providing for her family—that was where Buela thrived.

"Lorena, ¿ya le hablaste a tu mamá?" Tía Coco's voice carried out of the living room, over peals of laughter supplied by her sisters and their spouses. "I want to talk to my sister if you have not!"

Lola tried to tune her aunt out—maybe if she stayed quiet, no one would drag her away from the corner of the dining room where she'd been trying to translate one of the books Javi had given her. It was excruciatingly academic, so she spent more time second-guessing herself and looking up words and phrases on her phone than she did actually reading. The individual words made sense. Together, they were a riddle, and Lola had to read each sentence five times to understand its context. The moment when the meaning washed over her was both fascinating and infuriating.

"Lorena, are you there?" came Coco's voice again. "Why aren't you answering me?"

Lola minimized her translation app and pulled up the shortcut to call her mother. She walked to the rapidly filling living room and passed the phone to tía Coco, who wasted no time in trying to guilt her sister for not calling her enough the minute Letty picked up.

"Socorro, you try dealing with half the problems I solve every day," Mami's no-nonsense voice crackled back. "I manage an entire store of employees, customers who are worse than even you, and clean my house without any help. *You* can call me if you want to talk, and you'll be lucky if I pick up without falling asleep."

From where he had sunk into Buela's ancient couch, tío Chuy pointed his chin upward at the book under Lola's arm. "Oye, Lorenita, ¿qué estás leyendo?" She passed her uncle the textbook, and Chuy frowned as he flipped through it. "Leticia, how do you get your children to study so much?" he shouted at the phone. "I'll trade you Lorena for any of my daughters, go ahead and pick."

He made the offer with a wink, but Lola could sense a weariness in her uncle's voice. Mami said something about Chuy taking her son instead, which was the only invitation the two elder Gómez siblings needed to bicker and poke at each other, and Coco tried to regain what little dominance she once had over the conversation.

Her whole life, Lola had marveled over the significant age gap between her mother and her aunts and uncle for precisely this reason: There was an entire generation between the eldest and the youngest of Buela's children, yet they were unshakably close, and Letty and her siblings had never lost a beat of togetherness despite the distance that separated them. It was a kind of magic that family could pick up where they left off as if no time had passed.

Outside the window, two other sets of siblings tumbled out of the cars that had just pulled up. Lola weighed her options, then steeled her resolve and made her way toward the courtyard, where Cristina, Regina, Antonia, and Juana's sisters, Gabriela and Carmen, had gathered.

"¿Qué onda, Loli?" Gabriela asked, winking as she used her twin's nickname for their cousin.

Lola greeted her cousins with a wave, her eyes flitting toward Cristina, who had once again established herself as the most interesting person in the circle—and Lola's appearance clearly threatened that.

"¿Y tu novio, Lorenita?" Antonia asked, wasting no time in the effort to win her sister's approval.

"¿Novio?" Carmen asked.

"¿No sabías? Lorena and Río, that boy from Juana's restaurant, were going out. But he already moved on to somebody new." Antonia began telling the girls about Río and his apparent habit of flirting with almost anyone. "I thought he liked Regina a few months ago, but she's been dating Adrián for years, so—"

"Antonia, ya," came Cristina's sharp and impatient voice. "No one is dating Gregorio, so he's not important for this conversation, ¿cachas?"

Lola looked over at her cousin, feeling a mix of gratitude and confusion bloom somewhere beneath her lungs. Yet rather than smile, Cristina used her sister's stunned silence to pick up her story about what had happened at a nightclub she'd recently gone to. It was a meandering story that involved a detailed description of the four dresses she had considered before deciding on what she would wear, as well as a revolving cast of doormen, bartenders, and dance partners whose names Cristina barely cared to remember.

As Cristina droned on, Lola considered how little her cousins knew about her. How could they, when she barely gave them the chance to find out?

The group's overlapping laughter brought Lola back to the moment. While she didn't know what had been so funny, she got the sense that, for once, it hadn't been something she'd done or a verb tense she'd gotten wrong.

"Bueno," Carmen said, searching through her purse for her keys, "ya nos vamos. Gaby and I are just here to drop these three off. Loli, you want to go to La Rosa with us? I don't think Río is working today. It should be safe there."

"No, I think I'll stay. Your mom has my phone; she and tío Chuy were debating my mom about something when I left them inside."

"Better tía Letty than us," Gabriela said knowingly. "We'll probably get it later tonight. But if you're sure, Loli, nos vemos. ¿Okay?"

Lola waited in the courtyard as her cousins went back to their car, and Cristina looked her over again before heading into the house. She gave a small wave, and the other girl turned her head, her blond highlights glistening like a flare.

Maybe she and Cristina weren't meant to be both family and friends the way she was with Mari, she thought. That was all right. Sometimes friendships took root and sometimes they didn't, but that didn't make Lola and Cristina any less of the same family.

When Lola got her phone back from tía Coco almost thirty minutes later, two new notifications illuminated her screen: The first was from Ana, who had tagged her in a photo of way more luggage than any one person could possibly need for a week's vacation. **CDMX, here we goooo!** she had written in the caption, and already dozens of classmates had chimed in with how jealous they were, or how lucky Ana was, or with recommendations for some Instagram-famous restaurant they had seen on their feeds once. True to form, Ana had already liked every last one of the comments and was deep in conversation threads with several people. It was a habit she and Cristina had in common.

After reading through the comments and rolling her eyes at the number of classmates who were trying to talk Ana into smuggling them back bottles of tequila, Lola went to check the second notification.

Cristina had followed her back on Instagram.

CHAPTER 25

Ana's mother had booked a room in a nice hotel, but Lola hadn't known *how* nice it was until she looked it up during her break at La Rosa. It was located a few blocks north of the house in la Condesa where Rafa's party had been, on Reforma, the glittering street whose skyscrapers had struck Lola as being so otherworldly that night in the cab with Río. Now she was going to see that corner of the city up close.

"Why are you looking up Reforma?" Javi asked, peering over Lola's shoulder as he passed her usual seat at the end of the bar. "You're not going to find the cure for this curse of yours in one of those offices."

"Well, those books of yours are so dense, I might as well try another way," she said cheerily, determined not to let his dourness ruin her day.

But he didn't miss a beat, either. "The question is, do *you* really want to figure it out?" he asked, his voice dropping slightly so that no one else could hear the slight challenge in his tone.

Lola quickly tried to save face by offering up a different truth. "My best friend and her mom are here on vacation, and this is where they're staying." She showed him the hotel on her phone. "I'm supposed to visit them after work. We have a reservation at the Casa Azul."

"Qué padre," Javi intoned as he funneled ice into water glasses, more bored than impressed.

"Honestly, I think this is, like, the longest time Ana and I have spent apart since we've known each other . . . Why do I get the sense you have an opinion about where they're staying?" Lola asked, looking up from her phone.

Javi focused on arranging his table's drinks on his tray.

"My parents live near there. And my dad works right down the street. He has a view of el Ángel from his office window. He spent his whole life working for that view. He reminds me every time I visit him."

Lola looked up to see a scowl lingering on Javi's face. She considered asking more about his father, but while a difficult dad might be something they had in common, she'd rather remove the scowl than cause it to deepen if she could.

She put her phone down and assumed the sweetest voice she could muster, because by this point, getting on Javi's nerves was part of the fun. "So if you know the area, you wouldn't mind dropping me off after the shift change, would you? ¿Por favor?"

"If it stops you from using that voice. Ya te pareces a tu prima," he said, clearly enjoying Lola's reaction to the mention of Cristina. "I need to visit my dad anyway. He keeps calling. Why not take a look at his view while I'm there?"

And while he was still grimacing, the look was now mixed with a self-awareness that hadn't been there before.

The hotel lobby was modern and sterile, a feat of architecture with cold marble and colder metal glinting ominously. Lola was struck by how different it felt from her own temporary home with its plastered, painted walls and the dozens of family photos peeking from every corner. Buela's house burst with life, even when no one else was home—maybe this hotel had known it couldn't replicate that kind of energy, so it didn't even try.

Lola took her place in line for the reception desk, trying to connect to the Wi-Fi so she could tell Ana she was there. She was next in line to speak to the receptionist, a pretty woman with heavy makeup and hair slicked back into a severe, uniform-standard bun, when the elevator doors opened and a whirl of legs and track shorts came bounding over to Lola.

"Lo!" Ana exclaimed at a volume that reverberated off every one of the lobby's hard surfaces, almost tackling Lola where she stood. Lola gently maneuvered their bodies so that the man behind her didn't get knocked down in the process.

"I told you I'd get down here after you had that brilliant idea," Ana added, roping her arm across Lola's shoulders after their hug ended. "Yeah, it took a few weeks, and I'm missing so many hours of practice, but I told Coach I'd go running in that park around the corner, or the forest, or whatever it's called. It's named after bugs, right?"

"Chapulines are grasshoppers, so yes, Chapultepec."

"Yes! That's the one. Anyway, Coach made me promise to run every morning, and he keeps reminding me it's college season. If I hear about one more scout coming to practice, I might run away from the track forever, but every morning it is. The altitude is going to suck, though. And I promise, the runs aren't going to cut into any actual time here. I want to see everything. I want to meet everyone. We have to go to Frida's house, and maybe those canals again if you want to, and I want to eat everything on the menu at your cousin's restaurant . . ."

Ana barely took a breath as she rattled off her plans, her words washing over Lola comfortingly. An understanding settled between them—not the kind that matched vocabulary words with certain interpretations, but one where you could simply be. The kind that only existed between best friends.

Ana's phone beeped with incoming notifications. "Lo, why doesn't your cousin put La Rosa on Instagram?" she asked, swiping through her messages. "I wanted to look at the menu, but I couldn't find it anywhere."

"You can follow Rocío, but she changes the menu every week almost, depending on what she feels like cooking," Lola said, taking Ana's phone and pulling the right profile up. "It makes memorizing the specials impossible, and Javi always complains about it. But if you ask her nicely, she'll make this peach salsa that Juana says is sacrilegious. She has feelings about fruit in salsa, but it would be on the menu every week if she liked it. Everyone asks for it."

"Javi, huh?" Ana asked, pulling Lola through the lobby doors and toward the taxis idling outside the hotel. "And you're spending so much time with him because . . ."

"Because we *work* together, A. That's it. This is nothing like what happened with me and Río," Lola stressed. "Besides, that . . . happened, and I haven't felt sick since. So clearly I am not supposed to be into anyone. Especially someone who only tolerates me."

"Well, then maybe you cured yourself. Who needs boys anyway?" Ana hopped into the first waiting cab and froze. It was the first time Lola had ever seen her so visibly out of her element. "Uh, how do we get to Frida Kahlo's house?" she asked Lola.

The driver looked at Ana with confusion.

"Queremos ir a Coyoacán, a la Casa Azul, porfa," Lola said, and the engine revved in response.

Ana sat back in the seat, impressed. "Look at you, Espinoza. If only señora Smith could see you now."

"It's not señora Smith I have to be thinking about," Lola said. "It's my parents. They're the ones who sent me down here, remember?"

"But by now they have to know that you've gotten better, right? Haven't you showed off to your dad or anything?"

Lola paused. She and her father hadn't spoken at all

that summer. Not only was she unsure she could get through an entire conversation with him in any language, but a small, selfish part of her didn't want to give him the satisfaction of knowing that his punishment was working.

"Honestly, I've been too distracted with . . . this whole family curse thing," she said, catching the word *Río* just as it formed in the back of her mouth. How long was she allowed to nurse the sting of that afternoon in the alleyway, especially since, as he had so quickly pointed out, they hadn't technically been dating? "I don't know. Whether or not I can pass Spanish next semester feels like less of a priority."

Ana beamed. "Wow, Lo," she said after a moment. "Mexico has already changed you."

Lola looked at Ana with alarm. "What do you mean?"

"You're focusing on your actual life instead of your grades for once. And you gave directions when I didn't know how to," Ana said, nodding toward the taxi driver. "You would have never done that before."

"Well, I didn't *need* to do that before. You're good at finding your way around for us both."

"True, but . . . I don't know. It's different this time. It's like . . . Lola Espinoza has learned how to live."

Between a miraculous lack of traffic and some aggressive moves from their driver, it took less than an hour for the taxi to pull up in front of a building painted a pure, electric blue, with green windows and a red trim so bright, it looked almost orange. Lola paid the man with the tips she had in her pocket after Ana struggled momentarily with a debit card, and the two headed for the line outside the front door.

Inside, they were met with another burst of color as plants rushed from the ground in every direction, and a miniature pyramid in the same rusted red as the exterior trim took center stage in the courtyard. Reverently, the girls ducked into one room and then another. They were met with a gallery of artwork, followed by a kitchen finished in yellow and white, the ollas waiting for someone's family recipes, as if they were still used every day.

"Look at the tiles," Lola murmured, pointing to the names and birds inscribed at the top of the walls. *Frida* and *Diego*, immortalized in the home they had made their own.

Ana nodded somberly. "Imagine cooking without a microwave, though."

They passed through to the dining room and then to a bedroom marked as the place where Diego Rivera had slept. A hat and a coat hung in the corner of the room, almost as if the painter had stepped out momentarily and would be back for his things. Lola didn't know much about the couple's relationship other than the fact that it had been dramatic and tumultuous. There was something poignant about the idea that they each had a room to themselves, though—that they had found a way to be their own selves within the relationship, and that they were honest about their strife.

It wasn't until the girls found the four-poster bed that Kahlo herself had painted from, as well as the studio in the next room, that Ana lit up. She had insisted on paying the additional fee to take photos inside, intent on capturing the rooms from every angle—likely so she could have options later for her Instagram.

Lola thought back to the tourists at the pyramids, but she just as quickly felt the memory sour to regret in her mind. If anything, Ana had done more research for her trip than Lola had—in her texts, she'd said she was eager to explore parts of the city that Lola hadn't even known existed. Yet while Lola could not lay more claim to any part of it than Ana could, she still felt a flare of protectiveness for the spaces around them.

"This is so much cooler than going to *my* grandma's house in Texas," Ana marveled as they moved from the workroom back to the courtyard. "Did you know there's a Los Angeles there, too? And a San Diego. It's so confusing. Every time I go, it feels like we drive from diner to diner, and it's the same stuff for miles and miles. Which is great, don't get me wrong, but it's like . . . This is like . . . *really* Mexican."

"Ana," Lola countered. "That's because we're in Mexico. And Frida Kahlo is just one tiny part of it."

"I know. It's still different, though. Like, I know my mom's family is Mexican, but Texas has been the United States for so long that it's almost morphed into its own thing."

"That doesn't make you less Mexican," Lola said quickly. "Nothing could do that. Remember that time your aunt came to visit and made the best enchiladas I've ever had? Don't tell Juana that, though. She and

Rocío will try to one-up the recipe for the next month."

Ana nodded, placated enough to drop the conversation. But there it was again, that nebulous idea of authenticity, constantly threatening everything with tiny, prescriptive, limiting boxes.

"Hey," Lola said after a moment, nudging Ana slightly with her elbow. "Frida's dad was German. So in some ways, you have more in common with her than I do."

"Mixed-kid representation," Ana said, her voice almost light enought to mask the hollowness in it. It wasn't until they made their way to the exit that she added a small, "Thanks, Lo."

It was the softness of the gratitude that struck Lola most. Ana didn't know how to be quiet, and she was rarely self-conscious, which was a useful trait to have when you were one of the most popular kids in high school. Take the friendly crowds away, however, and there was a different Ana, one that Lola wanted to protect because no one else at school had ever seen her or even knew she existed.

"Come on," Lola said, flinging her arm around Ana's shoulders, which was difficult given the four inches of height her friend had on her. "I'll buy you a taco from a canasta lady. I think there's a market a few blocks over."

"See, I told you you're different here," Ana said. "And don't get me wrong, who you are back home is why we're friends, but I like this Lola."

"I'm the same me," Lola offered, but she understood what Ana meant. And she liked this version of herself, too.

CHAPTER 26

For two days, Lola tried her best to both visit and live in Mexico City—to meet Ana and her mother in the mornings for their next tourist activity before heading off to La Rosa for dinner shifts. And for two days, she hardly had time to open one of Javi's books, let alone think about the curse. But she did spend two days thinking about the worlds she was moving between, and how she was experiencing parts of a city she thought she knew well for the first time.

That was the difference between the Morris's vacation and her family's way of life: A vacation was an escape and a reason to see and do as much as possible in a finite amount of time. Living was slower, more deliberate—a mindset that made monuments melt into the background, turned them into everyday miracles waiting for someone to look up at them and remember how special they were. She had never been on a vacation the way Ana and Mrs. Morris—who insisted that Lola call her Estella—approached vacations, with the kind of meticulous spreadsheets and timekeeping that could rival Lola's study guides or Letty's Black Friday scheduling at work. There were lists of museums to visit and sub-lists of pieces to see in certain wings, as well as dozens of well-researched restaurant options and just as many neighborhoods and stores that a magazine or blogger had insisted were "must-sees." And the Morrises gravitated toward parts of the city filled with Americans, whether they were tourists or transplants who now called Mexico home.

"Lorena, what does your family like to do on the week-ends?" Estella asked early Thursday afternoon as she, Lola, and Ana made their way through the bottom floor of the castle at the center of Chapultepec park. "Is there anywhere they like to go for brunch?"

Lola briefly thought of the chain diners that her uncle sometimes escorted her grandmother to, with their uniform menus and elaborate bread service carts. She had a feeling that wasn't the kind of experience that Ana's mother meant. "Mostly we stay at my grandma's house," she said. "Everyone comes over; it's kind of like a ritual."

Estella nodded. "We used to do that at my great-aunt's house," she said, glancing over at a portrait of yet another long-dead president. "It was me and more cousins than I could count, trying to take the most attention away from one another."

"And then you moved to California, and now we only get to do that at Christmas," Ana said, wandering over from a mural she had been studying. "Mom, we have

292

tickets to the Barragán house tomorrow, right? Did you buy one for Lola?"

But at that moment, the museum's overextended guest Wi-Fi connected to Lola's phone, which pinged with an incoming WhatsApp message.

> JAI: The new work schedule for La Rosa is out
>
> Juana gave me three days off for the weekend
>
> I think it's a thank-you for teaching you Spanish

The smirk that fought at the corners of Lola's mouth was short-lived. Another server's name was all over the weekend schedule in Javi's place, as was Río's. Juana had given Lola just one double shift—lunch and dinner the following night—over the next three days. Lola was grateful for the time off, but that double shift also meant she couldn't join the Morrises for their next adventure.

"Lo, what's that look on your face?" Ana asked.

Lola closed Javi's message and put her phone back in her shorts pocket. "New work hours. So I might need to skip the next museum if that's okay."

"Yeah, it's *okay*." Ana laughed. "I don't want my vacation to get you fired. It'll be Mom-and-me time, right, Stel?"

"Which means you'll talk me into taking photos of you for Instagram until I get the exact right angle," Estella clarified for her daughter.

"You're my mother and you made those angles," Ana said. "Might as well get the best ones for the camera."

⌐

"So what are you going to do with your whole three days off?"

The remnants of Rocío's go-to salsa playlist drifted over the kitchen, mixing with the clink of silverware and plates stacked on top of each other. Somehow Juana had talked their grandmother into letting Lola stay for the full dinner shift, which meant that she now found herself stifling back a yawn as she shut down the kitchen at three in the morning.

Javi, meanwhile, was organizing a collection of paper bills on a gleaming countertop. The night had been busy, a musical-chairs game of new parties filling tables as soon as old ones left them. If Lola hadn't known any better, she would have thought Javi was pleased with himself.

He reached a hand out to pass Lola a few bills. "No sé. Sleep, visit my mother, maybe. Why?"

"What's this for?"

"Tips were good tonight. It feels right to share."

Lola nodded bashfully and slipped the pesos into her back pocket. "Gracias."

"De nada." A smile played on Javi's face, its curve making his cheekbones more pronounced. "Why do you want to know what I'm doing these next few days?"

Lola wrang the mop out in the bucket by the back door. It was the closest she'd been to the alleyway in over two weeks. "I'm just curious," she said. "If you prefer, we can listen to the music, like we always do in your car. But it feels . . . weird, I guess, to not know what you do with your time. Where do you go? What do you do? Those are normal things people know about each other."

"Is this the alternative to not talking in my car? An interview?"

"Fine, let's listen to more Marc Anthony and *not* talk. I love this song anyway."

Javi nodded. "It's my mother's favorite."

Lola looked up at him. The dimmed light of the kitchen cast itself on his face lazily, and though he looked tired from a full night of turnover, the shadows underscored that he was still in many ways a mystery. She could study him for months, maybe years, and still have more to learn.

"Do you need help with that?" Javi moved toward the heavy bucket and swung the door open. The sounds of the neighborhood bounced off the walls and into the restaurant, laughter mixing with the last few shouts of friends calling to one another. With a deep breath, Javi yanked the bucket up and over, making the soapy, dirty water splash against the bricks.

"I could have probably done that myself," Lola said.

"This is where you say gracias, and I say de nada," he said. "Again."

Lola rolled her eyes, and rolled them harder when Javi laughed. "Why don't you, like, leave the city for a few days? Pack the car and get out of here," she suggested.

Javi shrugged out of his black button-down and adjusted the T-shirt he wore under it. A muscle in his shoulder shifted below the cotton, and Lola averted her gaze. "And go where?"

"I don't know," she said, studying the grout between the tiles. "Where your mom's from, her hometown. When was the last time you went there or made memories of your own? You've got tip money; you can get gas and . . ."

"So the interview has stopped and now you give me orders instead."

Lola looked up and realized how intently Javi was staring at her. Like she was that textbook, and like he finally understood. She wasn't sure if she wanted to deflect from his attention or lean toward it.

"Do you want to come with me?"

Lola's words stuck to the roof of her mouth.

"Are you serious?"

"Sure. You've seen Mexico City, next we have Oaxaca. We can go once we're done here."

A single laugh escaped Lola's mouth. "Now?"

"We have a few days off work, and you leave Mexico in a few weeks. Why not?"

The question was an outstretched hand Lola didn't know if she should take. There were a thousand reasons why not, and several broadcast themselves in her mind at the same time. Her grandmother would never let her go if she asked, and the thought of asking her parents for their permission was enough to make Lola laugh. Besides, Ana was in town for two more nights, and she had asked to go to dinner at La Rosa together. Not once in their friendship had Lola ever ditched her.

But then again, she never really had anything to do other than tag along with Ana and her schemes.

She didn't have a plan, and they barely had a reason to go. But wasn't going just for the sake of it its own kind of living?

"I'd need to stop by the house for a few things," she heard herself say without quite realizing it. "You would, too."

"I have clothes in my car."

"And we'd have to be back before my parents found out. Which means we'd have to turn back, like, the second we arrived anywhere."

Javi's smile broke across his face and cast its own light in the room. "Is that yes?" he asked. "¿En serio?"

"En serio."

"So then we should get going before the traffic starts. You can pick the music, if you want to listen to more Marc Anthony."

Lola rolled her eyes a third time for good measure and rushed to Juana's office to grab her jacket and the tote bag she called a purse. Time was already against them, and it was a risk to say yes and to leave the city, no matter how close Javi and her cousin were. As she made sure she had all of her things, she felt a familiar buzz in the back of her skull that turned her thoughts to snow and made her want to sit down. She steadied herself and glanced at the altar, where three candles were burning with full force.

If there was ever something she shouldn't be doing, it was this. But all her life she'd done as she *should*. What her parents thought she should. What teachers thought she should. She never stopped to ask what she, Lola Espinoza, thought she should do. She didn't want to wonder *what if* in this moment. Or ever again in her life, if she could help it.

"I want to do this for me," she told la Virgencita, who smiled placidly down at the candles the same as she always did. "I need to at least try."

Lola wavered in front of the candles for a moment, unsure whether to blow them out. She had never seen Juana extinguish them—their flames were always dancing against the tall glass of their containers until they died out on their own. While she didn't know what some of the colors or designs meant, she didn't want to break whatever protection they offered, especially now, when she could use as much of it as possible.

So she left the candles burning, closed the door to the office behind her, and took a deep breath. There was an adventure waiting for her, and she wanted to make the most of it.

The keys clashed against each other and bit at Lola's palm as she tried to find the right ones for the front door. The last thing she needed was to wake the whole house up or, more specifically, for her grandmother to intercept her before she could grab her toothbrush and a change of clothes. So when she wrenched the heaviest key into the lock and sneaked inside, she took extra care to avoid the usual clanging that announced some new family member or another.

She should tell Ana where she was going, she thought. But she didn't reach for her phone. It wasn't that she didn't want to tell her best friend what she was up to. Selfishly, it was nice to be her own protagonist rather than react to someone else's life.

Lola scrambled around her room, trying to pull an outfit together that wasn't horribly mismatched. For once, she felt lucky that her clothes were so simple. Her fingers tried to tell the difference between her concealer and mascara tubes, but something in her stomach told her time was running out and she should hurry up.

No, that was her phone, buzzing against her body in her pocket. "Ya voy, Javier," she said quietly to herself as she crept back down the stairs. "No te enojes."

"Lorena, what are you doing?" came a voice from the dining room.

Mari sat at the table, books and notes splayed in front

of her. She must have fallen asleep in the chair she was sitting in, because she stretched awkwardly and looked somewhat dazed.

Her genius brain clicked the pieces into place in record time, however. "Lola, what are you doing? Where are you going?"

Lola sighed and took a breath.

"I'm going to Oaxaca," she said quickly. "Javi's outside, and . . ."

"Javi?" Mari interrupted. "You're running away with a boy? And you expect me to be okay with that?"

"I promise it will be fine. We're not eloping or whatever. I'll be back in, like, a day."

"This is about my mother's pinche curse, isn't it? He gave you some books and now he's trying to take you who knows where—"

"No, Mari. His mom is from there and he wants to spend more time there, and . . ."

Lola stopped short of saying what she wanted to: that the familiar static that tried to sever her brain from the rest of her body had come back and she wanted to see how much of it she could learn to live with. That she didn't want to let any curse, or any aunt, stop her. Even her favorite one.

"I think . . . I need to know what it's like to do something *I* want to do, not what everyone else wants me to do. Mari, this sounds weird, but this is the closest I've ever felt to . . . to understanding our family, and I . . ."

"Ya," Mari said, raising her hand to silence her niece. "I know."

"You do?"

"Sure. This family, there's so much going on that you can feel lost in the noise. Because los Gómez, we're loud, eh?" She laughed softly. "When will you be back?"

Lola exhaled, her breath catching up with her in a dizzying sweep. "Javi said the drive is about eight hours, and then we have to drive eight hours back. I promise to text you as often as I can; we'll be safe. Can you tell Buela . . . I don't know, that I went to Ana's hotel early or something? And that I'm staying the night?"

Mari waved toward the door and sighed. "You'd better go now before you wake your grandmother up. Don't worry, I didn't see anything. I was here studying for my test, which is what *I* want to do."

Lola looked at Mari gratefully before rushing back outside with her bag and the day-old rolls she had swiped at the last minute from the kitchen counter. The street was silent, making room for the buildings and the sparse trees lining the block to have their own conversations in the dark. Javi was once again leaning against the passenger-side door of his car, his hands casually slung in his pockets.

"Buenas noches to you, too," he said wryly, accepting the slightly stale bolillo Lola offered him. "There was no other food in your grandmother's famous kitchen?"

"It's the first thing I could grab, and besides, my

301

grandma is the cook, not me," Lola shot back. "I've been a little too busy hanging out with you to focus on her recipes."

"Do you want to drive back to La Rosa and put in some practice then?" Javi was smug as he walked over to the driver's side.

Lola made a face. "Please spare me the machismo if we have to be in the car for a whole day together."

"We don't have to go if you're already regretting this trip. It would save me a lot of gas, you know."

Lola briefly considered telling him to forget the entire plan and walking right back inside to Mari and her grandmother and the repetition of her life. But she wouldn't stop thinking about the what-if if she did, and turning around would feel like defeat.

"I won't make you listen to music you hate if you try to be a little more friendly," she said, settling into the passenger seat.

"Eh, we'll see how we do. You can be unfriendly, too, sometimes."

Lola glanced over to the driver's seat. There was a slight gleam in Javi's eye as he started the car and maneuvered it back out toward the main road.

"Speaking of friends, where is your . . ."

"Ana?" Lola asked. "She and her mom are going to the Barragán house tomorrow. Or today, really. You'd like her; she's as into museums as you are."

"And you don't like them?"

"I mean, they're interesting, but it's kind of over-whelming," Lola said. "It's so much information at once, it's like I'm studying for a test. Which I can do, but I would rather not for once, if you know what I mean."

"Most museums have a plan. There's a . . . How do you explain it? It flows. If you focus on each piece as it comes to you and then think about how it fits with the one before it, it's less confusing."

"That sounds kind of like a language."

"Más o menos," Javi said. "History is a language, depending . . ."

"On who is telling it, you've told me," Lola finished for him. "Maybe that's my problem. Languages are where I struggle."

"You're not as bad as you were before," Javi offered, and Lola felt a laugh jump out of her mouth.

"As I *was*?" she emphasized. "Wow, was that almost a compliment?"

"Are you taking it?"

"Are you going to stop me if I am?" Lola tried to get comfortable in the passenger seat, realizing she would likely need to sleep in it for at least a few hours. "So is that why you wanted to study history? To put everything in context?"

"I think it's important to remember where you came from, to make sure it doesn't leave you. That it isn't a stranger to you, that it isn't nothing. That includes the good things and the ugly ones, too."

By now, they were on the freeway, the buildings drawing closer in waves and then fading in the side-view mirror. The car made its way past one colonia after the next and toward the hills that bordered the valley. Because Lola didn't know exactly how far they had to go, she began marking their progress with each new song on the playlist she had picked at random from Javi's phone. By song four, she had stopped trying to categorize his taste. By song nine, she was resigning herself to constant surprise.

It was when the music switched to a Jenni Rivera song that Lola thought about her grandmother. In a few hours, Buela would be rushing about her kitchen, brewing the first pot of coffee for the day and asking Mari and Paty what they wanted for breakfast. She would be annoyed that her granddaughter had left without even saying good morning, perhaps even angry, but Lola would deal with that later.

They drove for hours as the sun first rose and then made itself comfortable in the dusty blue sky ahead of them. Cars joined and left the highway as they moved past towns and bus stops and a vast expanse of green. Lola stopped checking her phone for a surprise signal and found that nodding in and out of sleep drowned out the hum of fear in her brain.

Six hours into their drive, Javi pulled off the highway and into a makeshift parking lot. A row of tented taquerías was waiting for customers, their interiors open to the graveled road. Javi positioned his car under the shade of a sparse tree and let the guitarrón finish in the song they were listening to before he killed the engine.

"If I ask you to get us some tacos, are you okay to do that without me?" he said, handing Lola some bills. "Think of how the customers at La Rosa order, and do that, but less like the tourists, if you can." He grinned at his own joke and began making his way toward a separate building, which could only be the bathrooms, before Lola could think up a reply.

Better than the tourists. Well, that bar was on the floor. Even so, she walked past the tianguis, whose vendors called out to her about their specials. In one tent, a girl of about Lola's age was tending to a number of steaming pots, and Lola studied the handmade menu on the board behind her.

"Cuánto cuesta para . . . I mean, por . . ." Lola started nervously before taking a deep breath and trying again. Lola thought back to the differences between cuts of meat that Rocío had drilled into her, and the girl smiled helpfully as she loaded her customer up with two of everything she sold. Lola gave her more bills than was necessary and refused the change she was offered.

"Es su propina," she stressed.

Javi let out a low whistle as Lola approached the car,

arms laden with food. "If you need to eat so much, we could have stopped sooner," he said, taking some of the Styrofoam boxes out of her hands and spreading them across the trunk. He nodded for her to sit on the last remaining patch of car that wasn't claimed by their lunch while he leaned over the side.

"Juana would want us to try everything and report back to her," Lola observed, pulling herself up and choosing between tacos. "To make sure she has the best in the entire country, not just la Roma." The car was warm under her, but the branches above helped diffuse the worst of the sun's glare. "I can try to take some of them back if you're so worried about your money."

He shook his head, his mouth already stuffed with barbacoa. "No, this was a good idea," he said between chews. "Are you always so . . ."

"All or nothing? Yeah," Lola said, picking a taco filled with charred nopales. "That's kind of *my* whole deal. I told you, I only get A's so I can get into a good college so I can get a good job because that's what a good daughter does."

"I was going to say you always think about your family. But yes, you've given this speech to me before." Javi's eyebrow arched.

"I . . ." Lola searched for the right way to respond. Around her cousins and Río, she felt pressured to invent something to make them see her as a sparkly, interesting person, as someone they would like. Yet she knew that what Javi would like most was the truth. "Sorry. It's just the only thing I have going on in my life. I have to get everything right because that's what my parents expect of me. That's why they sacrificed so much, so that Tommy—my brother—and I could have a better life than they did."

"They've told you this?" Javi asked.

"They don't need to. It's what they want."

"If it's not what you want, you'll be chasing what *they* want forever."

Rather than answer him, Lola helped herself to another taco. Midbite, she stole a glance at Javi, who leaned against his car with ease.

He sounded so sure of his advice. But what did she want? What if it wasn't enough? And what expectation was he afraid of chasing forever?

"How did you—" she began to ask, but her words crashed into his own.

"Lola, I—"

He paused, waiting for her to finish.

"I was . . . wondering, do you ever think you'll work up the nerve to do what you want, even if your family hates it?"

Javi's brow furrowed. "I don't know," he said. "I'm learning how to do it every day. But I think I can live with my father's bad opinion. That is temporary. There are more important things."

The mention jammed at a button in Lola's brain. "Your dad! How did seeing him the other day go? Is he disappointed in you now for something?"

"Sure, but he usually is. The way it works with him, he is polite when there are people around, and he tells me to visit my mother this weekend. Other than that . . ." Javi shrugged. "Is your dad the same?"

Lola shook her head. "No, he's . . . Honestly, he's exhausted most of the time. My mom, too. They work so hard, and if I can be one less thing they worry about, maybe I'm doing something right."

There was another pause between them, punctuated only by the traffic rumbling over the road in the distance and a bird scratching at the tree above them.

"That's something I like about you, ¿sabes?" Javi said suddenly. Lola stared at him. "*You* work so hard to make the people around you happy. Even your cousin and her photos."

"You try saying no to Cristina about anything," Lola tried.

"You have to give yourself more credit, Lola. I don't think you do it because you don't have a choice. I think it's because you really do want them to be happy."

Lola didn't know what to say.

"It's rare," Javi added. "It's a good thing. I like it."

A car sputtered, and they could hear the rise and fall of voices joining the din of the food stalls. And while the sun was beating down on them and they were more than halfway to where they wanted to go, Lola also wouldn't have minded staying right there for the next few hours, or even days.

But Javi's voice brought Lola back to reality.

"I'm sorry, what?" she asked. "No, wait, en español. ¿Qué?"

He laughed softly. "I was saying, if this curse of yours lets you, when we get back, I can take you out. If your family lets you."

Lola studied Javi's face. His usual surliness, the wall that kept everyone at arm's length, was gone.

"Solo si quieres," he added. "Not because you think it will make me happy."

"What if the *curse* doesn't let me?" she asked softly. "What if I . . . can't do the things that would make *me* happy?"

Javi nodded, his eyes clouding almost immediately. "I understand," he said flatly. He shoved himself away from the car's warm body before she could say something to bring the hope back to his face. "Bueno, we should be driving again. There is more Mexico waiting for us."

Javi started the car and pulled back onto the highway, his playlist once again filling the silence between them. Yet when his arm found its way to the armrest, Lola reached out so that her hand found his. Almost immediately, their fingers intertwined, the static turning into a spark that kicked at Lola's chest. Javi didn't say anything, but Lola could feel either the pulse of his heart or the beat of the music through his palm, and neither she nor Javi let go.

CHAPTER 27

The eight-hour travel estimate stretched beyond its limits, each song adding handfuls of minutes to the timeline Javi had given Lola, who in turn had promised Mari. But where Lola should have been terrified to miss a curfew—even a self-imposed one—a growing sense of anticipation pushed at her heart. The good kind. The kind that felt like a promise.

It was four in the afternoon by the time they pulled into a small town high in the mountains, surrounded by trees threatening to grow through the buildings that had cropped up between them over the years. The spires of a church loomed above their heads, and Lola could hear children yelling at one another as they played. Their joy carried through the streets, but Lola couldn't understand what they were saying, as hard as she tried to listen.

"Es un idioma Zapoteco," Javi offered. "All of these mountains helped protect this land and its people from the conquistadors. So the languages survived, too. I know a little of what my mother spoke to me when I was very small, but you can try with your best Spanish."

Lola made a mental note to enunciate as well as she could. "Right, got it. I will be as careful as possible," she said, stretching as she got out of the car. The air hit her lungs in a clean blast, and Lola took in another deep breath. "So, is this your mother's hometown? Where do we go first?"

Javi stared at her and chuckled softly, as if the idea that they would need to do something once they arrived was brand-new to him. "Mitla is farther south, pero ¿sabes qué?" he asked. "I was so preoccupied with getting here—to anywhere in Oaxaca, really—I didn't think about what we would do once we arrived."

"Wait, we drove for half a day and you had no end goal?" Lola heard her own voice rise the way her mother's did whenever Tommy didn't want to clean his room, but she made no effort to soften it or bite it down.

"This was your idea," he said simply.

She opened her mouth to argue—really, she had every intention of arguing until he came up with a plan just to appease her—but laughter tumbled out instead.

She had questioned if going just for the sake of going wasn't reason enough. Now she had her answer.

"I thought I would know what I wanted to do . . . what I *should* do," Javi said. "Every part of Oaxaca is so different from Mexico City, and I don't remember much about Mitla other that what my mom showed me. I did not want to impose a plan onto a place that was different than my memory."

Lola could tell that his solemnness was sincere, but the fact that neither of them had thought things through only made their situation funnier to her. "You thought the town would, I don't know, speak to you and tell you when to stop the car, and the streets would dictate your next move?" she asked. "That we would get by on *vibes*? My grandmother is probably freaking out that I am gone right now, and you were like, '¿Por qué no?, let's hop in my car and give her a heart attack, I have tip money for gas.'"

"Is that your impression of me? That deep voice?"

Lola snapped her lips shut, worried that she had crossed a line and hurt Javi's feelings—until she saw the barely concealed grin on his face. The two of them burst out in a fresh peal of laughter together, startling a bird out of a nearby bush.

Javi shrugged with his whole body, his shoulders meeting a slightly sheepish grin. "I have spent my whole life knowing I have roots here, but maybe I don't know the first thing about it. Besides what is in my books," he said. The words landed with a weight. Like he was admitting the truth to himself as much as he was disclosing it to her.

Lola looked at Javi and saw no barrier or defense waiting for her. He was just Javi, and that was enough. "How did I not know that you're just as bad as I am at doing what you want rather than what's expected of you?"

He smiled. "Because when I do what is expected of me, I let everyone know I don't like it. You pretend you like it. I'm hiding in plain sight, mientras que tú . . ."

"I want to make people happy," she finished.

Javi turned to stare out at the hills surrounding them. They rose and fell for miles, protecting their secrets from outsiders. Maybe even from people who had known these roads their entire lives.

She watched him as he watched the horizon, and rearranged every judgment she had made against him in her mind. His formal posture, which had never wavered despite the drunk girls flirting with him at their brunches and the screaming toddlers who preferred to throw their quesadillas rather than eat them, softened against the skyline. And when Lola opened her mouth to talk, it wasn't because she wanted to break the silence they were so used to falling into together—she wanted to share with him, and to hear what he had to say.

"It's kind of funny, you know," she said, leaning against the car as she took in the vista. "I've spent weeks thinking about curses and spirits, and you've taught me so much, and . . . I mean, Dani did the egg thing, the limpia, but I haven't met a bruja myself. Unless someone in my family is a secret one, but my grandmother is so religious that I think she'd make them stop, but—"

"I'm going for a drink," Javi said, moving toward the road.

Lola balked. Had she read the moment entirely wrong? "Now?" she almost shouted at his retreating figure. "Aren't we supposed to wander the streets like we're in a movie montage or whatever?"

"You can join me if you want," came the reply, but Javi did not slow down or make it easy for her to catch up.

Lola hurried after him, toward a covered patio with chairs and rows of tables, the logos of various beer companies on mismatched plastic-coated tablecloths. Javi ordered a cerveza from the stocky man leaning against the back wall, who took his order and disappeared through an open doorway. Javi pulled an empty chair from its table and sat down.

"Is this really the time for a beer? We have to drive back, and I don't want to be the one doing it," Lola huffed.

"Cálmate," Javi said, a forced breeziness now in his voice. "You need to trust me on this. By the way, have you heard from your family?"

Lola pulled her phone from her back pocket. "No Wi-Fi service out here. I told my aunt where we were going, but I'm sure if I don't keep in touch with her, she'll kill both of us when we're back."

"Even me? Mari loves me best of anyone at La Rosa," Javi said. "If you want to borrow my phone to let her know you're safe, you can."

His tone was somewhat strained, but before Lola could ask him what his deal was this time, they were interrupted by the man, who set a chilly glass bottle in front of Javi. He paid and immediately picked up a conversation with the man, whose skin crinkled at his eyes and cheeks. Lola, an expert in knowing when a conversation was not meant for her, wandered away from them and back toward the street.

No, neither of them had thought the plan through entirely. In fact, she'd jumped at the first opportunity to rebel that was offered to her, and while she had told her aunt that it was to support Javi, she had a feeling somewhere inside herself that this trip could be the key to understanding all the feelings she'd been experiencing since her arrival in Mexico City. That doing something so out of character and breaking so cleanly with what was expected would squash her anxiety or knock the curse off its course. But the unsteady buzzing was growing in her head again, and the promise of adventure had been for nothing.

She would have to go home—well, she'd have to go back to Buela's house, and then eventually home. She would have to learn to live with the curse, no matter how little she was actually living. And she would shrink back to her old habits of doing what she was told, of making everyone else around her happy. Even if Javi said he liked that about her, she had a feeling he would be disappointed by what it meant she wouldn't let herself do.

Lola took a deep breath and turned to head back to the restaurant patio . . . just as Javi came rushing up to her with determination in his eyes.

"Javi, look, I . . ." she began as he he grabbed her hand and almost pulled her back toward the car. "What is going on?"

"A curandera lives four kilometers away. Benito told me how to get there," he said.

Lola balked. "Who is Benito?"

"He owns the restaurant. For someone who gets good marks in school, you aren't the quickest, ¿sabías?"

Lola made a face as he found his car keys in his pocket.

"Only the people who visit them are going to tell you where they are. They don't put advertisements out on the radio. You know someone who knows someone whose cousin's friend visited once, and if you are lucky, they have a tiendita for their velas and the basic things sick people might need. So if you find them, it means you were meant to find them. Do you understand?"

"You found . . ." Lola said slowly, the reality of his words dawning on her. "Javi, do you think this woman can . . ." She almost didn't want to say it in case she got her hopes up too much. "Could she break this curse for me?"

"This is how we find out, no?"

The pit in the bottom of Lola's stomach contracted tightly, trying to brace her against another rejection or dead end. She watched as the road ahead of them pulled them closer and closer to possibility.

"The first thing you do when we get there," Javi said, turning the music down as the car rattled along the road, "is agree on how much you need to pay her. How much money do you have with you?"

Lola grabbed for her bag, which had found a home at her feet on the car floor. "I've got the tips you gave me—is that enough? How much does breaking a curse cost?"

"Whatever it costs, it is important you decide together. She needs to tell you that you've paid her everything you owe her. The curse is one thing, Lola, but I'm not driving you anywhere if you have an unpaid debt, ¿me entiendes?"

His tone had shifted once again, to something somber and pragmatic. It made Lola want to sit up and remain on alert, but the car began to slow in front of a squat one-story house.

"This is it?" she asked. "This is the place Benito told you about?"

Javi nodded. "Ya llegamos."

The walk from where they had parked to the house's front gate was short, but Lola felt her heart pound with every step. A voice inside her kept telling her that she could turn around, that she and Javi could get back into the car, drive back to Mexico City, and forget about this day forever. But before she could suggest retreat, Javi rapped on the metal door.

After a minute, a woman wearing a white blouse and a full skirt appeared behind the gate. She looked about as old as Lola's tía Sofía. Her skin gleamed in the sun, and Lola was immediately struck by the kindness in her eyes. Javi explained something to her in a language that must have been Zapotec, and she nodded serenely when he gestured to Lola.

"Doña Teresa, ella es americana," he said switching to Spanish. "Su español es . . ."

But the woman halted Javi's explanation and beckoned to Lola. "Mija, ven conmigo," she said.

Lola stepped forward nervously, and Javi moved to follow before doña Teresa stopped him. He was at least half a foot taller than she was, but Lola got the sense that few people crossed her. From the brief moment of terror on his face, it was clear that Javi wasn't about to try.

"I'll wait here." He reached for Lola's hand and gave it a small squeeze of reassurance.

Lola's hand froze in Javi's, and he was the one who eventually let go so that she could follow doña Teresa into the house. The front room was smoky and warm and smelled faintly of chiles and salt. It was a comforting smell that reminded Lola of something she couldn't quite place, but that familiarity also calcified into fear in her stomach.

She took a deep breath and tried to find the words to explain to this woman why she had appeared at her front door. But the humming in her heart whispered to her that perhaps doña Teresa already knew.

"You didn't have to tell her my Spanish isn't good, you know," Lola said from where she sat curled in the passenger seat. They had been driving for three hours, and the sun had already set over the mountains. The only sound was Javi's car making its way up the highway, away from doña Teresa's house and back toward Lola's family.

She hadn't spoken a word until then. Her mind was too

busy thinking through what doña Teresa had told her and all of the things the woman had seemed unwilling to say.

Javi smiled out of the side of his mouth, but Lola also caught a faint sigh of relief as it escaped him.

"Actually, she stopped me before I could tell her," he said. "Besides, everyone needs a formal introduction."

"In the future, I'd like something a little less condescending."

"Bueno." Javi nodded. "I will remember that for the future." He adjusted his grip on the steering wheel. "So," he added, "are you going to tell me what happened, or is it between you and the santos?"

"Doña Teresa didn't tell me I had to keep it a secret," Lola said, shrugging slightly. "I just . . . I needed some time to think about everything. But she told me you weren't allowed to come in with us because it would have been too much . . . I think *energy* was her word. Like maybe the spirits, or whatever she works with, would have been confused."

"You understood this? Maybe your Spanish is better than what I've been telling people. I'll think about this new introduction for you."

Lola offered up a small, annoyed smile and looked out the window toward the horizon. They still had hours of driving ahead of them.

"Let me ask it differently," he said. "What do you want to tell me?"

Lola turned to look at Javi, his profile illuminated by

the headlights of passing cars as they drove north. He was the same boy who had dragged her out of the market almost two months ago, but there was something different about him now. Or perhaps the difference was in her. She hadn't needed him inside the curandera's house, but she had *wanted* him there. This had been his adventure, too, and she liked the idea of sharing it.

So Lola began to tell him about doña Teresa's room and how it was strewn with flowers and tapestries that dangled ominously above the multiple flickering candles on every surface. There had been figurines of saints almost everywhere she looked, as well as a statue of the Guadalupe that was identical in size to the one Buela had at the center of her altar. But what had struck Lola most was the comfort she found in the small, windowless room that smelled like sage and other earthy offerings.

"Mostly we just talked," she added. "Or, I talked, and she listened. She asked me why I was there, and I told her about the curse and everything Juana says about it, and the limpia Dani did and what the egg looked like when he cracked it open, with all those little dots in a line. She was really patient. She didn't rush me when I was having trouble figuring out the right words. And she didn't make me feel silly for believing in any of this. Because she believes it, too."

Lola paused, trying to name the feeling that felt so bottomless to her. If she wasn't careful, it would sound like resentment. "But she also told me I should talk to my grandmother, which . . . That's ridiculous. Buela talks at me about these . . . side quests of her life, and I barely understand on a good day. What is talking with my grandmother going to do about solving a curse?"

"Were you expecting something else?" Javi asked.

Lola shook her head. "I don't know what I was expecting. I know TV shows focus on rhymes and smoke and special effects . . . but this felt kind of like therapy or confession or something. It didn't feel like magic."

"Perhaps it is a combination of both, no?"

"Have you ever been?" Lola asked. "Not to doña Teresa, but to . . ."

"¿Una curandera? I went once," Javi said, lowering his chin slightly in memory. "It was some years ago. I didn't know what to do about school, and talking to my parents didn't help. I don't like confessing to priests; it was almost on a . . . how do you say un capricho?"

"A whim?"

"Mírate, thank you for translating for me. Yes, a whim. Like this trip. So I paid, we talked, and now here I am."

The car swerved as Javi pulled it off the road and into what looked like an abandoned field before he turned the car off. His dark eyes searched for Lola's in the dim light, and his hand wrapped around hers.

"Do you still think this curandería and these rituals control people's lives?"

"No . . . maybe? Not control exactly, but . . . honestly, I still don't know . . ." Lola let her voice drift into the night.

"Lola," Javi's voice was gentle, no mockery or rebuke, "that only happens if you let it."

She felt the impulse to pull away, to give in to the nerves that snaked down her neck and settled in her shoulders, but she fought the reflex as hard as she could.

"Why did you take me to her?" she asked, lifting her gaze to his. "I know we didn't have much time left, but we could have gone to see your family or to any of the places you remember from when you were little. You didn't have to make this trip all about me."

Javi flexed the fingers of the hand that still gripped the steering wheel, and exhaled. "There is so much of Oaxaca I want to see again—I want to stop in every town and talk to all of the people—and I will. I'll learn about it outside of my books. But finding her, helping you get your answers, that seemed like something to do before we had to drive back. I didn't want *not* having a plan to be for nothing."

"Doña Teresa asked me why I wanted to break the curse," Lola said. "And when I told her it was because I wanted to live my life, she asked if I had been doing that before I knew the curse existed."

Javi squeezed Lola's hand. Somewhere, an owl hooted in the distance. "¿Y qué dijiste?"

She thought back to the room that smelled like ritual and reverence, and to the curandera's soothing voice. Lola had tried to find the words, but either her Spanish or her emotions or both had failed her. She couldn't blame a curse for every time she had avoided one of her class-mate's parties or any of the times she'd chosen to study at lunch or work through homework and extra credit in an empty parking lot. Her world was small, not only because her parents were protective, but because their rules had made her afraid—of not living up to their expectations, of disappointing her family and especially her father.

And while she was now afraid that the boy sitting next to her would hurt her the way his friend had, Lola wasn't sure what scared her most: the idea of taking a risk and opening her heart to Javi, or the consequences of not doing so.

Of not living the way she wanted to.

It was a choice, she thought. The curse might always be there, but she was the one holding herself back.

"I told her no," she said. "I haven't. Ever. But I want to now."

So Lola leaned across the console that separated their seats and that felt like the final barrier between the life she had and the one she could want. For once, she made the first move. And when Javi's jaw tightened in surprise when her lips met his, Lola began to regret the impulse. Her mind raced for a way to pull away without making things even more awkward than they already were.

Before she could, she felt the force of his mouth kissing her back.

She half expected the sky to open up in a downpour or for lightning to strike the car, but neither happened. Javi's other hand found its way to her cheek, his thumb softly stroking her jawline. When she took a breath, his hand stayed there. She hoped it would remain there forever.

"I was wondering if you were going to do that," he said.

Lola blushed. "I'm sorry, I . . . I . . ." she tried.

He shook his head. "No, don't be. It saved me the work. Pero si me contagias . . ."

Javi paused, his words hanging ominously in the air. Lola kicked herself inwardly—if she got Javi sick, not only would she not forgive herself, but she'd be in charge of getting them back to Mexico City.

"No, you can't get sick," Lola said quickly. "We're hours away from home, and my grandmother would kill us both. I shouldn't have risked it. I'm so sorry."

"I was going to say it would be worth it," Javi said, pulling Lola back toward him. "I don't feel any warts, do you?"

Lola shook her head. "Does this mean the curse is broken?" she asked, acutely aware of how close their faces and bodies were.

"It means whatever you want it to mean, Lola."

This time, they both closed the distance between them.

CHAPTER 28

When Lola woke the next morning in a sparse room, it took a minute for the memory of where she was to come back to her: how Javi had suggested finding a place to stay the night after hours of driving had caught up to them both, and how they found a motel with a dusty parking lot and terra-cotta walls that felt worlds away from the hotel where Lola was supposedly staying with her best friend.

At first, Lola worried about not making it back to Mexico City before her grandmother realized Mari was covering for her, but Javi had been driving for so many hours and Lola could see he needed sleep. And while she thought about borrowing his phone and texting Ana to apologize for leaving town, giving her best friend Javi's number could turn into a very bad idea.

"I don't think I've ever spent so long without looking at my phone," she had told Javi over the leftover tacos, which had gone soggy and cold by the time they devoured them. What she had meant was, *I've never spent this long without talking to my best friend.*

"What's in your phone that is so important?" he asked.

She took a breath. "Basically my whole life, even though that's not really a lot. I saw you at the party," she added. "Surrounded by all those people, all those friends. You wouldn't even look at me if we went to high school together. But I think that's also because . . . I don't really let people look at me. I like fading into the background."

At this, Javi had shaken his head and offered Lola the last taco sloshing around the drippings at the bottom of the container. "People aren't so hard to be friends with," he said. "But I understand."

That was how he began telling Lola about who he had been in school, a scrawny kid who spent as much time reading the footnotes in his schoolbooks as he did joking around with his classmates. His friends now didn't understand why he couldn't get his mind off the idea of studying history, especially when he practically had a job at one of the biggest banks in Mexico waiting for him, but their jokes about Javier the tour guide came from a good place.

"You have to trust that people want what's best for you," he added. "A lot of them do, even if they show it badly. My friends don't know what it's like to lose their history, for it to become nothing to them, because it already is. So they joke, but I don't want my history to be nothing. Remembering it is a way for me to not be nothing, either."

"So let's just say you switched your major and you started studying history," Lola countered. Bemusement flickered in Javi's eyes. "What do you even want to do with that degree once you get it?"

"I could be a teacher, or work in politics. I could do anything with it." He nudged her lightly with an elbow. "I haven't thought that far yet. I can get by on . . . what did you call them? The vibes? If I get to that point."

His voice was warm and full of possibility, and its sound stayed with Lola through the rest of the night, even after Javi had insisted on rolling the thin bedspread between them as a barrier while they slept. And rather than worry about what waited for her at her grandmother's house, Lola drifted to sleep thinking about the opportunities that might open up if there was no road map, if being able to do anything meant she could try everything.

As they finished the last leg of their trip, the sky grew angrier and more agitated. What had begun as a rolling mix of gray clouds eventually met the smog of traffic as Javi drove deeper and deeper into the city. The drive reminded Lola of the first one she'd taken with Mari from the airport to her grandmother's house, though Mari, who lined up her next thought the minute the previous one escaped her mouth, and Javi, who appreciated the things that only silence could convey, couldn't have been more different.

"There will be lightning," Javi said as he pulled into an empty spot on the curb in front of Buela's house, his eyes flickering toward the top of the windshield. But even if Lola had been able to tell the clouds that threatened thunder from any others, she wouldn't have been able to look up. Instead, her eyes were fixed on the two small women standing at the driveway gate. Anger radiated from the top of Buela's cinnamon hair . . .

And Letty Espinoza's entire face was bleary with distress.

Her mother was here? In Mexico? How long had she been waiting for her daughter to return? Lola grabbed her bag and tried to disentangle herself from her seat belt, but her rushing made the task ten times more difficult.

"Javi, you should go," she said quickly, her voice rough with fear. She wanted to thank him for the adventure and apologize for misjudging him, but she didn't dare look back at him or spend a single millisecond longer in his car. The sooner he left, the less he would see of whatever she was walking into—the collective rage of the Gómez women.

She took two steps out of the car and onto the sidewalk, and her grandmother's voice filled the street.

"¿Dónde estabas?" Buela asked sharply enough to make at least one neighbor peer curiously out the window.

"Buela, yo . . ." Lola began, but she was cut off by her mother.

"¿Y quién es él?" Letty nodded in Javi's direction as Lola tried to move both her mother and grandmother farther into the courtyard and away from the car.

"Lorena Espinoza, no serás descarada," Buela huffed. "Mal hecho, hija de su madre."

Lola's face burned with shame. "No es nadie, Buela,"

she said. "Mom, what are you even doing here?"

But she looked back and realized Javi's car hadn't left the curb. He was standing halfway out the driver's side, watching the three generations of Gómez women with eyes that flashed like the sky above them, close enough to hear every word.

And that Lola had said that he was nobody.

She saw the door slam and heard the engine rev, and the car pulled away from the curb. It was too late for her to unsay the lie.

"Lorena Amelia, is that boy from Juana's restaurant?" Letty was dressed in workout capris and a denim jacket— her one and only travel outfit—and the ponytail holding her hair back shook with every word she spoke. "Why wasn't she watching you? I told Socorro letting you work there was a mistake."

Lola pushed her way through the driveway gate, tears springing to her eyes. "This isn't Juana's fault, Mom!" she groaned. "I made the decision to go, okay? Not Juana, not tía Coco, not Javier or anyone else at La Rosa, and working there has been the most fun I've had . . . literally any summer of my life. It was me. You should be mad at me."

The mention of La Rosa set Buela off about the ways her granddaughter's restaurant was more trouble than it was worth. And while it wasn't a conversation that Lola wanted to take part in—Juana worked so hard to keep the staff at La Rosa employed, and she was proud of the place she and Rocío had built together—she was more surprised when Letty turned her gaze onto *her* mother.

"Mamá, ya hiciste suficiente con tus espíritus."

Though it was not meant for her, the coldness in Letty's voice settled somewhere in Lola's spine. She had never seen her mother be anything but respectful to Buela, and now that deference shattered in the air around them.

"What spirits?" Lola choked out. "Mom, do you know about the curse, too?"

"Lorena, it's not a curse. Your grandmother, she . . ."

But before Letty could continue, Mari rushed out of the house toward her. Mari, who had known where Lola had gone, who not only hadn't stopped her but had promised to cover for her, who had been pushing Lola to go and do and see more than she had thought possible. Mari could have simply treated Lola like another one of her snotty nieces when she showed up at the airport. Instead, she'd given her a blueprint for what life as her own person, apart from her parents, could be like.

If there was one person Lola wanted to talk to about what she'd seen in doña Teresa's room, it was Mari.

But Mari had news for Lola, too. "Lorena, there was a fire," her aunt said. "The kitchen at La Rosa is gone."

⌒

Buela's house was exactly as Lola had left it two days prior. The chalky scent of fresh tortillas mixed with the lacquered tang of furniture cleaner, and people rushed in the front door and lingered for hours just as they always had. The sounds of the street outside chimed against one another more reliably than the clock told time. Everything was the same, but Lola felt different in this space now.

No, she *was* different—and between the news of the fire and her mother's surprise appearance, she wasn't sure what was real and what wasn't. She had defied her grandmother's orders, and therefore the orders of any adult in her life, for the first time. She had searched for an answer that wasn't in her schoolbooks and found a host of possibilities instead.

Her phone buzzed in her back pocket as it connected to Wi-Fi for the first time in over thirty-six hours. Avoiding the lectures her mother, grandmother, and aunt were waiting to give her would only mean she'd get longer lectures later, but she didn't care. She rushed upstairs and closed the door behind her, fumbling with her phone to text Javi. He would have to know what happened at La Rosa. And if someone told him during their trip, why hadn't he told her?

It was the candles. She hadn't blown them out, and one of them must have toppled over. And now the kitchen, and so much of what Juana and Rocío had worked for, was probably gone.

"So you have your phone. You couldn't use it to tell me you were alive?" Mari's voice was hoarse with exhaustion.

"I didn't have Wi-Fi; the motel we stayed at was . . ."

"¿Y qué? You couldn't use that boy's phone?"

"Mari, Javi isn't *that boy*. He helped me find a curandera who believed me when I told her about the curse, and . . ."

"It's because of you and *that boy* that I spent the past twenty-two hours telling la Señora and your mother not to call the police," Mari said, the measure in her tone forced. "I tried to tell her you were with the gringas, but Leticia wanted me to call your friend the second she landed, and then the hotel, and then she wanted to report you missing. Lorena, you could have been dead. You could have gotten *married* in secret."

"Okay, Mari, I think one of those is way worse than the other."

"We didn't know anything!"

Lola shut her phone off and sat down on her bed, which someone—Buela, probably—had made in the time between her departure the previous morning and now. A fresh stack of laundered clothes was waiting for her on top of her suitcase, and if she were to peek under her pillow, she'd find her pajamas waiting for her. None of these things were chores she was expected to do here. And she'd repaid that kindness with a reckless lie.

"Lo siento," she said quietly, only daring to meet her aunt's eye in the mirror that hung on the wall.

Mari nodded, the way her hands sat on her hips making her look identical to her oldest sister. "Sí, and it's good you showed up when you did. That woman would have the whole colonia looking for you in an hour," she said.

"In thirty minutes," Letty said from the doorway.

Lola avoided looking directly at her mother, feeling herself shrinking under the sudden attention. Tommy had always been more afraid of their mother than he was of their father, and now she understood why.

"Lorena, what were you thinking?" Letty asked.

Whether it was the confusion of seeing her mom in front of her, in Mexico, or the delirium of the past thirty-six hours, Lola felt something within her break.

"I wasn't, Mom, okay, is that what you want to hear?" she asked, not bothering to force the tears back. "That I wasn't thinking, that I was irresponsible, that you didn't raise me to be like this? Whatever speech you have for me, I'll say it myself if you want. I was just so . . . tired of this curse, and of feeling like I couldn't live my own life, that I needed to do something. Haven't you ever felt that way? Wasn't that why you left Mexico? To have a life of your own? Why can't I have the same thing?"

Letty said nothing, and the silence was worse than the reprimand Lola had been bracing for. At least yelling would mean that they matched each other in tone. At least it would have been the expected response. But no: Letty jerked her head at Mari, who sighed and followed her sister back out of the room.

And Lola was left in silence, and in a startling absence of the truth.

Her phone buzzed angrily yet again. She had sixty-seven unread text messages and one slightly stale Instagram notification: Javi had tagged her in a photo of the rolling mountains they had seen only a few hours ago, the sky as blue as the fields below were green.

And then there were the texts from Ana. Fifty-four of them, to be precise.

> **AM:** Hello?
>
> Are we still on for dinner?
>
> Espinoza?
>
> Hola??????
>
> Lola I'm beginning to get like... seriously worried
>
> And your mom isn't responding to my texts, either

Lola groaned. There was no way either her mother or her grandmother would let her leave the house tonight, not even for her best friend's last night in Mexico City. Quickly, she tapped out an apology.

> **LE:** I'm so sorry, I think I got grounded. I can't go.

> **AM:** ...
>
> What do you mean you think?
>
> Can you ask to be sure?
>
> We're going to Condesa tonight, are you sure you can't get out of it?
>
> Where even were you???

What if your grandma comes with us?
I can ask my mom

Lola, it's my last night here

> LE: I think if I invited my grandma,
> she'd ground me even longer

AM: So you're not even going to ask?
I came down here for you

> LE: I'm sorry, A

> I'll be home at the end of the summer

Ana had begun to type something, but those ominous dots disappeared as quickly as they appeared on Lola's screen, then started up again, then faded once more.

Lola put her phone down and buried her head in her pillow. She would have to go downstairs at some point—both to face her mother and grandmother and to ask as many questions as she could. Letty's fury at Buela haunted her, and the fear that she was to blame for the fire meant that whatever high she had felt from the past day and a half was gone.

Lola shut her eyes tight, trying to will herself back to the memories of even a few hours ago and the way Javi looked at her. Like how even without a plan, both of them ended up right where they needed to.

CHAPTER 29

If there was a first time for everything, that included being on the receiving end of Buela's outrage. For years, Lola had listened in on her mother's phone calls during which Buela would dole out grievances about various members of their family. Whether or not Lola understood the specific complaints was irrelevant; the older woman's tone was proof enough of her annoyance, or her anger, or, worst of all, her pettiness. Each time someone wronged her was another opportunity to give the performance of a lifetime, to anyone who would listen.

But now Lola picked up on something else, an undercurrent. She had missed it for years, perhaps because she had always been so amazed her grandmother could be so spiteful to her own family. There was a protectiveness that drove her grandmother's fury, and a righteousness whenever someone in the Gómez family betrayed themselves or their relatives. If she, la señora Cruz de Gómez, had been tasked with bringing these people into the messy and dangerous world, she would also task herself with shielding each one until the day she died . . . and perhaps even longer.

Which meant that now Lola was in double the trouble. And if she hadn't been the target, Lola would have found the routine both artful and extremely funny. Actors vying for an Oscar win, Lola thought, could take a few lessons from Buela on how to effectively deliver a searing monologue.

For the most part, it went like this: Buela would mutter to herself as she went about her chores, pretending that Lola wasn't in the room. Every so often, she punctuated that with a few key instances of pointing her finger first toward her granddaughter and then her oldest daughter, and talking with her hands and her voice in equal measure. Sometimes Lola would be subjected to yet another diatribe about why she was ungrateful, or thoughtless, or rude, as if she was the audience and not the target. Buela's words were sharp and melodic, a waterfall of criticisms that Lola could only half translate.

Even so, her grandmother jumped to help Lola grab a glass from the kitchen cabinet. Even so, she waved Lola off and fired up the comal to heat a tortilla for her, because she was the only member of her family allowed to touch her stove.

Those small moments made Buela's censure more bearable for Lola to endure and her disappointment that much more devastating.

Buela's indignation was only eclipsed by that of Letty Espinoza, who radiated disapproval in every direction and toward everyone in the Gómez house except tía Paty. Letty's mouth would constrict into a tighter and tighter line every time she looked at Lola or her mother, and the only words she spoke to Mari were commands to help her clear or set the table. It was the least Lola had ever heard her mother speak, and after one excrutiating night, Mari decided that something had to give.

"Ya, Leticia," she said pointedly over breakfast the next morning. "This family doesn't tell each other anything. You're better off changing that and telling your daughter something when it matters instead of telling her more of nothing."

"Our family talks more than any family I know," Letty replied, trying to pull rank through her voice. "Do I not call you every week, María? Am I not paying for your classes?"

"*Communicating* is different, Leticia. Hablamos pero no nos *decimos las cosas*."

"Mom, what is Mar . . . tía María talking about?" Lola asked, the oatmeal growing cold in her bowl.

Letty sighed and looked over her shoulder at the wall of portraits. The rosary Buela often used to pray with was draped over Lola's school picture from fourth grade, its red beads glinting against the glass. Hers was the only photo that preserved her as how she used to be. Juana and Cristina each beamed from their frames on the day of their graduations, and even Tommy's junior varsity soccer portrait was more recent than Lola's photo. She was the cousin frozen in time, an unselfconscious little girl with bangs and mismatched teeth. Lola felt an urge to shelter that memory version of herself, though she didn't quite know why.

"Lorena, your tía María thinks . . ."

"You think it, too, *Leticia*," Mari said as she stood with her empty bowl and moved toward the kitchen. "This isn't about me; this is about our family."

Mari left the room without looking back, letting her family sit in the truth only she was brave enough to say. Lola bit back the impulse to ask Mari to come back, to push Letty in a way she was afraid to. But with Mari as her proxy, she might never learn how to talk to her mother herself.

"Your grandmother . . ." Letty began slowly, the practicality in her voice wavering. Lola was still staring more at her suddenly unappetizing breakfast than at her mother. "She didn't want me to marry your father or to move to California. I was supposed to stay here and help her with my sisters, the way you do with Tommy sometimes. But I went anyway. Chuy says that's when la Señora started praying. When your abuelo died, she prayed more. I didn't come back for his funeral. I was angry with her for how she treated your father when we first met. I think I still am."

She nodded at the wall. "The mother María knows is

very different from my mother when I was her age. María knows a mother who protects because she is scared. Of what? The world, maybe. I don't know what she says in her prayers or what candles she's buying, but I think these prayers to keep her family close to her in whichever way she thinks is best, she repeats them over and over again. And the spirits listen. A little too hard, you know?"

Lola looked up at her mother, feeling the confusion in her throat like vomit. "Are you saying this is Buela's fault? *She's* the one who put the curse on everyone?"

"I don't think it's her fault, nena," Letty said with kindness in her voice. Even so, the nickname felt like a cheap endearment and stung like a betrayal. "Good intentions can get bigger than people mean them to be."

Lola felt the spoon handle dig into her palm as she gripped it. "So I'm supposed to just be okay with this?" she asked. "Now that Buela and her spirits missed each other's memos, I have to live my life the way she sees fit? You can't, like, talk her into reversing it or whatever?"

"Have you tried talking *your* mother out of whatever decision she's made?" Letty countered.

Lola glared openly at her mother for the first time in her life. No, she wouldn't dream of telling her what to do—she wasn't sure she'd ever be ungrounded if she did. But it felt so defeatist of Letty to accept things just as they were, to quietly accept what Buela said and did, and to expect Lola to do the same.

"I told you before you left, Lorena," Letty added to fill the silence. "No one thinks they know what everyone around them should be doing like family."

Lola stood on shaky legs and picked up her bowl as if she were on autopilot. "You knew what you wanted to do, so you did it," she said, her voice cracking and wavering like its connection to her brain was unstable. "And you pay for Mari's law school because it's what you wanted to do before you changed your mind and found a new dream. I'm so sick of the way this family treats that saying of yours like a rule. Like you have the right to judge everyone because we're related. The least you all could do is . . . is support Juana and her restaurant because she's doing what she wants to do. And you can let me figure out what I want to do with . . . with my whole life."

Letty said nothing. She was looking at her daughter's class photo. The younger version of Lola smiled up and out of her frame innocently, but the older, living one was tired of accepting her family's expectations without question.

"You're just as overprotective as Buela, and you won't even admit it," Lola added as she left the room. Because her grandmother might have spirits to help her, but her mother only had herself to answer for.

⌐

"You are so lucky tía Letty hasn't called Javier to yell at him, too, ¿sabes?" Juana asked the next day as she drove

Lola to La Rosa. This was the deal now: Lola was to stay at home for the indefinite future unless she was with another Gómez. It was a concession Buela made only after a compelling appeal by her second-oldest grand-daughter, who no longer needed Lola as a hostess but did not want to see her shut away in their grandmother's house, either.

Lola was grateful, but she had also been surprised that Juana even wanted to see her, let alone show her the wreckage of La Rosa's kitchen. She hadn't yet admitted that she was the one who left the candles burning, and their flames still flickered in her dreams like a threat.

Maybe Juana was showing her the damage to guilt her into a confession.

Juana's voice lifted a few octaves to mimic their grand-mother. "La niña desapareció," she added emphatically. "By six at night she was convinced you were gone forever. Pero if you married someone overnight, Javier would be an okay choice. His family is very rich, you know? He is not flashy like Linares, but you have to be rich to have a house in Coyoacán. And Dani approves of him. And he really likes you. I see the way he looks at you when he thinks no one is watching him."

Guilt seeped further between Lola's ribs, carving out space where muscles were supposed to be. "Can we please not talk about Javi?" She hadn't even felt like doing her makeup that day, and her hair was pulled into a halfhearted knot at the top of her head.

Juana made a motion that was half shrug and half gesture toward the traffic ahead of them. Mercifully, she said nothing.

Lola watched the now-familiar city as they moved through it. And while she tried to translate the billboards or focus on the song playing on the radio, her thoughts kept returning to her grandmother. Buela was the beating heart of their family, the center that everyone gravitated toward at the end of the day or the end of the week. For decades, her only and most important job had been to worry about her children, and then her grandchildren—how she would feed them, if they were safe, if they were happy.

Buela had been responsible for her granddaughter this summer, and, Lola thought, maybe family also meant you felt responsible for one another, no matter what. She had given Lola rules right at the outset of the summer, rules that kept her world sheltered and small. To protect her.

And Lola had acted like she knew better—no, she had ignored them entirely—and sped off without looking back.

A lump formed in Lola's throat, but before she could clear it, she heard her cousin shift in the seat next to her.

"I know la Señora doesn't like the restaurants, Loli," Juana said abruptly, though the way she didn't turn her head gave Lola the sense that she was speaking to herself as much as to her cousin. "She called me la Malinche when I told her I wanted to name the place after her. Actually, your aunt told her first. Buela would only talk at the back of my head for a week, about how I was taking the gringos' money and they were taking my dignity. And she wouldn't speak to Rocío for *months*. I think mi papá eventually told her to let me try, and if I failed, at least I would learn how to fail."

Lola pictured tío Zuma smiling his way through a conversation with his mother-in-law, probably offering more patience to the stubborn older woman than she deserved. He and tía Coco so believed in Juana's dreams that the restaurants had become their dream, too. A rush of admiration for her aunt and uncle mixed with the sympathy Lola felt for Juana herself, who had been fighting to keep a sudden heaviness out of her usually sunny voice.

Juana met Lola's gaze with her own. "You know why I did it, though? Why I named my restaurants after that woman?" Juana asked. She turned to Lola, a mischievous eyebrow raised. "I did it because caring for us is how Buela shows her love. It's the first thing I remember from when I was little. The cooking, the rules, waving her spoon around like it's a weapon, and threatening she'll swat you with it though she never did, every minute of it is her way of protecting us. I know it doesn't feel like it, Loli, but she'll sooner make you a tostada than she will say she's proud of you. That's how she was raised. So she shows how she feels instead. Even if she gets a little . . . with her spirits y todo."

"My mom told you Buela is behind the curse?"

Juana nodded. "I shouldn't be surprised it was her," she said. There was a pause that was inaccessible to Lola, a thimble of recognition of the bond Juana shared with her grandmother that was distinct from the one Lola had.

Cars honked at one another, and Juana waved one in front of her. Eventually she spoke again. "When she's gone, we'll have the memories and her recipes. Some people think that's a sad thing, but that's enough for me. We're her . . . no sé la palabra en inglés. Like a history for the future."

"You mean her legacy?"

Juana nodded. "My job isn't only to run a restaurant. It's to make sure this thing I named in her honor succeeds. This place is how I show my love back to her."

Juana motioned through the window. They had arrived at La Rosa, its warm front walls as inviting as ever. Inside, there would be no laughter and shouting, and the energy that had swept Lola up and into the fold from her first fateful shift would be gone. But there had been something more to La Rosa—from the photo of their grandfather that hung above the bar to the way Juana committed herself tirelessly to every inch of the place.

The restaurant was like their family. It was loud and dramatic, and someone was always overly invested in someone else's personal life, but it was also a community. And most of it was still standing, even after the fire.

"Juana, I'm so sorry. I should have blown out those

345

candles on your altar before I left," Lola blurted out. "The fire was my fault; you can tell your insurance it was your stupid cousin. I'll work next summer to make it up to you, I . . ."

Astonishingly, Juana laughed. "Someone lit the trash on fire in that pinche alley," she said simply. "My office is fine. Lorena, you are not responsible for everything that happens in this world."

The restaurant still smelled like smoke as Lola entered it, the char and injury seeping into the walls and the chairs and the floor. Lola barely dared to breathe in case she disturbed the unnatural quiet. But right as she turned the corner to the back corridor to see the full extent of the fire's damage, a nervous smile stretched across her face.

Javi was sweeping the floor, his body framed by a thick tarp tented awkwardly over a gaping hole in the wall. Lola had never seen brick burn. She wondered if it put up a fight or if it caught as quickly as some of the exhausted fields that stretched on for miles outside of Oxnard. That was how the farmers put them to rest before they could support any more strawberries or oranges, as well as the people who worked so hard to harvest them.

"So she is alive," he said. There was a kind of shine to Javi's voice, one where concern blended and softened his usual roughness. He straightened and put the broom aside. It leaned against the wall dutifully, waiting for whenever someone needed it next. "I tried to text you. I needed to make sure you were okay."

"Yeah, I . . ." Lola paused. There was so much she wanted to say, but she didn't know how. And this time it had nothing to do with the language. "Sorry, there's just been a lot going on."

The memory of the road trip came back to her in stills, like a camera shuttering between the high points. Of the leaves on the tree they had parked under, and the steady gaze of the man at the restaurant, and the way Javi's knuckles looked when his hand was entwined with Lola's.

But Lola was supposed to leave soon—in a week, if she could manage to talk her mother out of carting her home with her the next day. She had never passed any kind of final exam with her father as proctor, but the first day of the fall semester was drawing closer. Her senior year.

Another year she would be expected to receive straight A's and to choose homework over having a life.

Even the best summer had to come to an end. It was easier to close it proactively than to let it fade on its own. Maybe she and Javi could be friends—though friends wasn't what she really wanted.

"Is your grandmother mad at you?" Javi asked. "Tell her it was my fault. Or I can tell her. I can come by and explain for you."

"Javi, I . . ." Lola felt her voice break. "I don't think lying to her about whose idea it was is a good idea. I've got . . . I'm leaving next week and I have to pack and say goodbye to people."

Javi's posture changed again, growing imperceptibly straighter, the kind he reserved for patrons and his grand-mother. "Is this my goodbye, then?"

Lola could feel Javi trying to catch her gaze in his, but she couldn't bring herself to meet his eyes. "It might be easier if it is."

"Right," he said. "Of course."

He nodded past Lola's shoulder to where Juana lingered in the dining room. "Voy a prepararme para el trabajo de la noche," he told her cousin before moving back toward the office, maybe for his things, maybe simply to avoid the girl standing in front of him. "Adiós, Lorena."

There was no curse Lola could blame for Javi's departure. That was entirely her own fault.

CHAPTER 30

Letty left three days after she had arrived, adequately satisfied that her daughter was safe with her mother. Buela tightened her grip on Lola's world, and even Lola had to admit it was warranted. Besides, this small routine was nothing new to her. In many ways, it felt a lot like her life to and from school—the life that she would be returning to in a few weeks, in another country, with another set of responsibilities.

She found herself spending hours and hours watching YouTube videos and wiping versions of herself that didn't feel quite right off her face, only to start over. There was something comforting in knowing she could fix the mistakes she made with her contour, that she could dust off any glittery fallout and try again.

"I don't like to think of them as mistakes," Vanessa Corinne said as she adjusted an imprecise lipstick line on the bottom corner of her mouth with concealer and a brush. "Everything's a chance to practice. It's not a mistake if you learn to do it better next time. And if you're still bad at it next time, that means you're human."

Lola had never felt more human, or more alone.

Yet by some stroke of luck, Lola had talked her grand-mother into letting her visit the other La Rosa, the first location in the colonia Juárez. And while it looked similar to the place where Lola had spent hours tripping over words on the menu while talking to dozens and maybe hundreds of strangers, with the same hand-painted plates and light fixtures and colorful tile lining the bar, it also had an energy entirely its own.

She tried to take in as much of the restaurant as she could, imprinting the space on her memory. Sure, she could have taken a photo or two, but her phone couldn't capture the way the spices in Rocío's picadillo filled the room, and a video would only flatten the happy multi-lingual chatter to an indecipherable drone. The only way to preserve the memory was to hold tight to the moment as long as she could.

But the feeling of familiarity was marred just as quickly as it bubbled up inside Lola's heart: Río was working, which meant he would be the one to attend her if she sat at the corner of the bar as she had so many times before in la Roma.

"Do you want me to bring you your food?" Dani offered sympathetically as he nodded toward the back wall of the dining room, his smile barely masking a desire to tell Río to take himself out with the trash.

"No, don't worry about me," Lola said. "It would probably make things worse if I avoided him."

"Whatever you say, morrita," Dani said like he trusted her, and the fear Lola once had about facing Río melted away.

There was a kind of satisfaction in knowing that she'd done nothing wrong, that blaming herself was pointless. Sometimes things didn't work out the way she had prepared for, and it was up to her to react accordingly. She could study for hours and weeks and years, but nothing in her books could teach her how to live.

So she approached the bar, steeling herself to handle whatever Río had to say.

"Hey, American," he offered with a smile. "Isn't your summer almost over? Have you decided to stay with us forever yet?"

The breeziness with which he approached the conversation was momentarily unnerving. Río was able to charm his way through life and evade most of the consequences that came with careless decisions and a relative disregard for other people's feelings. Lola cared about what everyone else felt and thought, and she liked that about herself. They would have never worked.

"I think I should stick to high school for one more year," she replied lightly, scanning the dining room again. "Besides, Juana's already training my replacement. She's nice. I'm sure you two will get along great."

Río raised an eyebrow as he readied the last of the cocktails for a clearly thirsty table. Lola fought the urge to look away. He was still beautiful, and his nonchalance still stung.

"If you're suggesting that I am going to do the same thing with her, Lorena, I'm hurt," he said.

"I'm not suggesting you're going to do anything, Río." She picked the menu up and scanned the specials. Rocío must have gotten a good deal on ancho chiles, because they were listed prominently in every dish. "You're your own person; you can do what you want."

He pouted, the mock-hurt on his face transparent. "Can we not be friends, American?" he asked. "I don't want you to leave Mexico thinking badly of me."

Lola studied Río's face as if it would provide her with closure. Two months ago, she wouldn't have believed that he would so much as look her way. Now his attention was hardly worth much, especially if it wasn't sincere. He would only ever be another could-have-been to her, but this time she was choosing to walk away.

"Okay, then," she said. "I won't think of you at all."

Lola put the menu down and walked back out of the restaurant, exchanging a smile with Dani as she left. It wasn't until she was firmly outside that she let herself breathe, the exhale more freeing than she'd ever experienced it.

And while she wasn't supposed to go anywhere without another member of her family, she felt her legs pull her down the street and into the neighborhood. She wanted to experience Mexico City on her own terms for the first time all summer.

Just in case, she took her phone off airplane mode. The tiny bars of data strained to find a connection, and Lola tried to stop and take photos at interesting angles to see the city the way Javi might. But she was supposed to see it the way only she would, the way the Mexico City she knew was different from the Mexico City of his childhood and, even now, of his first few years of adulthood. The city she loved would always be different from anyone else's understanding of it, and theirs would always be partially distant to her.

She stopped in front of a small store with a window-pane door, wedged between open storefronts from which vendors beckoned at passersby. Something in Lola's heart told her to go inside. She reached for the door handle.

The room was quiet and filled with books jumbled in chaotic, intimate stacks. Layered over the scent of paper and ink was another, richer smell: Someone was burning incense, and it reminded Lola of the palo santo stick her grandmother had waved over her the night she learned about the curse, and of the rituals Mari followed when she was studying.

A woman appeared from behind an overflowing bookcase that divided the room, the gold ring in her nose glinting and accentuating her warm skin. She was humming to herself and looking at the two books in her hands, choosing between them.

"Buenas tardes," she said, nodding to Lola. She took a seat on a stool behind a register and opened one of the books, happy to read rather than hover over her new customer.

Lola returned the nod shyly and picked up a book whose crackled spine beckoned to her, the word *curanderismo* glinting on its cover.

"You are American?" the woman asked Lola, who blushed at the recognition. Was it that painfully obvious?

"Americans move differently from los defeños, even los chilangos," the woman said simply. "But I think you have something of los dos in you. It's in your shoulders, in your spirit."

She motioned to the book that had captured Lola's attention. "Curanderismo is a way of healing," she said. "I think you would call it folk medicine. Some people call it magic."

"I know," Lola said. "Someone . . . A friend told me about it this summer."

A smile played on the woman's lips.

"I'm sorry," Lola tried again. "This is a weird question to ask, but . . . do you think it's real? Magic and curses and everything?"

"Is it because you think you're cursed that you are here?" the woman asked.

Lola opened her mouth to reply, and shut it just as quickly. Even if this woman listened to everything she had seen and done that summer and walked with her through every memory and feeling, Lola was the only person who could answer her own question.

"To some people, believing is the first step to making things real," the woman said. "Curses, blessings, they come from the same energy. Some people want magic in their lives the way they need love. You can always learn more, but I think you already know everything you need to decide if you believe or if you don't."

She pulled the book gently out of Lola's hands, moved toward a small altar, and struck a match. It sparked ominously, as if to warn the woman that lighting a candle in a room filled with books was not the best idea. But the woman lit a long stick of incense and stuck it in a clay bowl filled with sand. A trail of smoke snaked upward to the ceiling. Lola recognized the smell of copal, warm and earthy and bright.

"What does that do?" Lola asked.

The woman smiled and motioned to the incense stick. "There are rituals that help bring comfort, and some that help with clarity. Some offer a . . . How do you say it? A reset. They clear the air."

Lola thought about her grandmother's palo santo. "What do you mean?" she asked. "From what?"

"Me, I like the rituals because I have to participate in my own cleansing," she said. "If I want to start fresh, I have to do the work, too. The saints can't do everything."

Lola let the words swirl around in her brain. Spirits and agency, together.

"¿Buscabas algún libro?" the woman asked.

"Not today, no. But thank you," Lola said before backing out of the store and into the sunlight, something like hope swelling in her chest.

CHAPTER 31

Lola's return flight was set for a Friday, two weeks before senior year was supposed to start. Her father's email—the first one he sent all summer—contained two attachments: a PDF of her plane ticket and a document detailing the three novels and one play her new English teacher expected her to read before the fall semester began. It was an underwhelming welcome to senior year.

Home would still be the same, but Lola wasn't. The girl who had gotten off the plane in Mexico City, the girl who had let everyone else dictate how she lived her life, was now a stranger to her.

Not because Lola planned on breaking the rules just to prove she could, nor because she wouldn't try to ace the first test of the year and every one after it. She could still do what was expected of her while holding tightly to the knowledge of who she was and what she wanted. And though Lola didn't have the answers to those questions yet, she was okay with figuring them out—she would spend the rest of her life doing it if she needed to.

Ana had been right. She was different now.

Ana, whose texts to Lola were short and polite, who said she was stressed about scouts coming to cross-country practice, even though Lola sensed there was something simmering beneath the packed practice schedule. Ana was breezy on even her worst day—she called it being pathologically chill—but there was something forced in the memes she chose to send, and those to which she responded.

Several times, Lola had opened their thread to read through a history of inside jokes that spanned years only to find that string of three dots at the bottom of the screen. But each time, whatever Ana was typing never materialized.

And each time Lola had typed and deleted explanations of her own, the words she found seemed a lot less like she was actually saying anything of substance, and more like talking. Like she was trying to fill a silence that wanted to be left alone.

The Sunday before Lola's flight was much like every other Sunday at Buela's house, but it also felt bigger and more important. Word had gotten out that la Señora was making tamales, and both Paty and Coco had been conscripted to help, which meant the house was already noisy by seven in the morning. Not even tío Chuy, who arrived several hours later with two of his daughters in tow, was spared from kneading the unforgiving masa in the crowded kitchen.

Between the nonstop grumbling coming from the back of the house and the cheerful, tinny sounds of Buela's ancient radio, the house was bustling with noise and laughter. From the living room, tío Zuma floated the idea of renting a mariachi troupe to serenade everyone that night, and began gathering donations for the endeavor as he and his wife kept the conversation going. Even Mari and Cristina chose not to pick at each other every second they could, their tandem laughter catching almost everyone off guard as it carried through the rooms.

More than once, Lola fought the bittersweet pang that threatened to make her cry. She'd let it wash over her later, maybe on the plane, where she could be anonymous and sad. First, it was time to celebrate.

"Lorena, if you come back next summer, bring more than your jeans and T-shirts, porfis?" Cristina asked, her words punctuating the tapping of her nails on her phone screen as she scrolled through her constant deluge of texts. "I can take you to lots of parties with me, but you can't wear the same dress every time."

"Or you could let her borrow some of your clothes, muñeca," Mari said. "You have enough to dress the entire family, even la Señora."

Lola gave Mari a grateful look, which the latter returned warmly. She'd chilled out significantly since the day Lola had returned from Oaxaca, because Mari was practical to a fault, and that included how much time she spent holding a grudge. Lola would miss her most out of everyone.

"But Lorena will have to return, ¿a poco no?" Regina's boyfriend, Adrián, interjected as the couple joined the table. "You have to see . . . Which one is he? Río? No, el otro. Javier?"

"Lorenita certainly had a busy summer," Cristina intoned, a domineering sneer creeping back into her voice.

The rest of the table ignored her.

Lola gave Adrián a small smile. "Javi and I . . . I don't think he'd want to see me," she said. "So if I come back—when I come back—it'll be to see family."

Mari snapped to attention, a flash of her mother's mindfulness in her eyes. "Lola, ¿qué pasó?"

Lola looked around the table for a moment before swallowing her pride. Even if she told Mari privately about meeting Javi in the hallway at La Rosa, the whole family would know about it in a manner of hours.

"I told him there's no point in us going out one last time. Because I'm leaving, so why bother, right? It would just have to end anyway."

"Ay, Lorena, what a heartbreaker. We should give you your own telenovela," Regina said sympathetically.

Mari rolled her eyes so hard, her neck followed. "¿Entonces? You let him walk away? And you can live with yourself like that? Lorena, that's not how Gómez women act."

"Sí, Gómez women never let you live any decision down,

no matter what you choose," Gabriela added. "Pregúntale a mi mamá."

"¡Exactamente!" Mari said, slapping her hand on the table for emphasis. "Lola, you did not have to hurt him."

"Mari, it wasn't worth it," Lola tried. "I'm leaving soon."

"So? Lola, I thought you were going after that silly curse so you could have the things you wanted." A hint of reproach lingered in Mari's voice. "And now you're going to let this one go? Have you learned nothing?"

"I mean, I think I learned some Spanish, and how to be an okay hostess, and . . ."

"Creo que ella necesita practicar," Regina intoned to her boyfriend, who laughed knowingly.

Mari ignored them. "The curse, if that's what you believe, is your excuse, and my mother's excuse, for controlling things that should not be controlled. That are impossible to control. Do not look at me like that, Lorena; you are doing it the same as she did, in your own stubborn way. You tell yourself these stories about how you struggle with everyone else's expectations of you, when your expectations are the biggest of all. And here you are again, pushing Javier away. You can't control your life, Lola. It is messy and it is scary, but that's because people are messy. And you need to accept that. You need to learn to enjoy it."

Mari's words echoed in Lola's head as tío Zuma's laugh boomed from the living room. It was impossible to say whether Mari had ever gotten an impromptu economics lesson from her brother-in-law, but Lola got the sense that Mari was the fourth kind of person, the prisoner who would trust the other person not to turn her in.

After a few minutes—during which Cristina maneuvered the conversation back to herself—Lola inched away from the group and toward the kitchen. Buela's children had excused themselves from the backbreaking business of tamal making, and the older woman was alone, methodically stirring a sauce in one of the three pots that bubbled on the stove. She had made enough food for the entire family and perhaps the entire neighborhood. All anyone had to do was stop by and ask.

Lola hadn't been alone with her grandmother since her return from Oaxaca, and she watched as the latter busied herself with the world she knew. Suddenly, confronting her and asking if those prayers had been worth it didn't seem to matter. What her grandmother did out of love didn't make her the ultimate authority on the matter. She was just a woman who was trying. And holding a grudge would hurt Lola as much as anyone else.

"Buela, ¿puedo ayudarte?" she asked gently.

"Claro, mi vida, ven aquí." Buela pulled Lola over to the stove and showed her how to stir the simmering mole gently, making sure to scrape the bottom of the pot so the ingredients neither separated nor burned. And as Lola followed her grandmother's directions, she took in the kitchen, the center of her grandmother's home and therefore the center of their family.

Just outside the door was laughter and joy, but there was happiness here, too. It was a quiet assuredness, a firm sense that more things were right than not, and that the things that weren't right would come out okay in the end. No matter how far away they might be, whether across town or through a customs line and thousands of miles away, they could come back to this, to Buela and to their family.

Lola looked up at a portrait of her grandfather, whose gaze had watched over her protectively through so many hours at La Rosa, which would be rebuilt and open again, she was sure. Yet this home was also La Rosa, she thought. The two spaces were so different, but they had each shown her so much.

"¿Buela?" Lola said after a moment as her grandmother bustled about the room, swapping steaming tamales out of a pot and plating them on an ever-growing mountain of corn husks.

"¿Sí, mi vida?"

"Gracias por todo."

Her grandmother smiled and went back to dropping more tamales into a waiting steamer, as if whatever her granddaughter was thanking her for was yet another given in her life.

CHAPTER 32

Lola stared at the phone in her hand, at the powerful, tiny computer that helped her keep up with everyone she had ever met. Through it, she could know what someone had for lunch that day if they posted it to Instagram, or scroll through years of outfits, inside jokes, song lyrics, and whatever other thoughts formed the emotional fingerprint of a person's life online. She could tell a lot about their mood from whatever they posted that day, or how they commented on other's posts, or what they liked before they moved on to the next square, the next thought, and the next curated glimpse into someone's life.

For years, she had watched her classmates broadcast every moment of their lives to one another, even as they sat next to each other in the cafeteria, or across from each other in a red plastic In-N-Out booth, or gathered together in the stands of a crowded football stadium. Even now, Lola knew who had gotten a new car that summer, and who had broken up and gotten back together several times over, and who was already stressing out about early-decision college applications.

But these were the public things, the details she was allowed to know, filtered for the maximum reaction.

Those were the things they talked about.

How they communicated was different.

There were things phones couldn't show a person, things that would somehow evade even the wittiest captions and most thoughtful text messages. There were things too special to share with everyone. How could someone make memories without committing them to pixels or film? How could they freeze a feeling so they could carry it with them forever?

Sure, Lola hadn't posted about the drive to Oaxaca and back because she didn't have Wi-Fi, and because she feared what would happen if her parents found out what she had done. But she also wanted the details of her and Javi's adventure—the way the trees competed with one another up and down the mountainside, and the way the sun had raced them toward the horizon, and how the salsa had dripped everywhere as they ate their roadside lunch—to stay a secret she shared with one other person.

And she wanted to hold on to it, and share it with him, just a little bit longer if she could.

I need to tell you something, she typed out, then deleted, then typed out again.

The words wouldn't magically appear on the screen for her—as with any of the dozens of papers she had ever written for school, she would have to write them herself.

> LE: That Friday when you were here, Javi and I drove to Oaxaca because he had always wanted to and I wasn't... Okay, I wasn't thinking at all
>
> I wanted to know what it was like to do something spontaneous for once, instead of following everyone else's rules
>
> My aunt covered for me and said I was staying with you overnight, but my grandma caught me with Javi when he dropped me off the next day
>
> That's why I didn't answer your texts, and why I couldn't go to dinner on your last night here
>
> I was selfish
>
> I'm sorry

A text bubble flickered on the opposite side of the conversation and disappeared.

As was the case lately, the text itself never came.

That was the other thing about phones: No matter how strong your connection, you couldn't force a conversation with someone who wasn't interested in having one.

"¡Lorena!" Mari's voice carried up from the first floor of Buela's house and to their bedroom, where Lola had been hunting down the clothes that had hidden themselves in every corner possible. It was Wednesday, and she had less than forty-eight hours to stuff her belongings into her suitcase. "¿Qué vas a hacer con estas cosas?"

Lola fished the dress she'd packed at her mother's advice from the bottom of a pile of neatly folded clothes in the closet. Buela must have thought it belonged to Mari, and besides, Lola hadn't had another reason to wear it since the night of the party.

She looked at the fabric in her hands and then up and around the room that had been her home for almost two and a half months, searching for proof that she had left some small mark in at least one corner of the city. Even if the swirling noise and movement meant that there was something more interesting going on somewhere else, she had been here. She had done something about her life.

"¡Lola! Come get your books or I'm throwing them out!"

Lola hurried downstairs and to the dining room. Mixed among Mari's law papers on the table were the books Javi had given Lola, stacked over a foot high. Lola's stomach sank at the sight of them.

"Are you not going to pack these, too?" Mari asked, barely looking up from her notes. "Why did you even bring that many books? Your mom was right, you study more than I do."

"Those aren't mine," Lola said after a moment. "They're Javi's; he gave them to me to research the curse."

Mari turned her full attention to Lola. "And did you find the answer in them?"

Lola thought back to everything Javi had shown her that summer, from the mercado to parts of the city she might not have discovered on her own. And despite their hours together, she had only begun to scratch the surface of the city's history—it wasn't something you could understand in a few days or even an entire summer, no matter how knowledgeable your guide.

But she also thought about the ease with which Javi had driven them around, his playlists and the way he turned the music up on certain songs, and the straightforwardness with which he had challenged Lola to not only try things that were new to her, but understand them, too.

"I think he helped me find the answer more than the books did," she said.

Mari was less than interested in Lola's reverie. "Well?" she asked. "You need to return them to him, no?"

"Maybe I'll drop them off with Juana; she can take them to La Rosa," Lola tried.

Mari scoffed and stretched in her chair. "You're impossible, you know that, Lola? Come on, get your things and take the books to my car. We'll return them to that boy right now."

"Mari, you don't even know where he lives. I couldn't even tell you how to get there."

"But your cousin la chismosa probably does."

Lola looked down at the books, bested by Mari's logic. If anyone would give up information that readily, it was going to be Juana.

That was how Lola found herself in the passenger seat of Mari's car, headed toward Doña Pilar's house as her last official errand before her flight home. Mari had chosen a particularly upbeat radio station to serve as the soundtrack while they drove, which offered up plenty of hype tracks for an impossible task. If Javi wasn't home, Lola would have to deal with his grandmother. She wasn't sure which option was less appealing or more likely to make her regret her final gesture.

Eventually, Mari pulled up to the correct street and let out a low whistle. "If you're not going to go in, I will," she said. "I want to see the inside of that house."

Lola took a breath and checked her reflection in the mirror—whether to buy time or because she cared what Javi thought of how she looked, she wasn't sure—before pulling the books from the back seat and balancing them in her arms. Javi had truly loaded her up with more texts than she would have been able to read in several summers, and the collection slowed her down as she made her way to the front gate.

It swung open before she could knock.

But it wasn't Javi's domineering grandmother who greeted her. It was his mother, and Lola was surprised by the way her heart cracked, a hairline break only she felt.

Maybe Javi was avoiding her inside the house. Maybe that afternoon at La Rosa was the last time she'd see him, the acrid staleness of the fire punctuating her goodbye like a nightmare.

"Lorena, ¿verdad?" Esperanza asked, her smile still not quite extending to her eyes. "Y usted, ¿qué quiere?"

Lola willed herself not to trip over her Spanish. "Estos son los libros de Javier," she said.

"Él no está aquí. Póngalos allí." Esperanza motioned to a small table in the entryway, just beyond the front door. Lola followed her, each step feeling like it stretched a mile.

Then she heard his voice from the street, the care he felt towards his mother unmistakable in the way he called to her. "Mamá, ya regresé."

Lola made sure the books wouldn't topple over on Doña Pilar's pristine tile floor before she turned around to face the boy who so often surprised her.

Javi stood on the sidewalk, his backpack slung over his shoulder. He nodded toward his mother, who clicked the gate behind Lola—apparently, gossip didn't run in Javi's family the way it did in hers.

"I'm only here to return your books. I'm going back to California on Friday," she said quietly, trying to keep a respectful distance. "I was going to leave them at the restaurant, but Juana told my aunt where you lived and . . ." She motioned down the street to where Mari's car was parked.

"So you're packed, then?" he asked in a voice he

reserved for the restaurant, the one he used on customers and strangers.

"Almost," she said, trying not to flinch at his tone. "I really am here to drop off your books. I promise I'll go now. I know what I said to you was . . . Honestly, it was shitty, and I wouldn't want to see me, either."

Javi pulled one hand out of his pocket and scratched the back of his head. "Why do you do that, Lola?"

"I don't know what you mean. I haven't done anyth—"

"You do, you assume the worst answer before I can tell you what I really think," he said.

Now it was Javi's turn to look sheepish. "At first, yes, I thought it would be better if you left before we saw each other again," he said after a moment, the honesty stinging. But he motioned to the bag on his shoulder. "I also have my classes, and I'm helping one of the professors at the . . . You call it the anthropology museum? I changed my studies."

"Javi, that's great!" Lola blurted out. "Now you can study what you really want to; you can be a teacher, or a . . . You can do whatever you want."

He nodded. "And what will you do in California?" he asked. "Now that you know you're not cursed?"

Lola let out a short laugh. "I don't think it matters if I'm cursed or not, especially if I'm the one getting in my own way."

"Is that something doña Teresa told you, or you learned it yourself?"

"Both? It's kind of obvious, right?" She took a deep breath. "Javi, I'm really sorry about what I said that morning at my grandmother's house. And at the restaurant the other day. You've been so helpful and . . . and you didn't deserve any of it.

"I thought I was protecting you. From my grandmother being angry, but also . . . I really thought maybe saying goodbye sooner rather than later would hurt less. But it didn't. At least not for me."

Javi shifted the heavy backpack and grinned. "Eh. Las abuelas love being angry about something. It gives them a reason to live," he said with a smile. He glanced toward the house, where his own grandmother was probably waiting to interrogate him the moment she could.

Cars sputtered past them down the cobblestone streets, interrupting the sounds of neighbors moving around their yards. Lola wished she had spent more time in Coyoacán, but it would take longer than a summer to learn its details from top to bottom, and her flight was leaving at the end of the week.

"You didn't drive me all over the city this summer because you really like history, did you?" she asked.

A mischievous gleam grew in Javi's eye. "I do like it," he said, and Lola's face fell before she could catch it. And before he said, "But it was also a good reason to spend time with you."

For once, Lola didn't want to run. She wanted to stand there with Javi as long as she could. She wanted to ask him about his classes and what he was most excited about in the semester to come. But she also wanted to talk to him about everything and nothing, and she would have been as happy to spend one last afternoon with him in total silence.

But Mari was waiting down the street, and Lola would have to go soon.

"Thank you," she said. "This summer was better than I thought it was going to be. That was because of you."

Maybe it was the *thank you* that caused Javi to take down whatever guard he'd put up on seeing her in his grandmother's doorway. Or maybe it was something more.

"There's next summer, too, Lola," he said. "Si quieres seguir practicando tu español."

"My dad would probably like that."

Javi laughed, and Lola warmed at the knowledge that she was the reason for that sound.

"And I'd like that, too," she added.

The smile Javi gave her was brighter than the paint on the buildings around them, brighter than the chrome on the cars parked at the curb, brighter than the sun.

CHAPTER 33

Practically speaking, saying goodbye to each member of the Gómez family was an almost endless parade of well wishes and reminders to say hello to Lola's mother and hints that they wanted to visit California.

Emotionally, it was devastating.

The aunts, uncles, and cousins that stopped by on Thursday night created a smaller group than the usual Sunday crowd, but the house was bustling anyway. Gabriela and Carmen wasted no time in dissecting recent soccer games with Lola's uncles, and tía Sofía's daughters teamed up to make Lola promise that she would take them to Disneylandia. Yolanda nudged her younger sisters to add a "¿Por favor?" every few minutes, making sure neither had forgotten the pleas they'd rehearsed.

"Mira, Lorena," tío Zuma said, his arm slung affectionately over the back of tía Coco's chair. "The next time you come, you bring your entire family with you. It will be all of us, the Mendozas, the Zuritas, and the Gómezes."

Tía Coco pursed her lips and shook her head ominously.

"Eso es imposible, mi vida," she told her husband. "La Señora no aprueba de su padre."

She spoke at a volume that was good for spreading gossip but less so for talking about which family members liked the others. And unfortunately for everyone at the table, Buela overheard her daughter's declaration right as she left the kitchen to join them.

The air evaporated from the room as she deliberately made her way to the empty chair next to Lola, who glanced over at the wall of photographs behind them. If her grandmother was still praying every day, Lola didn't know it—she had begun waiting to go downstairs until she was called for breakfast. It was easier not to know.

Slowly, the multiple side conversations picked back up, and it was when the room reached its usual level of commotion that Buela turned toward her granddaughter.

It wasn't that she didn't approve of her father, she said quietly enough so that only Lola could hear. She hadn't wanted her daughter to leave her, even if that was the best decision Letty could have made for herself at the time.

Lola understood what she meant before the words finished translating in her head. Letty was Rosa's oldest daughter. Perhaps it was a curse of its own kind that mothers had such a hard time giving up their daughters, and another that daughters might never fully disentangle themselves from the women who raised them. But for the first time in her life, Lola didn't resent that eventuality.

Throughout the night, Lola kept reminding herself not to give in to the tears threatening to spill. She hadn't expected to feel so sad about leaving, but her flight was taking off in fifteen hours, and a summer's worth of emotions had finally caught up with her. True, the people around her were always going to be her family, but she was struck by how readily they'd welcomed her into their world for no reason other than because they were family.

"Eres una Gómez, Lorena," tío Chuy offered before he left for the night. "Y bien mexicana, para siempre."

Lola hugged her uncle tightly. "Adiós . . . No, hasta luego," she said at the last minute. It was easier to offer a see-you-later than a goodbye.

Like almost everyone else on the plane, Lola hurried to turn her phone on the minute the wheels hit the tarmac and began to roll toward the gate. Chimes and alerts signaled incoming text messages and notifications, but Lola's phone stayed ominously silent. She had used the airport Wi-Fi in Mexico City to remind Ana that she was on her way home, but her best friend hadn't texted between takeoff and landing.

In fact, she hadn't texted once since Lola's confession and apology.

The silence wasn't without justification. But it was

also the first time Ana had ever been mad at her—she would sometimes be annoyed or even frustrated that Lola had excused herself early from yet another party, but never properly angry. What if they started the semester without talking? How long would the rupture stretch into senior year?

Lola was so caught up in dreaming up ways to show Ana that she was sorry that she barely noticed as she moved through customs or found her bags on the carousel, or even when her father's car pulled up to the curb. "Lorena, ¿ya estás lista?" he asked as he helped her load the bags into the trunk. It might not have been much of a greeting to other people, but it was par for the course for her dad. There was even a slight cheeriness in his tone, which Lola grasped at to momentarily forget about Ana.

"So?" Papi asked as he started the car, ignoring the impatient honks of cars behind him. "Can you speak Spanish now?"

A simple "Sí" bubbled up in Lola's mouth. Was there a way to tell her father that her summer had turned into something so much bigger than an extended Spanish lesson or that he had turned out to be right to send her to Mexico City after all? How to explain everything she'd learned, both about her family and herself? And there were some details, like where she had gone with Javi and why, that she wanted to hold on to a little while longer. Just for herself.

She turned the radio down and shifted in her seat to face her father. "Papi, why did you go to college in Mexico?" she asked.

Her father was silent as the car sped on. Just when Lola accepted that he wasn't through ignoring her, he responded.

"My whole life, your grandfather would talk about going to Mexico when he and your grandmother were finally citizens, back to where his parents were from." His voice was deliberate, as if he was trying to piece the answer together as he gave it. "But they had to work, and they did not make much money. So I told myself I would go for them. Everyone had moved away from Jalisco by then, so I went to the university in Mexico City instead."

"And that's where you met Mami, right?" Lola asked.

Thomas nodded. "Sí. It was also my first time leaving the United States. I had one cousin in Mexico City, and that was it. I had to figure everything out. Everyone called me gringo. I learned a lot in my classes, and I learned even more outside them. Your mother helped me with that. I met her, and I also met myself."

It was perhaps the longest speech Lola had ever heard her father give, and she sat with it as he fell back into his usual silence. He and her mother had worked hard—they had both been raised to respect and adhere to a certain work ethic, to believe that striving for more meant ensuring a kind of security that had evaded their parents. But the more she thought about it now, the more she realized that the work was also to ensure that she and her brother could do whatever they wanted to, that they could live with even fewer limitations than their parents did.

Her father would probably always be strict about grades—even throughout college, wherever she wound up going—but it was how he had been raised. His expectations were a tool kit more than they were a punishment. It was up to Lola and Tommy to apply what they needed and leave the rest.

"Gracias," she said, just loud enough to be heard over the still-soft radio.

"For what?" her father asked, but the slight nod of his head served as his "You're welcome."

Lola watched the palm trees and telephone poles as the car moved along the freeway. Already Mexico City seemed worlds away—the views and the sounds were so different, and there were only two people waiting for her at home rather than upward of a dozen—but it would also only take a plane ride to go back.

There, her family would pick up their conversations like she hadn't missed anything, and her grandmother would insist on cooking a multicourse feast for everyone, and Lola wouldn't be the outsider. And maybe her parents would be there, too.

Lola would find the right moment to tell her mother to call her grandmother and really talk, just like Mari had urged them to. It might take a while, even years, for them to repair whatever had shifted between them, but being honest was worth the risk.

Because families were connected by more than the house they shared or a last name or similar facial features. They were also fused together by a deep belief that the people around you care about one another, no matter what. A curse couldn't destroy that, nor could a border, or even years of disapproval and imposition mangled up with love. And whether Lola was in Oxnard or in Mexico City, she would be home.

CHAPTER 34

Lola turned in to the empty student parking lot and found her junior-year spot out of habit. In a week and a half, she would be given a new parking assignment, as well as a new locker and a new class schedule. She would be a senior, and in another year, she would be going off to college. Where she would go and what she would study, she had no idea. That was for a future version of herself to figure out—and anyway, she could always change her major if she wanted to.

For now, she relished the familiarity of her parking space and the habits she'd had at the beginning of the summer. Churro had spun himself dizzy with excitement when she entered the door and barely refused to leave Lola's side, and her suitcase had exploded in a semi-contained mess almost the second she had arrived home. Lola had ignored the piles of clothing in favor of the stack of assigned books she had curled up with for forty-eight hours, and as was *her* habit, Mami had chastised Lola more than once already for not cleaning.

"¡Mira este cuarto!" she had said the Sunday morning after Lola's return. "I know your grandmother wouldn't let you be so messy. And with a dog on your bed, too!"

"Mami, let me and Churro have this for right now. We missed each other."

Mami had huffed, but then she gave Lola a smile that indicated she understood.

But no amount of distraction or studying could keep Lola from worrying about the things that had changed. She tried to scroll through her Instagram, which now showcased Cristina's hyper-curated outfits and Rocío's beautifully plated twists on the food Lola had learned so well. And while her cousins responded to Lola's comments on their photos and asked her to come back soon, they weren't Ana.

Which is how Lola found herself walking toward the football field before school was even back in session, two giant iced coffees in her hands. The California sun beat down on the parched grass, and Lola heard both the soccer and football teams yelling at one another in an effort to push through the end of some hellish joint practice.

One of the members of the cross-country team shouted back at the boys to stop distracting them before cheering her own teammates to complete their laps. It was Ana, bouncing around the finish line, waiting for even the last girl, a tiny sophomore, to cross. Her unabashed friendliness was as boundless as her energy. It was Lola's favorite thing about her—the way she pulled everyone around her out of their shell.

"Hey, Espinoza!" a boy yelled. Lola paused at one of the gates that bordered the field to see Padilla waving at her from the turf. "When did you get back from Mexico? Did you bring me a souvenir?"

She returned the wave nervously, one of the coffee cups sloshing dangerously in her hand. Padilla's greeting had been enough to make almost everyone look her way— including Ana, whose arms were now crossed in front of her chest, a skeptical look on her face. It was only when Lola raised one of the coffees in her direction that Ana made her way over to the gate.

"You came back already?" Ana asked, her eyes darting from Lola to the coffee and back. It was well over ninety degrees out, and Lola had no idea how anyone could be convinced to run in such heat.

She handed over the small peace offering, beads of condensation dripping off its sides and onto the dirt below them. "I texted you from the airport," Lola said. "But you didn't respond, so I figured I would give you space."

Ana screwed her mouth together in a thin line. "You completely left town without telling me, and you only explained why over *text*. Just because my family likes doing touristy stuff doesn't mean Mexico isn't my heritage, too, you know. Did you even think of bringing me along?"

The words stung, but Lola deserved them. "It wasn't that," she said. "I wanted you to be there, I just . . . I also wanted something of my own for once, I guess. And I completely messed that up."

"You mean what's-his-name, the one who drove you all over the country?"

"Javi," Lola supplied quickly before catching herself. "I meant having an adventure of my own, the way everything is an adventure for you."

Ana took a long gulp of her coffee. "Only Lola Espinoza would get an A in almost every subject but an F in her social life," she said. "Maybe a D+ for trying."

"Well, and a C in Spanish."

Ana laughed, and for what felt like the first time in twenty minutes, a breath tumbled out of Lola's lungs.

Lola looked back to the field, where their classmates were beginning to pick up their equipment and carry it back to the locker rooms. Their good-natured shouting drifted upward with the heat, and Lola watched as the teammates who had been trying to beat one another five minutes prior began to merge together in a happy mass.

"I meant what I said on the way to the museum, you know," Ana added. "It's like you learned how to live for once. Now you need to learn how to do it . . . and clue me in every once in a while."

"If you have time right now, I'll tell you everything. Including everything the curandera told me when I was in Oaxaca."

Ana held her hand up in a stop motion. "Wait, are you still cursed? Because I don't know if I can be best friends with someone whose vibes are going to rub off on me . . ."

"If I am, it's because I'm the one in my own way," Lola said. "You have nothing to worry about."

"Oh, that makes me worry so much more."

The girls linked arms as they began to walk back to the parking lot, stopping at the track so Ana could pick up her things from where they lay on a bench. Lola used the time to explain everything she could, from the road trip and the meeting with doña Teresa, to the party where she'd seen Javi in his element for the first time. It had been a great summer—it had only been difficult to see that while it was happening, because so much was happening at once.

One of the football players yelled in their direction when they reached the steaming asphalt of the student parking lot. "Morris!" he called. "You coming to the bonfire tonight? Espinoza, you should come, too!"

Ana raised an eyebrow, a scheme already forming in her brain. "You think a beach party can beat a Mexico City party?" she asked.

"There's only one way for me to find out, right?"

Lola's willingness almost knocked Ana over.

"Yoooooo, Espinoza's coming to an actual party!" she announced to the entire parking lot. She lowered her voice and nudged Lola with an elbow. "Maybe someone on the soccer team will make you forget about those boys in Mexico."

"I forgot about one of them already," Lola said. "The other . . . I don't know."

Ana took an exaggerated sip of her coffee to show Lola she was listening. "Do we need to process, Lo? Should I pull a card?"

Lola shook her head. "It's fine, really. I guess I followed your lead on more than a few things. What would Ana Morris do, right?"

"The best advice I could have ever given you." Ana laughed. "But you know what else I would do?"

She held the beat dramatically, and it was only when Lola raised her eyebrows expectantly that Ana gave her a playful grin.

"I'd get the girl," she said.

Lola laughed and hugged Ana goodbye, promising not to bail on the bonfire. For the first time in her high school career, she meant it, too. Maybe senior year could be a little more balanced, a little more fun.

She took a deep breath and pulled out her phone.

> LE: I realized something . . . We never
> got to go on that date.

Lola tried to steady herself by leaning on her car and gripping her phone until her knuckles went pale. She didn't know what she would do if he ignored her text, but she also didn't know how she could live with herself if she didn't hit send.

It was the right thing to do, she told herself. Or if not the right thing, at least it was the honest thing. She had spent most of the summer—and her entire life, really—bottling up her feelings, and that hadn't worked. At least this, now, was a step in a different direction.

Her phone buzzed.

Slowly, she turned it over to look at its illuminated face.

JAI: ¿Regresas el próximo verano?

Lola smiled. Next summer was a lifetime away—who knew what kind of person she would be then and how different Javi might be as well. But for now, it was enough.

ACKNOWLEDGMENTS

Books are a marathon, not a sprint—and as a writer who was forged in the digital content mines, sprinting is all I have ever known until now. I'm grateful for Lola, Javi, the Espinozas, and the entire Gómez family for sticking with me through a pandemic and several jobs. They each taught me several things about them as I wrote them— and taught me so much more about myself.

Whether you picked up this book, bought it, borrowed it, gifted it or received it, or put it on hold at the library, thank you for spending even the smallest amount of time with this family and in this small window of Mexico City as I and Lola know it. If you took a chance on a language and a culture you're less than familiar with, thank you for trusting me. It was important that the Spanish, and the details of this day-to-day life, be presented just as they are—no italics, no translation, no isolation. That's how Spanish is spoken not just in Mexico and a lot of Latin America, but in so much of the US and the world. And I know that as much as representation can expand and affirm a person, it has its limits too—but if Lola and her family and friends resonated with you, that's as much of a gift to me as I hope it is to you.

Joelle Hobeika, Viana Siniscalchi, Josh Bank, and the Alloy team: thank you for teaching me how to write a book, and for believing that I could do it. I appreciate every email thread and your trust whenever I said, "I think I know how to fix it, but I can't explain it first." Thank you for letting me do by trying.

Zareen Jaffery, thank you for editing an editor (and also I am sorry). I am so grateful you wanted to help tell Lola's story, and that you understood the nuances of an everyday kind of magic. David Bowles, thank you so much for pushing me toward details that both make this story and make space for a multitude of identities within México. Ariela Rudy Zaltzman, Betsy Uhrig, and Bethany Bryan, thank you for your copy and continuity edits—for humbling me and holding me accountable. Tessa Meischeid, thank you for running with every "ok, so here's an idea" email I sent. And Selina McLemore, your edits, insight, and support came in at a critical low. Thank you for just getting it. I cannot stress enough how different this book is because of you, and it's all for the better.

John Paul Brammer, thank you for a better cover than I could have ever imagined. I am so grateful for even a small piece of your art. Anna Booth at Kokila, thank you for the wonderful cover design—the Mexican-pink color means everything. Asiya Ahmed, thank you for bearing with me through the painstaking effort that was bringing the Gómez-Cruz family tree to life. And José Olivarez, "Ode to Tortillas" unlocked a certain understanding in me. I'm so grateful you shared it with me for this book.

María Rodríguez Vallejo, your patience as I butchered my way through the Spanish language is infinite and gracious. Thank you so much for your guidance and corrections, as well as helping me hone the Gómez family's banter. I am so grateful to have shared my version of México with you.

Carly Piersol, you are simply the best. Thank you for helping me feel comfortable in a studio and in front of a camera.

The number of incomprehensibly understanding friends who have listened to me go completely galaxy-brained about my imaginary friends is long, and this is by no means exhaustive: Alice Morgan, Chasity Cooper, Christianna Silva, Danielle Quebrado, Dash Bennett, De Elizabeth, Francisco Martin, Gabrielle Korn, Jeanna Kadlec, Josh Gondelman, Julia Sodbinow, Kara Nesvig, Kelly McIntire, Kelsey Butler, Kyle Fenton, Kyle Vedder, Lindsey Rupp, Lisa Kennedy, Luppe Luppen, Maura Brannigan, Nick Montoya, Polly Mosendz, Sarah Solomon, Shane Duggan, Terron Moore, Tyler McCall, and Virginia Lowman, you have each been there in key ways. I don't know where I would be without community, and I don't intend to find out. Bolu Babalola, Elamin Abdelmahmoud, Matt Ortile, Rainesford Stauffer—and Gabrielle and Jeanna and Josh and Sarah again—thank you for showing me the way with writing and edits and publishing and putting in the work.

Nikita Walia: There are no words to convey how grateful I am for you. Your belief in me and in my ability to make good on saying, "Well, I guess I can write a book," is one of the top-three most valuable things in my life. (Holly and Olive are the other two.)

Luppe, thank you for reminding me it is always worth fighting for more—you get a second shout-out accordingly.

Also, squad forever.

J'Nay Reckard, I have promised you a paragraph of my gratitude since . . . well, since the beginning of this project. (More writers should thank their therapists.) Your advice and your ability to understand TikTok references has helped me press on even when I wanted to quit. Especially when I wanted to quit. Thank you so much for letting me cry over Zoom for hours, and for helping me work on the good, the fragile, and everything in between.

To every writer whom I've ever had the luck and honor of editing, and every editor who has trusted me with an assignment: Thank you for making me a better writer and a better editor, and for all the ways in which practicing one skill made me better at the other. Stella Bugbee and Phill Picardi, you each saw something in me that I didn't know was there all the way back when. Thank you for nudging me toward this path.

Jane Austen, thank you for the blueprint. Kiera

Knightly, Matthew McFadyen, and Joe Wright: Thank you for the adaptation I watched a [redacted] number of times as I wrote draft after draft. A bonus acknowledgement to Dario Marianelli, Jean-Yves Thibaudet, and the English Chamber Orchestra for the score I put on after I exhausted the movie. To every artist whose songs wound up on Lola, Javi, and even Río's playlists, thank you for putting me in the right headspace when I needed it. In other words, that's a thank-you to Selena and Celia and Daddy Yankee and Bad Bunny.

Lola's family is big and chaotic and full of love, but they don't hold a million candles to my own. Every time I go home to LA and every time I go to Mexico is a reminder of how much love is in the world for me, and my heart grows five times. Tía Irma, tío Alfonso, tía Eva, tío Adolfo, tía Araceli, tío Salvador, tía Elba, tía Lulu, tía Norma, tío Francisco, tía Diana, tío René y (ay, dios mío, vámonos) Claudia, Oscar, Jair, Nadia, Talina, Viridiana, Rodrigo, Mariana, César, Saul, Anapaula y Alan: para mi, ustedes son México. Pica, eres la mejor señora de mi vida. Mil gracias por tus tortillas, tus historias y tu cariño. Miriam, Manuel, Lilia, Joe, Doris, Scott, Sandra, Victor, Gael, and Mia: Thank you for being the surprise family that makes Los Angeles that much better. Analy, thank you for being my cool teen cousin when I needed to ask some old-person questions.

Natalie, I'm sorry you didn't get to hold this book, but I'm so grateful for how you believed in me all along.

Alex, thank you for Bash—also, thank you for being my incomprehensibly cool baby brother, and for letting me be your day one. You have always taught me how to chill out, even if I'm fundamentally incapable of it. Jessie, I love you so much in ways that are best expressed through sisterly bickering—but I love it better when we're not picking at each other, too, enana. I am so proud of you both.

Papi, you're the one I've always wanted to make proud, probably since I learned to walk. But you deserve more than an acknowledgment, because you were my sounding board and research assistant every step of the way for this book. It's because of you that I know I am de aquí y de allá—that I am, and can be, both.

Olga, thank you so much for the free HR advice, breaking down dad's 58-second phone calls with the detail they actually require, and all the bonus love.

Mom, I still remember every book you read to me when I was little, and all the ones I wanted you to read to me even after I could manage on my own. Everything I've done in my career can be traced back to that, and to you.

And to México—the land, the cultures, the people, then, now, and always. I am so grateful to know where my roots are and that there is always more to learn.